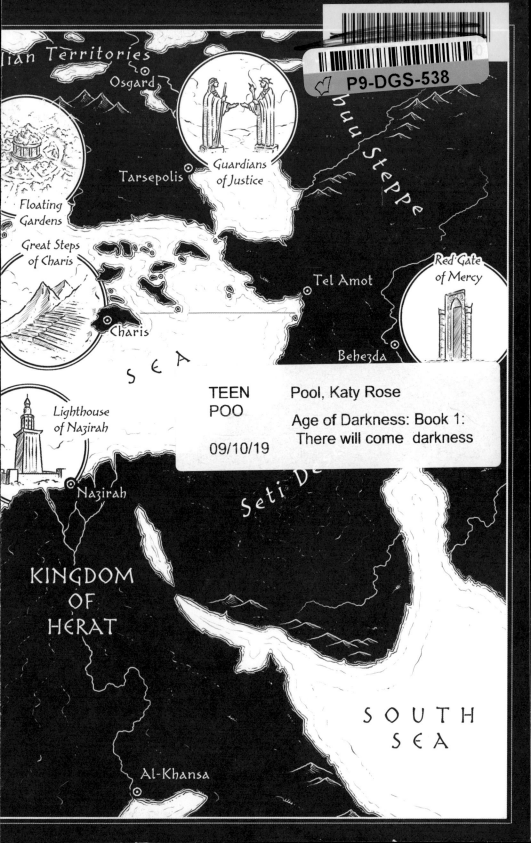

For Erica. Obviously.

Henry Holt and Company, *Publishers since 1866*
Henry Holt® is a registered trademark of Macmillan Publishing Group, LLC
120 Broadway, New York, NY 10271 • fiercereads.com

Text copyright © 2019 by Katy Pool.
Map illustration by Maxime Plasse.
All rights reserved.

Library of Congress Cataloging-in-Publication Data
Names: Pool, Katy Rose, author.
Title: There will come a darkness / Katy Rose Pool.
Description: First edition. | New York : Henry Holt and Company, 2019. | Summary: "For
  generations the Seven Prophets guided humanity with their visions, ending wars and
  uniting nations—until the day they vanished, leaving behind the promise of a looming
  Age of Darkness and the birth of a Prophet who could be the world's salvation . . . or the
  cause of its destruction"—Provided by publisher.
Identifiers: LCCN 2019017243 | ISBN 9781250211750 (hardcover)
Subjects: | CYAC: Fantasy.
Classification: LCC PZ7.1.P6435 Th 2019 | DDC [Fic]—dc23
LC record available at https://lccn.loc.gov/2019017243

Our books may be purchased in bulk for promotional, educational, or business use. Please
contact your local bookseller or the Macmillan Corporate and Premium Sales Department at
(800) 221-7945 ext. 5442 or by email at MacmillanSpecialMarkets@macmillan.com.

First edition, 2019 / Designed by Rich Deas and Mallory Grigg
Printed in the United States of America
10 9 8 7 6 5 4 3 2 1

THERE WILL COME A DARKNESS

AN AGE OF DARKNESS NOVEL

KATY ROSE POOL

Henry Holt and Company
New York

THE FOUR BODILY GRACES

THE GRACE OF HEART

Enhances strength, agility, speed, and senses
Wielded by: elite fighters

THE GRACE OF BLOOD

Gives and takes energy to heal or harm
Wielded by: healers

THE GRACE OF MIND

Creates objects imbued with unique properties
Wielded by: alchemists and artificers

THE GRACE OF SIGHT

Senses and locates living beings
Wielded by: scryers

I

HARBINGER

1

EPHYRA

IN THE MOONLIT ROOM OVERLOOKING THE CITY OF FAITH, A PRIEST KNELT before Ephyra and begged for his life.

"Please," he said. "I don't deserve to die. Please. I won't touch them anymore, I swear. Have mercy."

Around him, the lavish private room at the Thalassa Gardens taverna lay in disarray. A sumptuous feast spilled from overturned platters and filigreed pitchers. The white marble floor was littered with ripe berries and the smashed remains of a dozen tiny jewel-like bottles. A pool of blood-dark wine slowly spread toward the kneeling priest.

Ephyra crouched down, placing her palm upon the papery skin of his cheek.

"Oh, thank you!" the priest cried, tears springing into his eyes. "Thank you, blessed—"

"I wonder," Ephyra said. "Did your victims ever beg you for mercy? When you were leaving your bruises on their bodies, did they ever cry out in Behezda's name?"

He choked on a breath.

"They didn't, did they? You plied them with your monstrous potion to make them docile so you could hurt them without ever having to see their pain," she said. "But I want you to know that every mark you left on them left a mark on you, too."

"*Please.*"

A breeze rustled in from the open balcony doors behind Ephyra as she tilted the priest's chin toward her. "You've been marked for death. And death has come to collect."

His terror-struck eyes gazed up at Ephyra as she slid her hand to his throat, where she could feel the rapid tap-tap-tap of his pulse. She focused on the rush of blood beneath his flesh and drew the *esha* from his body.

The light drained from the priest's eyes as his lungs sputtered out their last breath. He collapsed to the floor. A handprint, as pale as the moon, glowed against the sallow skin of his throat. Dead, and only a single mark to show for it.

Drawing the dagger from her belt, Ephyra leaned over the corpse. The priest had not been alone when she'd found him. The two girls he'd had with him—hollow-eyed girls, their wrists mottled with green and purple bruises—had fled the moment Ephyra had told them to run, as if they couldn't help but obey.

Ephyra slid the tip of her blade into the flesh of the priest's throat, cutting a line of red through the pale handprint. As dark blood oozed out, she turned the dagger over and opened the compartment in its hilt to extract the vial within. She held it under the flow of his blood. The priest's desperate words had been a lie—he *did* deserve death. But that wasn't why she'd taken his life.

She had taken his life because she needed it.

The door burst open, startling Ephyra from her task. The vial slipped from her hand. She fumbled with it but caught it.

"Don't move!"

Three men spilled into the suite, one holding a crossbow, and the other two with sabers. Sentry. Ephyra wasn't surprised. Thalassa sat at the edge of Elea Square, just within the High City gates. She'd known from staking it out that the Sentry ran their foot patrols through the square every night. But they'd gotten here quicker than she'd expected.

The first Sentry through the door stopped short, staring at the priest's body, stunned. "He's dead!"

Ephyra sealed the vial of blood and hid it back within the dagger's hilt. She drew herself up, touching the black silk that covered the bottom of her face to make sure it was still in place.

"Come quietly," the first Sentry said slowly, "and you don't have to get hurt."

Ephyra's pulse hammered in her throat, but she made her voice calm. Fearless. "Take another step and there will be more than one body in this room."

The Sentry hesitated. "She's bluffing."

"No, she isn't," the one with the crossbow said nervously. He glanced down at the priest's corpse. "Look at the handprint. Just like the ones they found on the bodies in Tarsepolis."

"The Pale Hand," the third Sentry whispered, frozen as he stared at Ephyra.

"That's just street lore," the first Sentry said, but his voice was trembling slightly. "No one is so powerful that they can kill with only the Grace of Blood."

"What are you doing in Pallas Athos?" the third Sentry asked her. He stood with his chest out and his feet apart, as if staring down a beast. "Why have you come here?"

"You call this place the City of Faith," Ephyra said. "But corruption and evil fester behind these white walls. I will mark them the way

I mark my victims, so the rest of the world can see that the City of Faith is the city of the fallen."

This was a lie. Ephyra had not come to the City of Faith to stain it with blood. But only two other people in the world knew the real reason, and one of them was waiting for her.

She moved toward the window. The Sentry tensed, but none tried to go after her.

"You won't get away with killing a priest so easily," the first said. "When we tell the Conclave what you've done—"

"Tell them." She tugged her black hood over her head. "Tell them the Pale Hand came for the priest of Pallas. And tell them to pray that I don't come for them next."

She turned to the balcony, throwing open the satin drapes to the night and the moon that hung like a scythe in the sky.

The Sentry shouted after her, their blustering voices overlapping as Ephyra flew to the edge of the balcony and climbed over the marble balustrade. The world tipped—four stories below, the steps of Thalassa's entrance gleamed like ivory teeth in the moonlight. She gripped the edge of the balustrade and turned. To her left, the roof of the public baths sloped toward her.

Ephyra leapt, launching herself toward it. Squeezing her eyes shut, she tucked her knees and braced for impact. She hit the roof at a roll and waited for her own momentum to slow before picking herself up and racing across it, the voices of the Sentry and the lights of Thalassa fading into the night.

———

Ephyra moved through the mausoleum like a shadow. The sanctum was still and silent in the predawn darkness as she picked her way through broken marble and other rubble around the tiled scrying pool in the center, the only part of the shrine left unscorched. Above, the caved-in roof gave way to the sky.

The ruins of the mausoleum sat just outside the High City gates, close enough that Ephyra could easily sneak back into the Low City without drawing notice. She didn't know exactly when the mausoleum had been burned down, but it was all but abandoned now, making it the perfect hideout. She slipped through the scorched shrine into the crypt. The stairwell creaked and moaned as she climbed down and wrenched open the rotted wood door to the alcove that had served as her home for the past few weeks. Shedding her mask and hood, she crept inside.

The alcove used to be a storeroom for the acolyte caretakers who had tended to the shrine. Now it was abandoned, left for rats, rot, and for people like Ephyra who didn't mind the other two.

"You're late."

Ephyra peered through the darkened room to the bed that lay in the corner, shadowed by the tattered sheets that hung over it. Her sister's dark eyes peered back at her.

"I know," Ephyra said, folding the mask and hood over the back of the chair.

A book slid from Beru's chest as she sat up, its pages fluttering as it bounced onto the sheets. Her short, curly hair was raked up on one side. "Everything go all right?"

"Fine." No point telling how close her escape had been. It was done now. She forced a smile on her face. "Come on, Beru, you know my days of falling off slyhouse roofs are behind me. I'm better than that now."

When Ephyra had first assumed the mask of the Pale Hand, she hadn't been quite as good at sneaking around and climbing as she was now. Having the Grace of Blood didn't help her sneak into crime dens or scale rich merchants' balconies. She'd had to gain such skills the traditional way, spending countless nights honing her balance, reaction time, and strength, as well as gathering information necessary for specific targets. Beru had joined her, when she was well enough, racing Ephyra to see who could climb a fence faster or leap between roof-tops more quietly. They'd spent many nights stealing through the shadows, tailing behind a potential mark to learn vices and habits. After years of training and close calls, Ephyra knew how to get in and out of the dangerous situations she courted as the Pale Hand.

Beru returned her sister's smile weakly.

Ephyra's own smile faded, seeing the pain in Beru's eyes. "Come on," she said softly.

Beru lifted the rough blanket away from her body. Beneath it, she was shivering, her brown skin ashen in the low light. Tired lines had etched themselves into the skin below her bloodshot eyes.

Ephyra frowned, turning to the crate beside Beru's bed, where a shallow bowl rested. She opened the compartment in her dagger's hilt and poured the contents of the vial into the bowl. "We let this go for too long."

"It's fine," Beru hissed through clenched teeth. "I'm fine." She unwrapped the cotton from her left wrist, revealing the black handprint that marred the skin beneath it.

Ephyra pressed her hand into the bowl, coating it with wet blood. Placing her bloody palm over the dark handprint on her sister's skin, she closed her eyes and focused on the blood, guiding the *esha* she'd taken from the priest and directing it into her sister.

The blood Ephyra collected from her victims acted as a conduit to the *esha* she drained from them. If she were a properly trained healer, she would have known the correct patterns of binding that would tether her victims' *esha* to Beru. She wouldn't need to use the binding of blood.

Then again, if Ephyra were properly trained, she wouldn't have been killing in the first place. Healers with the Grace of Blood took an oath that forbid drawing *esha* from another person.

But this was the only way to keep her sister alive.

"There," Ephyra said, pressing a finger into Beru's skin, which was starting to lose that worrying grayish tinge. "All better."

For now, Beru didn't say, but Ephyra could see the words in her sister's eyes. Beru reached over and opened the drawer of the table beside the bed, withdrawing a thin black stylus. With careful, practiced motions, she pressed the stylus against her wrist, drawing a small, straight line there. It joined the thirteen others, permanently etched in alchemical ink.

Fourteen people killed. Fourteen lives cut short so that Beru could live.

It wasn't lost on Ephyra, the way Beru marked her skin each time Ephyra marked another victim. She could see the way the guilt ate at her sister after every death. The people Ephyra killed were far from innocent, but that didn't seem to matter to Beru.

"This could be the last time we have to do this," Ephyra said quietly.

This was the real reason they'd come to Pallas Athos. Somewhere in this city of fallen faith and crumbling temples, there was a person who knew a way to heal Beru for good. It was the only thing Ephyra had hoped for in the last five years.

Beru looked away.

"I brought you something else," Ephyra said, making her voice light. She reached into the little bag that hung at her belt and held out a glass bottle stopper she'd picked off the ground in the priest's room. "I thought you could use it for the bracelet you're making."

Beru took the bottle stopper, turning it over in her hand. It looked like a little jewel.

"You know I'm not going to let anything happen to you," Ephyra said, covering her sister's hand with her own.

"I know." Beru swallowed. "You're always worrying about me. Sometimes I think that's all you do. But, you know, I worry about you, too. Every time you're out there."

Ephyra tapped her finger against Beru's cheek in reproach. "I won't get hurt."

Beru brushed her thumb across the fourteen ink lines on her wrist. "That's not what I mean."

Ephyra drew her hand away. "Go to sleep."

Beru rolled over, and Ephyra climbed into the bed beside her. She lay listening to her sister's even breaths, thinking about the worry that Beru would not give name to. Ephyra worried, too, on nights like tonight, when she felt her victims' pulse slow and then stop, when she pulled the last dregs of life from them. Their eyes went dark, and Ephyra felt a sweet, sated relief, and in equal measure, a deep, inescapable fear—that killing monsters was turning her into one.

2

HASSAN

HASSAN TUGGED AT HIS TUNIC AS HE MADE HIS WAY UP THE SACRED ROAD. THE
servant he'd borrowed it from was a tad taller than he was, and it hung
awkwardly on Hassan's frame. He wasn't used to the clothing they wore
in Pallas Athos. The way it draped and flowed made him long for the
sturdiness of Herati brocade, for clothes that fastened shut and covered
his chest and throat.

But he would have been too conspicuous in his own clothes, and
all the effort he'd put into sneaking out of his aunt's villa would have
been for naught if he were recognized on the street. Not to mention the
danger he might be in.

That had been Aunt Lethia's reasoning, anyway, when Hassan had
first asked to leave the confines of her cliffside home.

"You came to this city to be safe," she had insisted. "The Witnesses
don't know for sure that the Prince of Herat escaped them in Nazirah,
and I intend to keep it that way as long as we can. The Hierophant
has influence even here, and I fear that if his followers knew you had
escaped, they would make it their mission to deliver you to him."

After two weeks of this argument, Hassan had decided to take matters into his own hands. His aunt had gone into the city for the afternoon, and Hassan had taken his chance. He was going to find out what was happening in his kingdom since he'd left—all the things his aunt didn't know, or wouldn't tell him.

The afternoon was warm, and the Sacred Road bustled with activity. Olive trees, the emblem of Pallas Athos, lined the limestone street all the way from the marina to the agora, then on to the Temple of Pallas, at the highest point of the city. Colonnaded porticos opened to shops, tavernas, and public baths on either side of the road.

The cold marble and austere limestone of this city made Hassan miss the bursting colors of Herat's capital, Nazirah—rich gold, warm ochre and carmine, verdant green, and vivid blue.

"You there! Stop!"

Hassan froze. He'd barely made it a mile from the villa, and already he'd been caught. Regret and embarrassment heated him.

But when he turned toward the voice, he realized they hadn't been addressing him. A butcher stood beside his market stall, calling out to someone else in the street. "Thief! Stop!"

Several other people stopped, looking around. But one small boy kept running, and before Hassan could decide what to do, the boy crashed straight into him.

Hassan stumbled but managed to catch the boy so that they didn't both tumble onto the paved street.

"Thief! Thief!" the butcher cried. "That's the thief!"

Hassan held the boy by the shoulders, taking in his tattered, knee-length pants and grimy face. He clutched a brown paper package to his chest. His dark features and bronze skin were unmistakably Herati—here was a child of Hassan's homeland. Hassan glanced back at the butcher, who was huffing his way over to them, red-faced.

"Thought you'd get away with it, did you?" the butcher said to the boy. "You won't like what they do to thieves in this city."

"I'm not a thief!" the boy growled, stepping out of Hassan's hold. "I paid for this."

Hassan turned to the butcher. "Is that true?"

"The boy gave me a meager few coins, not even half what that cut is worth!" the butcher said indignantly. "Thought I wouldn't notice and you could sneak off, did you?"

The boy shook his head. "I'm sorry! I thought it was enough. I counted, but all the money is different here, and I was confused."

"This sounds like a simple misunderstanding," Hassan said, putting on his most diplomatic smile. He reached into the coin purse that hung from his belt. "I'll make up what's owed. How much was it?"

The butcher eyed the boy. "Three virtues."

Hassan counted out three silver coins stamped with the olive tree of Pallas Athos and held them out to the butcher.

The butcher sneered, closing his hand around the money. "You refugees think you can get by on our charity forever."

Hassan seethed. A small part of him wished he could reveal who he was to this butcher, to publicly castigate him for saying such things to the Prince of Herat. Instead, with a smile fixed in place, he said, "Your charity inspires us all."

The butcher's jaw twitched, like he wasn't sure if Hassan was mocking him or not. With a grunt and a nod, he returned to his stall.

As soon as the butcher's back was turned, the boy spun away from Hassan.

Hassan caught him by the shoulder. "Slow down. We're not done here. You weren't really confused by the coins, were you?"

The boy looked up sharply.

"It's all right," Hassan said gently. "I'm sure you had a good reason."

"I wanted to get it for my mom," the boy said. "Lamb stew is her favorite. But we haven't had any since . . . since we left home. I thought if I could make it for her, it would make her feel like we were back there, and maybe she wouldn't cry so much."

Hassan couldn't help but think of his own mother, who *was* back home, though he would give anything to have her here with him. To comfort her, the way this boy, barely older than ten, wanted to comfort his own mother. To tell her everything would be all right. Or maybe to have her tell him that. If she was even still alive. *She is*, he thought. *She has to be.*

He swallowed, looking down at the boy. "We'd better get this back to her, then. You're in the camps, aren't you?"

The boy nodded. Together, they set off, Hassan's anticipation growing as they trekked up the final stretch of the Sacred Road. The High City of Pallas Athos had been built into a mountainside, three tiers stacked on top of one another like a towering crown. The Sacred Gate welcomed them to the highest tier, upon which the agora spread out, overlooking the entire city.

Above, the marble edifice of the Temple of Pallas gleamed, grander than any of the temples in Nazirah. Broad white steps led up the hillside to the temple portico, bracketed by rows of columns. Light spilled from the massive doors like a beacon.

This was one of the six great monuments of the world, where the founder of this city, the Prophet Pallas, had once given guidance to the priests who ruled, and spread the word of his prophecies to the rest of the world. According to *The History of the Six Prophetic Cities*, people from all over the Pelagos continent used to come to the agora on pilgrimage to the City of Faith, to consecrate themselves with chrism oil and leave offerings of incense and olive branches on the steps of the temple.

But no pilgrims had set foot here in the hundred years since the Prophets had disappeared. The structures of the agora—the storerooms, public baths, arenas, and acolytes' living quarters—had begun to crumble and grow over with weeds and tall grass.

Now, the agora was brimming with people and activity again. In the two weeks since the coup, Herati refugees had gathered here under the protection of the Archon Basileus and the Priests' Conclave of Pallas Athos. This was the reason Hassan had left the villa—to finally see with his own eyes the others who, like him, had escaped Nazirah. People like this boy.

The earthy scent of woodsmoke filled Hassan's nose as he and the boy passed through the Sacred Gate and into the makeshift village. Tents, lean-tos, and crudely built shelters crowded the spaces between the weathered structures. Scraps of cloth and debris littered the dirt-caked ground. The wails of crying children and the brusque tones of argument punctuated the air. Straight ahead, a long line of people spilled out from a colonnaded structure, carrying jugs and buckets full of water, moving carefully to ensure that not a single precious drop was wasted.

Hassan stopped, taking in the sight. He wasn't sure what he'd expected to find in the agora, but it wasn't *this*. He thought shamefully of the pristine gardens and palatial rooms in his aunt's villa, while here, just over a mile away, his own people were crammed into crumbling, ramshackle ruins.

Yet even in the overcrowded disarray, Hassan felt a pang of familiarity. The crowds were made up of dark-skinned desert settlers, and sun-bronzed delta folk like himself. He was struck by the thought that he could never have walked so casually into a place like this back home. There were celebrations like the Festival of the Flame and the Festival of the Flood, of course, but even then Hassan and the royal court were removed from the chaos and crowds, looking out from the palace steps or the royal barge on the Herat River.

Exhilaration and a strange sense of trepidation washed over him. This wasn't just the first time he was seeing his people since the coup— this was his first time seeing his people as one of them.

"Azizi!" a frantic voice broke through the din of the crowd surrounding the fountainhouse. A woman with plaited dark hair came rushing toward them, trailed by a silver-haired woman holding a baby at her hip.

Azizi ran at a tripping pace toward the black-haired woman, who was clearly his mother. She wrapped him up in an unrestrained embrace. Then she pulled away and began yelling at him, tears in her eyes, before sweeping him up in another tremendous hug.

"I'm sorry, Ma. I'm sorry," Hassan heard as he approached. Azizi looked plaintive.

"I told you not to leave the agora!" his mother scolded. "Anything could have happened to you."

Azizi looked like he was struggling valiantly not to cry.

The older woman sidled over to stand at Hassan's shoulder. "Where did you find him?"

"In the market, just outside the gate," Hassan replied. "He was buying lamb."

The woman made a soft noise as the child in her arms tried to squirm away. "He's a good kid." Then abruptly, she asked, "Are you a refugee, too?"

"No," Hassan lied quickly. "Just in the right place at the right time."

"But you are Herati."

"Yes," Hassan said, trying not to rouse her suspicion. "I live in the city. I came here to find out if there's been any more news out of Nazirah. I . . . I have family there. I need to know if they're safe."

"I'm so sorry," the woman said gravely. "There are too many of us who don't know what's happened to our loved ones back home. The Witnesses have stopped almost all the ships going in and out of the harbor. The only information we have is coming from whoever's managed to escape east, to the desert and the South Sea."

Hassan knew exactly how that felt. In his bedchambers in the villa, he had a leather-bound notebook filled with every measly piece of information he'd gained about what had happened to his city. He still didn't know what had happened to his parents. He wasn't sure if this was because his aunt Lethia herself didn't know, or because she was protecting him from the truth.

He didn't want to be protected. He just wanted to *know*, one way or another. He steeled himself as he asked, "What about the king and queen? Has there been any word about what happened to them?"

"The king and queen still live," the woman said. "The Hierophant has them captive somewhere, but they've been sighted in public at least twice since the coup."

Breath gusted out of Hassan's chest. He felt faint. He had needed to hear those words so badly. His parents were alive. They were still in Herat, though at the mercy of the leader of the Witnesses.

"There's no word about the prince," the woman continued. "He hasn't been seen in Nazirah since the coup. He's completely vanished. But many of us think he survived. That he managed to escape."

It was only by chance that Hassan hadn't been in his rooms when the Hierophant attacked the palace. He'd fallen asleep down in the library over a volume of *The Fall of the Novogardian Empire*, and he'd woken to the sounds of shouting voices and the smell of acrid smoke. One of his father's guards had found him there and snuck him out over the garden walls and down to the harbor, telling him his mother and father were waiting for him on one of the ships. By the time Hassan realized the guard had been lying, he was already sailing away from his city and the lighthouse that stood like a sentinel at its harbor.

"What is the Hierophant doing with the king and queen?" Hassan asked.

The woman shook her head. "I don't know. Some say he's keeping them alive to placate the populace. Others say he's using them to demonstrate his power—both to his followers and the Graced in Nazirah."

"His power?" he echoed, sensing she meant something more than just the command the Hierophant seemed to have over his followers.

"The Witnesses claim that the Hierophant can stop the Graced from using their abilities," the woman said. "That simply by being in his presence, the Graced are rendered powerless. His followers believe that if they prove themselves, the Hierophant will teach them to wield this power, too."

Hassan's jaw clenched. The thought of his mother and father being subjected to such a demonstration made Hassan feel sick with anger. He couldn't help but picture it—his mother, proud and tall, refusing to bend. His father, gentle and thoughtful, hiding his own fear for the sake of his people. The Hierophant, standing before them both, his face concealed by a gilded mask.

Hassan had never laid eyes on the man who had taken his country from him, but others told of the mask he wore—gold with a black sun carved into the center of its forehead, obscuring his face and identity.

Over the past five years, reports had built a picture of the masked man. A foreigner, preaching through the eastern regions of Herat. A skilled speaker, able to silence a room with a gesture or incite a riot with a word. It was said the Hierophant had once been an acolyte of the Temple of Pallas, but had turned his back on the Prophets and begun delivering his own message. He taught townsfolk that the powers of the Graced were unnatural and dangerous, his message gathering a following of others eager to blame the Graced for every ill suffered in their own lives.

Hassan could still remember how troubled his father had been as accounts of violence against the Graced poured in from every corner of the kingdom—and even from within Nazirah. In every attack, the perpetrators said the same thing. The Hierophant had told them to desecrate the village temple. The Hierophant had told them to burn down the healer's home. The Hierophant had told them they were purifying the world of the Graced.

The Hierophant.

"You should talk to the Herati acolytes," the woman said, nodding toward the Temple of Pallas. "They've been aiding the other refugees. If your family made it here, they'll know."

Hassan opened his mouth to thank her, but a bone-shattering shriek cut through the air. The people around them froze. Without pausing to think, Hassan sprinted through the crowd toward the temple. Two boys clipped past him, running in the opposite direction.

"Get the Sentry! Get the Sentry!" one of them yelled.

His alarm growing, Hassan pushed himself faster until he reached the steps of the Temple of Pallas. A crowd of people had formed there, as if waiting to ascend.

"Step back, old man!" a voice barked from the steps above.

Hassan craned his neck to see who had spoken. About two dozen men stood along the temple steps, holding hammers, sticks, and cudgels. They wore robes patterned with black and gold around the sleeve cuffs and hem, their hoods pushed back to reveal close-cropped hair. The one who'd spoken had a short gray beard.

Witnesses—followers of the Hierophant. Just the sight of them made anger roil in Hassan's stomach, and he found himself pushing through to the front of the crowd. At the top of the stairs, an old man, dressed in the light green and pale gold chiton of a Herati temple acolyte, stood facing the Witnesses.

"This temple is a holy refuge for those in need," the old man said, his voice quieter than that of the bearded Witness. "I will not allow you to desecrate it in the name of your lies and hatred."

"The only people seeking refuge here are the Graced," the bearded Witness hissed. "They taint the sacred energy of the world with their unnatural powers."

These last words seemed to be directed at two of the other Witnesses. They were younger. One, short and round-faced; the other, tall and gaunt. The short one clutched a pickax in his shaking hands. He almost looked frightened. But the tall one beside him looked eerily calm, except for his gray eyes, which gleamed with excitement. Instead of a black and gold robe, each wore a white cowl. Initiates, rather than full-fledged members.

The rest of the Witnesses seemed to be waiting for them to make their move.

The bearded Witness's voice grew louder as he continued. "This city is proof of the corruption of the Graced. The men who call themselves priests spend their time indulging their carnal vices and demanding tribute from the people of this city. A Graced killer is running rampant in the streets, taking lives. And now these cowardly Graced have come here, fleeing from the Immaculate One and his truth."

The Immaculate One. Hassan knew that phrase. It was what the Witnesses called the Hierophant.

"The Reckoning is coming," the bearded Witness said. "Soon your corrupt kings and false priests will fall, just like the abomination who sat on the throne of Herat. And the Immaculate One will reward his followers, even his newest disciples. Those who prove their commitment to his message earn the honor of wearing his mark." The Witness pushed his sleeve up. Burned into the back side of his varicose hand was the symbol of an eye with a black sun for its pupil. "This is your chance to show him your devotion to our cause and earn your mark. Make these abominations fear his name. Show them the truth of their corruption. Show them all so they cannot look away!"

The other Witnesses followed the man's lead, pushing up their sleeves to reveal the same mark burned into their skin.

The old acolyte stepped up to the round-faced initiate. "You don't need to do this," he said gently. "The Hierophant has preached lies to you, but you don't need to listen to them."

The round-faced initiate tightened his grip on the pickax, his eyes darting from the ringleader of the group to the crowd behind him.

Beside him, the tall, gaunt initiate sneered at the acolyte in disgust. "Your Prophets were the ones who preached lies. *I* will show the Immaculate One my devotion." Without another word, he stepped up to the acolyte and struck him across the face. The blow was hard enough to send the old man to his knees.

The crowd cried out. Hassan's blood surged in his veins, spurring him up the steps toward the Witnesses. The gaunt initiate turned and spat on the acolyte. Fury overwhelmed thought as Hassan seized the initiate by the cowl and punched him squarely in the face.

He heard the crowd gasp as the initiate stumbled back.

The bearded Witness stepped in front of him, whirling on Hassan. "Who in the Hierophant's name are you?"

"Someone you shouldn't anger," Hassan replied. "But it's much too late for that."

He was aching for a fight, and the Witnesses seemed ready to give it to him. They were kin to the zealots who had taken his kingdom and imprisoned his parents. And they were as close as Hassan was going to get to the Hierophant right now.

The gaunt initiate stepped up to him, lip curled in a snarl. "More Graced scum lording your ill-gotten power over the rest of us. Your Prophets cursed you when they gave you Grace."

Hassan flushed with rage—and shame. Because Hassan was *not* Graced. Though that fact did not lessen his rage at the Witnesses and their warped ideology. He wanted to correct the initiate—and, at the same time, he wanted to be feared by him, to be thought of as one of the chosen Graced.

In the Six Prophetic Cities and beyond, the Graced were revered for their abilities. The first of the Graced had been given their powers by the Prophets. Though there were only a few thousand Graced born every year, many of them occupied positions of power.

Every queen and king who had sat on the throne of Herat so far had possessed Grace. Hassan had spent much of his life wishing for one of the Four Bodily Graces to manifest in him. To be able to heal with the Grace of Blood, or scry with the Grace of Sight. To be like his father, with the Grace of Mind, able to create objects imbued with sacred *esha*, capable of wondrous things. Or like his mother, whose Grace of Heart made her as strong as an ox, as fast as a viper, able to see in the dark and hear a heartbeat from a thousand feet off.

As the years passed, Hassan's longing had grown more and more desperate. While Grace was known to manifest in people as old as seventeen, his parents and grandparents had discovered theirs before they were twelve. Now at sixteen, Hassan had long since shut away any hope that he was Graced. The initiate's words had brought all of that childhood shame bubbling back to the surface.

Hassan lunged at the gaunt initiate, his body acting out of pure fury. His arms reached out, hands flexed and ready to lock around the initiate's throat. But something collided sideways with him, and when Hassan turned, he saw the short, round-faced initiate above him.

He swung at Hassan again. Hassan ducked, catching himself on one knee. When he looked up, he saw that the tall, gaunt initiate had seized the old acolyte's robe.

"The Immaculate One will know the strength of my devotion!" the gaunt initiate cried, reaching for his belt and pulling out a glinting knife. "The Prophets are gone, and the Graced will follow!"

"*No!*" Hassan cried, leaping toward them. He shoved the acolyte hard, out of the way, and dove to tackle the gaunt initiate. But the initiate sidestepped and turned toward Hassan, blade flashing in his hand.

Though Hassan lacked her Graced speed and strength, his mother had taught him how to defend himself. He pivoted on his heel and flung his arm out toward the knife. The blade caught him just below the elbow, slicing into the flesh of his bare arm. Pain seared into him, but he did not let it jar his focus. With his other hand, he reached for the knife and forced it away from his body.

The gaunt initiate and he were in a deadlock, their grips pushing against each other, forcing the knife high. Warm blood dripped down toward Hassan's shoulder, his whole arm pulsing and hot with pain. He looked into the initiate's wide eyes. The deep, burning rage that had been left to fester for the past two weeks coursed through Hassan as he tore the knife away.

He looked down at the blade in his hand, overcome by the urge to plunge it straight into the initiate's heart. As if he could make him pay with blood for all the pain these people, and their leader, had caused his home.

But before he could act, an attack from behind knocked him forward. The knife clattered to the ground, and the world became a dizzying jumble as Hassan crashed onto the temple steps. He threw his arms up to protect himself as the other Witnesses advanced, brandishing their weapons.

But the blows never came. Hassan heard a sharp grunt and the sound of three bodies hitting the marble steps.

When he looked up, he saw only light.

On the steps, in the midst of three sprawled Witnesses, stood a girl. She was unmistakably Herati, shorter than Hassan but muscular, with smooth dark brown skin and thick black hair swept into a bun. The sides were cropped close to her head, in the style of Herati Legionnaires. The blinding light, he saw now, had been the reflection of the afternoon sun on the curved sword she held in her hands.

Two other Herati swordsmen flanked her, their eyes narrowed at the Witnesses, who quickly retreated.

"Get out of here now," she said to the Witnesses on the steps. Her voice was low and commanding. "If you set foot at this temple again, it will be the last place you ever go."

The Witnesses, who had seemed plenty bold when faced with an acolyte and unarmed refugees, were not as keen to face down Graced Herati Legionnaires with blades in their hands. They scattered down the temple stairs, looking over their shoulders as they fled.

Only the bearded Witness remained behind. He scraped himself off the steps. "The Reckoning is coming for you all!" he raged at the crowd as he turned to follow the others away from the temple.

"You scared them off," one of the other swordsmen said to the girl.

She shook her head. "They'll be back, just like rats. But we'll be ready for them."

"Oh, look," the other swordsman said, pointing down the steps of the temple. "The Sentry's here. Just in time to miss all the action."

Hassan turned to see the familiar light blue uniforms of the city Sentry as they marched through the dispersing crowd. In the time of the Prophets, the city and the Temple of Pallas had been protected by the Paladin of the Order of the Last Light—the Graced soldiers who served the Prophets. But when the Prophets disappeared, so had the Order, and now the city's protection fell to the Sentry, a cobbled-together force of Graceless mercenaries and hired swords.

"Are you all right?" the Herati girl asked.

It took Hassan a moment to realize the question was directed at him. He turned back toward the girl and then followed her gaze down to his arm. It was a mess of drying blood.

"It's just a scratch," he replied. His anger had kept the pain at bay, but looking at the wound made him feel suddenly queasy. The thrum of his earlier rage had dissipated to a low simmer. He felt a headache coming on.

"That was very stupid what you did," she said. In one fluid motion, she sheathed the curved blade at her belt. "Stupid, but brave."

Hassan's stomach flipped.

"I haven't seen you around the camps before," she said, tilting her head.

"I'm not a refugee," he blurted. "I'm a student here."

"A student," the girl repeated. "The Akademos is pretty far from here, isn't it?"

Hassan was saved from having to say more when the old acolyte appeared beside him.

"Emir!" the girl said. "You aren't hurt, are you?"

The acolyte waved her off. "No, no, I'm perfectly all right, Khepri. No need to fret." He turned to Hassan. "I believe you dropped something." He held out his hand.

"My compass!" Hassan reached for it.

"I couldn't help but notice it has a peculiar bearing," Emir said. "It points to the lighthouse of Nazirah, doesn't it?"

Hassan nodded slowly. The lighthouse was the symbol of Nazirah the Wise, the Prophet for whom Herat's capital was named, and whose prophecy had led to its founding.

Hassan's father had given the compass to him on the day he turned sixteen. He'd said he knew Hassan would keep the compass safe and, when the time came, he knew he'd keep the kingdom safe, too. Before that moment, Hassan had given up hope of succeeding his father as King of Herat.

"I can't," Hassan had choked out to his father. "I'm not—I don't have a Grace. Even if the scholars say there's still time for it to manifest, you and I both know it's too late."

His father had traced the compass's etched lighthouse with his thumb. "When the Prophet Nazirah founded this city, she saw a vision of this lighthouse, a beacon to learning and reason. She saw that as long as the lighthouse of Nazirah stood, the Seif line would rule the Kingdom of Herat. Your Grace could manifest tomorrow. Or never," he'd said. "But Grace or no Grace, you are my son. The heir to the Seif line. Should you ever lose faith in yourself, this compass will guide you back to it."

With his father's words echoing in his head, Hassan tucked the compass away and met the acolyte's curious gaze. Was that simple interest in his eyes, or something more knowing? Had he recognized Hassan?

"Nazirah?" the Herati girl said. "Are you from there?"

"It's my father's," he replied. It wasn't a lie. "He was born there."

Thinking of his father made Hassan's chest feel heavy. What would he say if he could see how Hassan had reacted today? Shame flooded him at how easily he had let his anger take over.

"I—I should go."

"You should see a healer," the Herati girl said. "There are some in the camps. I'm sure they would be glad to look at that arm for you, especially if they knew how you—"

"No," Hassan broke in. "Thank you. That's very kind, but I need to be getting back now."

Afternoon was cooling into evening, and Hassan knew he had less than an hour before his aunt's servants would call him to supper and realize he wasn't in his quarters. He needed time to get back and hide his wound.

"Well," the acolyte said warmly. "Perhaps you'll come again."

"Yes," Hassan said, his eyes on the Herati girl. "I mean, I'll try."

He hurried away from the temple and back to the Sacred Road. But as he reached the gate, he turned and looked up at the agora and the makeshift camps nestled beneath the Temple of Pallas. Behind him, the sun was sinking down below the shimmering turquoise sea, and Hassan could see the first campfires catch light, flickering to life, sending smoke into the sky like prayers.

3

ANTON

SOMETHING HAD HAPPENED AT THALASSA GARDENS.

There were always more Sentry in the streets once Anton passed through the gates that separated the Low City from the High City. But today, they were more than just noticeable. Dozens of Sentry dressed in pale blue uniforms emblazoned with a white olive tree clustered around the sides of the tavernas and public baths that lined Elea Square. An entire squad of them stood outside Thalassa, swords at their sides.

Anton nudged his way past whispering shopkeepers and other curious onlookers to where he could see a small knot of people wearing the same olive-green uniform he had on.

"Finally, you're here!" a cheerful voice crooned, seizing Anton's wrist and tugging him through the crowd toward the outer wall of Thalassa Gardens. "You picked a terrible day to come late to work."

"'Lo, Cosima," Anton said, blinking at his fellow server. "What's going on?"

Cosima took a drag of her cigarillo and blew a thick stream of valerian smoke directly into his face, her pale brown eyes lighting up. "There's been a murder."

"What—*here?*" Anton asked. "A guest?"

Cosima nodded, flicking ash from her cigarillo. "A *priest.* Armando Curio."

"Who?"

She rolled her eyes. "Of course. I forget you're not from here. Curio is one of the priests of the Temple of Pallas—but he's got a different reputation around here."

Thalassa Gardens was no stranger to members of the priest class with certain reputations. Since the city's founding, gambling halls, sly-houses, and other impious activities had been restricted to the Low City, where Anton lived. The High City, where the priests and the higher classes lived, was meant to be a paragon of virtue and piety. Maybe once it had been. But now, the priest class seemed only inter-ested in enriching themselves, indulging in their own vices and luxu-ries in places like Thalassa Gardens—places where those indulgences lurked beneath a veneer of respectability.

Cosima took another drag off her cigarillo. "I guess it's no surprise why he was chosen."

Anton glanced at her sharply. "What do you mean, 'chosen'?"

"They're saying," she drawled in the offhand tone she used when she wanted him to hang on to her every word, "that it was the Pale Hand who killed him."

"Who's saying?"

Cosima waved a hand vaguely through the smoke. "Stefanos says he saw them bring out the body. Pale handprint around the throat, just like the victims in Tarsepolis."

"Stefanos is an idiot," Anton said automatically. But his skin prick-led. This was the first Anton had heard of the Pale Hand in Pallas

Athos, but there had been whispers of mysterious deaths, marked by a single pale handprint, when he'd lived near Tarsepolis. He'd heard there were similar rumors in Charis, reaching back almost five years.

They all said the same thing—that the Pale Hand killed only those who deserved it.

"Why do you think she chose him?" Anton asked. "What did he do?"

"The usual," Cosima replied.

Meaning looting riches from the city's temples to throw lavish gatherings where the priests could eat and drink and satisfy themselves with whatever men and women caught their eye.

"And worse," she went on. "Curio had the Grace of Mind, and everyone said he was talented at alchemy. Except he wasn't making remedies or luck tinctures. The rumors say Curio's specialty was a draught that makes you docile and obedient. They say he used to go down into the Low City, find boys and girls there and tell them they'd been chosen to serve the temple. He'd drug them with the stuff and, well . . ."

Anton's stomach clenched. He knew the kinds of terrible things powerful men did to vulnerable people.

"What are you two whispering about?"

Anton turned to find none other than Stefanos sidling up to them. Simpering and self-important, Stefanos was a personal attendant at Thalassa whose guests seemed to like him as much as the rest of the staff detested him. He was constantly underfoot in the kitchens, demanding to taste the food to make sure it was up to scratch and bragging loudly about which priest or rich merchant he was attending that night. His sole redeeming quality was his penchant for losing large sums of money to Anton at the staff's after-hours canbarra game.

It didn't surprise Anton that Stefanos was taking this murder as an opportunity to make himself seem important.

Still, he was curious. "Cosima said you saw the body."

Stefanos glanced at Anton, his full lips stretched into a smirk. "That so?"

"Well?" Anton asked, raising his eyebrows. "Did you?"

Stefanos slung his arm around Anton's shoulders. "Look, I've seen a lot of messed-up stuff in my life. But that? In there? That was by far the most Tarseis-cursed thing I've ever seen. The guy didn't have a scratch on him. Just a *touch*, and he was—" He mimed getting his throat cut. "Makes you think—maybe it's time we open our eyes to how dangerous the Graced really are."

Anton shivered, despite himself.

"You're an idiot," Cosima said to Stefanos, echoing Anton's earlier sentiment.

Stefanos turned to her with a sneer. "You'd understand if you'd seen it."

"You sound like you're ready to shave your head like the rest of those hooded fanatics," Cosima said, blowing out another thread of smoke.

"The Prophets aren't here to curb the Graced anymore," Stefanos said. "We've seen the kinds of things the priests do here, just because they're Graced and they think that makes them better than us. And now we've got people like this Pale Hand running around, killing whoever they want with their unnatural powers."

"Wait, so are you saying that Curio deserved it, or that the Pale Hand should be stopped?" Cosima asked pointedly.

Stefanos's eyes flashed. "I'm saying that maybe the Witnesses are right. Maybe it's time the world finally was rid of the Graced."

Anton's throat felt suddenly tight. Stefanos was irritating, but Anton had never been frightened of him before. But now, Stefanos's dark expression chilled him. He didn't—couldn't—know that Anton was one of the very people he and the Witnesses wanted to see wiped away from the world. That like the priests of Pallas Athos and the Pale Hand, Anton was Graced.

Cosima punched Stefanos on the shoulder.

Stefanos jerked back, clutching at his arm. "Ow! What was that for?"

"To get you to stop running your stupid mouth," Cosima replied. "What's next? Are you gonna go burn down a shrine to prove your devotion to the Hierophant? They say anyone who joins the Witnesses has to commit an act of violence against the Graced."

"They're standing up to the Graced," Stefanos said. "Someone has to."

"Oh, really?" Cosima shot back. "And what about what Vasia told us last week at the canbarra game? About the man who butchered his own Graced children in the middle of the night to prove himself to the Witnesses. Or do you think those kids deserved that, since they were Graced?"

"That's just a rumor," Stefanos sneered. "That didn't really happen."

"Come on," Cosima said scathingly. "This Hierophant has got these people tattooing burning eyes onto their skin and convincing them that the Graced are corrupting the world. You really think something like that is beyond these zealots?"

"Whatever," Stefanos said. With a last sneer, he stomped off to regale the next group of Thalassa workers with his story. Cosima glanced at Anton as Stefanos retreated, worry flashing across her sharp features.

Anton put on a bland smile. "That guy really is an idiot."

"It figures he'd eat up all that crap the Witnesses preach," Cosima said, tossing the stub of her cigarillo onto the ground. "They're exactly like him—making up stupid horseshit to get attention. Falling all over themselves to gain the favor of whoever claims to have power."

"Yeah," Anton said, tacking on a laugh. It rang hollow to his ears, but Cosima didn't seem to notice.

"Come on," she said, playfully swatting at his head. "Let's go inside before we get yelled at. Or *I* get yelled at. Somehow you never do."

Anton ducked under her hand. "That's because everyone likes me."

"Can't imagine why."

The cheerful clank and clatter of dinner preparations enveloped them as they made their way through the kitchen to the servers' basins to wash up. Anton turned on the copper tap, letting warm water fill the bottom of the basin as he tried to clear his mind of the Pale Hand and the Witnesses. They had nothing to do with him. No one in this city even knew he was Graced. There was no reason that had to change.

"Oh, Anton!" a voice at his elbow piped brightly. "I've been waiting for you."

"Oh, *were* you?" Cosima said coyly.

Darius's round cheeks immediately flushed pink. The newest and youngest of the Thalassa servers, Darius had latched onto Anton almost immediately. Which Anton wouldn't have minded at all if it weren't for the fact that Darius seemed to become unaccountably terrible at his job when Anton was around. Hardly a day went by without Darius dropping a tray or crashing into a table in Anton's presence.

"I—I mean, because there's a guest," Darius stammered, avoiding Anton's eyes. "Who's asking for you."

"A *guest?*" Cosima crowed in delight. "Asking for Anton? What kind of guest?"

Aside from the occasional regulars who came in seeking something a little more than just dinner, no one had ever come to see Anton at Thalassa. This was unending disappointment to Cosima, who had never met another person's business she didn't want to stick her nose into.

"Um," Darius said, biting the edge of his lower lip. "A woman? She looked rich?"

"Of course she's rich," Cosima said dismissively. "What did she want?"

"I don't know?" Darius eyed Anton like he suspected he had the answer.

Anton looked down at the suds wreathed around his fingers. "Thank you, Darius." He turned and gave him his most charming smile. "You'd better get going. Don't let Arctus yell at you on my account."

Darius nodded, cheeks growing pinker, and scurried off, bumping into a tray of honey-drenched desserts on his retreat.

Anton reached to dry his hands, but Cosima snatched the towel before he could get it, leering. "Who's this guest, huh? You holding out on me? Engaging in some after-hours *entrepreneurship?*"

"Respectable boy like me?" Anton said, all wide-eyed innocence, plucking the towel from Cosima's hands.

"Come on, you're not going to tell me anything?"

He let an easy grin slip over his face as he tossed the towel into the basket. "I thought you found my air of mystery charming."

"You've mistaken me for Darius," Cosima snorted. "That poor besotted child."

Anton winked as he slid past her. "I'll see you at the canbarra game tonight."

Before she could answer, he ducked back through the kitchen, dodging a server with a tray piled with baskets of flatbread, and made his way through the doors. Incandescent lights glowed above the court-yard crowded with tables and chairs. Footbridges and tiled walkways crisscrossed over the tiered reflecting pools, shaded by broad-leafed trees and canopies of soft pink and gold cloth.

As he stepped into the gardens, he felt the familiar low, swelling hum that always enveloped him in crowds. He braced himself for the onslaught of each distinct *esha* emanating off each person seated in the courtyard, from the merchants, priests, and foreign dignitaries sipping alchemical wine, to the servers who whirled about them with trays of glazed lamb and the dancers who teased them in jewel-bright silks. Beneath their cacophonous chatter and the gentle melody of the lyre players was this: the pulse of the world that Anton alone could hear.

Well, not Anton *alone*. There were others like him who had the Grace of Sight, though few who were quite as attuned to the vibrations of the world's sacred energy. Anton had grown used to tuning it out, ignoring the ebb and flow of *esha*, but tonight, as he made his way through the gardens, he let it all in. He was searching for one in particular.

He felt it almost immediately—the high, clear bell ringing through him. It belonged, he knew, to the woman who sat at the table in the far corner of the courtyard, watching his approach with narrow eyes.

No one else would think this woman out of place at Thalassa, dressed as she was in an elegant gown of deep purple, a string of emeralds hanging off her long neck. But to Anton, she stuck out like an ace of crowns in a hand of canbarra. She looked exactly the same as she had the last time he had seen her—the same ink-black hair done up in an intricate coif, the same dark, round face that gave no hint at her age. The same *esha*, which felt like the clang of silver bells.

"Dining out alone?" he asked as he reached her table.

"Actually," the woman answered, "my dinner companion has just arrived."

She'd called herself Mrs. Tappan when they'd first met, but Anton knew by now how easily names slipped off her. He didn't know what her real name was, and she'd never offered it to him. Nor did he know what, precisely, she wanted with him. In his more sentimental moments, he could convince himself she genuinely wanted to help him. More often, he thought it just amused her to play games.

That was fine by him. Anton liked games.

"What do you want?"

She folded her hands neatly on top of the marble table. "I've heard the lamb here is exquisite."

"You know what I meant."

"I stopped by your charming little place last night," she commented, as though she hadn't heard him. "I'm sorry to have missed you. Working late, I suppose."

Anton was neither surprised the Nameless Woman had tried to drop in on him at home, nor that she knew where he lived.

"Though, I do wonder why, with this respectable employment, you haven't upgraded to something a bit less . . . *cozy*."

"This job is new," Anton lied. "I've barely made enough yet to pay off my last month of rent."

From the narrowing of her eyes, he knew she saw the lie for what it was, but he would not give her the satisfaction of saying the truth out loud. He could afford nicer rooms, but he'd kept his tiny flat in the Low City because it would be easy to leave behind if he had to. The past six months were the longest he'd remained in one place since he was a child, but that didn't mean Pallas Athos was his home.

"What do you want?" he asked again.

She sighed, as if his lack of decorum was a personal disappointment to her. "Fetch me a glass of wine, and we'll talk. Something from Endarrion if you have it. Nothing local—the wine here is swill."

Anton turned on his heel, hastening across the courtyard to the wine cellar. At the top of the stairs, he paused, considering whether or not he could just keep walking, out the door of the taverna, into the maze of streets, where he could lose her, and himself.

It wouldn't matter. She'd only track him down again.

The first time she'd done it had been over a year ago in a slyhouse in a canal town just south of Tarsepolis. Anton had spent six straight nights downstairs at the card table, filling his pockets with the coins of rich men who'd come to drink and gamble before they slipped off to enjoy the attentions of the boys and girls in the rooms above.

But on the seventh night that Anton had sat down at the card table, he'd found himself face-to-face with an elegant woman he'd never seen before.

Even then, her *esha* had felt different, distinct from the chorus of others that buzzed within the smoke-filled cardroom. It had reminded him of silver, bright but elusive. She'd poured him a drink and dealt out a hand of canbarra like she'd been waiting for him. Anton had wanted to get up and leave right then, but a quick glance to his side revealed two guards hovering at his elbow.

"Tell me," the woman had said. "How much money have you made at my card table these past few nights?"

He'd blinked at her. "I'm not cheating."

"I never said you were. I asked how much you'd made."

"Why?" Anton had asked. "Do you want to make me a better offer?"

One eyebrow arched, a thick swoop of amusement. "Tell me your name."

"I'm no one."

She had only smiled at him, and Anton had felt stripped bare beneath her gaze. "Anton," he'd said at last.

"And how old are you, Anton?"

His family had never really kept track of his age. Fifteen, perhaps? He knew it had been about four years since he'd run away from his father and grandmother's home. "Old enough."

The answer had amused her more. "Old enough? Whatever for?"

"I don't think you came here to reprimand and question me."

"Why, then? To punish you?"

"No." Anton's voice had been steady. "To use me."

He remembered how the liquid in her glass had gleamed like burnished brass as she took a slow sip. "And what are you best used for, Anton?"

"This is a slyhouse, isn't it?"

"Are you offering your services?" she'd asked. "Seducing rich, drunk men, playing at being their pet?"

"What," he'd said, flashing a smile. "You don't think I'd be any good at it?"

She'd actually laughed at that, a sound that reminded him of how her *esha* had felt, as clear as a bell. "I think it'd be rather a waste of your *abilities*."

A chill slid down Anton's spine.

"You have it wrong. I don't want to use you, Anton. I want to help you."

"How?" Anton had asked, not believing her for a second. No one helped you without getting something out of you in return. The past four years had taught him that much.

"This slyhouse is just for amusement," she'd said with a dismissive wave. "My real enterprise is my scrying agency."

"You're a bounty hunter."

She'd clucked her tongue. "I don't like that name. It makes it sound so terribly mercenary."

Bounty hunting *was* mercenary. Scrying agencies made the bulk of their money using the Grace of Sight to track down criminals and reaping the reward money for delivering them to whatever enforcers or city rulers wanted to bring them to justice. But there was also money to be made taking cases from anyone who wanted to find someone badly enough, criminal or not. For a steep price, a bounty hunter could find any person you wanted—people who, like Anton, did not want to be found.

"And are you here to—?" Fear had thumped beneath his ribs at the thought that this woman had been sent to find him. His grandmother was far too poor and miserable to do business with an elegant city woman like her, much less a bounty hunter. But there was someone else it could be.

"No one gave me your name," she'd said. "Although now I'm curious who you think would. A scorned lover, perhaps? You look like the type who isn't careful with hearts that aren't your own."

Anton's pulse had settled. "Then why are you telling me this?"

"I told you. I want to help you." Placing her glass on the table, she'd leaned toward him and said, in a voice like smoke, "I know what you are. It's time you stop hiding."

The thought had made him want to bolt out of the slyhouse and start running.

But he hadn't. Not that night.

Thalassa's lyre players were ending their song as he returned to the courtyard armed with a jug of red from a vineyard outside Endarrion. With the applause of the surrounding tables clattering in his ears, Anton poured the wine into a crystalline glass.

"Sit," the Nameless Woman said, waving a hand at the empty chair across from her. Anton stiffly took a seat as the sounds of scraping forks, indistinct chatter, and the bright first notes of a new song filled the silence between them.

"This certainly is nicer than the dumps I've seen you in before," she said approvingly. "It would seem you're doing well for yourself. A job, a roof over your head. Friends who have employers instead of madams."

He shrugged. On paper, at least, Anton was at last a functioning member of society.

She smirked, twirling her wrist so the light caught on the deep red wine in her glass. "Still. One can't help but feel like you're wasting your talents."

Anton blew out a breath, almost a laugh. "This again?"

She was one of only four people in the world who knew that Anton had the Grace of Sight. She was the one, after all, who'd given him his first lesson in scrying, teaching him how to focus on the vibrations of sacred energy around him, how to cast a lodestone into a scrying pool to seek out the frequency of someone's specific *esha*. His first and only lesson.

"I have a job for you."

"Not interested," he replied immediately.

"You haven't even heard what it is yet."

"Doesn't matter," he said. "You already know my answer."

"I do," she agreed, sipping at her wine. "But this isn't just any job. You're the only one who can do it."

The Grace of Sight was the rarest of the Graces, and even among those who had it, most were limited in what their scrying was capable of finding. But before she'd given Anton his one and only scrying lesson, she'd said she'd seen in him a capacity for great power—maybe even greater than hers. Sometimes, he even thought he could feel that power, too. The way he could sense *esha* without trying, the way he knew when someone was Graced and when they were not, the way he could differentiate between its frequencies with ease. It was instinctive.

"Except you know I *can't* do it," Anton replied. "You've known since that day."

The day she'd tried to harness his capacity, and Anton had wound up with lungs full of water and the realization that his power was shadowed by something else—the nightmares that brought him right back to the past he thought he'd left behind. The nightmares that were summoned whenever Anton tried to use his Grace. The Nameless Woman had seen what they'd done to him, had dragged him out of the scrying waters and watched him gasp for breath.

It was then that he'd started running again, even knowing that she was Graced, like him, and would find him again. And again. And again. It was, after all, what she did. In the canals of Valletta, in towns up and down the Pelagos coast—and now Pallas Athos. He'd no doubt she would chase him all over the Six Prophetic Cities if she had to. By now, the Nameless Woman's visits were expected. He hadn't learned to trust her, exactly, but in the last few years, she'd become one of the only things he could count on. Before her, the only invariable part of his life had been leaving it behind.

Every time she found him, she offered him the same proposition: learn to wield his Grace. Every time, Anton gave the same answer.

Since that day in the scrying pool, he'd done everything he could to build a wall between himself and his Grace. He'd learned how to keep the nightmares at bay. But the moment he tried to use his Grace, they bared their teeth again, like wolves drawn to blood.

The Nameless Woman took another sip of her wine. "One day, Anton, you'll have to get over your silly little fears."

"Are you done? Because as fun as catching up has been, I really need to get back to work." He started to rise, but she reached across the table, her palm flat over his hand, stilling him.

"I'm not done." Her tone had shifted—gone was the teasing lilt.

Her dark eyes burned into his. "You think I came all the way to the City of Faith just to hear a refusal?"

Anton's hand twitched beneath hers. "So if it's not for a job, then why did you come?"

"It is for a job," she said. "You *are* the job."

He went still. The thing he'd been afraid of, the thing he'd suspected the first time the Nameless Woman had found him, had come true. "Someone gave you my name?"

A trill of laughter spilled out from the table beside them, but the Nameless Woman's attention stayed focused on Anton. She nodded. "You know who it is?"

Anton's heart thudded painfully. "No."

"You're lying."

His palms itched with sweat, but the rest of him was ice-cold. She was right. He knew exactly who had given his name to her. The only other person in the world who would be looking for him.

"Oh," the Nameless Woman said over the rim of her glass. "Oh my. You're afraid. You're *terrified*."

Anton clenched his teeth, his breath coming out hot and quick as he gripped the edge of the marble table. "You can't let him know. You can't tell him where I am. Please."

"I can tell him he has bad information," she said. "He knows we can only do the job if the name is correct. I'll simply tell him he has the wrong one."

Anton shook his head. "Don't," he gasped. "Don't do that. He'll know you're lying."

"I'm a far better liar than you are."

The taste of ice burned his throat. "It doesn't matter. He'll know."

"If I turn down his case, he'll only take it elsewhere." She spoke gently now. "He may have done so already. Mrs. Tappan's Scrying

Agency may be the best, but there are others who would hang their own mothers for the kind of money he offered us."

Anton's mind stuttered over her words. The man looking for him had apparently amassed a great amount of money—enough to hire a bounty hunter with a reputation for taking on cases no one else could. It should have surprised Anton, but it didn't. Despite his humble beginnings, this man had always known exactly how to play his cards to get the biggest reward.

"One of them *will* find you, Anton. If they haven't already."

He was inside a nightmare, eleven years old, freezing water tearing into his lungs. Hands holding him below dark water.

He pushed away from the table in one rigid motion.

"Anton." The Nameless Woman grasped his wrist, her grip unexpectedly tight. "There are people who can help you . . . take care of this. You don't need to run again."

He could barely hear her words over his own thundering pulse. Pulling from her grasp, he darted across the courtyard, weaving through servers and laughing patrons to the staircase that led up to the roof. He climbed, nausea rising in him like a tide. As long as he kept moving, kept going up, it could not catch him.

There was no water.

There was no ice.

Only fear.

Warm night air rushed over him as he reached the roof. Above him, lit by the glow of a hundred distant fires, the Temple of Pallas looked out over the rest of the city. Anton flew to the edge of the roof. The marble balustrade was cold and solid in his grasp as he looked down past Thalassa's portico and the fountain and olive trees in the center of Elea Square. The long, pale stretch of the Sacred Road led all the way from the Temple of Pallas, through the main city gates and down into the Low City, where the streets grew narrow and dark, full of promise and danger.

Before his tiny flat there, Anton had spent many nights sleeping on roofs and in rafters, like a bird coming to roost. From high up, he could see everything that went on below, and none of it could touch him.

He was still afraid, but fear alone could not kill him.

He'd survived before, after all. The man who was looking for him, the man who had given his name to the Nameless Woman—Anton hadn't seen him since that day, out on the ice, the water so cold, darkness pressing in. He sometimes felt trapped in that nightmare, in the memory of what that man had tried to do.

But that scared, drowned boy—that wasn't who he was anymore. He'd left that boy for dead.

4

JUDE

THE SUN WAS JUST BEGINNING TO SET OVER KERAMEIKOS FORT AS JUDE MOVED through an extended koah sequence at the foot of the valley's highest waterfall. He stood effortlessly on one leg, his arms spreading and crossing fluidly in time with his breath. This koah sequence had five elements—balance, hearing, sight, speed, and focus. The narrow rock outcropping didn't offer much room for error, but that was why Jude liked this spot. When his focus was on his balance, his body, and his Grace, his thoughts dissipated like morning mist.

"I thought I might find you up here." A voice floated over the sound of rushing water, perfectly audible to Jude's Grace-enhanced hearing.

Jude finished the fifth form of the koah, shifting all his weight forward, his hands forming a triangle in front of him. He stepped into rest, his gaze finding the other Paladin standing below. "You know me too well."

Penrose's blue eyes lit up with a smile. "Seems your Year of Reflection didn't rid you of your old habits."

She'd said it in jest, but shame twinged in Jude's chest as he thought of the truth behind her words. He leapt down from his rock, landing neatly beside her at the edge of the pool. "I was just heading back."

"This is always where you come when you're nervous," Penrose said as they set off toward the fort.

Jude tensed. She really did know him too well.

"Don't worry, Jude," Penrose said. "Anyone would be. Especially after what's happened in Nazirah."

He swallowed. "The threat of the Hierophant is undeniable now. Before I left for my Year of Reflection, the Witnesses were just a fringe group of radicals. Or so I thought."

"When they were living out in the Seti desert, we had no way of knowing how many had joined the Hierophant," Penrose agreed.

A few years ago, the Witnesses and their masked leader had taken up residence in an abandoned temple in the middle of the Seti desert—a temple older than even the Prophets. It was one of the few surviving remnants of an ancient religion, when people worshipped an all-powerful god of creation.

The Order of the Last Light was keeping an eye on the Hierophant's activities and the rumors circulating around him. One rumor said the Hierophant had once been an acolyte who had renounced the Prophets and had begun preaching against them. Another said he had talked an entire squadron of Graced Herati soldiers into turning their swords on one another. According to his most fervent disciples, the Hierophant was so righteous, and so pure, that the Graced were rendered powerless simply by standing in the same room with him.

Jude and the rest of the Order doubted the truth of these rumors, but they had demonstrated the powerful nature of the Hierophant's following. The Hierophant was not just a man with dangerous ideas—he had made himself *into* an idea, a new figure to worship and follow now that the Prophets were gone.

"None of us thought they would take one of the Six Cities," Penrose said. "We underestimated just how fervently his followers believe his lies."

"'The deceiver ensnares the world with lies,'" Jude recited.

"'To death's pale hand the wicked fall,'" Penrose continued. "The bodies they've been finding marked with the pale handprint prove it. The first two harbingers are here. The Age of Darkness is approaching."

"Then how can this be the right time for me to become Keeper?" He hadn't exactly meant to voice the question—it had been bottled up in his mind since the moment he'd returned to Kerameikos. But once he asked, he knew he needed an answer. "Two of the three harbingers have arrived. They're not just a warning of what's to come. One of them—or all of them—could bring about the Age of Darkness. We need to find the Last Prophet before that happens, and it should be my father. Not me. Not *now*."

"Or perhaps that is why your father wants to do this now," Penrose said. "We're running out of time. Our acolytes are searching for the signs, but we've heard nothing through the scrying network. Maybe your father has grown desperate enough to find a new approach."

They crested the hill. Below, the spiral towers of Kerameikos Fort peeked out of pockets of mist trapped by the surrounding mountains. Waterfalls cascaded down from the face of a narrow gorge, flowing through the slender arches of the fortress's crossings and bridges.

Jude took in the sight of his home as he contemplated Penrose's words. "You think Father means to have me leave Kerameikos? To try to find the Prophet myself?"

With the exception of the Year of Reflection, when the Keeper of the Word's heir apparent retreated alone into the Gallian Mountains to affirm his faith and his duty to the Seven Prophets, the Paladin hadn't left Kerameikos Fort in a hundred years. But the Order was growing more desperate to find the Last Prophet. Maybe the only way to do it was for Jude and his Guard, once he chose them, to leave Kerameikos and find the Prophet themselves.

"Is that what you're worried about?" Penrose asked. "Leaving Kerameikos?"

"No." He was worried that if he left Kerameikos to find the Last Prophet, he would fail. Because despite what Penrose had said about it being the right time, about Jude's doubts being expected, he knew she was wrong. His doubts had not begun when he learned that Nazirah had been taken, or when he'd heard about the Pale Hand murders.

They'd begun when he was sixteen and realized there were things he wanted that a Keeper of the Word could never have. When he'd first felt that ache that pressed on him in silent, lonely moments. When Jude would close his eyes, desperate for the warmth of another person, the touch of their skin. A Keeper should not desire skin and warmth and breath, but Jude did. And nothing, not all of his training, not his Year of Reflection, not a desperate prayer to the long-gone Prophets, had changed that.

They crossed over the bridge that led into the fort itself. Above, thin wooden planks crisscrossed the river's banks, upon which Paladin balanced, silhouetted in the rising mist of the falls. Each of the Paladin wielded a long staff, which were used to parry, block, and attack one another. Some were perched as high as a tower, and some barely clear of the rushing water. A fall from the anchored beams would mean a watery death, but the Grace of Heart made the Paladin fleet-footed and sure, able to leap from one balanced plank to the next as they clashed in a dangerous dance.

"Then is it about choosing your Guard tomorrow?" Penrose asked. Her voice suddenly took on more urgency. "You know who you'll choose, don't you?"

It was every Keeper's first crucial task to choose the Paladin who would serve by their side. The Guard would take a special oath that bound them in duty to Jude for the rest of their lives. To be chosen for the Guard—to serve as advisor and comrade to the Keeper—was the highest honor for a Paladin. It was also a great responsibility. Breaking the oath of the Paladin Guard meant more than exile—it meant death.

"Worried I won't choose you?" Jude teased. He had always known Penrose would be one of his six. She'd known him since he was born, and though he'd been raised and taught by a number of different stewards and Paladin over the years, she was the one he was closest to. She'd been the one to teach Jude to control his Grace, coaching him through his koahs when he was still young. There was no family in the Order of the Last Light, but if there was, Penrose would be part of his.

"That's not what I meant," Penrose said, her voice taut with urgency. "I didn't just come find you this evening to see how you were doing. I came to tell you something."

Jude's Grace-enhanced hearing could hear her heartbeat pick up. Unease prickled down his spine. "About choosing the Guard?"

"I just want to make sure that when the time comes, you'll do what's best. That you won't let your judgment be clouded by—"

Jude didn't hear what she said next. He heard sound and sensed motion behind him. Quicker than thought, he leapt to the side to evade the oncoming strike. A flash of movement was all he saw of his attacker, but it was more than enough. Using his Grace-enhanced reflexes, Jude rebounded off the pillar of the bridge and launched himself at the unknown figure. Digging his heels into the ground, he threw out his arm to aim a firm blow to the other man's chest.

With a grunt, his attacker hit the ground.

"Well, I guess your reflexes haven't completely gone to shit without me."

Recognition struck Jude like a blade as he stared down at the person at his feet. Hector Navarro was no longer the reedy boy Jude had grown up with. His broad shoulders and chest tapered down to a trim waist and long, muscular legs. A shadow of hair now covered a jawline that had sharpened with time. But he wore the same infuriating, cocky smirk that had provoked a number of fights with the Order's other young wards.

The smirk Jude hadn't seen in over a year. The one he wasn't sure he'd ever see again.

"You're here," Jude said faintly. This, he realized, was what Penrose had been working up to telling him.

But before he could summon any more words, or do anything besides drink in the sight of his friend, Hector leapt from the ground, spinning to face Jude. And then they were off again—blow for blow, Graced speed and strength facing off in a coordinated dance they'd taught each other the steps to years ago.

Laughter bubbled out of Jude unbidden as he ducked under Hector's fist and swept a leg under him. Hector leapt at the precise right moment, knowing Jude's move almost before he did. Their agile back-and-forth devolved into roughhousing and then to playful punches, and then their arms were locked around each other, somewhere between shoving and embracing.

"I don't understand," Jude said, voice light with adrenaline, laughter, and the weight of Hector's broad hand on the back of his neck. "When I got back from my Year of Reflection, you were gone. The others all said you'd left, that you'd decided not to take your oath."

He didn't add that none of them had been surprised by Hector's departure. Hector had been a ward of the Order since he was thirteen, and his friendship with Jude had felt as inevitable as it was unlikely. Even as a young boy, Jude had striven to uphold the virtues instilled in him by the Order, while Hector had been more restless, more troublesome. While Jude cherished mornings spent in contemplative silence, long hours of training, and ascetic devotion to the Prophets, Hector had never seemed suited to the regimented life of a Paladin.

Though Hector had always said he would take up the cloak of the Order of the Last Light, some part of Jude had not believed it.

But now, Hector was here. He'd come *back*.

"I changed my mind," Hector said. As though it could be that simple. His lips quirked in an easy, self-deprecating grin—the kind of smile that he'd used countless times to get Jude to go along with his schemes and antics against his better judgment. "I figured if Jude Weatherbourne believed in me, I had to be worth something."

Jude shoved him again, and Hector batted his head down. Quickly they were swept back into their juvenile game. But it felt *good* to be playing it with Hector again, after all this time. As if all the worries about the Witnesses, the Pale Hand, the Prophet, could be wrenched from Jude's shoulders by Hector's capable hands.

"Penrose, tell Jude he needs to learn how to fight before he can be Keeper of the Word!" Hector called between gasps of laughter.

Jude glanced at Penrose and saw that she was no longer watching them with her well-practiced look of vague disapproval. Instead, she stood with her shoulders pulled back, gaze snapping to something behind him.

Jude did not need to turn to know that his father had arrived.

He sprang away from Hector and shot to Penrose's side.

"Son," Captain Weatherbourne said.

"Captain Weatherbourne," Jude replied, still a little breathless from wrestling.

All the joy of the reunion receded under the weight of his father's stare. Theron Weatherbourne was every bit as intimidating as he'd been in Jude's childhood. He had the same stony face, but his hair had grown grayer in the past year. Like Penrose and Jude, he wore a midnight blue cloak swept across his broad chest, fastened to one shoulder by a pin inlaid with a seven-pointed star pierced by a blade. A golden torc wound around the back of his neck, clasped at his collar.

"I see you've been informed of Navarro's return." He nodded at Hector.

"Sir," Hector said, bowing his head and touching his palm to his chest.

"Come, Jude," Captain Weatherbourne said. "There's something we must discuss."

Apprehension tripped in Jude's chest as Captain Weatherbourne swept away. It was rare for his father to seek him out like this. Theirs was a relationship based on duty rather than affection. The Paladin's oath forbade them from having children, except for the Keeper of the Word, whose duty was to perform the Ritual of Sacred Union in order to produce an heir. Jude's rearing had come primarily at the hands of Order stewards and Paladin, like Penrose.

Captain Weatherbourne kept a brisk pace as he led Jude up a steep pathway that wound through the fort, through ornate archways that mimicked the supple curves of the trees that stretched over them.

"Is this about Hector?" Jude asked. He recalled Penrose's words of caution. It was clear she thought that Jude would choose him to serve on the Paladin Guard—and that she didn't approve. His father probably felt the same.

"No," Captain Weatherbourne replied. "But the fact that you think an errant ward of the Order should be your most important concern on the eve of your ceremony makes me think perhaps we should discuss the matter."

Jude looked down, embarrassed.

"Hector hasn't told anyone why he left the Order," Captain Weatherbourne continued. "Nor, for that matter, why he returned. Nor, indeed, what he was doing while he was away."

Jude knew there were so many unanswered questions about Hector, but he couldn't deny that the sight of him back in Kerameikos Fort had felt like a breath of relief.

"I trust him," Jude said quietly. "Whatever it was he was doing, whatever it was he had to figure out, he came back." *He came back to me.*

Captain Weatherbourne glanced at him as they crossed another slender bridge, past a misting waterfall. Light fractured between them as Jude met his gaze. Tomorrow, he would take his father's place as Keeper of the Word. If he was ready, truly ready, then that meant his decisions, his judgment, had to be trusted. Including his judgment about Hector.

Captain Weatherbourne shook his head. "We all swear the same oath. To give up worldly desires. To serve the Prophets above all else. Above our lives. Above our hearts."

"I know," Jude replied. "If Hector is here, that means he's prepared to do that. I know it. He wouldn't take it lightly."

"I didn't mean Hector."

Blood rushed to Jude's face. Shame cracked him open, exposing the softest, weakest parts within.

"Even when you were boys, it was clear you two had an attachment to each other," Captain Weatherbourne said. "You kept your distance from the other wards, but not him."

Jude's mouth was dry. "You—you never said anything. You never—"

"You are hardly the first Paladin, or even the first Keeper of the Word, to have attachments," Captain Weatherbourne went on. "That is what the Year of Reflection is for, after all. To rise above your doubts. So have you?"

Jude didn't know how to answer.

"Tell me," Captain Weatherbourne said. "Whose place would he take?"

"What do you mean?"

"You already know who you'll choose for your Guard tomorrow," Captain Weatherbourne said. "I know how you are. You've known since you returned from the mountains. Tell me which of those six names would you take off the list for Navarro?"

Jude was silent for a long moment. "None of them," he said finally.

"Then you have your answer."

The river thundered beneath them as they crossed to a high rock outcropping, upon which the Temple of the Prophets stood. Water flowed on every side of the temple rotunda, streaming down the face of the cliff. They ascended the stairs that fanned up to the entrance of the temple. At the main archway, they each paused to dip their fingers into the bowls of consecrating oil and anoint themselves before crossing the threshold.

There were seven open archways in the temple walls, surrounding a sanctum dominated by a large stone pool in the shape of a seven-pointed star. Around the pool, marble stairs led up to an altar of pale silver. The temple walls stretched high above, studded with stones of slate gray, tempest green, deep red, and midnight black, from pupil-sized to as big as Jude's fist. They peered out at him like thousands of jeweled eyes. The oracle stones.

There were written copies of the prophecies in every library of the world, but only the Temple of the Prophets had the oracle stones themselves. Each of the stones had been cast into a scrying pool by one of the Prophets, preserving their visions of the future. Sometimes, these visions came as dreams; other times, as a prophetic trance. The oracle stones held the record of the prophecies that shaped the course of civilization and guided people through times of turmoil and strife.

Members of the Order of the Last Light were the trusted guardians of these prophecies, even now, one hundred years after the Seven Prophets disappeared. Even now that all their prophecies had been fulfilled.

All but one.

"Tomorrow is an important day, Jude. More than ever, you cannot be distracted," Captain Weatherbourne said, climbing the stairs to the altar that stood above the scrying pool. He lifted the silver box that lay on the altar and returned to Jude's side. He held the box out, and Jude, hesitating, opened it.

A smooth, pearlescent stone glowed softly inside. It was bigger than Jude's fist and traced with intricate spirals. A large crack ran through it, almost cleaving the stone in two.

Jude put his hand over the stone reverently. This was the last oracle stone the Prophets had ever cast. It contained their final prophecy. The prophecy that had been kept secret by the Order of the Last Light for a century. The prophecy that was still incomplete.

"The prophecy is unfolding," Captain Weatherbourne said. "The harbingers are here. The Age of Darkness is almost upon us. If we don't find the Last Prophet soon . . ." He didn't need to finish the thought.

Jude looked up from the oracle stone to his father's face. "You are the Keeper of the Word, Father. If the prophecy is unfolding, if the Age of Darkness is upon us, they need *you*. When we find the Prophet, he'll need someone experienced, someone knowledgeable, someone—"

"Enough," Captain Weatherbourne said. "I have been Keeper of the Word for thirty-three years. I have protected the secret of the last prophecy, the same way the Keepers that came before me did. But I was never meant to be the one to wield the Pinnacle Blade and protect the Last Prophet."

"I don't understand."

"My duty is complete," Captain Weatherbourne said, eyes bright with some emotion Jude had never seen before. "I have produced an heir to the Weatherbourne line. You, Jude. You are the one who is meant to protect the Last Prophet. I knew it on that day, sixteen years ago, when the sky lit up."

Jude shivered. He remembered that day, too. He could still remember the cold rub of the wind on his cheeks and how tiny he'd felt in the shadow of the monoliths. And above, the sky, lit like a glorious flame, ribbons of violet and red and gold shivering through it, their luminous dance calling out to the earth below. To those who knew the secret of the last prophecy, it was a day that had meant promise and hope. Promise that the Last Prophet had at last arrived to complete the final prophecy and show them how to stop the Age of Darkness.

In that moment, Jude had known, with a certainty that astonished him even now, that somehow, this bright, immense, enveloping thing was calling to him.

"You were just a child," his father said. "But I knew then. It was as if the Prophet had waited for you. When he finally arrived, his *esha* called out to you. You are meant to be his Keeper, to keep him safe so that he may save us all."

Jude felt paralyzed. His father believed in him. The Order, too. *Everyone knows you're destined for great things,* Hector used to say. It should have made Jude proud. But it was as if he had been climbing a great tower his whole life, toward a beacon of light, step after step after step, and now, with his destination in reach, the beacon flickered out and all he could see was the black abyss of the unknown.

"This is what I came to tell you, son," his father said. His face was brilliant with light and hope. "After sixteen years, our search is over. The Last Prophet has been found."

5

HASSAN

AFTER NARROWLY RETURNING IN TIME FOR SUPPER AFTER HIS FIRST VENTURE into the agora, Hassan couldn't stop thinking about what had happened—the Witnesses, the Herati acolyte who may have recognized him, and most of all, the Legionnaire standing over him on the steps of the temple like a prophesized hero from a story, curved sword gleaming in her hand.

He knew he had to go back, and when he did, he wanted more time than a stolen hour or two.

The opportunity arrived the very next day.

"Now don't sulk, Hassan, but I'll be dining out tonight."

Hassan looked up from *The History of the Six Prophetic Cities* to see his aunt standing in the broad open doorway of the balcony. Lethia Siskos was the elder sister of Hassan's father, though the two resembled each other very little. Lethia was a tall, bony woman, whose stern, lined face contrasted with her brother's warmer, softer features. But their eyes were the exact same shade of river green—and when Lethia rested those eyes on Hassan, he almost felt like his father was watching over him.

Lethia had married her husband, the previous Archon Basileus of Pallas Athos, long before Hassan was born, but she and her two sons had returned to visit the Palace of Herat often when Hassan was a child. Hassan had always greatly looked forward to their visits. Like him, Lethia and her sons were not Graced, and their presence in the palace had always made him feel less alone.

"I don't sulk," he said automatically, marking his place and closing the book.

"Then don't pout."

"Where are you going?" Hassan asked, mentally calculating how much time he would have while she was out.

"The Archon Basileus and the Basilinna invited me to dine at their estate," Lethia replied, leaning against the balcony balustrade. "Apparently, there's been some scandal with a priest murdered at one of the tavernas in the High City. They're saying it's connected to murders in other cities. The Archon is quite worked up about it."

"He's worried about a murder when the Witnesses are ruling Nazirah?" Hassan asked, his plans for sneaking out to the agora momentarily forgotten. "Has he given you an answer yet?"

Lethia's brow creased. "Not yet. He says he's sympathetic to what's happened in Nazirah, but that he's facing a backlash for allowing the refugees into the agora."

Hassan thought back to the way the butcher had sneered at Azizi. "The Temple of Pallas used to welcome pilgrims from all over the Pelagos into the agora. How is this any different?"

"Because it's been a hundred years since there were pilgrims in Pallas Athos," Lethia replied. "The priests are no longer interested in anything but protecting their own wealth and power. The only thing they care about is keeping the populace happy enough not to complain about their greed."

"Then the Archon Basileus should punish them," Hassan replied. That was what *he* would do, if this were Herat. Corruption brewed in every city, everywhere, and the only way to stamp it out was to act swiftly to remove those who abused their power. "He should dismiss the worst offenders from their stations. While he's at it, he should confiscate the tribute of the offenders and use it to feed the refugees."

"Spoken like a prince," Lethia said. "But Pallas Athos isn't Herat. The Archon Basileus doesn't have the power to remove the priests from their stations. They were originally chosen by Pallas himself."

"But Pallas is no longer here. None of the Prophets are."

"And the priests maintain that whoever Pallas chose has the authority to appoint their successors after the Prophets disappeared."

"A perfect recipe for corruption," Hassan said bitterly. Those who abused their power would only continue the cycle, rewarding the ones who enabled them.

"I told my husband repeatedly to contest this claim before he died. To set up a new system while he was still Archon," Lethia said. "He never listened—just like every time I tried to give him counsel. The corruption of the priests is entrenched in the city. They'll do whatever they must to maintain their power, empty as it is."

Hassan's stomach twisted. He had known when he came here that the priests were corrupt and self-serving, and that the Archon Basileus who ruled over them was an ineffectual figurehead. He was a fool for thinking they would help him.

"Don't the priests understand that the Witnesses pose a threat to them?" Hassan asked, anger building. "If the Witnesses gain a strong-hold in Nazirah, the other Cities are next. They've already begun to grow bolder in these very streets."

"And how, exactly, would you know that, Prince Hassan?"

"I—" He stopped, realizing that if he wanted to keep his visit to the agora a secret, he would have to tread lightly. "I hear the servants talking. They're worried about what's been happening here in Pallas Athos. The Witnesses burned down a shrine in the Low City a few weeks ago. They were even spotted outside the Temple of Pallas yesterday."

Lethia watched him with careful eyes, and then she sighed. "I can see how worked up you are about this, Hassan. And I agree with you. Of course I do. Nazirah is my city, too, even if it's been three decades since I lived there. I know how worried you are for your parents. I worry for my brother and the queen, too."

Hassan seethed, but his anger was more for himself than the Archon. "There has to be more I can do. Something to convince them, anyone, to help my people. I just feel so . . . useless." He brushed his fingers against his breast pocket, where the compass lay against his heart. His father was the one person who had never, for a moment, doubted that Hassan was capable of ruling one day. Thinking of his father's faith in him now made bitterness rise in his throat. "Father never should have named me his heir."

Lethia's voice was gentle as she drew closer. "What the Witnesses have done is not your fault."

"But I couldn't stop them," he said.

"And if you were Graced, you could have?"

He didn't answer. She was right, of course. The Graced were powerful, but they weren't invincible. Being Graced had not stopped his father and mother from being captured. Their Graces gave them power, yes, but it was also the reason that the Witnesses sought to depose them. And if the rumors were true about the Hierophant's ability to block the Graced from using their powers, there was no way they could protect themselves. Dread pitted Hassan's stomach at the thought.

Lethia's gaze slid away from him. "You should be glad, Prince Hassan, that your father did not deny you your birthright."

The words hung between them. As the eldest daughter of the Queen of Herat, Lethia should have been the next in line for the throne when her mother died. But like Hassan, Lethia had been born Graceless. Instead of being named queen, Lethia had been married off to the aging Archon Basileus of Pallas Athos. A man who, from what Hassan gathered, had never cared much for his wife, or her considerable skill at politics. When he'd died, his title had not passed to Lethia's sons, since they were not Graced, either.

"I asked my mother, once, if she'd ever considered naming me her heir," Lethia said. "All she said was that the happiest day of her life was the day your father's Grace manifested."

Hassan swallowed, not knowing what to say. Lethia had been passed over to become the Queen of Herat because she was Graceless. Now, despite being Graceless himself, Hassan was the heir.

"I suppose I shouldn't be too harsh on her," Lethia went on. "My mother grew up in those tumultuous decades just after the Prophets disappeared, when people feared any departure from tradition. But now, things are finally beginning to change. You are proof of that."

Hassan shook his head. "I don't deserve this birthright if I can't do anything to help my people."

"I wish there was more I could do, too," Lethia said. "I'll speak to the Archon again tonight, but I wouldn't get your hopes up."

Hassan closed his eyes. "Thank you for trying."

She smoothed a hand over his shoulder and then turned to descend the stairs to the central courtyard.

Hassan retreated inside, his mind drifting back to the agora and the conditions he'd seen in the refugee camps. Maybe he couldn't yet do anything for his people back home, but he could do something for the ones who were here.

"I'll be spending the evening in the library," Hassan informed the servants in his sitting room. "I shouldn't be disturbed. You can leave dinner for me here."

Fortunately, the servants had grown used to him at this point, and knew it was not out of the ordinary for him to lock himself in the library for hours on end. It was how he'd spent most of his time in Nazirah, too—burying himself in the histories of the Six Prophetic Cities, learning all he could about the resources of his country, about warfare and diplomacy—until he'd outread even his tutors from the Great Library.

Now, though, Hassan was tired of trying to arm himself with tales and facts. He wanted to *act*. So he took a volume from the library to enjoy outside in the dappled sunlight of the sitting garden. When he was sure the servants had left him to his own devices, he hopped the low garden wall and exited the villa's grounds.

He was becoming an expert at sneaking out.

The refugees largely ignored Hassan as he made his way into the agora, going about their business with grim resignation. He passed the long line of people waiting to gather water from the fountainhouse, spotting children as young as six and seven hauling jugs back to their camp-sites, many of them barefoot. Clouds of dirt and dust choked the air as a group of women beat out their tent canvases with sticks. Another woman with a broom was ineffectually trying to sweep the dirt from within her own shelter, an infant strapped to her back.

The crack of wood hitting wood cut through the din. Hassan's gaze was drawn to an open arena surrounded by crumbling columns, where a group of people stood watching three pairs of sparring fighters.

Hassan's eyes fell to the last of the sparring pairs—one of them was the same Legionnaire who'd saved him from the Witnesses at the temple. Instead of her curved Herati blade, she wielded a wooden practice sword that seemed to have been carved out of an olive branch.

"Defend your left side, Faran!" an onlooker cried out to her oppo-nent as the Legionnaire delivered a well-placed strike.

The opponent grunted, adjusting to the command. The Legionnaire feinted left again, and then struck him on the right. After a few more attacks she had him disarmed and flat on his back in the dirt.

"That's the match," the girl said, helping her opponent back to his feet before tossing the practice sword at him. "Next time, hold on to your weapon."

Her eyes flickered from her opponent to Hassan, behind him. "You're back," she said, cocking her head. "How's that arm?"

"It's fine." Her eyes on him made him feel like a fly trapped in warm honey. She wasn't pretty the way the delicate daughters at court or the alluring Herati flood dancers were pretty. She was *compelling*. Strong-jawed and muscular, she carried herself with strength—not just physi-cal strength, but a strength of spirit, a knowledge of herself that Hassan found intimidating.

"What was your name again?" she asked. A few dark strands of hair had escaped her bun and fell loosely against her cheek.

"Uh . . . Cirion." Unprepared to provide a name that was not his own, Hassan had chosen the first one he could think of—the name of his cousin, Lethia's eldest son.

"You here looking for more trouble, Cirion?" she asked. "What, are they not keeping you busy enough in your studies?"

Hassan had almost forgotten that he'd told her he was a student at the Akademos. "I guess not."

"Or maybe you're here looking for a lesson," she went on, a sly edge to her tone.

"Lesson?"

"That's right," she said. "I'm training the other refugees. The Sentry have been worse than useless at keeping the camps safe, so we've decided to take things into our own hands."

"Oh," Hassan said hastily. "Well, I suppose I shouldn't—"

"Come on," she said, nudging his shoulder. "If you're going to interrupt, you might as well learn something. Then maybe next time, I won't have to come in and save your ass."

A delighted laugh choked out of Hassan. No one had ever talked to him like that at the palace. "Oh, I don't know."

"What's the harm?" she needled. "I'll go easy on you."

He couldn't resist the confident gleam in her eyes. "Well, all right. As long as you go easy."

She backed away from Hassan, tossing a grin over her shoulder. "I'm Khepri, by the way."

He trailed after her as they wove between two pairs of sparring refugees, where a rack of wooden swords stood. She picked one up and tossed another at Hassan.

He caught it with one hand, looking up to see surprise flash across her face.

They positioned themselves between two other pairs of fighters in the arena. Khepri's expression was one of confident determination as she shifted back and took up a defensive stance, inviting Hassan to make the first move.

Hassan felt a smile break over his face as he shifted into an offensive stance. It had been a long while since he'd last sparred, but it felt good to use his body like this. Even though he didn't have the Grace of Heart, he'd always enjoyed strategy and physicality coming together for a common cause. His mother had taught him well enough to hold his own in a sword fight against anyone without the Grace of Heart.

Most days, he did everything he could not to think about where his mother might be now, or what was happening to her as a prisoner of the Hierophant. But if his sparring lessons had taught him anything, it was that his mother was a fighter. Wherever she was, she was fighting.

"I won't use any koahs," Khepri said.

"That sounds fair." Without using koahs, she wouldn't have the overwhelming advantage of Graced strength, speed, and enhanced senses.

She laughed. "Oh, it won't be *fair*. But maybe a bit more interesting."

Hassan made the first move, a strike heavy on the footwork, which kept his guard firmly intact. It was a hedge—he wanted to see how she would react.

She parried the blow and then, sweeping beneath his blade, countered it. Hassan blocked—and felt another spark of surprise from Khepri.

"You're a liar!" she exclaimed, sounding delighted. "You're no soft-handed scholar. You've fought before."

"Not all us scholars have soft hands," Hassan answered, wiping a bead of sweat from his forehead.

She attacked again, quicker than before. The force of the impact drove Hassan back, catching him wrong-footed.

Khepri didn't hesitate. She attacked yet again, taking advantage of his imbalance. He twisted away from her, the wooden sword singing past. They separated, regrouping. Khepri did not seem put off by the failure of her attack. In fact, she seemed pleased, and Hassan got the sense that she was just getting started.

He lunged forward and struck again, and Khepri's blade was there to meet his, without her ever having taken her eyes off his. He was beginning to feel the itch of competition thrum through his veins. He wanted to impress her, to show her he could keep up. They traded blows, attack and rejoinder, their blades whirling and clashing, pace ratcheting. Exhilaration sang through Hassan's blood. But even as Hassan met her blow for blow, he could see she was merely humoring him. Toying with him, even. She underestimated him.

He couldn't have that. With his next strike, he drove her back and then pretended to trip toward her. When she moved to take advantage of his apparent mistake, he stepped into her and swung down to buckle her stance.

She stumbled, catching herself on her sword to avoid winding up flat on her back.

Hassan gazed down at her, his own sword poised in front of her, a victorious smile creeping over his face. She swung up, and he blocked her sword with his own.

"All right," Khepri said, their swords crossed between them. "You're not bad."

And then, as he registered the grin on her face, Khepri kicked up, knocking the sword from his grip, and tackled him to the ground.

Hassan hit the dirt with a grunt, pinned there with his hips trapped between her knees.

Her triumphant face beamed down at him. "But I'm still better."

Hassan wanted to say something witty back, but Khepri was

breathing hard, and the effect of her exertion was . . . distracting. His face began to heat, but before he could truly embarrass himself, she climbed off him. He couldn't tell if he was relieved or disappointed.

She grasped his hand and pulled him to his feet with entirely too much ease. Graced strength.

"You said you wouldn't use your Grace," Hassan said.

"Fight's over."

"Then a rematch."

He was growing to like the sound of her laughter. "You think you're going to fare any better in round two?"

"You wouldn't begrudge a man for hoping, would you?"

"Hope should never be begrudged," Khepri said, and there was something unexpectedly soft in her voice, precious, like the slow unfurling of a river lily. "What about dinner, instead?"

Hassan hadn't expected that. He thought about how deeply he wanted to spend more time here—with the refugees, of course, but also with Khepri. "I'd like that."

She smiled at him, and Hassan realized their hands were still joined. She seemed to realize it, too, but rather than letting go, she turned his hand over, running her fingers lightly along his palm. His skin prickled, and he could feel himself beginning to flush.

"Still pretty soft," she murmured. She looked up, lips curling. "You'll have to build up those calluses if you want to beat me next time."

She dropped his hand and busied herself with picking up the practice swords, while Hassan stared after her. He shook himself, and as the sun sank into the sea, they set off together.

The smell of smoke filled the air as they made their way to the other side of the agora, where the campfires were just beginning to glow. As they approached the campfire Khepri shared, Hassan saw familiar faces: Azizi, his mother, and his baby sister. They, as well as the older woman Hassan had spoken with the day before, welcomed Hassan readily and put him to work peeling and seeding squash.

"You're lucky," said Azizi's mother, who'd introduced herself as Halima. "This is only the second time we've had fresh vegetables since we came here."

Hassan frowned, thinking of the many rich meals he'd enjoyed at his aunt's villa without even thinking about it. "Where does the food come from?"

"The temple acolytes have donated much of it," she said. "Enough to keep us all alive, for now. Some of the boys have gone into the surrounding hillsides to hunt for small game and birds. It's summer now, but I fear what will happen when winter comes."

"That's months from now," Hassan said, surprised. He wondered how many of the other refugees thought it would be months before they returned home.

Dinner seemed to be a communal affair—each campfire was shared by five or more families who all pooled resources and pitched in together while the children too young to help were corralled by one of the adults. Tonight, it was Khepri's turn on child duty. Every so often Hassan would look up from peeling squash to watch the children clambering all over her—climbing onto her back and launching themselves at her knees, which Khepri bore with admirable patience.

As the sky grew dark, they all gathered around the fire to eat. Though Hassan had only a few bites, leaving most of the food for the others, he could not remember the last time he'd enjoyed a meal so heartily—roasted squash and lentils seasoned with cracked pepper, served with sun-risen bread stuffed with nuts and figs. It was much simpler than the extravagant meals Hassan was used to in the royal palace, but everything smelled and tasted so much like home that his chest ached.

Having this tiny piece of Herat made him want all of it—he wanted to smell the perfume of blue river lilies and fresh sun-risen bread, feel thick river silt between his fingers, taste sweet pomegranate wine, hear the clamorous bells and drums of the graduating scholars parading down Ozmandith Road.

Over the course of the meal, Hassan learned more about what the lives of these families were like since they'd escaped Nazirah. The agora was already overcrowded, with two or three families sharing shelters built only for one. The fountainhouse near the Sacred Gate was the only source of fresh water for all of the camps, which meant much of the day was taken up by standing in long lines and there was never enough water for washing and cooking, which had led to an outbreak of lice early on. Most of the refugees had come to Pallas Athos with little more than the clothes on their backs, so even something as simple as soap or bowls was hard to come by.

Yet despite these hardships, and despite how little the priests of Pallas Athos had done to welcome the refugees to the city, there remained a sense of perseverance and hope. Despair loomed like a storm around them, but there was an unmistakable love and care in how they treated one another.

After they finished eating, Hassan and Khepri sat out by the glowing light of the fire. Azizi and the other Herati children chanted and ran circles around the glowing flames.

"I know this game!" Hassan exclaimed, grateful that despite everything these kids had gone through, they could still play and tease and laugh as the children back home did.

Beside him, Khepri let out a braying laugh. "Every Herati child plays this game."

"I didn't," Hassan said. "But I used to watch through the study window as the other children played it around the courtyard fountains."

"The study window?" she echoed incredulously. "Were you locked in a tower as a child?"

Hassan laughed, a little uneasy. "Something like that."

"All right, then," Khepri said, getting to her feet abruptly.

Hassan blinked as she held a hand out to him.

"Get up," she said. "We're playing."

He laughed, and Khepri pulled him to his feet. Cupping a hand around her mouth, she cried, "Ibis and heron, beware of me!"

"Crocodile, crocodile, let us be!" the children chorused back.

Khepri grinned at Hassan, and the two of them rushed toward the children, who shrieked with laughter and ran around the campfire. Khepri seized one little girl and lifted her to the sky. The girl cried out in delight. When Khepri set her back down, the girl cried, "Ibis and heron, beware of me!"

Hassan let himself get carried away in the childish game, the exhilaration of running, the thrill of being caught. Somehow, ten minutes later, every single child was chasing after him. They swarmed him at once, tackling him to the ground and piling on top.

"I yield, I yield!" Hassan cried, tears of laughter leaking from his eyes as Azizi ran a triumphant lap around him.

"Let him up, crocodiles," Khepri said, wading into the pile to drag Hassan out. She couldn't keep the laughter from her voice as she asked, "You all right?"

"I'm fine."

"Here, you've got a—" Khepri reached up to Hassan's hair, plucking a twig from it. "There."

He could feel himself flushing again. "You didn't warn me that this game is more grueling than a Legionnaire's training."

Khepri laughed, hooking her arm through his and steering him away from the kids. A chorus of *ooooohs* followed them as they headed toward a grass-covered outcropping.

"Are you going to *kiss?*" one girl demanded.

"*Eww!*" Azizi bellowed.

Hassan laughed helplessly, the children's jeers fading away as he and Khepri climbed the outcropping. It overlooked the agora on one side, and the entire city of Pallas Athos on the other.

"Those kids are worse than my brothers, I swear," Khepri grumbled, flopping down in the grass.

"Your brothers tease you?" Hassan asked, settling beside her.

"Relentlessly." She huffed out a breath, and then Hassan saw it— the tiny shift in her expression that told him her thoughts had turned to Nazirah.

Impulsively, he reached for her hand. "They're still in Nazirah, aren't they?"

Her eyes clouded with grief. "My whole family is."

He wanted to know everything that lay behind that look in her eyes. "How did you get out?"

She looked down at his hand but didn't move away. "My brothers were enlisted in the Legionnaires, like me. We found a merchant ship from Endarrion, who'd agreed to smuggle us. But on the night we were to leave, the Witnesses were at the harbor. They searched the ship while we hid inside. We knew they would find us, so my brothers surrendered. They managed to keep the Witnesses from finding me. They sacrificed themselves so that I could be free." She looked at Hassan with the same fierce gleam in her eyes that he'd seen when they'd first met. "Every day I wake up to that truth."

Hassan thought of his own family, his mother and father who were still prisoners, at the mercy of people who thought they were a corruption of nature. He knew the burden of being safe while those you loved were not. He knew how fear and anger choked you at every waking moment. How even as you slept, your mind never tired of torturing you with all the terrible things that could be happening, and all the things you should have done differently to stop them.

He wished there were a way to tell her all of that without revealing to her who he was. This grief was something they shared, and keeping it hidden from her pitted Hassan's gut with guilt.

"I'm sorry," he said, hating how inadequate those words were. He looked over her shoulder at the campsite and the children who were still running and laughing, evading their parents' half-hearted attempts to get them settled for bed.

"It's why I came here," Khepri said after a long moment. "They're taking refugees in Charis, too, but I came *here*. Where Prince Hassan is."

For a moment, Hassan couldn't speak. "How—how do you know that?"

"His aunt was wife to the late Archon Basileus," Khepri replied. "And if Prince Hassan really survived the coup like everyone said, he would have come here, where he had family and allies. I know it."

Hassan's heart was beating so hard he was sure that Khepri must have heard it. But she didn't seem to notice. Her eyes gleamed as they looked out at the city below, from the Sentry citadel and the Akademos in the second tier, to the sea of tiled roofs that covered the slope of the bottom tier, to the domed roof of the train station, in the Low City, beyond the gates.

"It feels right to be here," she said. "This is the City of Faith, after all. That's what led me here. Faith. When the Hierophant and the Witnesses took Nazirah, I wanted to tear them apart, and I didn't care what I had to sacrifice to do it. I let my hatred take over."

Hassan knew exactly what she meant. He had felt the hot pull of hatred outside the temple, facing down the Witnesses. And still, in the darkest part of his heart, he felt it when he thought of the Hierophant and his followers.

"But when I heard that Prince Hassan had survived the coup, my rage suddenly had a new purpose. I can't explain it, but . . . I knew I needed to come here. I came to the City of Faith to find the prince and help him retake our country."

"You think he can?" Hassan asked. He felt like a helpless scarab, pinned by her gaze, overwhelmed by the desire to tell her who he was. If anyone could have understood the way he felt, the way he longed for a home that had been violently wrenched from him, it was Khepri. This brave girl who'd come seeking him from his homeland.

She nodded. "I know it. The captain of my regiment in the Herati Legionnaires met him once. He said the prince has the best parts of his parents. The strength and courage of the queen, and the wisdom and compassion of the king."

Hassan closed his eyes briefly. The prince she described felt like another person entirely. What would she think when she found out the prince she believed could save his people was hiding in his aunt's villa, without a plan or any hope of freeing his country?

"What if he isn't here?" he asked. He swallowed. "What if you came all this way for nothing?"

The look she gave him was fleeting but bright, like the flash of a lightning bug over the banks of the Herat River. "It wouldn't have been for nothing."

Hassan felt her calloused palm over his hand as she leaned toward him. He stuttered in a breath, his eyes sliding shut.

"Cirion," she said softly.

Hassan squeezed his eyes shut and, hating himself, pulled away from her. As much as he wanted to let himself have this moment, unfettered by worry, he knew he couldn't. Not when it would be a lie. But he couldn't tell her the truth. Not now. The person she'd come looking for, the wise, courageous Prince of Herat who could lead his people to freedom—that wasn't Hassan. He was just another lost refugee, afraid and desperately hoping that there was someone who could show him the way.

6

ANTON

ANTON WOKE UP DROWNING. CHEST BURSTING, STARS BEHIND HIS EYES, A CALL ringing through his head—

His eyes flew open.

A gust of breath. Not water, but air. The stale air of his tiny tenement flat. It flooded his lungs as Anton lay twisted in sweat-damp sheets. He lifted trembling fingers to his throat and then pressed, counting each tap of his pulse against his fingertips.

It had been years since he'd dreamed of the lake. In the months after he left home, the bad dream had been a nightly visitor. The gray sky, the snow, the dark shape behind him as his feet carried him over the frozen lake. Ice cracking beneath him, cruel hands forcing him down as he thrashed in the freezing water.

Now, as he pushed himself up on his narrow bed, Anton felt as small and helpless as he had in that cold, biting water. He was restless, unmoored, feeling like at any moment the world could slide out from under him, plunging him back into the deep and the dark.

Warm wind shuddered in from the tiny window, lifting the edges of the curtain. Moonlight slanted into the room, casting rippling shadows on the wall.

And then Anton realized two things. He hadn't left his window open before he fell asleep.

And someone was in the room with him.

He felt their *esha* first, like the muted flutter of a moth's wings. It was unfamiliar—not the one he feared, the one belonging to the man that sought him. He drew in a sharp breath as his eyes fell on the shadow the stranger cast in the pale moonlight.

"I'm not here to hurt you."

It was a girl's voice—low and rough-edged. As Anton blinked at her in the dark, he saw that a silk mask covered the lower half of her face, leaving only two bright eyes peering at him from across the room.

He weighed his options. She was positioned beside the window, near the foot of the bed and across from the door. There was very little chance he could reach it before she did.

He would have to take her at her word.

"What do you want?" he asked.

She tilted her head. "You don't know who I am?"

"Should I?"

"The priest at Thalassa Gardens didn't, either."

Anton sucked in a breath. Of all the horrors he had ever imagined visiting him in the middle of the night, the Pale Hand was not one of them.

He made himself speak. "Are you here to kill me?"

Something like amusement flashed in her eyes. "Would you deserve it?"

Anton shook his head slowly.

"Then you've nothing to fear."

He thought back to his dream, to the warning about who was

looking for him, and wondered if the Pale Hand's words would ever be true.

"If you're not here to kill me, then what are you doing in my room?"

"I'm looking for Mrs. Tappan," she replied. "And I think perhaps you can help me find her."

Anton blinked in surprise. It wasn't hard to believe that somehow Mrs. Tappan was mixed up with a notorious killer—but usually, *she* was the one looking for someone.

"I don't know who that is," he lied, swinging his legs down to plant them on the floor beside his bed.

"This letter she left you at Thalassa Gardens says differently." In the dim light of the room, Anton saw her hold out an envelope. He could only guess that it bore the compass-rose seal of Mrs. Tappan's Scrying Agency. She must have left it for him after he'd fled.

"How did you get that?"

The Pale Hand drew nearer to the bed, still holding out the letter. "This is you, right? Anton?"

He reached for it, but she tugged it away. "Tell me where she is, and you get your letter."

"I don't know where she is."

"But you spoke with her last night."

Had it only been last night? The past day had gone by in a blur of nightmare and memory, so tightly woven in Anton's mind that he could scarcely pick them apart.

"How do you know that?"

He couldn't see her mouth beneath the mask, but he had the sense she might be smiling. "I met a few of your friends at Thalassa. They said a woman dined there last night with whom you had a very interesting-looking conversation. And that you disappeared not long after that."

He cursed Cosima for her insatiable nosiness and her inability to keep her mouth shut.

"So," the Pale Hand pressed, "what did you talk about?"

Anton lifted one shoulder. "She just likes to check up on me. See how I'm doing."

"You're not a very good liar."

"I'm not a liar."

"Then what *are* you?" she asked. "Mrs. Tappan doesn't do grunt work herself. She doesn't even show her face to most people. Why you?"

Instead of answering, he said, "That's not her real name, you know."

Names had a particular resonance with the *esha* of the person they belonged to. That was how scryers found their targets. For Anton, the sense was more acute. He couldn't exactly tell a person's name just from sensing their *esha*, but he could tell when a name didn't match. The name Mrs. Tappan had never resonated with her distinctive, bell-like *esha*.

"Then what is it?"

"I don't know," Anton replied. "But it's not that."

"How would you know that?" Her whole demeanor had changed, her eyes widening. "It's you, isn't it? The scryer she told us about. You're him. She said you could help me. That no other scryer can do what you can."

In a flash, it all began to make sense. The job the Nameless Woman had tried to offer him last night—it had come from the Pale Hand.

"Well, she lied," Anton said flatly. "I'm no one. I can't help you, so get out before I tell the Sentry exactly where they can find you."

She didn't move.

"I'm serious," he said, pushing past her to the door. "You have two minutes to get out."

Even if he felt a glimmer of curiosity—what did the Pale Hand want with *him?*—he wouldn't give in to it. The nightmares had already returned, and using his Grace would make them unbearable, he knew. It wasn't a road he was willing to go down, no matter what threats or promises the Pale Hand made.

But what she said next was not a threat or a promise. It was a question. "Who's Illya Aliyev?"

Shock froze him like ice. He hadn't heard that name spoken aloud in over five years. "Where did you hear that name?"

The Pale Hand held out the envelope again. This time, when Anton reached for it, she relinquished it.

The seal had already been broken, predictably. Anton tore into the letter inside, his eyes catching on the first line.

> *Illya Aliyev. Last known transaction: chartered passenger ship. Destination: Pallas Athos.*

There were a dozen full paragraphs below that Anton's eyes scanned over quickly. A full dossier on the man who was searching for him, researched, written up, and delivered. The man the Nameless Woman had warned him about at Thalassa Gardens. The man who haunted Anton's dreams.

He should be grateful that the Nameless Woman had gone through the trouble of getting that information to him. Grateful that she'd come to him in the first place, instead of giving Anton up and collecting her fee. But he didn't have it in him to feel grateful, not when he felt like he was choking on cold dread.

He'll only take his case elsewhere.

This meant he already had. He was *here*, in Pallas Athos. He probably knew exactly where Anton was. He could even be on his way now.

"If you're as powerful a scryer as she says," the Pale Hand said, "why do you need a bounty hunter's help to find him?"

"I don't," Anton replied, stuffing the letter back inside its envelope and crossing the room in three brisk strides. "And I'm not a powerful anything."

Kneeling at the wooden wine crates that passed for dresser drawers, he started digging for clothes. He knew he should have left Pallas Athos the moment the Nameless Woman had told him Illya was looking for him. He would leave now. Go somewhere far. Maybe across the Pelagos, to the eastern port of Tel Amot. To the deserts that stretched endlessly beyond it.

"What are you doing?" the Pale Hand asked as Anton haphazardly threw bundles of clothes into his pack.

"Leaving."

"It's the middle of the night."

"Then I need to hurry, don't I?" Anton replied. "Ships launch at dawn."

"You're in that big a hurry to find this person?"

The sound of footfalls echoed up from the cobbled street below Anton's window. The Pale Hand shrank into the shadows as Anton went to the window, keeping himself hidden behind the curtain.

More footfalls.

"Expecting someone?" the Pale Hand asked. Anton could see the panic in her eyes.

He drew the curtain back a half inch to peer outside. Half a dozen men stood at the mouth of the alley that ran outside his building, illuminated by the moon.

"Who is it?" the Pale Hand asked sharply.

Anton pressed his back flat against the wall, breathing hard. "Hired swords, I think."

They had to be Illya's. Mrs. Tappan had mentioned that she'd been offered a tempting amount of money to find him. If Illya had access to that kind of money—and Anton had no doubt he'd snaked his way into it somehow—then he'd have enough to hire men to do his dirty work.

The Pale Hand cursed beneath her breath. "Why wouldn't the Conclave just send the Sentry after me?"

"I don't think they're here for you," Anton said slowly.

"Then—You? Why?"

He swallowed. "That man," he said. "From the letter. Illya."

"The one you're looking for?"

He shook his head. "I'm not looking for him. He's looking for me."

And it seemed he'd already found him.

The Pale Hand's eyes locked with Anton's, and he could see the calculation in them, the same way he was sure she could see the desperation in his.

"Come with me," she said suddenly.

"What?"

"I know a place. It's safe. No one will be able to find you."

Anton hesitated.

"You have a better offer or something?"

He didn't. It wasn't like he had an abundance of close friends who would take it in stride if he showed up unannounced in the middle of the night. And if these hired swords had tracked him here, they could track him to Thalassa. They could even be staking it out now.

"Come on, kid. This offer expires the second those swords set foot in here."

"Are you working with him?" Anton asked.

"Working with—? You mean this Illya guy who's after you? No," she replied. "I told you, I came to find you because Mrs. Tappan said you could help me."

She didn't sound like she was lying, but accomplished liars rarely did.

"The way I see it, you have two choices: Stay here and see what these swords want with you. Or come with me."

"And do what?"

"Why don't we discuss that once there aren't half a dozen armed men breathing down our necks."

Anton considered his options. Trusting the Pale Hand was a gamble. But Anton's bets almost always paid off. "Fine. Let's go."

They stole into the corridor.

"There's another way out," Anton said. He led her down to the basement of the building, a cramped space filled with scuttling rats and cobwebs. They crept through the cellar and out the back door into an alley.

The Pale Hand edged along the side of the building. Anton followed. Shoulder to shoulder, they crouched with their backs against the wall, waiting for the last of the men to filter inside the building.

Anton slowed his breath and counted. The Pale Hand let out a soft curse.

"What is it?" Anton asked.

"They left some guards outside. Two men," she answered. "All right. Time to run."

Anton's heart kicked up. "They'll see us."

The Pale Hand crouched down, looking for something on the ground. "Perfect."

She held up a rock the size of her fist. Balancing it in one hand, she drew her arm back and threw the rock down the opposite end of the alley. It was too dark to see where it landed, but the resulting sound was loud enough to startle the guards into action.

The Pale Hand didn't waste any time. The moment their backs turned, she grabbed Anton's arm and set off at a run.

"Over there!" a voice called from behind them.

Anton wanted to see if the guard had spotted them, but the Pale Hand tugged him harder.

The sound of quickened footsteps gave him the answer. The guards were chasing after them.

At the end of the road, the Pale Hand took a hard left, and Anton followed her as she darted through the narrow streets.

"In here!" she cried. Anton skidded around the sharp turn and nearly ran into her.

She'd pried open the front window of a shop with a sign over the door emblazoned with a gear. The footsteps grew louder behind them. The choice was no choice at all. With the Pale Hand's help, he pulled himself up onto the window ledge. He felt around in the dark and found that there was a table below that seemed to be covered in various wires, gears, and glassware. He winced at the clatter and clash as they pulled themselves through the window.

Safely inside, they shuttered the window and then pressed their backs to the wall, out of sight. They sat there in the dark, breathing hard, waiting for the sound of running footsteps to pass by.

"Careful!" the Pale Hand warned as Anton stretched his legs out, jostling the table.

She caught a falling glass orb and froze. The guard's hurried footsteps thundered past the shop and faded into the distance.

Anton let out a breath.

Beside him, he heard the sound of soft tapping, and then a dim light filled the shop. It flickered and then grew brighter, and when he turned around he saw that the orb in the Pale Hand's palm was a small lamp glowing with incandescent light.

"What now?" he asked.

She looked at him, face half shadowed by the globe light. "Now," she said, "you come with me."

7

BERU

IN THE SECRET ALCOVE BELOW THE CRYPT OF PESISTRATOS, BERU PASSED THE night like she had so many others—with a cup of warm mint tea and the fervent hope that her sister would return alive.

Ephyra had gone into the black night alone many times before this, to face murderers and slavers and the most depraved men in the Six Prophetic Cities. Yet Beru felt more nervous now than she had on any of those nights. It was silly—she knew that. There was nothing to be frightened of when you were the most dangerous thing that stalked the streets.

But tonight, Beru had a different fear. Because tonight, the Pale Hand had not gone out looking for a victim. She had gone looking for help. If she succeeded, then this would be the last time Beru would have to wait and worry.

A year after the Pale Hand had begun killing, Beru had chosen the wrong victim. Usually, Ephyra took care of selecting their victims, but this time Beru had. The man she'd picked had a track record for visiting slyhouses and leaving his conquests literally in pieces. No one had seemed to care, because the slyhouses he frequented were in the poorest section of Tarsepolis. But Beru had cared. So had Ephyra.

So Ephyra had gone out, like she had so many nights before, and the Pale Hand had killed him.

The next morning, a letter had appeared tucked beneath the door of the abandoned wine cellar the sisters had been staying in.

The man you killed last night had a bounty on his head.
That bounty was mine. Next time, ask.

It wasn't signed, but there was a simple wax seal at the bottom, stamped in gold. A compass rose. When Ephyra and Beru had looked into it, they found that it was the symbol of Mrs. Tappan's Scrying Agency—a bounty-hunting outfit that, it turned out, was rather infamous in some circles.

Beru had been terrified at first. The message sounded like a threat, and it was clear that this Mrs. Tappan had managed to find them despite the fact that no one had seen the Pale Hand's face nor knew her name. Beru wanted to leave the city immediately, but Ephyra had stalled.

"'Next time, *ask*'?" she'd said. "For a threat, it's not exactly inspired."

The next day, they'd found out the letter hadn't been a threat. It was an offer. Another letter had appeared the next day, with a name and a crime: slave trading in Endarrion. A little digging had garnered the fact that the criminal in question also had a bounty on his head.

Three weeks later, they'd gotten another name.

It seemed the mysterious Mrs. Tappan was content to pass along some of her targets to the Pale Hand, no questions asked. They all seemed to be the worst kind of criminals—the murderers, slavers, and rapists.

Ephyra and Beru couldn't figure out *why* the bounty hunter was helping them. In most cases, the criminal's death meant that the bounty couldn't be collected. Yet the names still came, and no one, to Beru's relief, came after *them*.

And then, six weeks ago, another letter had appeared, tucked beneath the door of their haunt in Tarsepolis.

> *I know why you're doing this. And I know of a cure. A powerful artefact known as Eleazar's Chalice.*

> *I cannot find it for you, but there's someone who can. A scryer with the Grace of Sight, more powerful than any I've seen. More powerful than even mine. Go to Pallas Athos and await my next missive.*

All Beru had known of Pallas Athos was stories of what it had once been—the City of Faith, the center of the Six Prophetic Cities. When they'd arrived here, she had been shocked by what they'd found. The Low City, full of gamblers and thieves, and the High City, where priests preyed on children and left the city to rot. The City of Faith had turned out to be the perfect place for the Pale Hand.

They'd set themselves up in the half-destroyed, abandoned mausoleum of a minor priest and waited to hear from Mrs. Tappan again.

And waited.

And waited.

Then finally, today, they'd received their answer. A messenger had appeared inside the shrine, bearing an envelope marked with the seal of a compass rose.

This is it, Beru had thought. The letter that would determine their fate. The scryer that Mrs. Tappan had told them about, the person they'd come all the way to Pallas Athos for, had finally answered.

The answer was no.

"Maybe there *is* no scryer," Beru had said.

"Why would Mrs. Tappan lie to us?" Ephyra had asked.

"Why would she help us in the first place? She's a bounty hunter."

"The scryer is real," Ephyra had insisted. "They're *here*. And I'm going to find them."

"How?"

Ephyra had looked up at the retreating back of Mrs. Tappan's messenger, a determined glint in her eye. "Easy. The messenger is going to lead me to Mrs. Tappan, and Mrs. Tappan is going to lead me to her mysterious scryer."

"Ephyra . . ."

Ephyra's expression was soft as she reached out to tuck a coil of hair behind her sister's ear. "This is important, Beru. Life or death."

Beru looked into Ephyra's eyes and saw the earnest hope that lived there.

"We've come this far," Ephyra said.

"I know," Beru said. That was what scared her. They'd come this far—they'd thieved and killed for this long in the name of survival. They'd come this far—fourteen lives the Pale Hand had claimed. They'd come this far. How much farther would they have to go?

It was this question that plagued her now, five hours later, as she sat at the tiny table in their makeshift kitchen, shells, sea glass, and pottery shards strewn around her. This was what Beru always did when she couldn't sleep—she made jewelry and little trinkets out of whatever scraps she could find. It was something she and Ephyra had done as children, too, selling necklaces and bracelets to the traders who passed through their village. Now, this makeshift jewelry was their only source of money that didn't involve stealing.

The muffled echo of footsteps broke the dawn quiet. Beru froze, listening. The entrance to the alcove in the crypt was entirely hidden— you would only find it if you knew it was there.

She tracked the sound of the footsteps as they moved through the main sanctum and started down the hidden stairs. It had to be Ephyra. But evidently, she'd brought company.

A knock came at the door.

"It's me," Ephyra's voice called.

"Prove it."

Ephyra's long-suffering sigh sounded through the door. "Once, when you were eight years old, you found a barrel of dates that our mother was going to use to make wine. You ate half the barrel, and for the next three days, every time you went to the bathroom—"

Beru unlatched the door in a hurry and greeted her sister with a glare.

"Proof enough?" Ephyra asked.

"I hate you," Beru replied as Ephyra stepped nimbly past her into the room.

Leaving Beru to stare at the stranger in the doorway.

"So," the boy said, his eyes sweeping around the alcove, "the Pale Hand lives in a literal crypt. A little obvious, don't you think?"

The only possible explanation for his presence that Beru could come up with was that Ephyra had actually found the scryer, like she'd said she would. Which meant that the scryer was an utterly unassuming boy no older than herself. His pale skin and light hair marked him as foreign to Pallas Athos—probably from somewhere to the north, maybe the Novogardian Territories. His eyes were as dark as a grave.

As Beru regarded this boy, she realized he'd been doing the same to her. His gaze lingered on her arm, which was still on the door's latch. Beru had wrapped it tightly in cloth so the dark handprint was hidden, but the concealment itself was conspicuous.

Quickly, she tucked her arm behind her back and stepped aside to allow him in. "Would you like tea?"

"Do you have wine?" he countered hopefully.

"Sorry," Beru replied, retreating to the corner of the kitchen and busying herself with pouring the still-warm mint tea into three chipped clay cups. She stifled a laugh. This all felt absurd. It had been over five years since Ephyra and Beru had had a guest. Back in their village Medea, a trading stop just outside Tel Amot, hospitality had been a rule as impenetrable as law. Their mother would never have abided by having someone in their home without serving them something.

The boy took a seat on a cushion at the rickety wooden table, and Beru put a cup of tea down in front of him.

He didn't even glance at her now. His eyes were trained on Ephyra, and despite the ease with which he held himself, Beru could detect his wariness. Ephyra was watching him, too, propped against the wall, her arms crossed tight across her chest. Beru took a seat right in the middle of their staring contest.

"So," she said, blowing on her tea. "You're the scryer, then?"

Only then did the boy slide his gaze to her. "I'm just Anton."

"Anton," Beru said. She glanced at Ephyra. It was dangerous to let him in on even this much, to tell him who they were. Where they lived. But they'd come to Pallas Athos for no other reason than to find him, and it wasn't like they had another choice. "I'm Beru. Ephyra's sister."

"The Pale Hand has a sister," he mused.

"You have siblings, Anton?"

"Just one," he answered, his tone much too light.

Beru narrowed her eyes.

"All right," Ephyra said impatiently, "enough small talk. You know why I brought you here."

Anton eyed her over the rim of his teacup. "You said you need my help. Why?"

Beru glanced at Ephyra. If she was willing to trust this boy—trust him enough to tell him this much, at least—then Beru would follow her lead.

"You know who I am," Ephyra said. "What I've been doing."

"I think it's safe to say everyone knows what you've been doing."

"Yes," Ephyra said. "But no one knows why."

People spoke in fearful whispers of the bodies that turned up, marked by the Pale Hand. Everyone had their own ideas about what those bodies meant. A punishment for the wicked. A perversion of Grace. None of them knew the truth.

"I take their lives," Ephyra said slowly, "to save hers."

She looked at Beru, a silent understanding passing between them: They could tell this boy enough, but no more. Not the full truth. It was too dangerous.

"I've been sick," Beru said. "For a long time. Ephyra uses the *esha* from her victims to heal me. It's the only way to keep me alive."

"Why can't you go to a healer?"

"They can't help," Ephyra said flatly. There were other reasons—the danger of revealing who she was, the true nature of Beru's illness—that kept them from seeking help from anyone but the most unscrupulous. "Healers take an oath. If they knew what I'd done to keep Beru alive . . . even if they could help us, they wouldn't."

"And I can?"

"We've been looking for something that can help me," Beru said. "A powerful artefact said to enhance the power of the Grace of Blood. With it, maybe Ephyra can heal me for good, so I won't get sick again."

"They call it Eleazar's Chalice," Ephyra said, watching him closely. "Have you heard of it?"

He shook his head.

"You know about the Necromancer Wars," Ephyra said. This wasn't a question. Everyone knew of the Necromancer Wars—the most destructive war in history. Long before the Prophets disappeared, the Necromancer King had raised an army of revenants—dead brought back from the grave—to try to take over the Kingdom of Herat.

"The Necromancer King had the Grace of Blood," Ephyra went on. "The most powerful in centuries. Perhaps the most powerful since the beginning of the Graces. But not all that power was his own. Some of it, the Necromancer King had drawn from Eleazar's Chalice."

Anton blinked at her. "So basically," he said slowly, "you brought me back to your crypt to ask for my help in finding an ancient artefact that was once used to raise an army of the dead? Have I got that right?"

Ephyra didn't flinch. "Well, can you?"

"No."

"You're lying."

"I'm not," Anton answered. He looked suddenly vulnerable. "I'm really—I'm not lying to you."

"Mrs. Tappan told us you're the only one who can do something like this," Ephyra went on. "That you have a Grace more powerful than any she's seen. Was *she* lying to us?"

Anton let out a breath. "No, she wasn't."

"She said you might be reluctant," Ephyra allowed.

"Reluctant," Anton echoed dully. "Right."

"That's not how you would put it?" Beru asked.

"Not exactly."

"You know I risked a lot, bringing you here," Ephyra said. "I didn't have to do that. I could have left you for those hired swords."

Beru whipped around to stare at her. "What hired swords?"

"Later," Ephyra said curtly. Then, to Anton, "All I'm saying is that if this person who's after you wants to find you so badly, I don't have to stand in their way. In fact, I might be better off helping him."

She leveled him with what Beru called the Pale Hand stare.

"Is she always this persuasive?" Anton asked Beru.

Ephyra's eyes flashed. "Why don't you ask that dead priest how persuasive I can be?"

"Ephyra," Beru said. "Let me talk to him."

Ephyra shot her a questioning look. Beru gave her a slight nod. They weren't going to get anywhere with this boy by threatening him. But Beru thought that maybe—*maybe*—she could get through to him. Because beneath the sarcasm and put-on confidence was something she recognized. Fear.

Ephyra went to the doorway and lingered there a moment before disappearing up the stairs.

Beru turned back to Anton. "Look, I don't know what your story is. I'm not asking. I just need you to understand something."

Anton nodded. And Beru saw it again—the shadow of fear passing over his face. Not panic, not terror—nothing so immediate as that. But a deep, unrelenting dread that lived quietly in every breath. She'd recognized it in him only because she knew it so well in herself.

"The thing I'm most scared of," Beru went on. "It's not getting sick again. It's not dying. It's not even Ephyra dying."

She had his full attention now, his dark eyes fixed on hers.

"There was a time before Ephyra became the Pale Hand. Back when Ephyra and I were just two girls. Orphans. All we had was each other. I guess it wasn't so different from now."

She and Ephyra didn't discuss their past anymore—too much guilt lay there. But there wasn't a day that went by that Beru didn't think about it and wonder if her own life was worth what she and her sister had paid for it.

"But back then, there was a family," Beru said. "They took us in, in a fishing village on Charis Island. They were kind to us, fed us, gave us shelter. Even loved us. In time, I think they would have come to see us as their own. They had two sons. A boy around Ephyra's age, and another a little older."

A memory of the months spent with that family glimmered to life in her mind. The two brothers sparring with wooden swords in the thistle-infested yard. Their mother stirring a bubbling pot and breathing in warm steam that smelled of lemon and herbs and a hint of spicy peppers. Their father unloading his fishing gear on the front stoop. The corners of his eyes crinkling when Beru and Ephyra blew past him in a footrace that took them over the spigot, around the chicken coop, and into the front yard. And when dinner was served, all of them filing one by one back inside, like ants returning to their anthill.

The memory blurred together with the memories of Beru's own parents, until she could not recall if it had been her own mother or this one who'd plaited flowers in her hair and taught her the proper way to catch a chicken. They were a patch of bright sunlight in her shadowed past. But the memory that came next, the memory of what she and Ephyra had done to that family, eclipsed it.

"A few months after they took us in, I got sick. And it wasn't the first time. Back in our old village, Medea, I'd been sick with the same illness that took our parents but I . . . I recovered. We thought that it was over, but a few months after that family took us in, the sickness came for me again. And soon, I realized I was dying." She broke off, swallowing. "The father left to find me a healer. But I was getting worse quickly, and before he returned, Ephyra decided to heal me herself. And it worked. I got better. But that day, the mother of that family took ill suddenly and died—or at least, that's what we all thought."

Though it had been years, Beru still felt a wash of fresh horror roll over her when she recalled it.

"After a few months, the sickness came once more. And again, Ephyra healed me. This time, the eldest son died. That's when we realized what was really happening. That *we* were the cause of it." Beru trembled. "The father realized it, too. He was beside himself with grief, terrified that Ephyra would kill his only surviving son. He threatened us. Threatened me, thinking somehow if he took my life, his eldest son and his wife would live again. And Ephyra, she—"

It all came back in a nauseating flash. The father lunging toward Beru. Ephyra throwing her hands against his chest to stop him. The pale handprint that had bloomed on his skin.

"She killed him," Beru whispered. "It was instinct. She was protecting me, and she still couldn't control her powers."

"What happened to the other boy?" Anton asked. "The youngest son?"

Beru shook her head. "We don't know. After the father died, we left. When I got sick again, we decided. Not another innocent death. Not because of me. So Ephyra became the Pale Hand."

"And that's what you fear the most?" Anton asked slowly. "That more innocent people will die because of you?"

She nodded but didn't tell him the rest. That innocent or guilty didn't matter to her—every life the Pale Hand took weighed on Beru's conscience.

"My sickness is getting worse," she said. "It happens faster now. It used to take months for me to start getting weak after Ephyra healed me. Now it's weeks. I know that someday—maybe even soon—we'll be as desperate as we were that day in the fishing village. And it won't matter what someone has done or hasn't done. Only that their life can be traded for mine."

"But if you find Eleazar's Chalice . . ." Anton trailed off.

"Then no one else has to die." *Then,* Beru thought, *we'll be free.*

"And you won't have to be afraid anymore," Anton said quietly.

Beru nodded. She knew that Ephyra might be angry that she had told Anton this story. They had no reason to trust him.

And yet, despite that, Beru felt like she could. Or felt, at least, like Anton might understand in some small way the things they had been through. She could tell that he, too, was haunted by his past. Maybe he understood what this felt like—that the harder you chased freedom, the further away it seemed.

"So," Beru said, "will you help us?"

Anton stared at her for a long moment, pressing his lips together. "I don't know. I don't know if I even *can.* It's been a long time since I used my Grace, and . . . well, let's just say you aren't the only one with things in your past you'd rather not remember."

"You know she wasn't serious," Beru said. "When she said she'd turn you over to the people who are after you. She wouldn't really do that. That's not who she is."

Anton lifted one shoulder in a gesture approximating a shrug.

"You don't have to decide right now," Beru said. "But I'm guessing you don't want to go back home if those people are still out there looking for you. You can stay here for now, if you like."

She could see him hesitate. But it seemed his weariness won out, because he then nodded and helped Beru drag the cushions at the table across the floor to create a makeshift pallet.

"Get some rest," she said. She waited a moment until he was settled down with his eyes closed, and then crept over to the door and eased it open.

Ephyra was standing on the other side. "What did you—?"

Beru held her finger up to her lips and pushed Ephyra back out into the dark stone passage that led to the mausoleum. She closed the door behind them.

"What did you tell him?" Ephyra asked.

"I told him about the family," Beru answered. She didn't need to specify which family. She and Ephyra almost never spoke of them, but the memory was always there, haunting every note of their days.

"And nothing else?"

"Of course nothing else," Beru said. "But he's not stupid, Ephyra. At some point he's going to start asking questions."

"Then until we find the Chalice, we can't let him leave," Ephyra said. "It's too dangerous."

"And if he decides he won't help us?" Beru said. "We can't just keep him here forever."

"We won't," Ephyra said, a grim finality to her words.

Beru reeled back from her. "You can't just *kill* him, Ephyra!"

"I'm the Pale Hand," Ephyra replied. "I'll do what I must."

Beru pulled away, retreating down the dark, cold stone passage.

"Beru, wait—"

"I can't talk to you right now," Beru said, pushing on.

She loved her sister more than anyone else in the world. She knew Ephyra felt the same way. She would do anything for her sister.

But that was what scared Beru the most.

She couldn't help but feel like whatever happened now, there were only two ways their story could end—either Ephyra was going to lose Beru, or Beru was going to lose her.

8

ANTON

ANTON DREAMED, BUT NOT OF THE LAKE. HE DREAMED OF FACES SHADOWED BY hoods, eyes with pupils of black suns. He saw pale handprints scorched against his skin.

"Kid! Hey—kid! Wake up!"

Anton jerked himself up, ready to flee. His gaze fell on the Pale Hand, crouched uncertainly beside his pallet of cushions.

The last few hours rushed over him. The Pale Hand in his flat. Fleeing from Illya's hired men. Falling asleep in the dark and damp alcove in the destroyed mausoleum.

"You were shaking," she said. "Bad dream?"

"What other kind is there?" He rubbed at his eyes. "How long was I asleep?"

"A few hours," she replied. "It's midafternoon."

"Where's your sister?"

"She left to get food," Ephyra replied. At Anton's frown, she laughed. "Oh, come on. You're not scared to be here with me alone, are you?"

"Not scared," he replied. "She's just much nicer than you are."

Ephyra laughed again. The way she laughed was unexpected—loud, unbridled, open. "That's not saying much. She'll be back any moment now, if that puts your mind at ease. You sticking around?"

Anton folded his arms over his knees. "Do I have a choice?"

"We're not holding you hostage here," Ephyra said. "But I seem to recall that I saved your life last night."

"Oh, please. I heard what you said," he replied. When she fell silent, he continued. "When you were talking out in the stairwell this morning? You must have thought I was asleep."

Ephyra's expression didn't change. She just watched him, arms crossed in front of her chest.

"You think it's too dangerous to let me go." He swallowed. "You brought me here knowing that you weren't going to let me go alive."

Beru might believe that her sister wasn't capable of doing something like that, but Anton was no stranger to the taste of desperation, how it trapped you in its claws and forced you to sacrifice even the things you thought you held dear. He'd been on his own since he was eleven years old, and in that time he'd traded parts of himself—dignity, virtue, a clear conscience, if he'd ever had those things—to save the whole. He hadn't balked once.

So when Ephyra threatened to turn him over to the people hunting him, when she told her sister that she might kill him if he didn't help them, he believed her.

"You know why I brought you here," Ephyra said. "I need your help to keep my sister alive."

"And if I refuse? You'll let me leave?"

Before she could answer, the sound of footsteps echoed from the secret staircase. A moment later, the door shuddered open and Beru shouldered her way in, carrying a basket of potatoes and flatbread.

She paused awkwardly in the doorway and looked between them. "What's going on?" Worry edged her voice.

Ephyra's eyes were fixed on Anton. Expectant.

He knew what his answer had to be. He met Beru's gaze. "I've decided I'm going to help you."

It had been almost a year since Anton had last used his Grace, but the moment he stepped into the scrying pool, he felt a familiar quickening of his heart. The shock of cold water on his legs wrenched a gasp from his throat. He was already shivering. In his left hand, he clutched the only gift he'd ever received in his sixteen years, given to him by the Nameless Woman the last time she'd dropped in on him. A lodestone, no bigger than an apple, smooth and gray and utterly unremarkable.

At the edges of his awareness, he felt the *esha* of the two sisters who stood in the empty mausoleum with him. Ephyra's—that same fluttering vibration he'd felt when she'd snuck into his room. And Beru's. There was something off about her *esha*. Anton had first noticed it in the crypt. There was a strange cloudiness to it, like the muffled ringing of a bell. Like it was no longer a whole, unbroken sound.

"I've never seen someone scry before," Ephyra said from behind him. "How does it work?"

Anton was hardly an expert. Everything he knew about the specifics of the Grace of Sight, he'd learned from Mrs. Tappan. For all the good it did him.

"Each of the Four Bodily Graces has a different way of interacting with *esha*," he said. "You, for instance, can give and take *esha* from living things because you have the Grace of Blood. People with the Grace of Heart can enhance their own *esha* to make themselves stronger and faster. Alchemists and artificers, with the Grace of Mind, can imbue ordinary materials with *esha* to make them do the impossible. Incandescent lights that glow without a flame, or wine that cures seasickness, for instance."

"But the Grace of Sight doesn't let you give *esha*, or enhance it, or transform it," Ephyra said.

"No," Anton agreed. "I can't manipulate *esha*, but I can sense it. All *esha* in the world vibrates at different frequencies. I can feel those vibrations. Even right now. Scrying lets me home in on them, search through the patterns of *esha* that flow throughout the world. Usually, scryers can just find people. But what you're looking for—an artefact that was once used to raise the dead—that's something only an artificer could have made, meaning it's imbued with *esha*."

"So since all artefacts are imbued with *esha*, you can find them?" Beru asked.

"Not quite," Anton said. "Scryers need one important thing to find an artefact or person—their name. A person's name binds their *esha* to them. That's why we have Naming Days. Unlike people, though, most everyday artefacts don't have names. But the rare ones do, because names help bind *esha* to the artefacts and make them more powerful."

"Like Eleazar's Chalice," Ephyra said.

"Right," he replied, looking down. He didn't tell her this was all theoretical. If most scryers had the kind of ability Anton did, they could have made themselves rich tracking down lost, powerful artefacts from prophecies past.

"And what's the purpose of the water and the stone?" Beru asked.

"It's a way to focus and direct my Grace," he said. "Like the movements of the koahs do for the Grace of Heart. Or the patterns of binding for the Grace of Blood."

The stillness of a scrying pool, the Nameless Woman had taught him, helps the scryer focus. The ripples of the lodestone echo the vibrations of *esha*, amplifying them so a trained scryer can parse them out.

Anton waded out into the center of the scrying pool. He took a breath and tossed the lodestone into the water. At once, the water began to churn, shifting and swirling.

He closed his eyes and followed the ripples of the lodestone through the currents of *esha* that made up the world. He let the thrum of these currents wash over him, let his awareness of his body, his *self*, go slack as he reached out into the fabric of this shivering world. He did not direct the *esha* but let it direct him, letting it pull him deeper and deeper into the weaving currents, into the winding paths of sacred energy. But as the currents pulled him deeper, something else tugged, too.

The memory. The lake.

Hands grasped at him. Ice shot through him. *No, no, no!* He could shake it off, he told himself. He could do this. He felt his way along the current, as if tugging himself along a thread, with many thousands of other threads splintering and twisting together.

Anton swayed, the water churning.

He felt the dark maw of the frozen lake hungering for him. The water thrashed violently, as though shaken by a terrible storm. He collapsed with a splash, gasping, as the water surged over him. The scrying pool transformed into cracked ice, the broken columns into rows of towering trees.

He was knee-deep in snow, salty tears stinging at his eyes, pinned and struggling, struggling, struggling.

"*Stop!*" he begged. "*Stop it, please!*"

He was free, racing to the middle of the lake, wind cutting across his cheeks, laughter rattling behind him. He ran as the ice cracked beneath his feet, ran and ran and ran, but he could not escape the widening chasm of the lake.

He plunged down into icy water. Fingers pressed into his skin. Above him was a face, its mouth a wide smiling gash.

Knife-cold water rushed over him. His lungs clenched painfully. There was no sign of the surface as he thrashed, the water dark all around him. He was floating; he was sinking. His lungs succumbed to the pressure. His heart slowed. His eyes drifted shut.

There was only one thing now. Not the water, not the cold. Not that terrible laughing face. There was only his Grace, ringing through his bones, filling his veins, gripping him with cold, bony fingers, dragging him down, down, down into the darkness, down into the black pit, and he knew if he opened his eyes he would see it, the thing that wanted to consume him, wanted to destroy him, wanted to—

Anton woke.

The mausoleum was still. He lay halfway in the scrying pool, his body doubled over the edge. Sunlight slanted through the broken roof above.

Beru knelt beside him, worry creasing her brow. Ephyra hovered over her shoulder, watching with barely concealed impatience.

"Did it work?" she asked.

He shook his head and pulled himself up and over the edge of the scrying pool. "I couldn't. I'm sorry."

"What happened?" Beru asked.

For a moment, her face looked like it was twisted into a ghastly scream, but when Anton blinked, her expression was normal again. Concerned.

"I—I tried to tell you. I can't use my Grace without seeing—" He tried to shape the words.

Without seeing my brother holding me under the water.

The memory of the lake flashed behind his eyes, like the snapping of teeth.

"Without seeing what?" Ephyra pressed.

He got to his feet. "I'm sorry," he said. "I won't tell anyone about you, I won't ever mention you, but I can't—this was a mistake. I'm sorry."

He ran from the scrying pool, tripping over loose stones and rubble from the dilapidated mausoleum walls as Ephyra called out after him. "What did you see?"

The words chased him out into the evening air, echoing in his mind long after the mausoleum disappeared from sight.

He thought he'd left his past behind, but it had come looking for him. And now he knew. He was still that scared, drowning boy. He always would be.

9

JUDE

JUDE WAS AWAKE BEFORE THE SUN ON THE MORNING HE WAS TO BECOME Keeper of the Word. He had barely slept, his body a knot of nerves and anticipation, his father's words running through his mind.

The Last Prophet has been found.

Their hundred-year wait, over. Their sixteen-year search, at an end. The Last Prophet, waiting for Jude in the City of Faith.

A sharp rap on the door of his room in the barracks pulled him from thoughts of the Prophet. He bolted from his narrow bed and wrenched the door open. His eyes widened at the sight of Hector standing on the other side.

"What are you doing here?" Jude asked.

Hector raised his eyebrows. "I can't believe it's only been a year, and already you've forgotten our routine."

Jude blinked. Before he had left for the Year of Reflection, he and Hector used to wake up every morning to practice koahs as the sun rose. Back then, though, Jude had always been the one dragging a reluctant Hector out of bed in the predawn twilight.

Hector grinned like he'd read Jude's thoughts. "Thought I'd come wake you up for a change. Though I realize now that was never going to happen."

"Today's the ceremony," Jude blurted.

Once the sun ascended over the valley, the Paladin would all gather in the Circle of Stones, the complex of monoliths that overlooked the rest of the fort, to witness Jude choose the six others who would serve as the Paladin Guard and go with him to the Prophet.

"We have time," Hector said. He waited outside as Jude changed into the full Paladin uniform—soft, flexible boots, slim dark gray pants, a stiff shirt that fastened down the side, overlaid with Grace-forged armor as thin as silk, and a midnight blue cloak that swept across the shoulders. After today, he would wear this uniform not just as a member of the Paladin, but as their leader.

"Ready?" Hector asked as Jude emerged.

"For koahs? Yes. For everything else . . ."

"You'll be great," Hector said, offering a smile as they wound through the quiet fort, making their way up the path to the highest waterfall in the valley. "What else did your father say about the Last Prophet?"

The night before, Captain Weatherbourne had called all the Paladin to gather in the great hall to tell them the news.

"He was found by an acolyte," Jude replied. "One of ours. Father says he trusts this man more than almost any other."

There were many acolytes who still served the temples of the Prophets, even now that they stood empty. The acolytes had no authority; they simply maintained the temples and helped perform namings, weddings, and funerals for the public. A small number of these acolytes throughout the Six Prophetic Cities had taken secret oaths to the Order of the Last Light. These acolytes had another, hidden duty—to search for signs of the Last Prophet and alert the Order in Kerameikos if anything turned up. They passed this duty on to their apprentices, choosing carefully from those who had demonstrated their devotion to the Prophets' legacy. There were few deemed worthy of holding the secrets of the Order.

"The acolyte sent a message yesterday through the scrying network, saying he had found the Prophet in Pallas Athos," Jude went on. "He told us they fit all the signs, but nothing else, not even their name. It's safest this way. We can't risk anyone knowing what we're in Pallas Athos for. *Who* we're there for."

This was why the last prophecy had been kept a secret for so long. To keep anyone except the Order of the Last Light from looking for the Prophet.

"I can't believe the Prophet is in Pallas Athos," Hector said. "What was it they used to say about fate and irony being friends?"

"Father says it's fitting," Jude replied. "The Last Prophet is finally found in the very city our predecessors left one hundred years ago."

"So the Order of the Last Light will make their return to the City of Faith," Hector said. "I guess this means you're leaving again soon."

"Tonight," Jude said. "We'll leave the fort and camp in Delos until morning." The journey would take them five days in all. Once in the hidden cove of Delos, a ship with Grace-woven sails would carry them along the rocky coast and into the Pelagos Sea to dock in Pallas Athos.

Jude had grown up hearing tales of the city upon the hill, the city where the Order of the Last Light had served the Prophets for over two millennia. He had hoped, one day, he might see its marble columns for himself. That he might walk the curving limestone path of the Sacred Road, following the rows of olive trees to the steps of the Temple of Pallas. The City of Faith called to him from the stories of the Paladin, and now, at last, he would go there and meet his destiny.

"This is really it, isn't it?" Hector said, gazing out at the fort below. "All of the Paladin are gathered to see you become Keeper of the Word and choose the Paladin Guard. You know who you'll choose?"

"I've had my entire life to think about it."

"Penrose, of course."

"Of course." Jude hesitated, glancing at Hector. "But sometimes people can surprise you."

Hector looked away. "You're not the only one who was surprised I came back."

A cold discomfort gripped Jude. He did not want to be one more in a string of people who had doubted Hector. "I did hope for it," he said.

They came to a stop at the foot of the highest fall, the same spot where Penrose had found Jude the day before. He'd spent almost every morning of his teenage years in this place, with Hector. It was where Jude went when he needed to center himself. The flowing falls and the view of the river valley calmed his thoughts. Being here now with Hector, on the morning he was to become Keeper of the Word, felt right.

He glanced at Hector again and couldn't stop himself from asking, "Why did you leave?"

The question fluttered between them like a leaf on a breeze. A long moment passed, and Jude thought Hector might not answer.

But then, his voice quiet against the sound of the waterfall, he said, "I needed answers. Answers I couldn't get here."

Jude's chest clenched. The words wounded him, but he couldn't understand why. He had so many more questions—where Hector had gone, what answers he'd been seeking, what had made him return. He stepped toward Hector. "Did you find them?"

Hector's eyes were the same black as the predawn sky. "I hope so. I think so. I want to be here, Jude."

Jude couldn't tear his eyes away. He wanted to know everything, every second Hector had spent apart from him. But he would let Hector keep those secrets. What mattered was not that Hector had left—it was that he'd come back.

"This is where you belong," Jude said. "It has been since the day the acolytes brought you here."

The Order's acolytes had found Hector on the island of Charis. Orphaned at the age of thirteen, Hector had taking refuge in the Temple of Keric. His Grace had already manifested at that point, and the acolytes had brought him to Kerameikos Fort when they'd seen he had the Grace of Heart. Jude had always felt like it was fate that had brought Hector to the Order. To Jude.

Maybe it had taken leaving Kerameikos for Hector to realize that he'd always belonged there.

A thin, rueful smile stretched across Hector's face. "It really is so easy for you, isn't it?" He shook his head with a laugh. "You've always been so certain. Of everything."

No, I'm not, Jude thought desperately. He was about to become Keeper. The Prophet had been found; Jude was days away from meeting him. But the same doubts plagued him, and they only seemed to grow. Part of him was glad Hector didn't seem to see it—but another part of him wished he didn't have to bear those feelings alone.

"It's why you've always been better at koahs than me," Hector said, leaping onto a rock beneath the waterfall. "I'm still a better fighter, though."

"We'll have to put that to the test," Jude replied, leaping onto the rock, beside Hector.

"Anytime."

They began to slowly move through the ten standard koahs. The specific sequences of breath and movement drew power from their Graces to enhance their physical bodies. There were koahs for strength, balance, speed, for each of the five senses, for endurance, and for focus. Each had three parts: breath, movement, and intention—the unwavering purpose beneath it all, the core reason one drew *esha* from the world and channeled it with their Grace. The greater the commitment to this intention, the more powerfully the Grace of Heart could be wielded.

This was what Hector meant. Jude's intention, the purpose for which he wielded his Grace, was his devotion to the Word of the Prophets. He tried to think of this and nothing else as he moved through the fluid second sequence, his Grace growing warm within him.

But he couldn't deny it was difficult with Hector so near. This was the only time Jude got to see him like this—focused, intent, unwavering. When they practiced koahs, it was with slow deliberation, every movement timed with their breath, every posture perfectly shaped. It wasn't like the lightning-quick koahs one performed during a fight— these koahs were a meditation, a way to strengthen their connection to the sacred energy of the world.

As he and Hector moved into a lunging form, raising one arm and stretching the other back, Jude imagined that the invisible, unknowable ripples of *esha* flowed between them, connecting them.

The sky began to lighten in the east as they completed the last set of koahs.

"Sun will come up soon," Hector said as they came to rest, hands pressed against their chests. "Guess it's time."

They hiked back down to the fort in silence. Usually, it would already be milling with activity at this early hour, stewards going about their duties in the kitchens, stables, and armory, and the Paladin beginning their practice in the training yard. But this morning, the barracks were empty, the kitchens silent. Everyone was gathered in the Circle of Stones, waiting for Jude.

"Navarro."

Jude looked up to find Penrose waiting for them at the heelstone that marked the entrance of the Circle. She looked surprised to find Hector there.

"You should join the others," she said.

Hector sent one last glance at Jude and then left his side to enter the Circle of Stones.

Jude searched for judgment in Penrose's eyes. "You should join them, too," he said.

Penrose hesitated. For a moment, he thought she might press him about Hector. She'd clearly wanted to the day before. But all she said was, "The choices you make now are no longer your own. They are the choices of the Keeper of the Word, sworn protector of the Last Prophet."

"I know." Penrose's words felt like a warning, one he wasn't sure he knew how to abide.

"May the light of the Prophets guide you," Penrose said, and left his side to join the other Paladin.

Jude's apprehension grew as he looked up at the towering monoliths of the Seven Prophets that surrounded the Circle of Stones. Endarra the Fair, in a crown of laurel; Keric the Charitable, presenting his coin; Pallas the Faithful, with his hands clasped around an olive branch; Nazirah the Wise, carrying the torch of knowledge; Tarseis the Just, weighing with his scales; Behezda the Merciful, her hand outstretched; and the faceless Wanderer. Seven statues for the seven wisest men and women of ancient times, who had sought the knowledge of the fate of the world so that they might better serve their people. Who had given their people the power of the Four Bodily Graces. Who had lived for over two thousand years, guiding them in their destinies.

In their shadows stood four hundred of the most powerful Graced warriors from the Inshuu steppe to the delta of Herat, their dark blue cloaks drawn across their breasts, the silver of their light armor gleaming in the dawn light.

Jude felt their eyes on him as he crossed into the silent Circle of Stones, each gaze a weight that dragged with every step. With his own doubts flickering through his mind, he couldn't help but wonder what the other Paladin saw—a boy, or a leader worthy of the mantle of Keeper of the Word?

He took his place beside his father as the sun broke over the mountains, beaming light through the arch that marked the west edge of the Circle of Stones, illuminating everything in brilliant gold.

"Today," Jude's father proclaimed, "we gather in the Circle of Stones to anoint Jude Adlai Weatherbourne as Keeper of the Word and captain of the Paladin Guard."

The Paladin bowed their heads, touching their foreheads to the hilts of their swords.

Captain Weatherbourne turned to Jude. "Do you swear to fulfill the duties of your office, to uphold the virtues of chastity, austerity, obedience, and to devote yourself, your Grace, and your life to the Order of the Last Light?"

Jude's hands trembled, but his voice remained sure. "I do swear."

His father lifted a torc of twisted gold and said, "This torc was crafted to symbolize our obedience to the will of the Prophets. With it, I bind you in service of the Last Prophet, to preserve the legacy of the Seven and the truth of their Word." He placed the twisted gold wreath around Jude's neck, fastening it at his throat. The metal hung heavy and cold against his skin.

Next, his father picked up a silver and pewter reliquary, lifting its delicate top and dipping his fingers inside. "This chrism was consecrated by the great alchemists to strengthen our connection to the *esha* that flows through each of us."

Jude closed his eyes and felt his father draw the cool consecrating oil over the ridge of his brow.

"With it, I anoint you, Jude Adlai Weatherbourne, Keeper of the Word and captain of the Paladin Guard."

Jude looked up at his father's face, which even on this solemn occasion could not completely hide the pride he held in his son. Yesterday, his father had spoken of Jude's destiny with conviction—how he had known when Jude was just a child that this moment would come. He shut his eyes, wondering if his father would still look at him like that if he knew the weakness buried in his heart.

Last, his father raised the sheathed Pinnacle Blade between his hands. "This sword was forged to strengthen the Grace of the first Keeper of the Word. It must be wielded for one purpose, and one purpose alone—to protect the Last Prophet."

Jude's hands shook even harder as his father lowered the sword into them. As his fingers curled around the intricate hilt and sheath, Jude felt his Grace swell within him, as if he were moving through a koah. This sword had hung at his father's side for over three decades, his constant companion. As it had hung at the side of every Keeper of the Word before him. In Jude's hands, it was another expectation, another promise he desperately hoped he knew how to keep. Another weight he wasn't sure he could bear.

He drew in breath and stepped forward, looking out at the sea of faces before him. "As captain of the Paladin Guard, it is my duty to call to service the six Paladin who will join me as guardians of the Last Prophet. I call Moria Penrose."

Penrose emerged from the crowd, striding between the great stones of the inner circle before coming to a stop in front of Jude. She knelt there, presenting her sheathed sword to him.

"Moria Penrose, I hereby name you servant of the Word and guardian of the Last Prophet," Jude said, taking her sword and unsheathing it, laying the flat of the blade on her shoulder. "Your duty to the Prophet shall be your life, for you shall not live if you do not serve. Do you swear to uphold this holy duty?"

"I do swear."

Captain Weatherbourne secured a silver torc around her neck and then spoke again. "Rise and take your place beside the Keeper of the Word."

Next was Andreas Petrossian, the oldest of the Paladin Jude had chosen, known for his blunt honesty and practical mind. After Petrossian came Yarik and Annuka, a brother and sister who had joined the Order after their tribe on the Inshuu steppe slowly broke apart. Both were deadly fighters alone, but it was their power together that made them truly unstoppable.

The fifth to join the Guard was Bashiri Osei, a giant of a man who, like Hector and so many others, had grown up as a ward of the Order, finding new purpose and place after a childhood marked by suffering.

And then it was time for Jude to make his last choice, to call the final member of the Guard who would stand beside him as he faced his destiny. He looked out at the crowd and let his gaze linger on Hector, his thoughts turning back to a time that felt as long ago and as far off as if it had been another life.

It was the last night they'd had together, on the eve of the day Jude had left to start his Year of Reflection. Hector had stolen a jug of wine from the Order's storerooms, and he and Jude had snuck out of the fort and onto the Andor Bridge, overlooking the river.

They had talked and joked and goaded each other, until finally Hector had turned and asked, his eyes bright, "What would you do if you could do anything you wanted? If you didn't become Keeper of the Word. If you were just some nobody somewhere."

Had anyone else in his life ever asked Jude this question, he would have considered it nothing short of a betrayal of the Order. He had one purpose in this life, and even at eighteen, about to be on his own and away from his father and the Paladin for the first time, he knew he must devote himself to it completely. But though his destiny was the only future ahead of him, it had still felt far off, a beacon glowing faintly in the distance. And something in the way Hector had smiled in the soft moonlight, and the way they'd held themselves close at the edge of the bridge made Jude say, "I'd go to the oasis of Al-Khansa. I'd drink pomegranate wine and ride elephants and send blue lily blossoms into the flooding river."

He hadn't known where it had come from. He had certainly never thought he'd possessed any deep longing to cross the world to Al-Khansa. Frankly, the idea of being near an elephant rather frightened him. But somehow, grinning at Hector, it had seemed like the only answer he could possibly give.

"What about you?" he'd asked.

Hector had laughed, deep and full-throated. "I'd go with you, of course."

He had never forgotten that moment on the bridge, and the way Hector had cast his future with Jude's. As if it were always meant to be that way. Al-Khansa was a foolish fantasy, but the thought of Hector at his side was not.

Jude had told his father that there was no one on his list he would replace with Hector, and that had been the truth. Because there was no sixth name. There was only an empty place that Jude had kept open in the hope he would one day fill it with the person who had been at his side from the start.

He took a breath and spoke the final name. "I call Hector Navarro."

Hector's expression was hidden from Jude as he stepped out from the crowd and came to kneel before him as the others had. The conferring words, now spoken softly to the crown of Hector's head, held the weight of real questions.

Jude's heartbeat quickened as he reached the end. "Do you swear to uphold this holy duty?"

Hector looked up, his eyes meeting Jude's. The moment hung between them, breathless, vast.

Then Hector spoke. "I do swear."

He rose, and Jude's father secured the silver torc around his neck, marking him as the sixth and final member of the Paladin Guard.

"Rise, and take your place beside the Keeper of the Word."

Hector did.

Over Hector's shoulder, Jude's father's face was troubled. But no matter what his father thought, Jude knew that Hector belonged there, at his side, for the rest of their lives. He couldn't have chosen anyone else.

His father broke his gaze, looking out at the rest of the Paladin. "The seven guardians of the Last Prophet stand before you, the new Paladin Guard called to take their place beside the Keeper of the Word. Raise your swords and pledge your faith in them."

A sea of blades lifted to the sky.

Jude glanced beside him, Penrose on his left and Hector on his right. And ahead the Prophet, the City of Faith, and their destiny.

10

EPHYRA

THE CRYPT SHOULDN'T HAVE BEEN EMPTY.

Ephyra stood in the rotted doorway. No matter how many times she swept her eyes over the cold stone floors and moth-eaten sheets, Beru never materialized.

It was almost midmorning. This was when Ephyra normally returned from training or scouting her next victim. They usually ate breakfast together, tossing chunks of flatbread for the other to catch with her mouth, arguing over who was the better pickpocket. (It was Beru.) Sometimes, Beru would leave early for the market to sell the jewelry she'd made, but all of her beads, shells, and other trinkets were still on the table.

Beru was nowhere to be found. If Ephyra didn't know for a fact that Anton had been holed up in some seedy taverna in the marina district, she would be convinced that he'd led the Sentry straight to them. Her stomach plummeted as she pictured it—swordsmen barging into the crypt in the middle of the night and hauling Beru away. But there were no signs of struggle in the crypt, and nothing upstairs in the mausoleum had been out of place, either.

And then came the other fear—the one that Ephyra tried desperately to bury each time it rose. The fear that no one had come for Beru. That she was gone because she'd chosen to leave.

"Sweet Endarra, you scared me!"

Ephyra whirled at the sound of her sister's voice, heart pounding.

Beru stood halfway down the secret staircase. "What are you doing just *standing* there, Ephyra?" she demanded, trotting down the rest of the way and brushing past her sister to go inside.

"What am *I* doing?" Ephyra retorted. "What are *you* doing? I came back, and you weren't here!"

Beru unhooked her small coin purse and shrugged out of her overcoat. "I'm not allowed to go outside now?"

"We always tell each other when we go out," Ephyra said, circling the table to face her sister. "That's the rule."

Beru leveled her with a perfect icy stare, and Ephyra realized she'd made a mistake.

"Oh, is it?" Beru said. "Is that the rule you've been following when you've been staying out all hours of the day and sneaking out every night? I honestly didn't think you'd notice I was gone, what with how little I've seen *you* these past few days."

"I—That's different," Ephyra argued feebly. "I was just—"

"Save it for someone who hasn't listened to your horseshit for the last sixteen years," Beru said. "I know what you're doing. You're tracking that scryer you kidnapped."

"Kidnapped?" Ephyra protested. "Don't you mean rescued?"

Beru was not amused. "Are you still following him?"

"It's possible I've checked up on him once or twice," Ephyra said.

The night Anton had left, she'd followed him down to the marina district, where he'd entered a dilapidated taverna that stank of fish and smoke and sweat. That had been four days ago, and she'd yet to see him emerge. "It's just to make sure he hasn't told anyone about us."

Beru's lips drew together.

"I'm not going to hurt him," Ephyra said. "But we can't just let him go and *hope* he keeps quiet. We have to be ready if someone else finds out about us. We've already drawn too much attention to ourselves. It's not just the Sentry that worries me. The Witnesses are all around this city. I've heard them say the Pale Hand is an abomination. I don't even want to think about what they might do if they found out about you."

"I get it. I don't think he would tell anyone about us, but I get why you're worried. That's actually what I wanted to talk to you about." She heaved a sigh, throwing her overcoat across the table. As it landed, an envelope slid out of the pocket. A cream-colored sheet of paper fluttered to the ground.

Ephyra stooped to pick it up.

"Wait, Ephyra—"

But it was too late.

"Train tickets?" Ephyra said, staring down at the paper in her hand. Her disbelief grew when she saw the destination. "You bought train tickets to Tel Amot? *Why?*"

Slowly, Beru raised her eyes. "I think we should leave."

"You want to give up."

"There's nothing to give up *on*," Beru protested, plucking the tickets from Ephyra's hand. "Pallas Athos was a dead end. We came here to find the scryer, but he can't help us. There's no reason to stay."

"And you think going back there, to Tel Amot, isn't a dead end?"

Ephyra replied incredulously. "Of all the places you could have chosen—"

"What if we're not meant to find the Chalice?" Beru said. She lowered her gaze immediately, as though she wished she hadn't said it.

Ephyra flinched like she'd been struck. "What are you talking about?"

"What if . . ."

"What if what?" The words came out as a challenge. There were things she suspected that Beru thought about, things that neither of them wanted to say out loud. Things that Ephyra feared more than the Sentry, more than the Witnesses.

"I don't know," Beru said, her voice going high, like she was trying not to break into tears. "Mom and Dad never wanted you to use your Grace, remember?"

Ephyra remembered. Her parents hadn't reacted well when her Grace manifested. Beru had been dazzled by it—Ephyra discovering she could revive the drooping plants in the yard and mend the wing of a fallen sparrow. But she still recalled her mother and father's ashen-faced expressions as they gently told her not to tell anyone else in the village about what she could do.

Beru wore the same expression now.

"What's your point?" Ephyra asked.

Beru let out a breath, her whole body going slack. "Maybe . . . Maybe the Witnesses are right. What we're doing is unnatural. Using your Grace to keep me alive when we both know—"

"No," Ephyra said sharply, and Beru fell silent, her eyes widening at her sister's harsh tone. "The Witnesses are wrong. They just want to scare the Graced because they're terrified of us. It has nothing to do with me, or with you, or what we've done."

Beru's grip tightened on the train tickets. "Ephyra—"

"We're going to find Eleazar's Chalice, Beru," Ephyra barreled on. "We're going to cure you. We didn't come this close only to give up."

Beru called out after her, but Ephyra was already out the door. Anton was the only person who could help them, and Ephyra knew exactly where to find him.

This time, she wouldn't let him refuse.

11

ANTON

ANTON'S LUCK HAD RUN OUT.

The beady-eyed sailor across from him was silent, his twice-broken nose nearly purple with anger. Exhaling noisily, the sailor threw his cards down and slapped the table. "Admit you cheated!"

Two of the man's crewmates stepped up behind Anton, close enough that he could smell the valerian smoke on their clothes and the stink of wine on their breath. Anton drummed his fingers over his own cards. Three aces and a poet of crowns beamed up, declaring his overwhelming victory.

He had spent four wine-soaked days in the dusty parlor of this taverna, charming and gambling the coin out of men like this one. It was a poor substitute for the after-hours game at Thalassa, but Anton couldn't return there, not now that he knew Illya was looking for him.

Besides, he was used to making do. He needed something to distract him from the nightmare that lurked at the edge of his mind. The past few nights, since he'd tried to scry in the burned-out mausoleum, the dream had only gotten worse. He woke up choking. Everywhere he looked, he saw his brother's face.

But there was nothing like a few rounds of canbarra to clear his mind—and fill his purse. A few hands more, and he would have what he needed to leave Pallas Athos for good.

If he didn't get himself killed first.

Anton glanced at the large sailors from the corner of his eye. "You're right," he said with a sigh. "Playing against someone so wildly outmatched is unfair. I apologize for not realizing just how stupid you really are."

There was a moment of dead silence, and then his opponent lunged across the table. Anton leapt up, and at the same time, his opponent's crewmate yanked him back by the collar.

Anton held up his hands. "What," he said mildly, "stupid *and* no sense of humor?"

His opponent planted his hands on the table, spreading his arms to make himself look larger. He leaned forward. "You think you're so smart, but you're just a dirty little cheat." Spittle flew from between yellowed teeth, landing wetly on Anton's cheek.

Anton shut his eyes.

"Now," the man said slowly, "how about a real apology?"

Anton heard their rumbling laughter, punctuated with hacking coughs, and felt hot, moist breath against his neck. He tried not to squirm as his mind conjured another image from the depths of his memories—his brother leaning over him, breath on the back of Anton's neck as he pressed him into the ground.

I'm not letting you go until you say you're sorry. Say you're sorry, Anton.

"You should take your hands off him if you want to keep them," a voice said, cold and cutting in the din of the parlor. A familiar *esha*, like the ripple of a moth's wings, hit Anton.

"Who the *shit* are you?" the sailor growled, whirling.

Anton peered around the man's broad form to take in the sight of Ephyra standing before them, flicking her dagger idly in the low light.

"Trust me," she said. "You don't want the answer."

The man turned to stare down at Anton.

"You really don't," he confirmed.

And this was what finally snapped the man from anger to violence. With a growl, he swiped a meaty fist at Anton. Anton ducked, but the fist caught him below the jaw and sent him sprawling back onto a chair, which flipped over and crashed to the floor.

"What in the Six Cities do you think you're doing?" another voice roared. Anton glanced up to find the proprietor of the card parlor standing like a hulking beast in the doorway. "Break any more of my furniture, and I'll break your face."

"I'd like to see you try!" the sailor bellowed.

A glass of brown ale flew across the room, shattering against the doorframe where the proprietor stood. Chaos erupted. Anton clambered to his knees in an effort to crawl away to safety, but his opponent spotted him and cried, "Get the little cheat!"

A foot caught Anton in the gut, and he let out a wheeze of pain. That was a bruised rib or two, at least. He rolled to the side as a man's boot came crunching down onto the floor.

A hard yank on the back of his tunic, and Anton was on his feet. Ephyra kept her hand clenched around his tunic as she deftly wove through the raucous cardroom—by now, some of the other players, drunk and unable to distinguish friend from foe, had turned on one another.

At last, Ephyra pulled Anton behind a stairwell, hidden from view.

"Are you all right?" she asked, her brown eyes blazing in the dim light. "That looked bad."

Anton touched his three fingers to the tender, swelling underside of his jaw. "I've had worse nights."

"Nights?" she echoed. "It's not even noon."

Anton blinked, taking in the dusty sunlight streaming under the door that led out to the marina.

"Oh," he said. In this part of the city, sailors and wanderers turned up at all hours. Each day he'd spent trying to get lost here had bled into the next.

"You're in that bad of shape, huh?"

"I'm fine." So he'd lost track of time. What did that matter?

"You haven't been sleeping."

Realizing she was still holding on to his tunic, he primly plucked her hand off. "I said, I'm fine."

"And would you have been fine if that guy and his friends shattered you like that glass?" she asked. "Either you're actually that stupid, or you're out here looking for trouble."

"Doesn't concern you either way, does it?"

She sighed. "Kid, come on. Come back to the crypt with me and we'll get you sorted out."

His jaw tightened. "I'm not—I'm not going back there."

"We can talk about your . . . whatever that was with your scrying later. For right now, you need to—"

But Anton did not hear the rest of her sentence. Everything, from the sound of Ephyra's voice to the din of the sailors still fighting in the other room, seemed to fade into the background as a pulse of *esha* flowed through him like a sudden gale.

His breath caught in his throat. The *esha* thrummed, so distinct from those of the myriad of buzzing people around him. He could almost taste it, like the air before a thunderstorm. It felt somehow *familiar*. Except Anton was absolutely certain he'd never felt it before.

Without knowing quite what he was doing, he pushed past Ephyra and burst through the door into the hot morning sun.

"Hey!" Ephyra's shout was faint behind him. "Where are you going?"

He squinted in the light, briefly glancing around at the street before setting off at a furious clip. He flew past apothecaries displaying bright amber tinctures and tackle shops with fishmongers proudly offering the catch of the day, and wove alongside merchants, sailors, and tourists come to see the once-great City of Faith.

All around, the buzz of *esha* mingled together, a low hum vibrating from every direction, but so quiet, so indistinct, compared to the one that rang in Anton's blood. The strange *esha* grew stronger, like a wind picking up, and Anton quickened his pace along the Sacred Road. As he approached the bustling marina square, the crowd thickened, choking the arcaded entryways. There were far more people pouring into the square than out. It was clear something was happening—something noteworthy, to draw this large a crowd.

Still, he was barely aware of the other bodies around him as he stood suspended in the crowd, the *esha* surging like a storm.

A sharp jab to the gut brought him back. He turned to see a pair of kids—younger than he was, but not by much—jostling past him through an archway.

"Stop elbowing me!"

"Come *on*, I wanna see!"

Snatches of conversation filtered through the crowd.

"... arrived this morning ... silver sails ..."

"... disappeared after the Prophets ..."

"... haven't been seen in a hundred years ..."

Hands grasped at Anton. He seized up, frozen, as a woman pulled him abruptly against her bony chest.

"They've returned! They've finally returned, after all this time!" she cried out euphorically. Her long fingers were latched onto his shoulders, shaking him, tears streaming from her cataract-clouded eyes. "Praise the Prophets! Praise Faithful Pallas! The Order of the Last Light is here!"

Anton tore himself out of the woman's arms.

"The Prophets will return now, don't you see?" she said. "They haven't abandoned us. They have answered our prayers! They'll save this city!"

Terror gripped him, the kind he felt in the depths of his nightmare. With the stormlike *esha* still bellowing around him, he shoved the woman away as hard as he could. She stumbled into the crowd, jostling the other spectators.

"Watch it!" someone yelled.

He fled from the crowd, darting into an alleyway behind the shops that lined the square. He leaned against a limestone wall, his breath catching in his chest, two distinct and directly opposed desires blooming within him. One was to find whomever the thundering *esha* belonged to. The other was to turn around and run as far and as fast as he could.

Anton did neither. He pressed his fingers against his throat and started to count the beats of his pulse.

When he looked up, Ephyra was standing in front of him. He hadn't realized she'd followed him.

"I thought you were trying to run away," she said.

"I was." Anton's pulse tapped against his fingers.

"You look like you're about to faint."

"I was doing that, too."

She squinted at him. "What's got you so freaked out?"

Anton glanced up at her and then slid his gaze to a shop's back balcony.

It wasn't difficult to climb up.

"I was just asking!" Ephyra cried after him.

He ignored her, edging around the side of the balcony to climb on top of the arcade that fed into the square. He felt Ephyra close behind, climbing even more quickly and easily onto the covered walkway.

From here, they could see the entire square and the brilliant turquoise waters of the marina beyond it. Amid the vast merchant ships and the red-sailed clippers floating in the harbor, a ship with silver sails was docked at one of the main wharfs. Its hull was a graceful sweep of pale white, the bow tapered and slender. Sunlight glinted brilliantly off the silver sails, so luminous Anton almost couldn't gaze directly at them.

The crowd standing just beyond the wharf began to part, making way for seven figures dressed in deep blue cloaks emblazoned with the symbol of a seven-pointed star pierced by a blade. Swords of silver hung from each of their waists. The people crowded in the square craned their necks to catch a glimpse of the swordsmen, their incredulity and wonder palpable. Some of them seemed to be crying in elation.

A hundred years had passed since anyone from the Order was last seen. There were traces of them left throughout Pallas Athos, the city they'd called their headquarters for centuries, until the Prophets disappeared. Some people theorized that the Order had disappeared along with them. Others thought that the Order had simply disbanded, until none of its members were left. And some believed they'd gone into hiding, retreating to a secret fortress.

The group of seven Paladin were now making their way through the crowd toward the head of the Sacred Road. Spectators had gathered all along the road to watch their procession, spilling up the curve of the lime-washed street all the way through the High City to the Temple of Pallas high on the hill.

"I thought the Order was long gone," Ephyra said, beside Anton.

The mysterious *esha* surged in his veins. He wasn't sure he could speak.

"Why do you think they're back?"

Anton shook his head. He tore his gaze away from the Paladin. The mysterious *esha* at last began to ebb, leaving him like a passing storm. Whoever it belonged to had left the immediate area of the marina square, and Anton didn't know if it was relief or despair that filled his chest.

"I don't know," he answered Ephyra at last. He thought about what the woman on the street had said. *The Prophets will return now.* But she was just a superstitious old woman. There was no way that could be true. He turned away from the square. "What does it matter?"

"Wait," Ephyra said, getting up after him. "You're not leaving."

Anton turned to pull himself back onto the roof, but Ephyra's hand shot out to grab his arm, holding fast.

"You're not leaving," she said, a threat in her voice this time.

He looked down at her hand wrapped around his arm. If she wanted to, she could kill him right now. Hold on to his arm, draw the *esha* from his body, and leave a pale handprint there, just like her other victims. He glanced at her face and saw that she was staring at her hand. Was she wondering, like he was, whether or not she would do it?

"Look," Anton said slowly. "It's not that I don't want to help you and your sister. I tried."

"So try again."

He shook his head. "It's not going to change anything. There's something wrong with my Grace. And it's only getting worse."

First, the nightmares. Then, the way his memory had overtaken him in the scrying pool. Now, here, that strange storm of *esha* overwhelming him like nothing ever had.

"What do you mean, something's wrong with your Grace?" Ephyra asked. "What happened exactly, when you tried to scry for the Chalice? What did you see?"

He closed his eyes. "The same thing I always see. A frozen lake."

"A lake," Ephyra repeated. "That's all?"

"The lake where I almost drowned."

Ephyra let go of his arm. "What are you talking about?"

It had been a long time since Anton had told anyone about his nightmares, about the memory that kept him clutched inside its claws. But he was keeping a secret of hers now, and maybe if she thought she had a secret of his, they would be even. Maybe if she knew what he was running from, she'd let him go.

"It was winter," he began. "The lake was frozen over. I was playing outside in the snow when my brother found me. He chased me out onto the ice, and it broke beneath me. I reached for him, and he . . . he pushed me under."

Anton opened his eyes and saw Ephyra staring at him. She looked horror-struck.

"How could someone do that?" she said.

Anton looked away. "I wouldn't think cruelty and murder would surprise the Pale Hand."

"He was your *brother*," Ephyra said, as if that changed anything. As if cruel people, wicked people, could not be blood.

"We grew up in the Novogardian Territories," Anton said. He could still remember the shivering winters, the hunger that pitted his insides. "Life is different there. The Graced are much rarer, and there's superstition about them. Novogardians believe all kinds of things about them—about us."

"You mean like the Witnesses?"

Anton shook his head. "The Witnesses hate the Graced and

believe they are a corruption of nature. But northerners don't hate the Graced—they revere them. They don't believe the Prophets gave us our powers—they believe they were given to us by an ancient god, and that those powers give us the divine right to rule. My brother and I were raised by our grandmother, and she believed that, too. She was Graceless. So was her son, my father. So was my brother. And then I was born. My Grace manifested early, and once it did . . . it was all my grandmother cared about."

"And your brother resented that," Ephyra said.

"Yes, but—it wasn't just that," Anton said. "Most people, when they hurt you, they do it for a reason. To get you to do what they want. Or because they're angry and they need a way to lash out. But my brother . . . he hurt me because he liked it. It brought him joy to make me feel pain, to make me terrified, to make me beg him to stop."

And how Anton had begged.

You want me to stop? Illya would say. *Then stop me. Aren't you the one with Grace? Show me how powerful you are, Anton.*

"It was like a game to him, one that I could never learn the rules to." Anton shut his eyes again. "I've spent my whole life trying to put the things he did behind me."

"But when you use your Grace, you're forced to relive them," Ephyra said. "Is that what happened when you were scrying?"

He nodded. "For a while, I'd gotten better. I was able to control the nightmares. But when I try to scry, it's like I'm back there, at the lake. I'm helpless. All I can feel is my brother's hands forcing me under . . . That's why I couldn't help you. That's why I have to leave."

"And your brother . . . he sent those men after you the other night?" Ephyra asked. "What does he want with you?"

That was the question Anton hadn't been able to answer, though it had haunted him since the moment the Nameless Woman had showed up at Thalassa.

"I think he just couldn't stand the fact that I got away," he said at last. "It must have felt like he lost, knowing he couldn't hurt me anymore. And he never lost. He's looking for me so he can make me pay for running away."

"So your plan is just to keep running?" Ephyra asked. "Hope he doesn't find you again, and live in fear of the moment that he does?"

"It's not like I have another choice."

A sea breeze swept past them, ruffling Ephyra's dark curls. "What if you did?" she asked softly. "What if you could stop running? What if you could be rid of that fear, for good?"

Anton took a half step back. "What are you talking about?"

"You can help us—help Beru. And I can help you, too."

"How?"

Her eyes caught his. "Sooner or later, the Pale Hand will claim another victim in this city."

The moment felt like a held breath. Anton had never considered it before, what it would be like to live without the constant fear at his back. To know that his brother was gone—truly gone, never to torment him again.

"You can keep running forever," Ephyra said. "You can spend your entire life looking over your shoulder, waiting for your past to catch up to you. Or you can stop running and finally face it. That sounds like the choice to me."

Anton dug his nails into his palm. "I just want to breathe without feeling like I'm drowning."

"I just want to find a way to keep my sister alive," Ephyra replied. "We can help each other. You can't use your Grace while your brother still lives. But if he was gone . . ."

If his brother was gone, would Anton be free of his memories, free of the nightmare that kept him in its teeth?

"I can't be sure whether that would change anything," he said. "Whether I'd be able to use my Grace, let alone find Eleazar's Chalice for you."

"But you might," Ephyra said. "And that's better than what we have without you, which is nothing."

She reached out again, but she didn't grab him this time. She was offering her hand.

"We can help each other," she said.

Anton looked past her, out onto the shining waves cresting just beyond the harbor. Part of him still wanted nothing more than to leave everything behind—the threat of his brother, the Pale Hand, the mysterious *esha* he'd sensed in the marina. To leave this city of broken faith and not look back. It was what he always did.

But Ephyra was right. He'd always be looking over his shoulder. The nightmare, the memory, the lake—they would always be a shadow closing in on him. He was in the icy water still, suspended in those few moments of darkness. He could either succumb to it and let himself sink, or he could reach for the surface.

He took Ephyra's hand. "Then it's a deal."

12

HASSAN

HASSAN STIFLED A YAWN AS HE SLID HIS TEACUP UNDER THE SAMOVAR. IN THE past five days, he'd managed to sneak out to the agora twice more, bringing whatever food and extra clothing he could. He'd made up some lie about collecting them from other Akademos students when Khepri had asked about it. He'd spent his time there doing various jobs around the camps—collecting firewood, minding the children, and cleaning up some of the debris littered around.

Mostly, though, he spent more time with Khepri. She seemed to have a hand in almost every aspect of the camps—from training the refugees to fixing tents to distributing food—and had no compunction about putting Hassan to work. *No one* had ever ordered him around before, and each confidently issued command hit him with surprise and a curious sort of delight. For the first time since the coup—for the first time in his whole life, really—Hassan felt *useful*.

On his most recent visit, he had stopped in the marketplace on his way and traded a set of gold coat fasteners for a dozen wheelbarrows from the woodworker. He'd then gone to the potter and cleaned out his inventory, carefully stacking the bowls and jugs in the wheelbarrows.

"What's all this?" Khepri had asked when Hassan had shown up with the potter's apprentice and a dozen other kids he'd hired to take the wheelbarrows into the agora.

"Halima was saying she sometimes spends three hours a day waiting in line for water," Hassan had said, directing the kids to line the wheelbarrows up against the side of the fountainhouse. "What if instead you assigned some of your trainees to deliver the water?"

"Oh," Khepri had said, drumming her fingers on the side of one of the wheelbarrows.

"What?" Hassan had asked, suddenly worried that he'd overstepped or that she was starting to get suspicious of him.

But she'd just smiled, shaking her head, and then went to get the trainees.

Hassan had woken up thinking about the curve of that smile.

"You missed breakfast this morning," Lethia said, spooning a tiny dab of jewel-red chutney onto her plate.

"Sorry," Hassan replied automatically, stirring the tea idly with a little gold spoon. He'd pressed his luck last night, staying out almost until dawn. But he didn't regret it—those moments, shared between him and the other Herati refugees, had been more necessary to him than the food he now ate or, indeed, a full night's sleep.

"I suppose you must have been tired after being out all night," Lethia went on conversationally.

Hassan froze.

"You couldn't possibly think I was unaware of your little jaunts to the agora, did you?"

He had, in fact, been certain she was unaware.

"You're not exactly a master of deception, Hassan," Lethia went on, her tone still light and jesting. "Oh, for Keric's sake, you can speak. I'm not angry."

"You're not?"

"I'm not pleased with you, either," she conceded. "I just wish you weren't so careless. You're lucky I knew you snuck off. I spoke with the Sentry captain and had them double the foot patrols around the Sacred Gate."

"You can do that?" Hassan asked. Since the death of her husband almost a decade ago, Lethia held no official power in Pallas Athos, but it seemed he'd underestimated the pull she still had.

"I asked the captain as a personal favor to me," Lethia said. "I thought it wise after that incident outside the temple with the Witnesses."

"You knew about that, too?" Hassan asked, dismayed.

Lethia gave him a withering look over the brim of her teacup. "There's little that goes on in this city I'm not aware of. Which reminds me—evidently, the Order of the Last Light arrived in the harbor earlier today."

Hassan nearly choked on his tea. "What do you mean, they arrived in the harbor? The Order hasn't been in Pallas Athos for a hundred years."

"Well, evidently, they're here now. They were seen entering the High City."

Hassan's eyes widened. He knew that the Order had once been the holy protectors of Pallas Athos. They'd watched over the city and the pilgrims who flocked there to visit the Temple of Pallas. Their abrupt departure, right after the Prophets' disappearance, had caused decades of turmoil in Pallas Athos, turning it from a city of faith and safety to one of danger and vice. Hassan had always thought that members of the Order had slowly died off after leaving.

"Why would they return here after all this time?" he wondered.

"No one seems to know, not even the priests. Which makes them furious, of course," Lethia said with a small smile.

"Lady Lethia," a servant said from the doorway. "There's a messenger waiting in the courtyard."

"Can't you see I'm having tea with my nephew? Tell them to wait."

"They said it was quite urgent," the servant said timidly.

"Urgent to them, perhaps," Lethia said with a little scoff, making a shooing motion with her hand.

The servant didn't move. "They said they've come on behalf of the Order of the Last Light."

Lethia's eyebrows shot up.

Hassan gaped at the servant. "The Order of the Last Light wants to talk to Aunt Lethia?"

The servant shook his head. "Not Lady Lethia. They want to see *you*, Your Grace."

"*Me?*"

"Do they really think they can just waltz back to this city after all this time, stirring up all this excitement, and then summon the Crown Prince of Herat whenever they like?" Lethia demanded. "The arrogance of the Graced astounds me sometimes, truly. How did they even know he was here?"

It was a good question, but Hassan had plenty more of his own. And only one way to answer them.

"Where are you going?" Lethia asked as he stood up from the table.

"To find out what's going on."

"They can't just summon you like a commoner," Lethia snapped. "They lost that right a hundred years ago, when they turned their backs on the world."

"I'm not exactly overwhelmed with important appointments," Hassan replied. "If the Order of the Last Light has finally returned to Pallas Athos, it must be for an important reason. The timing is too coincidental—it must have something to do with the Witnesses and Nazirah."

Lethia frowned at him. "Oh, very well. It's not as though I've been able to stop you from going where you like whenever you like. But you're letting the Sentry escort you this time. I won't take no for an answer."

Hassan considered. No doubt the Witnesses in Pallas Athos had learned of the Order's arrival. Whether there would be another attack in reaction to them, he didn't know. But it wasn't worth the risk, especially since the temple was so close to the refugees.

"All right," he said to his aunt. "I'll take two guards."

"Five," she said, bargaining.

"Three."

"Fine."

A half hour later found Hassan sweating beneath the midafternoon sun as the messenger and three Sentry escorted him through the limestone streets. A few curious stares followed them as they marched up the Sacred Road to the agora, but most quickly lost interest.

The marketplace just below the agora was emptier than Hassan had ever seen it. As he passed through the Sacred Gate, he saw that the people usually found in the markets had come to the foot of the temple. The Order's arrival had stirred everyone up, refugees and citizens alike.

He kept his eyes on the messenger leading him through the crowd. The Sentry kept a wide perimeter around him—wide enough that hopefully no one would see him and recognize him as the curious and slightly awkward university student who'd been hanging around the camps the past few evenings.

"Cirion!"

Hassan flinched, closing his eyes briefly as Khepri's voice cracked across the crowd. He kept his head down, hoping she would think she'd been mistaken.

"Cirion!" she called out again, her voice nearer.

"Miss, we need you to step back," one of the Sentry said firmly.

"I'm just trying to speak to my friend over there—"

Hassan turned to where Khepri was being kept back. One of the Sentry glanced over his shoulder at him.

"Do you know this woman?"

Hassan watched Khepri's expression slide from amusement to confusion. "Yes," he answered the Sentry. "I know her. It's all right—you can let her through."

The Sentry stepped aside, but Khepri didn't move.

Her brow creased in confusion. "Why are there armed Sentry with you?"

Several different lies came to the tip of Hassan's tongue, each of them believable enough. But he couldn't bring himself to dispense them. He didn't want to keep lying to her.

"Your Grace," the Order's messenger said at his elbow. "We really mustn't delay."

"Your Grace?" Khepri echoed. "Cirion, what's going on?"

"I'm so sorry," Hassan said in a rush. "I didn't mean to deceive you. I should have told you the truth from the start. My name isn't Cirion."

He stepped toward her, but she stepped back.

"You're . . ." The words seemed to catch in her throat. "You're the prince. Aren't you?"

Hassan swallowed. "I wanted to tell you."

Khepri let out a wild, choked-off laugh as she took a step back. "You—This whole time, you . . ." She shook her head in disbelief.

"Khepri," he said, drawing toward her.

She looked up at him, her shoulders slumped and her mouth twisted. She wasn't just angry. She was hurt. "I—I have to go."

"Wait, if I could just—"

"I have to go," she said again, steadier. She turned away, and Hassan moved to follow her, unsure what he could say to make things right but knowing he didn't want her to leave like this.

Two of the Sentry guards converged to block his path.

"I have to speak to her," Hassan said. "The Order of the Last Light can wait."

He felt a gentle touch on his elbow and turned to see the Order's messenger beside him. "Your Grace," she said. "I don't think you'll want to delay this meeting."

Hassan looked from Khepri's retreating form to the Temple of Pallas, where the Order waited. The desire to chase after her warred with the need to know why the Order of the Last Light was here. If it had something to do with the Witnesses . . . with Herat . . . then even Khepri, in her confusion, would want him to find out.

"All right," he said at last to the messenger. "Take me to the Order."

The messenger led them to the temple. Anticipation churned in Hassan's stomach as they ascended the marble steps. Two wide, flat bowls of chrism oil flanked the open doors. Between them stood the Herati acolyte Emir.

"Your Grace," he said, kneeling.

"You recognized me that day in the agora, didn't you?" Hassan asked him.

Emir bowed his head. "Please, enter the house of Pallas."

Hassan wet the tips of his fingers to consecrate himself before entering, but when the Sentry guards with him moved to do the same, the acolyte stood and held up his hand.

"The Order summoned only the prince," Emir said in a clear, flat voice that brooked no argument.

Hassan nodded at the Sentry to affirm the acolyte's order, and then stepped through the threshold alone.

Sunlight ribboned into the sanctum from the open roof, illuminating the seven Paladin who stood in the center. Two men with the darker skin of the Seti desert stood side by side with a man and a woman who shared the pale complexion and dark hair of the Inshuu steppe. In front of them, a woman with the freckled, copper-haired coloring common to Endarrion stood beside a man who was clearly island-born—Charisian, if Hassan were to guess. At the head of the group was a man—more of a boy, really—whose tawny skin and dark hair made him look like a native of Pallas Athos.

For some reason, Hassan had expected everyone in the Order of the Last Light to look alike, but these people were as varied as the scholars who came from far and wide to Nazirah. What they had in common were the silver torcs around their necks, the dark blue cloaks draped over their shoulders, and the reverent expressions on their faces.

Emir stepped forward between them. "Your Grace, I present to you the Paladin Guard of the Order of the Last Light, and their leader, Captain Jude Weatherbourne, Keeper of the Word. Captain Weatherbourne, this is Prince Hassan Seif, heir to the throne of Herat."

The Paladin Guard knelt as one.

With his head bowed toward the ground, the youngest-looking

Paladin at the head of the group said, "Your Grace, I . . ." He cleared his throat. "I have been waiting to meet you for a very long time. Since the day you were born."

He lifted his gaze, and again Hassan was surprised by how much younger he was than most of the others. Yet he was the one who'd been introduced as their leader. The Keeper of the Word.

"Why?" Hassan asked. "And what has made you return to this city?"

The Paladin stood.

"We came to tell you something," Captain Weatherbourne said. "A secret the Order of the Last Light has protected for a century. And now that we've found you—"

"You were looking for me?"

"We didn't know it was you we were looking for," Captain Weatherbourne said. "Not until recently."

Hassan's patience waned. He should have expected that talking to a hermetic group of swordsmen would be like talking to the most opaque philosophers of the Great Library. "What do you mean, you didn't know it was me?"

"Jude," the copper-haired Paladin woman said urgently. "Perhaps it's best if he hears it now."

Hassan bristled. "Hears *what*?"

Captain Weatherbourne's gaze was unwavering and bright as he answered. "The final prophecy of the Seven Prophets."

Hassan blinked. "The prophecy of King Vasili was fulfilled over a century ago. What relevance could that possibly have?"

King Vasili, the last king of the Novogardian Empire. Afflicted with a strange madness, the king had waged a war against the Six Prophetic Cities when he'd learned that the Prophets had predicted he would be the last Graced heir of his line. But no one can defy their fate for long, and King Vasili's war had ended the Novogardian Empire for good, fulfilling the Prophets' final prophecy. The story had always haunted Hassan, a stark warning of what had happened the last time a powerful kingdom had failed to produce a Graced heir.

"The prophecy of the Raving King was not the Prophets' final prophecy," Captain Weatherbourne said. "The rest of the world believes it was, but there was another prophecy they made before they disappeared. You will be the first person outside the covenant of the Order to hear it."

Hassan stared at him, his mind whirring to make sense of it all. A secret that had been kept. A promise that the Prophets had left to the world. And for some reason, they wanted *him* to hear it.

"Does it involve the Witnesses? Nazirah?"

Captain Weatherbourne didn't answer, and instead took a silver filigreed box handed to him by one of the other Paladin. Nestled inside was a pale stone, cracked nearly in two, with intricate fractal designs etched over its surface.

Captain Weatherbourne held the stone out to Emir, who plucked it from the box with careful hands.

"What is that?" Hassan asked as Emir took the stone to the edge of the scrying pool.

Captain Weatherbourne looked up at him. "An oracle stone."

"I've never seen one in person before," Hassan said, his voice hushed. A real oracle stone, like in the stories of old.

Captain Weatherbourne nodded to Emir, who raised the stone high and cast it into the scrying pool with a small splash. The water rippled out from the stone and began to swirl. A faint glow lit the pool from below, and a low hum filled the sanctum, echoing off the walls, growing steadily louder.

The echoes began to sound like whispers. They coalesced into seven voices, speaking as one.

"When the Age of Prophets wanes
And the fate of the world lies in shadow,
Only our final prophecy remains,
Given to the guardian, the Keeper of the Word.

"The deceiver ensnares the world with lies,
To death's pale hand the wicked fall,
That which sleeps in the dust shall rise,
And in their wake will come a darkness.

"But born beneath a light-streaked sky,
An heir with the blessed Sight,
A promise of the past undone,
The shadowed future made bright.

"The final piece of our prophecy revealed
In vision of Grace and fire
To bring the age of dark to yield
Or break the world entire."

The whispers echoed through the sanctum until they dissolved into a low hum. The glowing water faded, and the pool returned to stillness.

Silence overtook the sanctum. Hassan knew that he was the only one present who was hearing the prophecy for the first time, but he could feel the effect of these words, kept secret for so long, in each of their carefully held breaths, in the reverence in their gazes.

It was a moment before it struck Hassan that they were all staring at *him.*

Captain Weatherbourne was the first to speak. "You were born on the summer solstice sixteen years ago. On that night, the sky glowed with celestial light."

Hassan watched the Paladin leader's face, feeling as though he stood on the precipice of a vast truth that could unmake him.

"Prince Hassan, you are the Last Prophet."

II

OATH

13

JUDE

JUDE WAS NINE YEARS OLD WHEN PENROSE TAUGHT HIM HIS FIRST KOAH. EVERY koah of the Grace of Heart, she'd told him, had three parts. Breath, which focused your Grace and drew *esha* from the earth. Movement, which channeled it into power. And intention—the one unwavering purpose beneath it, the true north that guided it all.

For every koah, Jude's intention was the same. It had not changed since the first time he'd felt his Grace humming within him. Always, his true north was this moment. He had sworn to himself that when it came, he would cast off whatever doubts, whatever fear, whatever longing had clouded his heart before. He would rise to meet his destiny full only of faith and unwavering devotion.

"I'm a-a Prophet?" the prince said. "That doesn't make any sense. The Prophets are gone. They've been gone for a century. How can there be—How can *I* be—?"

"You heard the prophecy," Jude said. "When the Prophets disappeared, they left it behind as a promise that a new Prophet would be born. And we believe that Prophet is you."

There was so much else he wanted to say. That his and the prince's destinies were bound together. That he could still remember everything about the day the prince had come into the world, and the way the sky had lit up in a storm of light.

But the words died in his throat, and Jude went silent. The moment was here now, the moment he had anticipated since he was born.

And Jude felt no different than before.

This is it, he realized. *This is all you get.*

He had thought that finally looking into the face of the Prophet would fill him with all the things he had lacked. But those were the thoughts of a child. A child who had looked up at lights in the sky and thought that they were meant for him.

He was a man grown now, and he knew the truth. His destiny was finally here, and it did not care whether or not he was ready for it.

14

HASSAN

HASSAN GAPED IN THE SILENCE OF THE TEMPLE. THE WORDS THE PALADIN leader had spoken rang in his head, over and over again until they ceased to sound like words, just a long dulcet buzz of nonsense.

It *was* nonsense. Absurd. Hassan felt like laughing.

"There must be some mistake," he said at last, looking from Captain Weatherbourne to the acolyte and back again, as if one of them would suddenly come to their senses and realize that what they were saying was impossible.

"There is no mistake," Emir said. "You fit the signs."

"Signs?" Hassan said. "You mean the things in the prophecy? The lights in the sky?"

Hassan knew the story of the auspicious lights that had illuminated the sky when he was born. The Herati had interpreted it as a sign that he would grow into a wise and worthy ruler. They had celebrated for five days and five nights, and on every year thereafter, they lit the sky with firecrackers and flares to commemorate the occasion.

No one had imagined that it was part of a secret prophecy.

Hassan shook his head. "I can't have been the only child born on that day."

"That certainly would have made our jobs easier," Emir said with a small smile. "But you're right. After that day, I had only suspicions. Enough to keep a close eye on the young Prince of Herat, waiting for another sign. And then, two and half weeks ago, it came."

Two and a half weeks ago. Hassan went cold. "You mean when the Witnesses took Nazirah."

"Yes," Emir replied. "That is when I knew. The Witnesses broke the Seif line in Herat. Their coup went against one of the earliest prophecies made by the Seven Prophets—the prophecy of Nazirah."

As long as the lighthouse of Nazirah stands, the Seif line shall rule. Hassan touched the compass in his pocket lightly. These were the words he always came back to, the prophecy that secured his place as heir.

"Prophecies can't be undone," Hassan said uncertainly. "Can they?"

"It's never happened before," Captain Weatherbourne replied. "But the Prophets have never predicted it before, either. The Order's scholars have scoured the records of every prophecy ever made, and they've failed to find a single one that did not unfold as the Prophets foretold. Your family's prophecy is the first and only one that's ever been broken. Which makes it the second sign that you are the Last Prophet. 'A promise of the past undone.'"

"But *I* didn't undo it. The Hierophant did!"

"But you—or rather, your family—were the subject of the prophecy of Nazirah," Emir said. "Therefore, it was your destiny that was undone."

Hassan swallowed. "So that's two signs. But what of the third? 'An heir with the blessed Sight.' The Prophet is supposed to have the Grace of Sight. I don't have a Grace at all."

He let the statement hang there.

"But you are an heir," Emir said. "And not yet seventeen. There is still time for your Grace to manifest."

Hassan's mouth went dry. He'd spent years trying to drive such thoughts from his head, thinking them a foolish fantasy. To have that fantasy suddenly dangled in front of him again after all this time was agonizing.

"By the time my father was twelve," Hassan said, "he was creating locks that could be opened by voice and a clock that predicts the weather. My mother was nine when she discovered she could lift a man thrice her size. It's too late for me."

"I don't think that's the case," the copper-haired Paladin said. "The Grace of Sight tends to manifest later than the other Graces."

That was true, and something Hassan had considered often. He'd always assumed, however, that the Grace of Sight was simply more difficult to detect than the other Graces, and thus more likely to go unnoticed for longer. But maybe there was more to it than that.

"Some scholars even say that the Prophet Nazirah, the very founder of your homeland, was sixteen when she received her first vision," the copper-haired Paladin went on.

"Your Grace," Captain Weatherbourne said abruptly. "The acolytes of our Order have been searching for the Last Prophet for a hundred years. Never in that time have we encountered *anyone* who fit the signs as you do. We would not have come all this way if we didn't believe it was you."

The other Paladin were all staring at Hassan, their expressions certain and unwavering. In the face of their palpable belief, his doubt began to waver.

"And what do you intend to do now that you're here?" he asked.

"We intend to keep you safe," Captain Weatherbourne said. "To wait for you to fulfill the prophecy and show us how to stop the Age of Darkness."

"The Age of Darkness," Hassan said. "What is it?"

Captain Weatherbourne hesitated, glancing at the other members of the Guard before he forged on. "The end of the Graced."

"And with it, the destruction of our civilization," the copper-haired Paladin woman said. "When the Prophets disappeared, there were decades of turmoil that followed. Wars broke out between allied cities. Disease and natural disasters followed. In the past, the people of the Six Prophetic Cities could weather these hardships, because the prophecies let them anticipate what was to come. But without the Prophets, the world panicked."

Hassan nodded. He knew all this, had read extensively on the history of the past century. Even Herat, one of the most stable regions, had experienced this upheaval. His grandmother's rule had begun with the kingdom near rebellion.

"Still, none of that compares to what will happen if the Graced are gone, too," the Paladin continued. "No one with the Grace of Blood to heal the sick and injured. No one with the Grace of Mind to keep lights aglow and trains running and messages sent from one city to another. No one with the Grace of Heart to protect the weak. It will be chaos, a thousand times the magnitude of what had happened when the Prophets left."

And in the midst of that chaos would be the perfect time for a ruthless despot to seize power. Especially one as charismatic and shrewd as the Hierophant.

Hassan's heart sank. "The end of the Graced," he said. "Isn't that what the Witnesses want? Are you saying that the Hierophant's plan—what they call the Reckoning—is real?"

Captain Weatherbourne bowed his head. "We think so. Whatever the Hierophant is planning is what the Prophets saw in their final prophecy."

"But how do you know that?"

"Because it's already beginning," Captain Weatherbourne said. "The prophecy speaks of three things that can bring about the Age of Darkness. A Deceiver, the Pale Hand of Death, and one who would rise from the dust."

"We believe the Deceiver is the Hierophant himself," the copper-haired Paladin said. "He has convinced his followers that the Prophets were wicked and that the Graced must be destroyed. His followers have committed hundreds of horrific acts in his name—burning down shrines, desecrating temples, even killing Graced children. All based on the lies he tells them."

"And the Pale Hand," Hassan said, recalling the murder Lethia had mentioned the other afternoon. The one that had spooked the priests and the Archon so badly. "I've heard of that. Bodies turning up marked by a pale handprint. That's part of the prophecy, too?"

Captain Weatherbourne nodded. "All of these things are connected. All of them mean that the last prophecy is unfolding. One of them, or perhaps all of them together, will bring about the Age of Darkness."

"What about the Witnesses?" Hassan asked. "Do they know that their Reckoning was predicted by the Prophets? Does the Hierophant?"

"No," Captain Weatherbourne replied. "The Order has kept the prophecy a secret to all but its own sworn members. No one else in the world knows what the Prophets saw before they disappeared."

Anger flared in Hassan's gut. "But if you've known this would happen—if you knew this Age of Darkness was coming—why did you keep it a secret?"

"It was a choice made by the Keeper of the Word after the Prophets disappeared," Captain Weatherbourne answered. "She knew that if the prophecy were common knowledge, the Last Prophet would not be safe. Others would search for him. So she chose to keep the contents of the prophecy secret, until the Order of the Last Light could find the Prophet. Could find *you*."

"And now that you've found me?"

"The prophecy must be completed."

Hassan shook his head. "But what does that mean?"

"There is a reason that this prophecy is the last one. It was the last thing the Prophets *could* see," Captain Weatherbourne replied. "Their powers of Sight extended only as far as our present time. Beyond that, they were as blind as the rest of us. They could see the Age of Darkness, but not how to stop it. Only you can see that."

Hassan recalled what Khepri had said to him the first night in the refugee camps. That Prince Hassan was going to take back his country from the Witnesses. He had doubted himself then, and he doubted himself now. He was supposed to be a prince, not a Prophet. How could he set the world right again when he could not even defend his own country?

"But *how* do I see it?" he asked.

"The Prophets each received their visions in their own way," the copper-haired Paladin said. "Some in dreams. Some in trances. The visions of the Prophets are rarely predictable. They come when the time is right—not before, and not after. Fate does not reveal its hand quickly."

"So we just wait," Hassan said, his voice dulling. He was tired of waiting. "And what if it never comes?"

"It will," Captain Weatherbourne said firmly. "I know this must be a lot to take in right now. Particularly so soon after you had to flee your country. But know that we left Kerameikos Fort to be here. To protect you. Each of us swore an oath that we would serve you. That is what we've come here to do."

The swordsman's words grated on him. The Order claimed they served *him*, but they said nothing of his people. "And if I were not the Prophet?" he asked slowly. "Would you still be hiding in your fortress? Or would you be here, fighting back against the Witnesses?"

"We serve the Prophet," Captain Weatherbourne said again.

Hassan turned away. "I think it might be best if I returned to my aunt's villa now. As you said, this is . . . a lot to take in."

Captain Weatherbourne nodded. "Of course." He turned to the acolyte, Emir. "Thank you for all that you've done. Your service to the Order will be remembered. We'll speak again soon."

Emir nodded, and the Guard fell into line, heading toward the temple doors.

"Wait," Hassan said. "What are you doing?"

"You said you wanted to return to your aunt's villa," Captain Weatherbourne said patiently.

"Yes, but I brought Sentry to escort me back," Hassan replied. "I don't need you to accompany me."

It was Captain Weatherbourne's turn to be confused. "Your Grace, perhaps I was not clear. I am the Keeper of the Word. This is the Paladin Guard. We are here to protect you. Where you go, we go."

Hassan just stared at him. It was finally beginning to sink in. An hour ago, he had been summoned to the Temple of Pallas by a group of people who hadn't been seen in a century, without the faintest idea why. Now, he was no longer Hassan Seif, Crown Prince of Herat. He was Hassan Seif, subject of a secret prophecy.

The last and only hope to stop the Age of Darkness.

15

ANTON

THE MESSAGE TOLD ILLYA TO MEET ANTON IN THE TEMPLE OF TARSEIS AT MID-night. Ephyra had left it inside Anton's flat in the marina district. They knew the flat was still being watched by the men Illya had hired, so it wouldn't be long before the message was discovered.

All they needed to do was wait.

Anton and Ephyra stood shoulder to shoulder in the dark sanctum of the Temple of Tarseis. Night had fallen over the city like a shroud, and Anton felt smothered by the quiet.

They'd chosen the temple because of its location just within the walls of the High City. Anton knew it was a risk to do this where Sentry foot soldiers patrolled every night, but with the Sentry around, there was less danger that Illya would bring his hired swords with him to ambush them. The Sentry would be quick to notice a half dozen armed swordsmen roaming the streets near the temple, but Anton's knowledge of the city's back alleys and Ephyra's knowledge of the Sentry patrol routes meant they themselves could avoid detection.

"When you do this usually . . . I mean, when you kill someone as the Pale Hand . . . what happens?" Anton asked, keeping his voice hushed in the quiet of the sanctum.

"I break in. Or I sneak in. Make sure they're alone." Ephyra's smile was slow, like poison. "Then I tell the poor bastards why I'm there."

"You talk to them?"

"Everyone should have their last words."

A sick sort of curiosity came over him. "What do they say?"

"You're about to find out," she said, before retreating into the shadows.

Anton felt his brother's approach before he saw him. The low buzz of his *esha* rattled through him like teeth in a glass jar. He looked to the temple doors. On the portico stood the person that he had prayed every day for the past five years never to see again.

Moonlight spilled across a broad, pale forehead. Bright gold eyes peered down a straight nose, so similar to his own. Anton would know that face anywhere. He had spent a long time trying to purge its image from his mind.

"Brother," Illya said. The sound of his voice was ice in Anton's veins. "It's been a long time."

The last time Anton had seen him, they'd both been in threadbare rags, perpetually cold, perpetually grubby. Now, Illya looked like one of the guests Anton might serve at Thalassa Gardens. Anton had no trouble believing that the man in front of him had the means to hire a scrying agency and furnish himself with hired swords.

"Not long enough," Anton answered. "Why were you looking for me?"

Illya answered without hesitation. "I wanted to make sure you were safe."

"Safe?" Anton was nearly speechless with disbelief. "You've never cared about that. I haven't forgotten what you tried to do to me."

"I've changed," Illya said, boots clicking against stone as he stepped farther into the sanctum. "I look back at the vicious, rage-filled creature who hurt you, and I no longer recognize him. All I've wanted since you left was to find you and tell you how sorry I am for the things I did."

For the first time, it occurred to Anton to wonder what had happened to Illya in the years since the lake. If the man who stood in front of him now truly was different, somehow, than the boy he'd been. He certainly looked different, in his trim gray Endarrion coat and polished boots. But beneath the fine clothing, there remained something derelict in Illya's appearance. A hunger in his eyes, a desperation that Anton saw only because he knew it so well.

"The things you did," Anton said. "You *tortured* me. You told me you were going to kill me. You—" Fear halted his tongue. There was no language for the kind of terror he had lived in.

Illya paled. "I was a child."

"So was I."

Illya's head dipped forward, shadowing his face from view. "I cannot excuse what I did. I know that. But you know that I suffered, too. You don't know how it felt, being an unwanted, useless son, just like our father. Worthless, because of what I was. What I *wasn't*. While you were the chosen son, destined to rescue our family from squalor and restore us to glory."

Illya had been cast aside, the Graceless firstborn living in the shadow of his younger brother.

"I never wanted to be that," Anton said. "Every night, I wished that someone would take my Grace away, so she would let me be. So that you would stop hating me."

Something flickered in Illya's expression, something so close to remorse that Anton felt bewildered for a moment. Could someone as cruel as his brother feel true remorse?

Anton wouldn't let himself believe it. Illya might have found a way to rise from their bleak childhood, to trick the world into giving him what he wanted, the way he'd tricked Anton so many times, but it was all a clever ruse. The beast might have been caged, but it still lived.

"I did hate you," Illya said after a pause. "But once you were gone, I saw that it wasn't you I hated, truly. It was them. After you left, I left, too. I never looked back. Father's probably drunk himself to death, and as for our dear old grandmother . . . well, if you can survive on spite alone, I imagine she's right where we left her."

If Anton thought back far enough, he could remember a time when he and Illya had been united in the stark, cold reality of their home. Side by side against their drunk, useless father and their cruel grandmother, a woman so devoid of kindness she made wolves look nurturing. Anton could remember the exact day it had all changed. Illya had gotten lost outside during a storm. And when the snow died down, Anton had led their grandmother straight to him, guided there by Illya's *esha*.

The next day, Illya had twisted Anton's arm behind his back until he cried. From then on, it was clear—Anton had lost his only ally. His only true family.

"I got out, just like you," Illya said softly. "I went to Osgard, and then to Endarrion, searching for a place where I could be something more than the unwanted son. It took time, but . . . I saw how wrong I was. I saw how I let jealousy twist me."

"Don't tell me you want to apologize now," Anton said. "Don't tell me you've changed. Don't tell me you can ever, *ever* escape the things you did to me. Because I can't."

Illya's golden eyes dimmed. "Anton, I . . . I know I was cruel. I hurt you. I wanted you to suffer. But the things I said to you, the things I threatened—I would never have killed you. Never."

"Liar," Anton said, his jaw clenching.

"Anton, I swear—"

"*You tried to drown me!*" Anton shouted. "You led me to that frozen lake, and when the ice broke beneath me, you tried to hold me under."

Illya's face twisted in surprise, then sorrow. "Is that what you think happened? That day, on the lake, I *saved* you. You fell in, and I dragged you from the freezing water. I thought—You weren't even breathing. Your skin was so blue. But then you coughed, and breathed, and that was the moment—that's when I knew I had to start protecting you. That I had to be the brother I should have been from the start. But you left before I had the chance."

"Stop," Anton said. "Stop lying."

"I'm not lying, Anton."

"*Stop!*" Anton yelled, and in his mind, he heard the yell of his eleven-year-old self, as his brother pushed him beneath the water, beneath the ice.

Stop! Illya's voice rang in Anton's head, sharp and panicked, like the rattle of his *esha*, as Anton's lungs seized, as his vision went dark. *Please, stop!*

No. It was Anton pleading, Anton begging, pathetic. Wanting Illya to let go, wanting to be free, wanting to sink below the water.

No.

He wanted to be safe. The only way to be safe was for Illya to be gone. Even standing in front of him was messing with his head. He had to make it stop.

"Oh, Anton," Illya said, with a look of pity. "You still don't know what you're running from, do you?"

16

EPHYRA

EPHYRA STEPPED OUT OF THE SHADOWS AS ANTON FELL TO HIS KNEES IN THE middle of the temple sanctum.

"Who's there?" Illya cried as Ephyra knelt beside Anton's trembling form.

"A deal is a deal," she said to Anton. "Just say the word."

"Who are you?" Illya asked, fixing his gold eyes on Ephyra.

She stood, leveling him with the Pale Hand's coldest stare. "You shouldn't have come looking for him," she said. "You shouldn't have sent those men after him."

"What?" Illya said. "I didn't send anyone after him. I came here to *protect* him."

Behind her, Anton let out a harsh sound, sharper than a laugh. He climbed back to his feet. "Protect me from what?"

Illya's brow creased. "From the Witnesses, Anton. From anyone who would try to hurt you because of what you are."

"You mean like you did?"

"There are people out there who are worse than I was," Illya replied, his voice shaking ever so slightly. "Things are different now than they used to be. The Witnesses aren't just a fringe group of fanatics. People believe what they say. That they will bring a Reckoning for the Graced. Now that they've taken Nazirah, they say the other Prophetic Cities are next. Charis. Tarsepolis. Behezda. It's the reason I started looking for you. To make sure you were safe."

"I'll never be safe," Anton replied. "Not if you're still here."

Ephyra looked between the two brothers. She'd killed plenty of men like Illya before. Men who swore they'd never done the terrible things that she knew they had. Men who used their last breaths to plead and pretend they'd changed. This Illya Aliyev was no different. From what Anton had told her, about the lake, about their childhood, Illya was as cruel as they came. He deserved death just as much as the Pale Hand's other victims.

But Ephyra didn't move. It wasn't that she bought Illya's remorse. It wasn't the softness in his shoulders that held her back. It wasn't the anguish in his eyes—it was the uncertainty in Anton's.

You still don't know what you're running from, do you? Illya had asked.

Ephyra wondered if that was true. The way Anton had looked after he'd tried to scry for the Chalice, and then again this morning at the harbor, spoke of a kind of fear she wasn't sure she fully understood. And she didn't think Anton understood it, either.

A sudden barrage of footsteps sounded outside the temple.

"Is that the Sentry?" Ephyra asked.

Anton's eyes were wide. "There shouldn't be a patrol here for another hour." He whirled on his brother. "Did you tip them off? Did you call them here?"

"Why would I do that?" Illya asked, eyes wide in a way that made the resemblance between him and Anton apparent.

A ghostly light appeared outside.

Ephyra glanced at Illya, torn. If they let him go now, they wouldn't get another chance. Anton might never be able to control his Grace. Which meant Ephyra might never find Eleazar's Chalice.

But if she was caught and the Sentry decided to lock her in their citadel, there would be no one to heal Beru again when she began to fade. She could risk her own life, but she couldn't risk Beru's.

She grabbed Anton's wrist, making her decision. She dragged him through the sanctum, through the arched entryway onto the steps.

A high, loud whistle pierced the air. A blinding light shone on the two of them, stopping them in their tracks.

"They're robbing the temple!"

"Stop where you are, thieves!"

Shielding her eyes, Ephyra turned back toward the temple. Illya had already melted into the darkness.

"Move, and we shoot!" the Sentry shouted.

There were over a dozen of them, their crossbows drawn in front of them. Too many for Ephyra to take on by herself without risking leaving innocent bodies behind. They closed in, pinning her and Anton on the temple steps. The scrape of swords being drawn rang through her ears.

"By decree of the Priests' Conclave of Pallas Athos, you're under arrest."

17

HASSAN

HASSAN WOKE EARLY THE NEXT MORNING AND DRESSED QUICKLY FOR BREAKfast. He assumed Lethia wouldn't miss this opportunity to show her hospitality to the Paladin Guard, and when he arrived at the terrace courtyard, he was not disappointed. The breakfast table was overladen with pastries stuffed with dates and chopped nuts, glass bowls of thickened cream drizzled with honey, pitchers full of jewel-colored nectars, and silver pots of rose tea.

Five Paladin in dark blue cloaks stood around the feast, looking more prepared for battle than for a morning meal.

Lethia was placid and welcoming at the head of the table, though Hassan did not miss the slight quirk of her lips that indicated she was annoyed by his lateness. The night before, when he had arrived back at the villa with the Guard in tow, she'd welcomed them with equanimity but confusion. The Guard had been reluctant to let Hassan tell Lethia everything they'd told him in the temple, but he had insisted. Lethia had kept him safe these last two and a half weeks and had kept his presence in the city a secret. He was sure she could be trusted to keep this secret, too.

While she hadn't expressed any doubt in front of the Paladin, Hassan could tell as she listened to their claims that she was skeptical. For that matter, so was he.

"Good morning, Your Grace," the copper-haired Paladin said to him as he took his place at the head of the table.

"Good morning," Hassan replied. It was a moment before he realized that Captain Weatherbourne wasn't present.

"Captain Weatherbourne sends his apologies," the woman went on, as if anticipating Hassan's question. "The Sentry sent word requesting to speak with him at the citadel. I'll be in charge of your safety while he and Navarro are gone."

"Thank you, uh . . ."

"Penrose," she said with a brief smile.

Penrose. He mouthed the name to himself, vowing to remember it.

After a stilted conversation over breakfast, Lethia suggested he give the Paladin a tour of the gardens. Hassan had planned to sequester himself in the library all afternoon and read whatever he could find about the Order—but then he realized he was probably better off just asking them anyway, so he agreed.

"So," he said, once they were all gathered in the gardens, enjoying the cascading fountains. "You all lived at Kerameikos Fort? What's it like there?"

"Quieter," replied the swordsman called Petrossian. He looked like the oldest of the Guard, and evidently wasn't fond of idle chatter.

Osei, a larger man with skin as dark as ink, added, "Colder."

Hassan heard a snort of laughter and was surprised to see it had come from the two tall, pale Paladin who'd been exceptionally quiet at breakfast. Penrose had introduced them as Annuka and Yarik.

"Desert dweller," Annuka said, nodding at Osei. "No good with cold."

Osei cracked a grin. He had a face suited for smiling. "Not all of us were raised drinking snowmelt instead of mother's milk."

"You're from the Inshuu steppe, aren't you?" Hassan asked Annuka.

"The Qarashi tribe," she answered.

"Why did you leave?"

Annuka frowned. "Many tribes on the Inshuu steppe rely on the herds of wild oxen. But the oxen have been dying off. In one very bad winter, half our herd died. The other tribes came to raid us. Yarik and I fought them, many times, but it didn't matter. Without the oxen, our tribe was dying. The others left, married into new tribes. When it was just Yarik and me left, the other tribes called a Janaal."

Hassan remembered learning about the Inshuu practice of Janaal when a delegation of the largest Inshuu tribes had visited Nazirah. It was a way of encouraging more intermixing of tribes—the best fighters from each tribe would compete, and if they were defeated, they joined the tribe of the victor.

"None of the others could defeat us," Yarik said. "And on the last day of the Janaal, a new opponent stepped into the ring. Not a tribesman. An acolyte. She told us about the Order of the Last Light. She offered us something to fight for again, though we would have to give up our allegiance to our tribe. But we no longer had a tribe. So we went and found new purpose."

The Paladin's tone was simple, straightforward, but Hassan could see the pain behind her words, and in the tenseness of her brother's shoulders. They had lost their entire tribe, and with it, their place in the world.

"Were any of you born in Kerameikos?" he asked.

Penrose shook her head. "The oaths do not permit members of the

Order from having children. With the exception of the Keeper, who does so only to continue the Weatherbourne line."

"Then how have you persisted over the past century?"

"Are you always this curious?" Petrossian muttered.

"'The Crown of Herat fits best on a curious head,'" Hassan quoted. "That's what the scholars say."

"Your question is astute," Penrose said, giving Petrossian a look of admonishment. "The Order's numbers have dwindled, it's true, but we have acolytes all over the world who find new members. Most come to us as children, like Osei and Navarro. Some come later in life, like Yarik and Annuka."

"The Order takes children?"

"Orphans," Osei said. "But we do not swear the oath until we reach adulthood and choose to do so willingly."

"But you all did," Hassan said. "You all chose this."

"Yes," Penrose said. "For me, it was a calling. My whole life, I had felt drawn to the stories of the Order of the Last Light. Though I believed them to be long gone, I felt a deep connection with their noble purpose, so far removed from anything I knew as the daughter of poor farmers in the countryside outside of Endarrion. When my parents discovered I had the Grace of Heart, they sold me to a woman who would train me to become a dancer."

Dancing, Hassan knew, was one of the most prized occupations in Endarrion, a city that valued beauty and aesthetics over strength or scholarship.

"I knew dancing was not my purpose. I hated the idea of performing for the people of Endarrion, who enjoyed luxury and beautiful things, while the farmers in the surrounding countryside starved," Penrose went on. "When I reached the city, I went to the Temple of Endarra to seek guidance, hoping somehow the Prophets had a plan for me. One of the acolytes in the temple heard me praying, and told me the thing I'd most wanted to hear—that the Order of the Last Light still existed, and that I could join them. I left that night."

Hassan was beginning to understand the people who made up the Paladin Guard. All of them, it seemed, had been forsaken by their homes in one way or another. All of them had been touched by turmoil. All of them had sought purpose. In that sense, they weren't so different from him, or from any of the refugees in the agora.

Penrose's eyes suddenly narrowed, her whole body going still.

In a flash, Petrossian was at her side. "I hear it, too."

Hassan glanced around to find all five of the Guard with their hands at their swords, as if awaiting a threat.

With a slight nod, Penrose signaled Yarik and Annuka. They swiftly parted from the rest of the group, heading down the garden path that led to the villa's outer courtyard.

"What's going on?" Hassan asked. The remaining three members of the Guard—Petrossian, Penrose and Osei—formed a triangle around him.

"There's someone trying to enter the villa grounds," Penrose replied. An undercurrent of tension belied her light tone. "Not to worry. That's what we're here for."

Immediately, Hassan's mind leapt to the Witnesses. After the spectacle the Order had caused yesterday, and Hassan's appearance at the Temple of Pallas, they had more than one reason to show up here.

An uneasy few minutes passed, and then Annuka reappeared at the end of the path.

"What is it?" Hassan asked.

Annuka directed her reply to Penrose. "It's a girl. A Herati refugee, I believe. She was denied entry by one of the servants and then climbed over the wall."

It had to be Khepri.

"Wait here," Penrose said.

The words were scarcely out of her mouth before Hassan was pushing ahead of her, hastening down the path. Let them try and stop him.

When he reached the courtyard wall, he spotted Yarik's hulking form by the main archway that led outside. In front of him, her wrists held by one of Yarik's large hands, was Khepri.

"Release her at once," Hassan said, summoning his best commanding voice.

"Your Grace—"

"At once," Hassan repeated. The voice must have been more effective than he thought, because Yarik dropped Khepri's wrists and shuffled away.

Khepri's eyes were trained intently, distractingly, on Hassan. Slowly, she sank into a bow.

"Your Grace," she said. The words sounded perfectly deferential, but he could swear there was a challenge in them.

"Please," he said. "You don't have to kneel."

"But this is the proper way for a subject of Herat to greet her prince, is it not?" Khepri asked, her tone perfectly poised, her eyes lowered.

A cold bead of sweat trickled down the back of Hassan's neck. "It is."

"Perhaps, then, there is some other way I should pay respect to a prince who, until yesterday, claimed to be a student at the Akademos by the name of Cirion."

There was no mistaking her tone this time. Hassan gritted his teeth. "I offer my apologies, but I did not think it safe to—"

"You concealed the truth of your identity, even after I told you why I had come to Pallas Athos." Khepri's eyes cut up to his. "You kept it from me."

Heat flooded him, and with it, shame. "I did not intend to deceive you."

"But you did."

"And I have now apologized for it," he replied, growing frustrated. "Twice—yesterday in the agora, and again now. I am sorry I lied about who I was, but the truth is, I am the Prince of Herat, and, as such, I will not permit you to speak to me in such a manner."

"I don't need an apology," Khepri said. "And I will speak to you how I like."

His eyes widened at her brashness, and the Guard, seemingly as one, moved toward her.

"No," Hassan said, holding them off with a raised hand. "She is free to speak."

A faint flush colored Khepri's cheeks and neck, but she forged on.

"I have risked my life many times over, crossed the sea to get here. Because I want—I *need*—to know how we can take Herat back from the Witnesses. I came to fight for my country. I thought that's what you wanted, too."

Hassan flinched as though she had struck him. "It is what I want. More than anything. But what the Witnesses want—it's more than just our country. There is more at stake here."

"More at stake? You have no idea," Khepri said. "You weren't there after the Witnesses took the city. You don't know what they did to us."

The words tightened like a noose around his throat. Each day since the coup, he had been mired in sick dread, not knowing what the Witnesses and the Hierophant had been doing to his parents, and to the others captured along with them. "What are you talking about?"

"I want to show you something," Khepri said. "And if, after you see it, you still don't think I understand the threat the Witnesses pose, then I'll leave you alone."

He didn't want Khepri to leave—not when she was his one real connection to his home. Not when she was standing here in front of him, eyes burning like twin suns.

"All right," Hassan said. "I'll come."

"You won't go anywhere without the Paladin Guard," Penrose interjected.

Hassan had almost forgotten they were there.

"So it's true," Khepri said, staring over his shoulder at Penrose. "They said that the Order of the Last Light had returned to Pallas Athos. No one knows why."

Penrose glanced quickly at Hassan. "We're here because of the Witnesses," she said. "We've had our sights on the Hierophant for quite some time, and what's happened in Nazirah is of great concern to the Order."

Khepri's eyes darkened at the word *Witnesses*. "Then you should come, too. Whatever you've heard about the Hierophant, I promise you—the truth is much worse."

18

JUDE

THE CITADEL OF PALLAS ATHOS STOOD ON A BARE OUTCROPPING OF ROCK THAT stretched up from the city's second-highest tier. From here, Jude could see clear across the city, from the gleaming limestone edifices of the High City to the poorer neighborhoods that spread out between the mountainside and the harbor.

He and Hector met the Sentry captain in the citadel's central court-yard, a wide hexagonal yard paved in limestone, surrounded by all the main Sentry buildings—the holding cells, the trainee barracks, and the prisoners' tower.

"Great," the captain grumbled as he approached. "I ask to meet with the Keeper of the Word, and he sends a gelding in his place."

Jude felt his face heat and opened his mouth to correct the captain.

But Hector spoke first. "That *is* the Keeper of the Word you're talking to, so I'd show some respect if I were you."

The captain swept his gaze over Jude, clearly unimpressed. "You're the Keeper? Huh. Well, in that case, let's get to it. I don't have all day." He marched across the courtyard.

Hector caught Jude's eye as they followed, shaking his head with a small smile. It made Jude feel marginally better about the captain's error.

"The Archon Basileus asked me to meet with you," the captain explained as he led them up the stairs to the citadel's perimeter wall.

"He couldn't meet with us himself?" Jude asked.

The captain snorted. "You'll learn pretty quickly that no one in this city does much of anything themselves, unless it's getting drunk with whores."

Jude flinched. "What do you mean? The Priests' Conclave governs this city. They set the example of piety and faith for the city—for the world."

The captain snorted again. "Sure, maybe that was the case a hundred years ago, when this city *had* faith. Now all it has is leeches sucking at its marrow."

Jude felt winded by the captain's words, and the bland way he'd spoken them. If what the captain had said was even partially true, Pallas Athos was a far cry from the beacon of faith and holiness it had been when the Order was still there. The thought that the City of Faith had become a pit of vice sent something snaking unpleasantly through Jude's stomach. It violated everything the Order believed, that he himself tried so desperately to uphold.

"What—Does that offend you?" the captain asked, glancing over his shoulder at Jude's face. "What do you think happened to this city after the Order abandoned it? Or have you all just been pretending the Prophets never left and everything's stayed the same since?"

"We're not pretending anything," Jude said sharply.

"Captain," Hector said, cutting in. "We know the Order hasn't been here to defend the city in a long time. But with all due respect, we're here now."

A flood of gratitude swelled in Jude's chest.

"What does that mean, exactly?" the captain asked. "That you want Pallas Athos to go back to the way it was before? It's too late. When you left, this city had no one to defend its people. The priests don't care what happens here as long as they can continue to do whatever they like. It's fallen to the Sentry to keep things in order, but we're not Graced like you."

For the first time in his life, Jude wondered whether his predecessors had made a mistake. The Paladin were the servants of the Prophets, and they had left to protect their last secret. But what if, in leaving, they had abandoned the Prophets' subjects at the moment they'd been most needed? Were they then to blame for how hollow the City of Faith had become?

"Truth be told," the captain went on, nodding to a pair of Sentry bustling past along the perimeter wall, "thanks to this Pale Hand nonsense, the Sentry is stretched pretty thin at the moment, what with the extra patrols around the High City."

"Pale Hand?" Jude asked.

Beside him, Hector stopped suddenly, leaning against the wall.

"That's right," the captain replied, turning back to them. "A priest was murdered last week, with a pale handprint on his body. Real mysterious. We've had our men out every night looking for the culprit, but so far nothing's turned up. And apparently, we're not the first city the Pale Hand has plagued."

"We've heard about the deaths in other cities," Jude said carefully. "But I didn't know there had been one here in Pallas Athos."

And so close to the Last Prophet.

Hector had gone very still. Jude looked over and saw that his dark eyes were fixed intently on the Sentry captain.

The captain glanced between the two of them. "I'm rather surprised you've heard about a handful of mysterious murders, yet you seem to know nothing about what happened to this city since you all left."

Jude swallowed. "The information we have is perhaps a bit incomplete," he said. Whatever was happening beyond the walls of Kerameikos Fort hadn't mattered to the Order unless it had to do with finding the Prophet. He wondered what else the Order had ignored.

"Well, I guess I better get to why I asked you here in the first place," the captain said.

"The priests want to know why we've returned," Hector said.

"Actually," the captain replied, "I'd say just about everyone wants to know why you've returned."

The prophecy and the truth about Prince Hassan were far too precious to share. So Jude settled on a half truth. "The Order is very concerned with the growing strength and influence of the Hierophant. The Witnesses now have a large presence in almost every one of the Six Prophetic Cities. The Hierophant has gone from leading a handful of desperate followers to now forcibly capturing the capital of Herat."

The captain nodded. "We've noticed. The Witnesses have been growing in numbers for a while, but with the arrival of the Herati refugees, they've started making themselves more visible. Just a few weeks ago, they burned down a priest's shrine at the edge of the High City. And they've been coming around the Temple of Pallas. They all say the Hierophant used to be an acolyte of a temple. You know anything about that?"

"I don't believe it," Jude replied. "It's a lie, designed to make his followers believe he is an authority on the Prophets and the Graced. When he tells them that the powers of the Graced are corrupt, they believe him."

"So he's just some kind of charlatan?" the captain asked. "An opportunist spewing whatever lies will get him power?"

Jude hesitated. "He is deceiving them, but I think his zealotry is real. He truly hates the Graced and wants to see them gone."

The Hierophant was the Deceiver, a master of embellishment and lies, whose goal was to get others to follow him. But at the core of his lies seemed to be a real belief—that if he could end the Graced, the world would be better for it.

"So this Reckoning thing the Witnesses are always shouting about is real?" the captain asked. "And that's why you came out of hiding?"

Jude bristled. The Order wasn't *hiding* at Kerameikos. They'd been waiting.

Before he could decide what to say that would satisfy the captain's question without giving too much away, a clamorous toll of bells rang out around them. They clanged in a distinctive pattern—one long chime, then two short, and over again. The sound of running footsteps and indistinctly barked orders followed.

"What do those bells mean?" Hector shouted over the cacophony.

The captain's expression was agitated. "It means one of our prisoners is trying to escape."

The man's lack of urgency confused Jude. "Does this happen frequently?"

"Not frequently, no," the captain replied. "Not to worry. A prisoner loose in here won't get very far."

A sudden yell rose up from the practice yard below as an indistinct black-clad figure streaked through it. Three Sentry guards limped behind in various states of disarray.

Without thinking, Jude performed two quick koahs and launched himself two stories down from the perimeter wall. From the corner of his eye, he saw Hector touch down beside him.

Jude immediately moved to the edge of the yard to cut off the runner. He saw now that it was a girl who looked like she could be from the arid eastern Pelagos. Determination creased her face as she ran, and when she caught sight of him, she veered behind a rack of wooden practice swords.

Before Jude could react, he saw Hector take a flying leap to land directly in front of the girl, hemming her in. Seeing that her plan had backfired, the girl skidded to a halt and tried instead to dive over a low wall that separated the yard from the walkway below.

Hector moved as quick as lightning, seizing her by the arm and dragging her back. She struggled ferociously against his grip until Hector grabbed her other arm, swinging her around so the two were face-to-face.

Jude watched with confusion and concern as Hector's eyes widened, shock bolting over his face. He went still, his grip on the girl going slack.

She took the opportunity to tear herself away and run right past him toward the gates.

But it was too late. More Sentry guards came pouring into the yard, surrounding her. The girl reeled back but didn't put up much of a fight as the guards seized her and bound her hands behind her.

"An escape attempt's not going to look very good for you," the one behind her said. "Should've stayed in your cell."

The Sentry couldn't see her glare, but Jude did.

"Keep her bound at all times," one of the others said as they started to shuffle her out of the yard.

Jude crossed the yard to where Hector stood, still frozen with his hands out in front of him, his face bloodless and stricken.

"Hector?" Jude asked tentatively. "What is it?"

"That prisoner," Hector said, but he wasn't talking to Jude. He was speaking to the Sentry captain who had descended from the perimeter wall to draw up beside them. "Who was she?"

The captain shook his head. "Not sure. The patrol around the High City walls brought her in. Found her and one other person in the Temple of Tarseis. Trying to rob it, we think."

The girl and the guards were no longer visible, but Hector's gaze was focused on the gate they'd gone through.

"Hector," Jude said in a low, urgent tone. "What's going on?"

"That's no temple robber," Hector said. "That's the Pale Hand."

The Sentry captain looked startled. "What? Can't be. We told you, we've had our men out every night since the murder searching for the Pale Hand."

"Well, it looks like you found her."

The Sentry captain frowned, his bushy eyebrows knitting together. He looked as bewildered as Jude felt.

But Hector was as sure as a storm. "Let me talk to her, and I'll prove it."

The Sentry captain glanced at Jude, as if waiting for him to respond first. When he didn't, the captain blew out a breath and said, "I'll see what I can do."

He swept away from them, and the moment they were alone in the yard, Jude turned to Hector. "Tell me what's going on."

"That's the Pale Hand, Jude. I know it."

"How could you know that?" Jude asked, searching Hector's face.

"Because I've seen her," Hector replied.

"What?" Jude said. That couldn't be true. "What are you talking about?"

"I saw the Pale Hand," Hector said again. "Five years ago."

Five years ago. Before Hector had been found by the Order's acolytes in the Temple of Keric. Before Hector's parents had died.

Jude stepped back, horror seeping down his spine. "Your parents . . ."

"I still remember the handprint she left on my father's chest," Hector said, his eyes hollow and haunted. "I can still see it when I lie awake at night."

Jude had known that Hector was an orphan, but the time before he had arrived in Kerameikos was something they never discussed.

"Why didn't you tell me?" Jude asked. "All those years at Kerameikos, you never told me how your parents died."

At the dawn of their friendship, Jude had tried to coax the tale out of Hector, thinking he could offer him comfort. But every time Jude had brought up the subject of his past, Hector had closed off, becoming distant and cold. Jude had eventually stopped asking altogether.

Hector looked down. "I didn't—I didn't know how."

"But you've known who the Pale Hand is this whole time?" Jude asked. "And you kept it from me—from the Order?"

"It wasn't like that," Hector said. "When my parents died, I didn't know anything about the prophecy. Even after coming to Kerameikos, I didn't know that the Pale Hand had any connection to it. Not until after you left for your Year of Reflection, and I turned eighteen."

Of course. As the heir to the Keeper of the Word, Jude had known the full contents of the prophecy since he was a child. However, the other wards raised in Kerameikos like Hector didn't learn the exact words of the prophecy until they came of age. Hector would have learned the words of the prophecy just after Jude went on his Year of Reflection. Was that what had made him leave?

"And this . . . girl," Jude said. "This prisoner. You're sure it's the same person? You only saw her for a moment."

"Jude," Hector said, his dark eyes steady. "It was her."

To death's pale hand the wicked fall. The second harbinger of the Age of Darkness. Here, in the same city as the Prophet.

"All right," Jude said. "We'll speak with her. Find out the truth."

Hector nodded, moving past him back into the open yard. Jude hesitated. He was asking a lot of Hector. If he was right, then that meant Jude was asking him to face his parents' killer. Was he asking too much?

He shook off his doubts as he followed. Hector had sworn his oath, the same as Jude. His duty was to the prophecy. To the Last Prophet. Whatever other feelings he had, he would have to set them aside.

19

EPHYRA

THE CLANKING MECHANICAL NOISE OF THE ARTIFICED LIFT BROKE THROUGH the oppressive silence of Ephyra's cell.

It had been about an hour since her escape attempt. Her *first* escape attempt, because she wasn't about to give up now. Although the initial failure had made the task more challenging—they'd moved her from the holding cells to the prisoners' tower. The only way out was through the lift that ran down the center of the tower. That was definitely a problem. As were the chains clamped around her wrists.

The clanking of the lift ceased, and next Ephyra heard the ratcheting click of a wheel turning and the outer door moving to align with one of the twelve cells. When the clicking ceased, the door of her cell rasped open like a dying man's last breath. The two swordsmen from the practice yard stood on the other side. Instead of the white and blue uniform of the Sentry, they wore torcs around their throats and dark blue cloaks pinned with a distinctive brooch—a seven-pointed star pierced by a blade.

She'd seen that symbol—yesterday, in fact. These men had arrived in the harbor on the ship with silver sails. The Order of the Last Light.

Now they were standing in the cell, staring at her. Ephyra stared back.

The one closer to her, who had green eyes and a small dimple in his chin, broke the silence first. "A priest died in this city last week. The guard who saw the body said there was a pale handprint on his throat. Would you happen to know anything about that?"

Ephyra had to fight to hide her reaction. Her heart pounded furiously. The Sentry had only accused her of robbing a temple—they'd said nothing about the Pale Hand. Was it possible that these swordsmen knew it was her?

She forced a laugh. "First, I robbed a temple. Now, I murdered a priest? What are you going to accuse me of next—kidnapping the Archon's son?"

The other swordsman, the intense dark-eyed one who'd caught her in the yard, stepped toward her suddenly. "Tell us what you're doing in Pallas Athos."

Familiarity pricked at Ephyra. "What are *you* doing here? Aren't you Paladin supposed to be gone, or in hiding, or whatever it is you did after the Prophets disappeared? What are you doing in this city?"

"That doesn't concern you," the dark-eyed man said.

"Well, maybe my business doesn't concern you."

"Your *business* is killing," he spat. "You killed that priest, and he wasn't the first. Tell me—how many lives has the Pale Hand claimed?"

Ephyra met his dark gaze. The feeling of familiarity grew stronger.

"It really is you," he said, shaking his head slowly. "After all these years. I thought I'd never set eyes on you again. But here you are."

He let out a hollow laugh that sucked the air from Ephyra's lungs.

Suddenly, she realized she knew exactly who he was.

Hector Navarro. The boy she'd orphaned all those years ago to save Beru's life. She'd always wondered what had happened to him, after she had taken everything he had. After she had killed his parents, his brother.

"I searched for you," Hector said. "I spent *months* trying to find you. And while I chased down every rumor of the Pale Hand, I thought of this moment. Of how it would feel to finally face you."

The other swordsman touched Hector's shoulder, concern and confusion etched into his soft features.

Hector shook him off and raised his eyes back to Ephyra. "Don't you have anything to say?"

She didn't. She had nothing, no words to convey how devastating it was to sit there staring up at him. Remembering him. Of all the deaths she'd caused over the years, these were the ones that still gutted her.

"You killed my family. Admit it!"

Ephyra flinched as he lunged at her, but the other swordsman held him back with the full force of his own body.

"Hector!" It had the bark of an order.

Hector's eyes were pinned on Ephyra, his whole body tense and ready to strike.

"Get some air," the other swordsman said. "Now."

Hector relented, and then with a last torrential glance at Ephyra, he whirled out of the cell, back into the guardroom.

As the low groan of the lift sounded from outside the cell, the other swordsman turned and fixed Ephyra with a searching stare. If she had thought this swordsman was softer than Hector, she realized now she'd been wrong. There was steel in that stare.

"Is he right? Are you really the one who killed those people? Are you the Pale Hand?"

Ephyra said nothing.

"Are you?"

"If I was, do you think I'd still be here?" she asked. "Someone who could do that . . . who could kill those people without remorse, they wouldn't hesitate to kill you, or a few Sentry guards, would they?"

The swordsman pressed his lips together tightly.

"Your friend looked upset," Ephyra said. "Maybe you should go find him. It's not like I'm going anywhere."

The swordsman glanced to the door and then back to her, his expression torn. After a moment, he turned on his heel and followed Hector out.

The door clanged shut behind him, leaving her awash in her own questions. Questions like, What was Hector Navarro, the youngest son of the family she'd killed all those years ago, doing with the Order of the Last Light?

And what did the Order of the Last Light want with *her?*

20

HASSAN

HASSAN RETURNED TO THE AGORA FOR THE SIXTH TIME IN AS MANY DAYS. BUT this time, instead of curiosity or longing, it was dread that drove his every step.

Khepri brought them to a tent that had been erected in the style of the desert nomads, with a wide hexagonal base and a gradually sloping roof made of woven palm fronds. She held aside the dried river reeds that hung over the entrance, motioning Hassan and Penrose inside.

It was dark and warm within the tent. Baskets piled with dried roots and flowers hung from the vaulted ceiling, while soft pallets and cushions lay strewn across the floor. Three women, old enough to be Hassan's grandmother, bustled inside, laying out valerian root on a camelskin and grinding some kind of fragrant leaves into a bowl. One of them paused her ministrations, looking up as they entered.

"Prophet's blessings, Sekhet," Khepri greeted.

"Prophet's blessings, Khepri," the woman replied.

"Prophet's blessings," Hassan said. "I am Hassan Seif. This is Penrose."

"Your Grace!" the woman cried, falling to one knee and lowering her head. "I—We had no idea—"

"Please," Hassan said, holding up a hand. "You may stand."

The woman didn't move.

"We're here to see Reza," Khepri said. "I wanted the prince to meet him."

Sekhet's eyes cut up to Khepri. "Are you sure that's wise?"

"The prince needs to see him," Khepri said firmly.

The old woman hesitated a moment longer. Some kind of unspoken communication passed between her and Khepri, and then she nodded and got to her feet. "Of course. This way." She led them to one of the curtained-off sections of the tent. "Idalia is with him right now, but you can go right in."

Nerves buzzed in Hassan's chest as he followed behind Khepri. She drew the curtain aside, letting him step through and then Penrose. As Hassan's eyes fell on the thick pallet laid out before him and the figure that lay on top of it, it took all of his control not to recoil.

The man on the pallet was a patchwork of scars and blistered flesh. It was sloughing off in layers, revealing weeping pink sores beneath. Sickly pale skin covered half his face down to his collarbone. Tiny white scars, like fissures or the cracks in shattered glass, crept away from the burns, covering the rest of his body. He looked like he might have once worn the same hairstyle as Khepri—the close-shaved sides of the Herati Legionnaires—but it was now growing in thin, uneven patches. His mouth hung slack, breaths coming in shallow, rattling bursts. It was hard to imagine this frail, gasping man had ever been a soldier.

Hassan's stomach clenched with pity and a tinge of revulsion, which he tried to swallow down, ashamed. Khepri knelt beside the pallet.

"Reza," Khepri said, a soft smile on her face. She laid her hand gently on top of his. "It's me, Khepri."

Reza gave a pitiful groan in response.

Khepri looked up at the healer next to him, a short, dark-skinned woman with a round face. "Has there been any change?"

The healer shook her head. "The burns themselves are almost healed, though he will bear the scars. But the pain . . ."

A dry breath rasped from between Reza's lips. "Please . . ."

Khepri started to get up from his side, but Reza's hand suddenly gripped hers. Hassan moved toward them without thinking, but Khepri held up her other hand, signaling him to wait.

"Please," Reza said again, his eyes now wide, staring at her. No, not *at* her. Through her. His eyes were blank, unseeing. "I can't . . . The pain . . . Please . . ."

"It's all right," Khepri soothed. "It's going to be all right."

"Isn't there something you can do?" Penrose asked, looking over at the healer. "The burns—"

"It's not the burns that hurt him," the healer said, shaking her head.

"*No*," Reza moaned. "No, no, no, no . . . It's gone. It's all gone. I can't feel it. I can't . . . *It's gone!* They took it. There's nothing left. *Nothing.*" He dropped Khepri's hand, arm falling limply to his side as he began to shake. Soft, almost inhuman whimpers escaped from his throat. The sounds were unbearable, the desperate, rattling gasps of a man on the edge of delirium. Hassan thought he had seen suffering, but he could not fathom what he saw in front of him now. He rooted himself to the ground, wanting desperately to flee.

"I think that's enough for now," the healer said quietly.

Khepri got to her feet, turning away from Reza and ushering Hassan and Penrose out through the curtain.

It was a moment before Hassan found his voice. "What . . . what happened to him?"

He could still hear Reza's bitten-back moans of pain. Khepri took Hassan's arm, leading him out of the tent.

"They call it Godfire," she said at last. She addressed both him and Penrose as she spoke. "It burns the Grace out of you."

Hassan swallowed roughly, his eyes stinging. The dull horror in Khepri's voice and the echoes of Reza's agonized moans told him everything he needed to know.

"The Witnesses did that?" he asked. Khepri nodded, and an anger like Hassan hadn't felt since the morning of the coup wrenched at his gut. "Was it during the coup?"

Khepri shook her head. "They didn't use it in the coup, but they've been secretly experimenting with it ever since. The Hierophant himself watches while his followers take captured Graced soldiers and hold them in the flame. Seeing what it does to them. How long it takes to burn their Graces out."

Reza's blank stare flashed through Hassan's mind. He imagined what it would be like to be burned slowly, your skin blistering, able to do nothing but scream. Rage roared in his chest, until he felt he might choke on it.

"We heard rumors that the Hierophant could stop someone from using their Grace," Penrose said. "But to burn it out of them? Permanently? None of us thought that was possible. We've never heard of such a thing."

"How . . . how many?" Hassan asked. "How many people did they do that to?"

Khepri shook her head. "We don't know. We think Reza is the only one who survived."

"The only one?" Penrose asked. "They burned the others to death?"

"Some," Khepri said. "The others took their own lives. They say that losing your Grace is the worst kind of agony. It's not like losing a piece of your body . . . It's like losing a piece of your *self*. I've seen what Reza has been through, and it's like there's a hollowness that's slowly shredding him from inside out. Our Graces aren't just our power—they're our connection to the world. Without them we're just . . . ash."

Hassan's skin prickled. He hadn't even known he *had* a Grace until a day ago. Would losing it really feel like that? It was hard to imagine, but Reza's agony told him everything.

What the Hierophant had done was nothing short of monstrous.

"Do you know how they made this . . . Godfire?" Penrose asked.

Khepri shook her head. "When Reza escaped, he showed us where they were keeping it, but I don't think it was *made*. Not by the Witnesses, at least. The story goes that the Hierophant found it in the temple ruins in the desert where he took his most devoted followers. That's why they call it Godfire—they say the flame was left at the altar of that ancient deity."

"Another lie, I'm sure," Penrose said. "No one has worshipped the old god in over two thousand years. I'd bet before the Hierophant took it over, no one had set foot in those ruins for nearly that long."

Khepri shook her head. "Well, wherever the flame came from, it's in Nazirah now. We think there's only one source, a single white flame that burns continuously. Before I escaped, we were going to try to put it out."

"What happened?" Hassan asked.

"Reza told us they were keeping the Godfire in the High Temple of Nazirah," Khepri said. "My other comrades snuck up there in the cover of night. My brothers and I remained outside the temple to stand guard while they doused the flame." She closed her eyes. "I remember how dark it was. A moonless night."

Hassan moved toward Khepri as her face twisted.

"A patrol of Witnesses carrying Godfire torches found us outside the temple. My brothers and I fought them off. One of the Witnesses knocked over a font of chrism oil. He dropped his torch in it, and—"

She broke off, her eyes going wide and distant, as though she were back at the High Temple, reliving that night.

"There was a blinding flash of light, brighter than the sun, and a sound like the earth cracking. We were thrown to the ground, and all I could see was smoke and white flames pouring from where the temple had once stood. My brothers and I ran. And our comrades inside . . . they never made it out."

She met Hassan's gaze, her eyes clouded with pain.

Penrose let out a soft breath. "This is worse than anything we imagined."

"It's worse than even that," Khepri said. "Because now that they've tested it, we know what the Witnesses plan to do with Godfire. Taking the city was just the first step. The next is igniting it. They're going to burn out the Grace of everyone who remains there. Then . . . well, they'll do the same to the rest of the world, if they have their way."

"The Reckoning," Hassan said quietly, his voice shaking. He remembered the words of the Witnesses at the Temple of Pallas. *The Prophets are gone, and the Graced will follow.*

He closed his eyes and saw pale flames rippling across his beloved city, leaving charred ashes in their wake. He saw his mother's face, twisted in agony. He heard his father's bone-shaking scream. He pictured finally reuniting with them, only to have them turn and look right through him with Reza's empty gaze.

"We need to know everything we can about Godfire," Penrose said briskly. "I want to speak more to your healer. Prince Hassan?"

"I'll stay here." He could not return to the dark tent. To Reza's hollow gaze and haunting pleas. To the visions of agony and fire that flashed through his mind when he thought of his parents.

Penrose disappeared into the tent without another word. Khepri made to follow her, but Hassan reached out and grasped her wrist, halting her.

"Why didn't you say anything about this to me before?" he asked roughly. "I mean, when you—" He bit off the end, too angry to continue.

"When I didn't know who you were?"

"Yes," Hassan said, releasing her. "Did you not trust me?" He knew what a hypocrite he was being. He had no right to feel hurt that Khepri had not trusted him right away, not when he'd been lying to her. But his anger was stronger than his logic.

Khepri just shook her head, her eyes soft. "It wasn't that."

"Then why?"

"I—" She swallowed. "It was selfish."

"Selfish?" Hassan wasn't sure he'd ever met a less selfish person in his life.

"It doesn't matter," she said, her tone edged with desperation. "You know now. This is what we face. The Hierophant and his Witnesses are going to burn the Grace out of every last man, woman, and child in Nazirah. That is the promise he's made his followers, and he won't hesitate to deliver it. Unless someone stops him."

Hassan looked up at her. "Someone? You mean me?"

"I mean *us*," Khepri replied. "I didn't come here to run away from Nazirah. I came to find an army to take it back. All of us did. And we want the Prince of Herat to lead us."

It was a stunning image to behold—he and Khepri, leading an army into Nazirah and striking down the Witnesses in one fell swoop. Retaking Nazirah. Toppling the Hierophant. Ensuring the safety of Herat, of his family, and all the Graced. He wanted it so badly, wanted everything Khepri did.

But Hassan had read every volume on martial history in the Great Library, had studied with some of the greatest military minds in Herat, and he knew that no matter how much he wanted a way to take back his city, what Khepri was suggesting was impossible.

"If Godfire is as powerful a weapon as you say, we won't have any hope of stopping the Witnesses with a few hundred soldiers," he said.

"It's better than sitting here, across the sea, doing nothing," Khepri replied. "We're willing to risk our lives to save our people. Aren't you?"

He knew the answer he wanted to give. The answer that would quell the anger shaking in his bones. But the sight of Penrose returning from within the tent stopped him. The Paladin Guard was here to protect him. To keep the Prophet safe. He couldn't risk his life just to save the people of Herat when the entire fate of the Graced, and the world, rested on his shoulders.

He wished he could explain this all to Khepri, to tell her the reason for his hesitation. But the Order wasn't ready to let loose the secret of the last prophecy.

"We should return to the villa," Penrose said gently.

Hassan nodded, but he was still looking at Khepri.

"Make whatever choice you want, Prince Hassan," she said. "But I'm going to fight."

She turned and marched back down the row of tents. Hassan watched her go, his heart sputtering like the point of a compass that had lost its bearing.

21

JUDE

JUDE FOUND HECTOR STANDING BENEATH AN OLIVE TREE IN THE SENTRY PRAC-
tice yard, limned by the pale wash of the evening sky.

When they'd first reunited at Kerameikos, Jude had been relieved
by how easily they had picked up their friendship again, and how like
his younger self Hector still was. Now, Jude wondered how much of
what he saw when he looked at him was colored by their past. If Hector
had never come to Kerameikos as a child, if the two boys had not grown
up getting in and out of trouble together, what might Jude see when he
looked at this man?

"This is why you left, wasn't it?" he asked. When Jude had chosen
his Guard, he'd decided that he didn't need to know why Hector had
left. The only thing that had mattered was that he'd returned. But that
had been a mistake.

"After you went on your Year of Reflection, the rumors about the
Pale Hand reached us at Kerameikos," Hector said. "I knew—I *knew*
that it was her. The girl who killed my family. I was . . . obsessed. I left

Kerameikos to track her, from Charis to Tarsepolis. I came up with nothing. I gave up on ever finding her. But now here she is."

"Hector, I know you said you were sure, but it's been five years since you saw her," Jude said. "You were young, you'd just been through a great trauma, and—"

"You heard her heart beat faster the moment you mentioned the Pale Hand," Hector said. "You know I'm right. I know what she really is, and I can prove it. We can stop her."

"She could have just been scared," Jude said. "And besides that, she's a prisoner. There's nothing she can do from inside that cell."

Hector's hand clenched the hilt of his sword, knuckles white. "She's dangerous, Jude. I've seen what she can do. It's . . . it's unnatural. We can't let her live."

"What are you saying?" Jude asked. "You want to kill her?"

"She's the second harbinger of the Age of Darkness. The prophecy is clear what her destiny is."

"No, it isn't," Jude said. "Until the prophecy is completed, we don't know what role any of the harbingers will play in the Age of Darkness. Or what would happen if one of them dies. We must be patient, and trust in the Prophet."

Hector shook his head, staring out at the empty yard. "Where she goes, darkness follows. Allowing her to live a moment longer is a grave mistake."

Jude had never heard this cold, furious tone from Hector before. Carefully, he asked, "Are you saying this because you think she'll bring the Age of Darkness? Or is it because you want revenge for your parents' death?"

Hector whirled on him, eyes blazing. "So what if I do? I see my family every night in my dreams. My mother's withered body. My brother's lifeless stare. That pale handprint on my father's silent, still chest."

Jude's chest clenched tight with the thought of a young Hector, still just a boy, waking to find the cold bodies of every person he had ever loved. He swallowed, forcing his voice to be steady. Calm. The voice of the Keeper of the Word. "You are a Paladin of the Order of the Last Light. Your allegiance is to the Order, to the Prophet. You cannot allow grief to cloud your judgment."

Hector looked away again, toward the olive tree. When he spoke, the harsh edge of anger was gone. "I can't just separate out my feelings the way you can, Jude. Everything that happened before you chose me for the Guard, it's not like it's just *over*. It still matters. It's been years, but whenever I close my eyes, I can hear their voices. They call out to me, begging me to help them."

His grief was a fist closing over Jude's own heart. Hector had not trusted him with this. He had kept this pain secreted away for all these years, had borne it alone rather than bare himself to Jude.

But Hector wasn't the only one to blame for the distance between them. Because as much as Jude wanted, more than anything, to be Hector's friend, there had always been something else between them—the unspoken understanding that one day Jude would be his leader, too.

Hector's eyes shuttered closed. "I don't know how to make it stop."

"You must," Jude said, guilt clawing at his throat even as he spoke the words.

"I've tried. I have. I have devoted myself to the Order. I took my oath, just like you wanted me to. But this feeling will never go away." He looked back at Jude, his eyes haunted. "I can't just keep pretending it will."

"It's not always easy for me, either," Jude said before he could stop himself. "Putting aside everything for our cause. For the Prophet."

Hector smiled. A twisted wretch of a smile. "Don't be stupid, Jude. You were born to this life. I had to learn it. I had a family, and she *took them* from me. She took the people who loved me, the *only* people who loved me, and you'll never know what that feels like, because you never had that, and you never will."

Jude stiffened, sucking in a breath as if he'd been struck. Hector was right, of course. Jude didn't have a family. He had the Order. He had his father, who'd sired him but had little hand in raising him. Jude was his son, his successor, but the bonds of family meant nothing to the Order. Jude knew this. He'd always known it. But Hector's words rang in Jude's ears, a truth he'd never named before.

"I'm sorry," Hector said, shaking his head. "I didn't mean—"

"No," Jude said. "I . . . You're right. I don't understand."

"It's just . . . now that I've seen her, now that I know she's here—" Hector looked away from Jude, his jaw set and his shoulders tight.

Jude wasn't sure what more he could offer, how to navigate Hector's grief and the line that had been drawn between them. He touched Hector's shoulder. "Hector . . ." But the look in Hector's eyes—haunted, wary—stopped him.

"I know who you want me to be, Jude. But I don't know if I have it in me."

"You do," Jude said, desperation drawing his voice taut. "You can. I chose you to be in my Guard because I believe that. I believe in you."

Hector tensed beneath Jude's hand. Finally, he looked up. "You won't tell them, will you? The Guard? I don't want them to look at me like—"

"I won't," Jude promised. "I wouldn't."

Hector nodded and looked down at the hand on his shoulder. Jude withdrew it quickly. But before he could say anything else, offer anything more, Hector turned away and walked off into the darkening evening alone.

Jude curled his fingers over the palm that had touched Hector's shoulder. Hector had kept his grief locked away from Jude, but his was not the only heart that held secrets.

There had been a moment, before the Prophet, before his training, before he was Keeper of the Word, when Jude had finally realized his own secret. When all the doubts he'd ever felt about himself and his destiny had finally made sense. A moment, once, beneath a swollen summer moon, when his heart had given itself away.

He and Hector had decided to take a dip at midnight—Hector's idea, of course, but Jude had been only too eager to play along. They'd snuck out from the barracks, winding through the fort to where the rush of the river was diverted into a gentler stream.

They'd stripped down to their underclothes under the great stretch of stars and flung themselves off the top of a waterfall. Despite the summer month, the water had still been bitingly cold—Jude remembered that, even now. And he remembered how Hector's back had glistened in the moonlight when he slid out of the water and collapsed onto the bank, grinning as Jude fell beside him.

It had been quiet—so quiet all Jude could hear was the rustle of the trees, the murmur of water sliding over stone, the gentle thumping of two hearts—his own and Hector's. It occurred to him that Hector could surely hear them both, too, and the thought quickened his heartbeat. When Hector turned on his side to look at him, brows drawn over luminous dark eyes, Jude was sure his disobedient heart would leap straight out of his chest and flop to the ground between them.

And then Hector had gotten up and walked back to the water, leaving Jude behind on the bank.

They hadn't spoken of it, not that night or any night since. Perhaps it was something Hector had forgotten, their diverging lives and the passing of time making a sieve of his memories. Or perhaps even then, lying in the moonlight beside him, he hadn't understood that, in the space of a few heartbeats, Jude's entire world had been upended.

Jude was no longer the boy he'd been then. He had mastered his Grace, completed his training, taken his oath. He had found the Last Prophet.

But when he closed his eyes, he could still hear the frantic pounding of his heart against the cage of his ribs.

22

HASSAN

CAPTAIN WEATHERBOURNE AND HECTOR NAVARRO DIDN'T RETURN TO THE villa until after supper. Hassan called them and the rest of the Guard into the library and told them what Khepri had showed him in the agora.

"Godfire." Captain Weatherbourne spoke the word as though it were a curse, his expression troubled. "How did they even get such a weapon?"

"Khepri says they may have found it at the altar of an ancient temple in the desert. There's no way to know for certain, but we do know that they mean to use it on the rest of the Graced in Nazirah," Hassan said. "And the rest of the world, too, if we don't stop them now. The Hierophant isn't going to wait for the rest of the prophecy to unfold before he acts. We can't, either. Not if we want to stop him."

"No," Petrossian said firmly. "Only two of the harbingers have surfaced. If we try to stop the Hierophant before we know the rest of the prophecy, we might end up helping him bring the Age of Darkness."

"Meanwhile, the people of my country are at his mercy." Fear bubbled up in Hassan's throat as he thought again of his mother and father. The image of Reza's charred body flashed through his mind, and he felt sick.

"I understand your desire to attack, but we can't risk the Witnesses getting ahold of you, not before we know the end of the prophecy," Captain Weatherbourne said firmly.

The irony was not lost on Hassan—that in order to prevent destruction, first he must let it unfold. But he could not trust, as the Paladin did, that the end of the prophecy would reveal itself to him. The Age of Darkness loomed, and he didn't know how to stop it. He had no idea where to begin.

"You're asking me to turn my back on my people," he said.

"No," Captain Weatherbourne replied. "I ask only for your patience. The world waited a hundred years for you to be born. We waited another sixteen to find you. We all can wait a little while longer, until we know the way forward."

"Perhaps," Hassan said, pushing himself to his feet, "if you all had done something instead of waiting, we wouldn't be here now."

Though he knew the Order wasn't to blame for the coup, it felt good to lash out. But as he watched Captain Weatherbourne go pale, he regretted the harsh words.

"Perhaps it would be best to continue this discussion in the morning," Penrose said, stepping toward them.

Captain Weatherbourne nodded. "It is getting late." His eyes darted to the side of the room, where the Paladin named Hector stood with his arms crossed in front of him. "We could all use some sleep."

But sleep evaded Hassan that night. He hadn't managed a full night of rest since before the coup, but tonight the restlessness was worse. He did not want the peace of slumber, did not want to absolve himself of the guilt of bedding down safe in his aunt's villa while his people lived in terror and fought for their lives in Nazirah. Every time he closed his eyes, he felt the same crackling anger he'd felt on the steps of the Temple of Pallas, facing the Witnesses. Anger at them, at the Order, at himself.

The hour grew later, and still he sat awake, rereading the third volume of Scholar Sufyan's *History of the Six Prophetic Cities*, which he'd taken from his aunt's library the first day he'd arrived in Pallas Athos. Whenever his thoughts began to spiral, he'd reread his favorite chapters—"The Winter Bloom of Endarrion," "The Treaty of the Six," "General Ezeli's Last Stand." He had a collection of first edition volumes at home, gifted to him on his fourteenth name day by the head librarian of Nazirah. But those books had been left behind, along with so much else.

Tonight, he paged to the chapter he'd read so many times he almost knew it by heart: "The Founding of Nazirah." The thread that connected across two thousand years to Hassan's own present. A vision of a tower of light shining across the Pelagos Sea led the Prophet Nazirah to the beaches of the southern Pelagos coast at the mouth of a great river. She had made her prophecy on that land—that it would soon become the center of knowledge, learning, and wisdom in the Pelagos, a kingdom of many peoples, attracting the brightest minds and the most powerful Graced. As long as the lighthouse stood on its shores, the Seif line would rule this land, the Kingdom of Herat.

Hassan's tired eyes blurred as he set the book down. Nazirah's lighthouse still stood, but the Seif line had fallen. The prophecy had been broken, just as the acolyte Emir had said. The Witnesses had undone it.

A promise of the past undone.

Nazirah had been ripped away from Hassan. The prophecy of his ancestors had shattered that day. But could it all mean what the acolyte said—that Hassan's destiny was greater than what the Prophet

Nazirah had seen two millennia ago? That his own prophecy would carve a new path to the future?

He closed his eyes, trying to calm his still-whirring mind and let himself sleep. Images of the lighthouse, of golden laurel crowns and banners waving down Ozmandith Road swirled together with the words of the final prophecy as he began to drift.

The city of Nazirah spread out below him. This was not the same Nazirah that Hassan had left—this city had been overrun by fear and shadow. Figures paraded between the building facades along the main stretch of Ozmandith Road. They wore white cloaks and carried torches of pale flame that cast ghastly shadows along the sandstone street.

Godfire.

Smoke poured from the torches, curling up from the procession and blanketing the once-shining domes and towers of Nazirah's cityscape.

Hassan set his hands down on the solid stone parapet before him. He looked up and realized he was standing on the observation deck of the lighthouse of Nazirah. His back was to its flame, his face toward the harbor. To his left stood Khepri, curved sword strapped to her side, eyes burning fiercely. On his other side stood Emir the acolyte, his gentle face alight with fervent hope.

The soldier and the man of faith. Between them, Hassan, their leader. The Last Prophet.

Glimmering in the harbor were ships with sails the same color as the moonlight glinting off the smooth, dark water. Soldiers poured off the ships and onto the shore. Their forces met the procession of Witnesses and their turncoat soldiers and mercenaries, a sea of green, gold, and dark blue overtaking black and white. The flames alight in the Witnesses' hands flickered out like dying stars.

Hassan blinked and found himself inside the throne room of the Palace of Herat. Gilded columns depicting colorful scenes from Herat's great history lined the aisle that led up to the throne, which sat atop a golden pyramid. On each of its four faces, water spewed from the mouths of animal-shaped spigots into the moat at the base. Behind the pyramid, a painted falcon stretched its wings across the back wall, crowned by the golden sunlight that spilled into the room.

Dawn had come.

All around him, subjects from all over the kingdom knelt before the throne of Herat. And on the throne sat Hassan himself, a crown of golden laurel on his head, the royal scepter in his hand.

Nazirah was his once more.

"Prince Hassan! *Hassan!*"

He woke with a start. The incandescent lamp beside the bed cast a hazy glow. Someone gripped his right arm tightly, and when Hassan turned over with a groan, he saw that it was Lethia, wrapped up in a silvery-blue silk sleeping robe, her lined face grim with worry as she knelt beside his bed.

His heart beat like a drum as he took in the sight of Penrose standing behind her.

"What's going on?" Hassan asked, pushing himself up in his bed. He'd been roused frantically like this once before—the very last time he'd woken in the Palace of Herat.

"You were thrashing," Lethia said, cupping the side of his face with one bony hand. "Penrose sent for me. Were you dreaming?"

The drumbeat of his heart picked up. "I . . . I saw . . ."

Penrose pushed herself toward the bed, standing by Lethia's shoulder. "What did you see?" she asked, her eyes gleaming in the lamplight.

"Nazirah," Hassan replied. He closed his eyes, summoning the image. It came back to him, vivid, *real.* "I saw Nazirah. I was standing at the top of the lighthouse, watching an army—*my* army—defeat the Witnesses. I saw myself sitting on the throne. It was a dream, but it felt real. It felt *true.*"

He opened his eyes to find that Penrose had moved closer, like a moth drawn in to the flame of Hassan's words.

"What is it?" he asked, scanning her face for some hint of a reaction. "Was that . . . what was that? It wasn't just a dream. It was . . ."

The shadowed future made bright.

Hassan had seen it. The breaking dawn over Nazirah. The end to a darkness brought about by the Witnesses.

"It was a vision," Penrose said, awe blooming across her face. "You saw how to stop the Age of Darkness."

23

JUDE

JUDE WAS ALREADY AWAKE WHEN PENROSE'S RAPID FOOTSTEPS POUNDED down the hall. Truthfully, he'd been awake for hours. Sleep had never come easy to him and now, in an unfamiliar place and with the other half of his destiny just down the hall, it deserted him completely.

But it wasn't the Last Prophet or the Pale Hand that kept him awake. It was Hector. No matter how far his thoughts strayed, they always seemed to return to this: the secrets that Hector had kept from him, and the secrets he had kept from Hector.

So when he heard Penrose's hasty approach, the first thing he felt was relief—whatever had brought her sprinting into his room at this early hour, it would distract him from the torture of his thoughts.

The door burst open, pale light streaming inside. "Jude! Wake up!"

Jude's feet hit the cold marble floor. "I'm awake. What's going on?"

Penrose faltered in the doorway. "It's the Prophet." She sounded out of breath, though the short journey down the hall couldn't possibly have winded her.

Jude sprang to his feet. "Is everything all right?"

"He's not hurt," Penrose said hastily. "He woke up suddenly. He was thrashing. Talking in his sleep. When he came to, he said he'd had a dream. About Nazirah, about taking the city back from the Witnesses."

"A dream," Jude said slowly.

"Not just a dream." Penrose's eyes met his. "A *vision*."

Jude was pulling his boots and cloak on before he'd processed what was happening. His thoughts were a raging storm, but these swift, familiar actions grounded him.

The end of the final prophecy. The answer to the darkness promised. Could it be?

He turned back to Penrose. "Have you woken the Guard?"

"I came here first."

Of course. Jude was Keeper of the Word, and she needed orders. He nodded and strode to the door. "I'll get Hector and Petrossian. Wake the others."

They split at the hallway, Jude going right and Penrose, across. He could hear her tapping at Osei's door as he passed.

He went to Petrossian's room first, though it was farther away. Petrossian woke quickly and didn't question Jude when he told him to report directly to the prince's chambers.

Then Jude was back out in the hallway, facing Hector's door, heart thumping. He willed it to stay steady. He was just waking up his friend.

Not his friend, he reminded himself. A member of his Guard. He needed to be clear about that, starting now. If what Penrose said was true, if the prince truly had seen a vision . . . the devotion of the Keeper of the Word had to be absolute. Unwavering. There could be no more distractions.

"Hector," he called, hesitating with his hand on the twisted iron door handle. "Are you awake?"

There was no reply from within. Jude realized that though he could hear Penrose's low murmur across the hall, and farther down, the creak of Yarik's joints as he stretched, there was only silence on the other side of Hector's door. No low thump of a heartbeat. No sigh of breath.

Jude's pulse picked up as he pushed the door open.

The bed was neatly made, the curtains drawn back to the night sky. Hector's uniform and sword were gone. And so was Hector.

"Where is Navarro?"

Penrose's voice sounded from the open door behind Jude.

Jude shook his head, panic gathering in his chest. He knelt by the wooden chest at the foot of the empty bed and opened the lid. Inside, the dark blue cloak of the Paladin Guard lay folded, left there with intention.

"Jude?" Penrose's voice was careful behind him.

Jude reached for the left-behind cloak, as if somehow by grasping it between his fingers, he could pull Hector back to him. No matter how much he'd wanted to believe that Hector would overcome his grief, the truth pitted his gut. Yesterday, Hector had come face-to-face with the darkest shadow of his past. He was not fine. He might never be.

"He went back to the citadel," Jude said, rising. He was almost certain of it.

He may not have known the details of Hector's past, but he still knew *him*, better than anyone else in the world. Jude left wounds alone to heal. Hector was different. He would pick at the seams of a scab until it ripped open again.

"Why would he do that without telling you?" Penrose asked, her expression tightening with alarm.

Jude hesitated. Telling her the truth would mean breaking his word to Hector. But she deserved to know. "Last night, Hector told me why he left Kerameikos. When he was a child, his entire family was killed by a girl with the Grace of Blood. A girl who left pale handprints on their bodies."

Penrose's mouth fell open. "Hector's family was killed by the Pale Hand?"

"He left the Order to go searching for her."

Her eyes narrowed. "What does that have to do with the citadel?"

"Yesterday, when we went to speak to the captain of the Sentry, we saw a prisoner there. Someone they'd caught in the Temple of Tarseis the night before. Hector recognized her immediately. He said it was the girl who killed his family."

"The Pale Hand is here?"

"I don't know," Jude answered. "She wouldn't admit it. It's been years since Hector has seen her. But he was convinced."

"What is he going to do?"

"I don't—" Jude jerked his head sharply. "I don't know." He paused, the next thought cresting like sunlight breaking through a storm. "But I have to stop him."

"Right now, the Last Prophet is down the hall waiting for you."

"I have to find Hector before he does something foolish." Jude knew how preposterous it sounded. But somehow, that only made him more certain of the decision. "I won't be gone long. The Guard will be under your command until I return."

He started to brush past Penrose through the doorway, but she held fast to his wrist.

"*Send someone else,*" she said. "The Prophet needs you now."

Jude shook his head. "No, I can't—I—It has to be me. I'm the only one who can. If I can speak to him, I know he'll see sense."

"What if he doesn't?" Penrose asked, her grip tightening. "If he disobeys the Keeper of the Word, that is desertion. You know that. You know what the punishment will be for him. What the punishment is for any Paladin."

Jude swallowed. The oaths of the Paladin were clear. If Hector broke them, it would be a sentence of death. And Jude would be the one to deliver it.

"It won't come to that," he said, although his heart was less sure than his words. "It won't."

24

EPHYRA

THE CELL DOOR SCRAPED OPEN, STARTLING EPHYRA AWAKE. DIZZY WITH THE remnants of sleep, she scrambled to her feet, yanking awkwardly on her chains for leverage. In the doorway, shadowed by dim light, stood Hector Navarro.

His fingers were wrapped around the hilt of his sword. Ephyra had no way to defend herself. Except the usual way. Her palms tingled with anticipation.

"How did you get in here?" she demanded.

"It's just the two of us," Hector said, stepping inside the cell at last. "So you can drop the act."

"Where's the other swordsman?" He'd reined Hector in before.

"He's not here," Hector replied tersely. "I told you."

Ephyra swallowed.

"I've been looking for you for a long time," Hector went on. "Long enough to know how many lives you've taken since you killed my family. How many people you've left your mark on."

"Then you know none of those people were innocent," Ephyra said, her voice shaking. "I only kill those who deserve it. Those who are cruel, who use their power to hurt others."

"Ah, yes. The Pale Hand only kills the wicked. How strange that that didn't seem to matter when you took my family's lives. They were innocent, but that didn't stop you from killing them. Do you even remember them?"

Forcing her eyes to meet his, she whispered, "Yes."

His mouth curled into a snarl. "My mother. My father. My brother. They took you in, showed you kindness. And you murdered them."

"I didn't—" She stopped. Nothing she could say would change what she had done, and if she could go back and choose again, she knew she would still choose Beru. "It was an accident."

"I don't believe that," Hector said. "You take lives because you *can*. You think you are a god. But you're not. Who are you to decide who lives and who dies? How does a monster know who is and is not her own kind?"

Ephyra sucked in a panicked breath as Hector's expression shifted back to that pinned, flat look. The one that chilled her more than explosive anger ever could.

"You know, I used to wonder why I didn't die, too. Why was I spared?" Hector asked. "After five long years, I finally know the answer. I survived because I'm supposed to stop you. Everything in my life has led to this moment. Fate has decided my purpose for me. To make sure the Pale Hand never reaches for another life again."

Ephyra pressed herself back against the wall, ignoring the bite of the chains straining on her wrists.

Hector's hand tightened over the hilt of his sword, his eyes wild. She could almost see the thoughts racing through his mind. He could cut her down right here, right now. He could spill her blood in this cell and put an end to the Pale Hand.

"You've never killed anyone before, have you?" Ephyra asked softly. "It's easier than you'd think. Harder, too. Or maybe that's just me."

"I'm not going to kill you."

Ephyra let out a breath, but his tone kept her from relief.

"Not yet," he said. "First, I'm going to show everyone what you are. I'm going to prove to the world that you are the Pale Hand."

"Prove it?" Ephyra asked. "How are you going to do that?"

"You're going to tell them," Hector said. "The Sentry. The Order of the Last Light. The world will know exactly what you are."

"I won't admit anything."

Hector's eyes narrowed. He was silent for a long moment. Then quietly, he said, "You have a sister. I remember her."

Ephyra stiffened and then tried to smooth her expression. "I haven't seen my sister in years."

"You're lying," Hector said at once. "You would never leave her. She's somewhere in this city, too."

Ephyra took a deep breath, regrouping. She couldn't let him see how scared she was. This was the one thing that could undo her. Hector could threaten Ephyra's life all he wanted, but Beru—

He couldn't touch her.

"She's innocent," Ephyra said. "Like your family was. Would you really threaten an innocent life?"

Something flashed through Hector's eyes. Maybe she had finally broken through the haze of grief and anger for a moment. Maybe she could get him to look at what he was doing and realize he'd gone too far.

"I hope it won't come to that," he said at last. "This is bigger than one life. If you refuse to admit to the world what you are, then whatever happens is on your conscience."

Ephyra would give up her own life if it came to that. But if Hector got to Beru, if he found out that Ephyra had killed all those people for her, that his family had died because of her . . .

She could see the chasm of his grief, and knew what pain like that could make you do.

"You won't find her," she said in a low, snarling voice. "You can search the whole city."

Hector's gaze was dark and furious. "Then I'll search the whole city," he answered. "And I know exactly where to start."

25

ANTON

ANTON'S CELL WAS UNBEARABLY COLD. THE KIND OF COLD THAT MADE HIS bones brittle and his joints ache, that left a chill in his spine like someone had hollowed out the warm blood and flesh. The kind of cold he hadn't felt since he'd lived on the streets. The kind of cold that drove men to desperation in search of a way to escape its cruel fingers.

He had to get out of here. Illya was still out there, and now he knew exactly where Anton was. He would find a way to come for him. But his brother wasn't the only thing Anton was worried about. During the long stretch of hours when Anton had been locked in here, he'd felt the thundering *esha* again. The same one he'd felt at the harbor, drowning out the low buzz of all others, as powerful and unyielding as a storm on the horizon.

It made him feel more trapped than the walls of his cell—though whether he wanted to flee from the *esha* or run to it, he still didn't know. He just knew he had to get out. They couldn't keep him here forever. He hadn't actually done anything wrong. They would realize that eventually, and then they would let him go. And Anton would run again. Run fast, run far. It had been a mistake to imagine he could ever do anything else.

Footsteps outside his cell signaled another guard change. Except, Anton realized with a jolt, the guards had just changed, not an hour ago.

The cell door burst open, and Anton pressed himself back, certain that he was once again about to see the face that haunted his dreams.

But instead of his brother, a swordsman towered in the doorway. His *esha* hit Anton like the scrape of hard rock against steel. He didn't look like the other guards who had come to question him. This man, with burning coal-dark eyes, looked like he had come for blood.

Anton supposed this should scare him. It did, but his fear was matched by relief. Because no matter who this swordsman was, no matter what he wanted, he wasn't Illya.

"Hello," Anton said pleasantly, peeling himself from the wall.

The swordsman stepped inside, boots thudding against the cell floor.

"I already told the Sentry I wasn't trying to rob that temple," Anton said. "So if you're here to—"

"Stop," the swordsman said gruffly. "I'm not here on behalf of the Sentry."

This, Anton had guessed.

"My name is Hector Navarro. I've been searching for the Pale Hand for a very long time."

"The what?" Anton asked, affecting as much guileless innocence as he could muster. "I don't know what that is."

"Do not lie to me," Navarro said. "The Paladin of the Order of the Last Light are trained in many powerful techniques of the Grace of Heart. Our senses are heightened beyond any other Graced swordsmen you've ever encountered."

Anton tried to keep his expression neutral. "And?"

Navarro's face pinched in irritation. "I can hear your heartbeat. I can smell the sweat on your skin. I can sense the tiniest shift in tension, in your breath. These things tell me that you're lying to me. Now tell me—you came here with the Pale Hand, didn't you?"

Anton pressed his lips together.

"*Didn't you?*"

"Fine." Anton sighed, raising his eyes to the ceiling. "Yes. Fine. I did. We're old pals, me and the Pale Hand."

"She has a sister," Navarro said slowly. "I need to find her. Tell me where she is, and I won't hurt you."

"And if I refuse, you'll—what? Kill me?" Anton was not new to having his life threatened. "I haven't actually done anything wrong."

"As I said, I am not the Sentry. It doesn't matter to me what you have or haven't done." Navarro unsheathed his sword slowly, letting Anton's gaze linger on the curve of its blade. "Tell me where her sister is."

Anton raised his eyes from the sword to Navarro's face. He was afraid, but not of the blade. "What are you going to do to her?"

"Nothing," Navarro replied. "If the Pale Hand cooperates."

"What if she doesn't?"

Quicker than a blink, Navarro's blade was at Anton's throat. "You should first worry about your own cooperation."

Anton raised his chin. "You're not going to kill me." He'd faced men like Navarro before—men steeped in anger and a little fear, looking for something to make them feel in control again.

"You think not?" Navarro asked. There was something strangely open in his dark eyes, like he himself wasn't sure how far he'd go.

Anton felt the blade pinch against his flesh as he swallowed. Strangely, he was calm. This was a danger that was real, right in front of him. A danger that, one way or another, would end.

And though Anton was the one at this man's mercy, it was *his* choice what would happen next.

"Look," he said. "We both have a problem here. You want to find the Pale Hand's sister, and I want to get out of here. Seems like we can help each other."

"You'll tell me where she is?"

"No." The blade pressed harder. "But I can show you."

Navarro took a step back, putting a blessed few inches between his sword and Anton's throat.

Anton exhaled. "Get me out of here, and I'll take you to her."

"You're playing games while the fate of the world hangs in the balance," Hector told him. "Whatever she is to you, it's not worth what will happen if I don't find her."

"If the fate of the world really hangs in the balance, then what does one prisoner going free matter?"

The swordsman's gaze flickered to the door and then back to Anton. "Someone's coming."

"Then I guess you better decide quick."

With a groan of frustration, Navarro sheathed his blade and grabbed Anton by the shoulder, shoving him toward the open door.

26

JUDE

WHAT WOULD YOU DO IF YOU COULD DO ANYTHING YOU WANTED?

The question flashed through Jude's mind as he tore through the Sentry barracks to the entrance of the holding cells. This was the question Hector had asked him that night, over a year ago, when the future had stretched endlessly ahead of them. It was the question that had surfaced in Jude's mind when he'd chosen Hector as the sixth member of his Guard. It was the question that, when Hector had answered it, had cemented their roles in life. Hector and Jude, side by side.

I'd go with you, of course.

But Jude knew, now, what Hector's real answer was. Unburdened by the oath he'd sworn to the Order, unshackled from Jude's expectations, Hector felt called by another cause. He had not been born a soldier of faith, the way Jude had. He had been born a son, and made an orphan, and that was a wound that ran deeper than Jude could fathom. Even if Hector swore he was doing this because of the last prophecy, Jude knew the truth. It was grief, not faith, that drove him.

A Sentry stopped Jude just outside the prisoners' tower. He recognized her from the Pale Hand's near escape the day before.

"Captain Weatherbourne," she addressed him. "There's been an incident."

Jude drew up short. A thousand awful scenarios chased through his mind. "What happened?"

"The guards on duty early this morning were found unconscious in the guardroom. One of the prisoners is missing."

Jude tensed. "The one we spoke to yesterday?"

To his surprise, the Sentry shook her head. "No. The boy she was with when we found them. We're investigating what—"

"Take me up there," Jude demanded.

The Sentry hesitated.

"Those prisoners are of particular interest to the Order of the Last Light. It's imperative that I speak with the girl again," Jude said, summoning whatever scrap of gravitas his father had passed on to him. "Take me up there."

"All right," the Sentry said. "This way."

She led him into the lift. It was a tense few minutes of waiting for it to ascend into the tower, and then for the Sentry to open the girl's cell.

The Sentry stood back, and Jude stepped forward, wrenching open the heavy iron door.

Inside, the girl Hector called the Pale Hand was already on her feet. Before she could say a word or the Sentry could follow him into the cell, Jude turned and slammed the door shut.

He whirled back on her. "Where is he?"

She looked so different from the girl they'd interviewed just the day before. Despite her imprisonment, she had been calm, collected.

Overnight, she had transformed into a desperate tangle of nerves and panic.

If Jude had thought he could find anger or hatred in his heart for this girl who had caused Hector so much pain, one look at her—shackled hands pressed to her gasping chest—dispelled that notion.

"He was here, wasn't he?" Jude tried again. "Hector Navarro, I mean. He came back down here this morning."

She nodded haltingly.

"Did he try to hurt you?" The words felt wrenched out of him. He could not imagine Hector being cruel, but he had seen the hollow, haunted look in his eyes when he looked at this girl.

She didn't answer, her eyes bright with furious unshed tears.

"Please," Jude begged. "Tell me what happened."

"How do I know you're not just going to help him?" Her voice was scraped raw. "You're with the Order of the Last Light, too."

Frustration ignited his chest. He didn't have time for her suspicion. He had to find Hector and bring him back before this mistake became irrevocable.

"I'm not here as captain of the Paladin Guard. I came here to find my friend. Whatever happens after that—"

"You mean, whether or not you decide to kill me?"

Jude's eyes widened. "Is that what he said he was going to do?"

"He said he was going to try to prove to you that I'm the Pale Hand," she said. "The killing part was implied."

"I won't hurt you," Jude said. "Where is Hector now?"

She stared at him in silence as Jude's frustration grew.

"The other prisoner who was brought here with you," he said. "The boy. The guards say he's gone missing. What does Hector want with him?"

She pressed her lips together. Sucking in a shaking breath, she said, "He knows where my sister is."

"And what does Hector want with your sister?"

"To use her against me," she said. "To hurt her, if I don't comply with him."

Jude's chest seized. He knew that Hector wanted revenge, but this? To hurt an innocent girl, just because he believed her sister was responsible for his family's death?

It was the grief talking. Hector would not really do such a thing. Jude gripped his sword, reordering his thoughts to face the problem at hand. He would not consider what might happen if he didn't find Hector.

"The other prisoner—do you think he'll help Hector?" Jude asked. "Would he betray you just like that?"

"I . . . I don't know," the girl replied. "He might. He doesn't owe me anything, and I don't trust him."

"Then you need to tell me where they're going."

She met his gaze squarely. "Take me with you."

"You know I can't do that," Jude said. "Just tell me where he went. I swear to you, I won't let him hurt anyone. I will find him, and I will make him see reason."

"How will you do that?" she spat. "He won't see reason. He's blinded by—"

"Grief," Jude finished quietly. "I know. There is a code that we live by, an oath that we take, and that oath does not allow for grief or revenge. He has broken it by leaving, and if he carries out what you say he intends to do—" He stopped. He would not allow himself to think of Hector that way. "I swear to you, I will not let that happen."

"I don't care about your stupid oath," she bit out. "I care about my sister. So *please*—" She broke off raggedly, pressing a palm to her chest as if she could press the panic away.

Jude saw in her face what lay behind her ferocity and rage. Fear.

"Please."

"I won't let him hurt your sister," he said. "There is no honor in revenge, for you or him."

Her eyes searched his. "You think a lot of that. Honor."

Jude bowed his head in agreement.

"Then I need your word, that whatever happens, whatever Hector says about me, about my sister—" Her voice cracked. "Give me your word that you'll protect her."

He could promise her this much, at least. Death should not be dispensed so readily. "I'm responsible for Hector's life. For his choices, his actions. I will not let him hurt your sister."

"Swear to me," she said, her eyes flashing. "The way you swore your oath."

His fingers twitched at the edge of his cloak. The oath of the Paladin was sacred.

"Swear to me!"

Jude dropped to one knee, laying the Pinnacle Blade across his hands. "I do swear."

She studied him for a long, hard moment before she said, "She's in a burned-down shrine just outside the High City, by the South Gate. Find her before Navarro does."

He nodded and stood. Whatever was going through Hector's mind now, he knew that he would regret it if he hurt an innocent girl. He would find them before it was too late.

"I don't know anything about you," the prisoner said. "But I'm trusting you to do this for me. Keep her safe."

"For your sister's sake," Jude said. "And Hector's."

27

HASSAN

WHILE HE WAITED FOR PENROSE TO FETCH THE REST OF THE GUARD, HASSAN called two of Lethia's servants and sent them to the agora.

"There's a girl. A soldier," he told them. "Khepri." He described to them where her tent was located. "Find her and bring her here."

"Just what are you up to, Hassan?" Lethia asked when the servants had left.

Hassan glanced at his aunt. "She was in my dream. My vision."

"Vision?" Lethia repeated, doubt suffusing her tone. "You don't really think—"

Penrose appeared in the doorway, looking harried and tense. Behind her, the rest of the Guard filtered in. Once again, two of them were missing.

"Where is Captain Weatherbourne?" Hassan asked.

"He had to take care of some more business with the Sentry," Penrose replied. Her gaze didn't quite meet his.

"What business?" Hassan's mind darkened with the possibilities— maybe the Witnesses had done something, destroyed a temple in the night or threatened the lives of the refugees.

"Nothing you need concern yourself with," Penrose answered tightly. "He put me in command in his absence. I know that if he were here, he would say that this is too important to wait. Tell us what you saw, Prince Hassan."

Hassan straightened up, looking out at the other members of the Guard.

"I . . . I had a dream last night," he began unsteadily. "A vision."

He felt the room shift as soon as he said it. Penrose must have told the Guard about his dream already, but hearing him say those words sent a tremor through the room, a collective intake of breath, a hopeful silence.

Somehow, Hassan had tapped into the Sight that had been bestowed on him at birth. Somehow, his power had revealed itself, at just the moment he needed it most. He had asked for guidance, and his own heart, his own Grace, had answered.

Petrossian broke the silence. "What did you see?"

Hassan took a deep breath and, as best as he could, described his vision to the Guard. He watched their faces as he spoke about standing on the deck of the lighthouse of Nazirah, watching as the Witnesses were overrun by his troops, sitting on the throne of Herat and looking out at his subjects.

"It could have just been a dream," Lethia interjected gently. "With everything that's happened in the past few days, I wouldn't be surprised if the Witnesses and Nazirah and Godfire were showing up in your sleep."

"No," Hassan said. "I've dreamt about the Witnesses and the coup since it happened, but this was different. Those dreams were confusing, twisting in my mind. But this was . . . almost solid. The details are so vivid, even now. More like a memory than a dream. I felt this pull, like I knew this is what I was supposed to do. It feels right, doesn't it? Returning to Nazirah and taking on the Witnesses is my destiny."

"'The final piece of our prophecy revealed in vision of Grace and fire,'" Penrose recited. She turned to the rest of the Guard. "This is what the Seven Prophets could not see. This is the answer we have been searching for. The way to stop the Age of Darkness."

"I hope you understand what you're saying," Lethia said, her voice crackling with ire. "*If* this prophecy is in fact real, and *if* Hassan's dream was truly a vision, then you're asking him to put himself in a great deal of danger."

"*We* ask nothing," Penrose replied. "Prince Hassan's vision has shown us the path forward. He must return to Nazirah."

The thought made Hassan's chest clench. Return to Nazirah. It was all he'd wanted since arriving in Pallas Athos.

"What if you're wrong?" Lethia asked. "Hassan is the sole heir to the throne of Herat. If something happens to him—"

"Nothing will happen to me," Hassan said. "Aunt Lethia, listen."

She rose from the settee. "I hope you're right about this. I truly do. But I fear that these people who say they are sworn to protect you may not truly have your safety in mind. I fear that they will lead you astray."

Penrose's eyes flashed at this. "The safety of the Prophet is our only priority. We would never do anything to endanger him."

Lethia's cool gaze flickered to Penrose before settling back on Hassan. "I beg that you think everything over carefully before you make any decisions just because some Graced swordsmen who haven't been seen in a century tell you it's your destiny. If not for your own sake, then for the sake of our country."

Hassan felt as if Lethia had struck him. "I am doing this for Herat.

All of this is for Herat. It's more than anything you've done for our country."

Lethia's eyes narrowed. "Your temper makes a fool of you, Hassan," she said. "I am only trying to help. I know you have hope. I just don't want you to put it in the wrong place."

Hassan regretted his harsh words, but he could not bring himself to take them back, even as Lethia walked out the door.

He felt a loss at her absence. The day before, Lethia had seemed skeptical of the prophecy, but he'd thought that, like him, she was simply taking time to adjust to what they'd learned. A part of him had even wondered if Lethia's resistance came from her own past of growing up without Grace. He'd never asked her directly, if she used to wish for Grace the way he did, but he thought she must have. Perhaps she'd felt a twinge of envy on learning that Hassan had gotten what he'd wanted. If their positions were reversed, he was certain he would feel that way.

"So what does this all mean?" Osei asked, breaking the awkward silence.

Penrose raised her chin. "We must go to Nazirah."

"How? When?" Petrossian asked. "What does the vision tell us about how to stop the Witnesses?"

Hassan opened his mouth to reply, but a sharp rap on the door interrupted him.

"Who is that?" Annuka asked, looking alarmed.

The door opened, and a servant entered.

"Miss Khepri Fakhoury is here, by request of His Grace Prince Hassan."

Hassan stood. "Send her in."

"Prince Hassan—" Penrose's objection was cut short as Khepri stepped into the room.

Everything went quiet inside Hassan's mind at the sight of her, his anger and frustration melting away. An image from his dream flickered before him—Khepri standing by his side at the lighthouse of Nazirah, fierce and luminous in the flame's light.

She swept into a bow. "Your Grace."

"What is she doing here?"

Hassan barely heard Petrossian's question. He was still staring at Khepri. "You were there. You were right there, at my side."

Their eyes met. "Your Grace?"

I knew I needed to come here, she'd said that first night in the agora. The moonlight had cast a glow across her face, making her look like one of the golden statues that lined the Hall of Kings in the Palace of Herat. *I came here to find the prince and help him retake our country.*

She had believed in him then, even before she knew him. Believed in him enough to risk everything and come to Pallas Athos to find him. It was fate. He hadn't realized it then, but he knew it now. She had come to find him so that they could retake Herat, because that was what was meant to happen.

With Khepri here in front of him, it was all so clear.

"You were there." He drew toward her. She got to her feet uncertainly, allowing Hassan to take her by the wrist. "On the lighthouse, overlooking the city."

"What do you mean, on the lighthouse?"

Hassan glanced at the Guard behind him. He knew that they had wanted to keep the secret of the last prophecy, but that was before his vision.

Before he'd completed the prophecy.

"Khepri," he said. "The Paladin Guard aren't just here because of the Witnesses. They came here because of me. Because for a century, the Order of the Last Light has kept a secret from the rest of the world."

"Your Grace," Petrossian cut in. "You cannot simply reveal—"

Penrose silenced him with a look. With a nod at Hassan, she told Khepri, "When the Prophets disappeared, they left one final prophecy. An unfinished prophecy. It was entrusted to the Order of the Last Light, to be kept secret until it could be completed."

In a patient, matter-of-fact tone, Penrose explained about the harbingers, the Age of Darkness, and the Last Prophet, who would stop it. Khepri listened without interrupting.

"Khepri," Hassan said when Penrose was done. "*I* am the Last Prophet. And now I finally know what we need to do to stop the Age of Darkness. We have to go to Nazirah with the refugee army. Your army."

"Army?" Osei asked.

Hassan turned to the Guard. "Khepri has been training the refugees in the agora. An army of Graced fighters who have as much reason to fight the Witnesses as I. They want to help me retake Nazirah and drive them from the Kingdom of Herat."

Khepri's gaze caught on his, and Hassan could see the burgeoning hope in her eyes.

"And that's exactly what we're going to do," he said, the words coming easily to him now that he was looking at Khepri. "Storm the harbor of Nazirah. Overtake the Witnesses. The way to stop the Age of Darkness is to save Nazirah."

Khepri's eyes widened. "But yesterday, in the agora, you said—"

"I didn't know," Hassan said. "I didn't know then what I was supposed to do. What I was. I do now. I *know* what we're meant to do. I saw it."

"I—You're serious?" Khepri asked. "Yesterday you told me there was no hope of stopping the Witnesses with a few hundred soldiers.

But now . . . You really saw it, didn't you? This vision. The salvation of our kingdom."

"Yes." He met her gaze, and the spark that flickered between them burned all other doubts away. "And it wasn't just the refugee army I saw. I saw ships. With silver sails. A whole fleet of them."

"The Order's fleet," Penrose said.

"Osei told me your numbers have dwindled since the Prophets disappeared, but there are still hundreds of Paladin, aren't there?" Hassan asked.

Penrose nodded. "There are hundreds of us sworn to protect the Prophet from harm. If your vision is to come to pass, and I believe that it will, then our path is clear." She knelt in one swift motion, her hand going to the hilt of her sword. "Our swords, and all the swords of the Paladin of the Order of the Last Light, are yours to wield."

The rest of the Guard followed, dropping to one knee. Hassan was not unused to people bowing to him, but this felt different. There was a weight, a promise of something that he had only just begun to grasp. He was more than a prince now, and this was more than allegiance.

"I stand with the Prophet," Penrose said, lifting her chin.

"I stand with the Prophet," the other members of the Guard echoed.

Khepri raised her chin. "I stand with you, Prince Hassan. Wherever that may lead."

For the first time since the Hierophant had taken Nazirah, Hassan saw the path forward. Everything that had happened since the coup—the Witnesses in the agora, the revelation of the last prophecy, Khepri—was leading to this. At last, he knew what he needed to do. At last, he had people to stand with him.

But with that thought came an edge of apprehension. No longer was his own path the only thing at stake. Now, there was Khepri and the refugee army. There was the Paladin Guard and the Order of the Last Light.

He was finally the leader he'd never thought he could be. The leader his father had seen in him. He could only hope he didn't lead them all astray.

28

BERU

SOMETHING HAD GONE WRONG. BERU KNEW IT IN HER BONES. THE THING SHE'D worried about, night after night, that Ephyra would one day leave and not return, had finally happened.

She wasn't sure exactly what her sister had meant when she'd said she had to go to the Temple of Tarseis to "take care of something," but it had now been over a day since she'd left. Worry ate at her gut.

Their argument was still fresh in Beru's mind. Ephyra believed they could still find Eleazar's Chalice and cure her. Maybe she was right. But in case she wasn't, Beru still had the train tickets tucked into her pocket. If Anton couldn't find the Chalice, they were going home. As soon as Ephyra came back.

She has to be all right, Beru told herself, running her fingers over the beads and shells of the bracelet she'd just finished making. They stopped on the tiny glass bottle stopper Ephyra had brought her.

The sound of footsteps coming down through the mausoleum broke through her anxious thoughts. Beru's body went slack with relief. Ephyra was back. She didn't have to leave without her.

As the footsteps came nearer, Beru detected a second set. *Anton.*

She hurried to the door and unlatched it quickly. She didn't want another moment spent not knowing Ephyra was safe.

But when the door swung open, it wasn't her sister who stood there.

She recognized him instantly. It had been over five years, and in that time, he had transformed from a bright and lively little boy into this ferocious, intense man.

Somehow, impossibly, Hector Navarro was here.

He stood frozen, looking as shocked to see her as she was to see him.

"It's all right," Anton said, stepping out from behind Hector.

"What are you doing with him?" Beru asked, her voice shaking as she looked between them. "Where's Ephyra?"

It was Hector who answered. "Your sister is where she belongs."

Beru's blood went cold.

"It's not what you think," Anton cut in quickly. "We were caught by the Sentry in the temple. They thought we were there to rob the priests, so they put us in cells. She's all right."

"How could you let this happen?" Beru asked Anton. She didn't know if she meant Ephyra getting imprisoned or Hector standing in front of her like a vengeful spirit. Both were unfathomable.

"Your sister is a killer," Hector said. "She deserves to be locked up. And I'm going to make sure she never takes another life."

"Beru," Anton said, stepping toward her. He looked like a wreck—hair standing up, deep lines beneath his eyes. "I'm sorry."

Hector threw out his arm to hold Anton back. "You did as I asked. You're free to go."

Beru heard the words not as an offer, but as an order.

Anton glanced from her to Hector. "I'm not going to leave you with her." His voice shook slightly, but Beru had to give him credit for trying.

"Just go, Anton," she said quietly.

His gaze jumped to her, startled. "What if he tries to hurt you?"

Maybe I would deserve it, Beru thought. "The time for worrying about that would have been *before* you brought him here," she said, her voice cold. "This is between us now. Leave."

Anton cast her another haunted, helpless look before slowly turning away. She watched him disappear through the door, leaving her and Hector alone.

A chill shivered down Beru's back. She tugged at the edge of the wrapping that covered the black handprint on her wrist. "How did you even find us after all this time?"

Hector shook his head slowly, his eyes lost and far away. "I didn't. Fate brought me here so that I could stop her. And you're going to help me."

"Why would I help you hurt my sister?" Fear bled into anger.

"Because," Hector said, "you're the only person aside from me who knows the truth about what she's done. That the Pale Hand doesn't just kill the wicked. She's killed innocent people—people like my family. If someone doesn't stop her, more will die."

"What are you talking about?"

"Where she goes, darkness follows," Hector said. "You know the truth about your sister. You know what she's done. If you tell everyone, they'll believe you. She is an agent of evil. A harbinger of darkness."

"That isn't true," Beru said fiercely. "You don't know what you're talking about."

"I was there when she killed my family. So were you."

She closed her eyes. She knew if Ephyra were here, she'd never let Beru do what she was about to. "You don't know the whole story."

"The whole story?" Hector repeated. "My family took your sister in, and she killed them in cold blood. I had to bury their bodies. *That's* the story."

Beru shook her head. "It was an accident. She wasn't trying to hurt anyone."

"She *killed* them."

"She was trying to heal me," Beru said desperately. "She—she didn't know what she was doing. She took *esha* from them by mistake. It wasn't her fault. It was mine."

Hector reeled back, staring at her.

"Do you remember how I got sick right before your mother died?"

Hector's hands balled into fists so tight they shook.

"I'm the reason your family is dead," Beru said. "Don't blame Ephyra. It was my fault. All of it. I'm the reason the Pale Hand exists. If it weren't for me, Ephyra would never have taken a single life."

Hector's eyes narrowed. "Then atone," he said. "Stop your sister from killing anyone else."

His words struck to the core of her, because some part of her knew he was right. If Beru were truly remorseful for the deaths she'd caused, she would have done more than argue with Ephyra about it. She would have found a way to stop it.

It wasn't the first time she'd had this thought. Every time Ephyra put on her mask and went out as the Pale Hand, it crept into her mind.

"Come with me," Hector said, holding his palm out to her. "Help me show everyone what the Pale Hand has done. Help me stop her."

Beru looked at his hand and then at the curtain behind him.

"I will never," she said, her voice trembling, "*ever* betray my sister."

She reached up and yanked down the curtain. Hector lunged forward, seizing her by the arm as the falling curtain twisted around them.

"Just let me go!" Beru cried, stumbling back against the table, dragging Hector with her. She threw her other arm back, reaching for something—anything—to help. Her fingers closed around a pair of brass pliers. In one jagged motion, she jabbed them at Hector's shoulder.

He moved to block her, yanking her arm back by the wrapping around her wrist. The cloth unraveled, and Hector froze, staring.

Beru followed his gaze. The wrapping trailed off her like a snake's shed skin. Exposed beneath it was the dark handprint branded into her arm.

Hector's grip tightened as he slowly turned it toward him.

"'To death's pale hand the wicked fall,'" he said, eyes locked on the handprint. "'That which sleeps in the dust shall rise.'" He looked up at her face. "It's you."

Beru squeezed her eyes shut. She didn't know what Hector's words meant, but there was a horror in his eyes she couldn't bear to see.

He let go of her wrist, backing away. "*Revenant.*"

The word hissed through the air between them like smoke.

She clutched her wrist to her chest, as if by hiding the mark she could cover the truth of what she was. But it was too late. Just as the pale handprints marked Ephyra's victims, the dark handprint marked Beru.

Hector had seen it, and he knew what it meant.

The reason Ephyra took lives to heal Beru. The reason their stolen *esha* always left her. It was because she wasn't just sick. Five years ago, Beru had died.

And Ephyra had brought her back to life.

She heard the scrape of metal and opened her eyes. In the dim light of the alcove, Hector stood above her, his sword in his hand.

"Wh-what are you doing?"

"You rose from the dead," Hector said. "You're the third harbinger. You're going to bring about the Age of Darkness."

Hector's words lanced through her, though she scarcely understood what they meant.

He raised his sword. All Beru could do was stare, frozen, as the blade glinted above her.

But then—a flash of movement, and suddenly a body collided with Hector, knocking him away.

Anton. He'd come back.

Hector stumbled forward into the table. The bug-eaten wood creaked beneath his weight and collapsed, sending him crashing to the floor in a heap of jagged wood and dust. A rain of beads and seashells scattered to the floor.

Beru gaped for a moment, until Anton turned and seized her wrist, tugging her toward the stairwell.

"Come on!"

Beru stumbled after him, grabbing her overcoat as they fled through the doorway. Together, they raced up the narrow stone steps and through the passage that led them out into the ruined sanctum.

"Thanks for coming back," Beru said breathlessly, tugging on the coat.

"Seemed like a good moment," Anton said as they veered up and into the mausoleum. Dusty light poured through the half-caved-in roof. "Sorry I—well, you know."

"You can make it up to me by taking me to Ephyra."

"*What?*" Anton said. "We can't go back there."

Beru stopped short, bringing them both to a halt. "I can't just leave her!"

"That cell may be the safest place for her right now," Anton said. "That swordsman doesn't have any proof she's the Pale Hand. That's why he was looking for you. The best thing you can do is stay away from the citadel."

Anton was right. If Beru showed up there, Hector wouldn't even need her to say anything. One look at the dark handprint that marked her wrist, and everyone would know that not only was Ephyra the Pale Hand, she was also a necromancer.

"You need to get as far away from here as you can," Anton said. "If they can't prove Ephyra's the Pale Hand, they'll have to let her go."

Rapid footsteps echoed up from the crypt. Hector was right behind them.

"Get out of here *now*," Anton said, his eyes wide and trained on the stairs they'd just ascended.

Reaching into the front fold of her overcoat, Beru drew out the train tickets.

"I need you to do something for me," she said seriously, holding one of them out to Anton. "Find a way to get this to Ephyra."

Anton reached for it. "I can't promise anything, but I'll try. Now go!"

Beru turned and ran for the gaping hole in the wall that had once been the door. She didn't look back.

29

ANTON

ANTON WHIRLED AS NAVARRO'S DISSONANT *ESHA* CRASHED OVER HIM. RAGE poured off the Paladin like smoke as he emerged from the passage below and stepped into the shadowed sanctum.

"Where is she?" he demanded, eyes scanning over smashed tiles and blackened reliquaries. "Where did she go?"

Anton took a breath and moved to block the exit. Beru could get out of the city if he could buy her just a little more time. He owed her that much.

"You don't know what you're doing," Navarro said. "Move aside."

"She's innocent."

"Innocent?" Navarro repeated. "You don't know what she is, do you?"

Anton didn't answer.

"That girl you call innocent is a creature of death," Navarro said. "A revenant. Resurrected by her sister."

It seemed impossible. Revenants were from stories, the frightening creatures that had once laid waste to the Kingdom of Herat under the command of the Necromancer King.

But then again, Beru and Ephyra had been searching for Eleazar's Chalice, the artefact that had imbued the Necromancer King with enough power to create an army of the undead. Why would they need that, if what Navarro was saying wasn't true?

Navarro glanced at Anton's hand. "What is that?"

Anton's grip tightened on the ticket that Beru had handed him just moments ago. He moved to tuck it away, but Navarro snatched it quicker than Anton could react.

"Tel Amot," Navarro said, eyes scanning over it. Then, almost to himself, "Why is she going there?"

Anton dove for the ticket. Navarro knocked him to the ground without a trace of effort.

"Thank you for this," Navarro said, tucking the ticket away.

"You said you weren't going to hurt her. You said no harm would come to her."

Navarro peered down at him. "Did you not hear what I said? She's a revenant."

"So what?" The words came out before Anton could stop them. "You're going to kill her for what she is? For something she never chose?"

Navarro's eyes flashed as he advanced. "You know nothing of what you speak."

Anton scrambled to his feet, putting himself once again between Navarro and the exit.

"Move aside," Navarro said. "Despite that stunt you pulled downstairs, I don't want to hurt you."

Anton stayed put.

Navarro stepped back. "If you won't move," he said, drawing his sword slowly from its sheath with a metallic scrape, "then I'll make you."

Sunlight glinted on the edge of the blade.

And then, through the fear that spiked his veins like ice, Anton felt it. The *esha* that had been haunting him since that morning in the marina. The one that had swept over him again when he was locked in the tower in the citadel. It was closer now than it had been then, almost palpable in the room. Navarro and the blade in his hand seemed to bleed into the background, as the *esha* reverberated around Anton, taut and charged like a sudden drop in air pressure.

He looked back at Navarro to find him staring, sword still gleaming between them, confusion shadowing over his face. For a moment, Anton thought that somehow Navarro felt the *esha*, too, but then the sound of hurried footsteps rebounded from the portico, followed by a voice echoing into the sanctum.

"*Hector!*"

Navarro cursed, sheathing his sword. A split second later, he grabbed Anton by the front of his tunic, throwing him back against the crumbling side of the scrying pool. Anton stumbled, grappling against the slippery stone for purchase. The *esha* grew stronger, like a gathering storm.

"Hector!"

In the gaping opening of the sanctum, a second swordsman appeared, dark-haired and compact, his sword still sheathed at his hip. The light pouring in through the threshold blurred the edges of him, glowing. Not quite real.

He turned, fixing Anton with a gaze that swept through him like fire.

Anton's knees threatened to collapse from under him. He could not look away from the swordsman, could not stop his Grace from rippling out to feel his *esha*. The same one he had felt in the marina, and in the cell, only now it was right here, filling the sanctum with torrential power, pulling his Grace into the eye of the storm.

Every particle of air around them stood at attention, like the whole world had shifted, reordering itself with them at the center. Anton's Grace thrummed in his body, pulsing out and back, reverberating off the gusts of the swordsman's *esha*. Like it was calling out to him, reaching for him. Like it recognized him.

30

JUDE

JUDE'S GAZE SNAPPED FROM THE BOY HUNCHED AGAINST THE EDGE OF THE scrying pool back to Hector.

Hector looked stunned. "What are you doing here?"

Jude stepped into the sanctum toward his friend. Whatever was going through Hector's mind now, he was still Hector. "I could ask you the same thing."

Hector's jaw tensed. "I told you last night. I have to stop the Pale Hand."

"By going after her sister? An innocent girl? This—this *revenge*, it won't heal you, Hector."

"I didn't come here for revenge," Hector said. "That innocent girl? She's a revenant, Jude. A revenant that the Pale Hand created. She's the third harbinger of the Age of Darkness. 'That which sleeps in the dust shall rise.'"

Jude's mind reeled. Hector sounded so certain. But he knew that Hector was also grappling with grief, fury, and helplessness. He might be wrong.

But even if what he said was true, that was just more reason for him to return to the rest of the Guard. Tell them what he knew, so they could, together, decide how to handle it.

"Hector," Jude said, moving toward him. "I believe you. Come back to the Guard with me. We'll figure out what to do."

"I *have* to stop her, Jude. You, of all people, should understand that."

Jude stopped an arm's length from Hector. "What does that mean?"

"You know what your destiny is. You always have," Hector replied. "I thought—I thought that it was mine, too. Finding the Prophet and—and—"

"It still *is*."

Hector shook his head. "I searched for the Pale Hand for almost a year. After all that time, after I gave up, after I returned to the Order, now, *now* is when I find her. The moment you finally find the Prophet is the same moment that I finally cross paths with the Pale Hand again. That *means* something. It must."

"Yes." Jude reached a hesitant hand to clasp Hector on the shoulder. "It means there are two paths in front of you. One that leads to your past. The other to your future. It's up to you to choose."

Hector shuddered beneath Jude's touch. "You're right," he croaked. His hands came up to clasp Jude's shoulders, and Jude felt relief ripple over him.

Until Hector's grip tightened and he shoved Jude back toward the gaping threshold. In a hollow voice, he said, "I've made my choice."

He turned and leapt onto the toppled pillar that leaned across the middle of the sanctum. He raced up it to the sanctum's half-collapsed inner wall.

"*Hector!*" The name ripped out of Jude as he leapt after him.

Hector disappeared behind the wall, then reappeared as he took a flying leap up to the edge of the buckled-in roof.

Jude drew in breath and raced after him. The smoke-blackened stone slipped beneath him, but he kept moving, leaping from the pillar to the half-destroyed roof. The damage from the fire had left it a patchwork of crumbling stone and gaping holes.

Hector stood at the edge, his eyes scanning, searching the streets below. Jude concentrated on the placement of his steps as he crossed over toward him, careful to avoid the parts of the roof that had already collapsed or seemed unstable.

"Hector, don't do this."

"You don't understand. You *can't*." Wind swirled between them. "And you know what? I envy you, Jude. I do. You'll never have to know how it feels to lose your family. Go back to the Guard, back to the Prophet. That is your place—it always has been. This is mine. I will follow the revenant all the way to Tel Amot if I must. I swore an oath to my dead family that I would set right what had been done to them."

"You swore an oath to obey and serve the Order!" The words bellowed out of him. "You swore an oath to *me*."

Hector's eyes narrowed. "This has nothing to do with you. I should never have accepted a position in your Guard."

Anger flared, sudden and sharp. Jude launched forward, slamming into Hector. Hector reared back, throwing his fist toward Jude's jaw. It collided with a sickening crack that rang through his entire skull. This was not the elegant, practiced combat of a Paladin soldier. Nor was it the playful, juvenile wrestling Hector had greeted him with at Kerameikos. This was a fistfight, a brawl, born of hurt and consuming anger.

"You selfish"—Jude jabbed an elbow into Hector's throat—"*ungrateful*—"

Hector's leg swept his feet from under him. Jude caught himself, stumbling before he toppled into a sheer drop.

"Me, selfish?" Hector shot back, charging at him again. He swung a fist, and Jude raised his hand to catch the blow.

This was no different from the way Hector used to act out. Picking fights, mouthing off, behaving as though the rules of their world had been put there for him to break.

Jude tightened his grip on Hector's fist. "I chose you, Hector! Against my father's wishes, against Penrose's advice. I *chose* you."

"I never asked you to!" Hector replied. "I never wanted you to. But when have you ever cared about what I wanted?"

He swung at Jude with his other hand, and then they were grappling, pulling at clothes and hair and skin. Grasping Hector's shirt, Jude drew him close, pinning him against the edge of the roof.

Even cornered, Hector had never been one to back down. He looked fiercely into Jude's eyes and bit out, "You have *always* asked more of me than I knew how to give."

It hit Jude harder than any blow from Hector's fists.

Jude's grip slackened, and Hector pushed himself away from the edge of the roof, breathing heavily. Jude was suddenly, excruciatingly aware of the sound of his own heartbeat. Anger burned low in his gut, but the rest of him felt numb. He closed his eyes. He wasn't a boy any longer. He was Keeper of the Word. Leader of the Paladin Guard. He knew his duty.

When he opened his eyes, Hector had turned away.

"If you don't return with me, then I will have no choice," Jude said to Hector's back. "As captain of the Paladin Guard, I will have to dispense punishment for the desertion of your sworn duty." The words were firm, but his heart thundered out their lie.

Hector stopped, and for a moment, hope welled inside Jude that his words had jolted Hector back to his right mind.

But then Hector spun, unsheathing his sword like lightning. Jude didn't move. The blade sang through the air—and then stopped, inches from Jude's throat.

"You're going to end me?" Hector asked, his eyes as sharp as his blade. "How are you going to do that when you can't even draw your sword against me?"

Jude reached for his hilt. A flare of energy hit his Grace, as if the Pinnacle Blade was responding to him. Chastising him. As if it knew its true purpose was to protect the Last Prophet and was warning him he could not draw it for the first time now.

But even without the blade's warning, Jude knew that he could not draw his sword on Hector, no matter the purpose. He let his hand fall back to his side.

"Just let me go, Jude." The words came out a desperate plea.

"I *can't.*"

Hector's eyes met his, and something flickered through them, something that felt akin to the ugly shame that twisted Jude's gut. Like the shock of cold water on a warm summer night, they flashed with sudden understanding. The thread that had been fraying between them for years snapped.

The ground shifted under them. Before Jude could say anything, before he could begin to put words to the secret that had slipped into the light, the stones beneath his feet gave way.

He registered, vaguely, the sound of Hector calling his name as the world spun out of place. The roof crumbled beneath him, plunging him down to the dark sanctum below.

31

BERU

BERU'S HEART POUNDED AS SHE BOARDED THE TRAIN. ONCE THEY PULLED OUT of Pallas Athos Station, it would be the first time she was separated from Ephyra in her entire life.

Yet despite the fear and uncertainty, there was a small seed of excitement. Ever since she was a little girl growing up in the dusty town of Medea, she had always wanted to ride the Armillary Rail. Some said it was the greatest feat of Graced engineering the Six Prophetic Cities had ever seen. It had been built almost two hundred years ago by the world's most skilled Graced artificers to connect five of the Six Prophetic Cities over land, making it possible for landlocked Endarrion and Behezda to reach the other cities in under a week. Since then, the Armillary Rail had expanded considerably, with routes weaving in and out of the countryside, connecting trade routes and ports. Every day, it brought hundreds of foreign travelers to Tel Amot. Occasionally, a handful them would find their way to Beru's village, bringing with them stories of the Six Prophetic Cities and beyond.

Now, Beru was one of those people, returning to Tel Amot with knowledge and stories of all the other places where she and Ephyra had lived the last five years. She looked around at the rest of the passengers—the father pointing out the gleaming gears and brasswork on the train car to his tiny daughter, the brand-new traveler trailing behind the porter with a dazed expression, the young couple walking hand in hand through the compartments to the tearoom car.

Beru wondered what it would be like to be one of these people. To luxuriate in arrival and departure, in the flashing of the world going by through a window. To live on time that was not stolen, but her own.

The train whistle blew, startling her from her thoughts, and a moment later they had begun to move, whisking smoothly over the tracks. The attendant poured her tea, and Beru let the cup cool, trying not to think about where she was headed and what she was leaving behind.

The door of the compartment shucked open. The sight of Hector Navarro standing there stole every scrap of wonder from her mind.

He'd found her again. And this time, there was no one to stand between them.

As he prowled inside the car, Beru thought back, not to the last time she'd seen him, but to the first. She and Ephyra had arrived from the city of Charis with his parents and walked the seven miles to their seaside village. Hector's older brother, Marinos, had welcomed them at the bottom of the walkway and ushered them into the cramped cottage for a dinner of fresh-caught fish, pickled vegetables, and warm bread. It was more food than Beru and Ephyra had eaten in months.

Halfway through the meal, the youngest Navarro son had raced into the house in a swirl of sand and seagrass. He sat down, tore off a strip of flatbread and, before Beru even had a chance to introduce herself, cheerfully began describing the turtle nest he'd discovered in a tidal pool. She could still remember his face as it had been then—cheeks still plump with baby fat, the dark pink flush of exertion creeping up to his ears, the way his hair plastered against his forehead, damp with sweat and sea spray. And those eyes, as dark as coals. Even in the awkward thrall of youth, Hector had been striking.

Now, as she sat at the back of the train car sipping tea, Beru watched as those eyes found her. She couldn't read his face at all as he sat down across from her. Was that pain in his eyes? Fear? Hatred? Between them, a bronze teapot wafted mint-scented steam.

When he didn't say anything, she asked, "Shall I call for more tea?"

She reached for the teapot. His hand shot across the table, catching her wrist. She'd rewrapped it, but they both knew what lay beneath the thin layer of cloth. She watched him closely, feeling strangely calm as she waited to see his next move.

His hand was warm and rough against her wrist. He wasn't even holding on tightly—to anyone else sitting in the train car, it might even look like he was being tender. If they didn't look too closely. Beru swallowed as the pad of his thumb dragged over the delicate bones of her wrist to rest against her pulse.

"I'm still flesh and blood," she said. "Same as I was before. Same as you."

His eyes flashed, and he jerked his hand back from her wrist as if he'd been burned. "We are not the same."

She looked down, surprised by how much his words hurt. "How did you find me?"

His jaw tightened. He let out a breath, and for a moment Beru was sure she'd be treated to more stubborn silence. "The train ticket you left," he said at last. "I took it from your friend. Why Tel Amot?"

The coast flashed by through the window. Beru didn't know how to answer his question. She could have gone back to Tarsepolis, to Valletta, to any number of other cities. She had chosen Tel Amot. That sunbaked, dust-cracked land where she had begun. And where she had ended.

"Why? For the same reason you want to kill me," she said. "I thought if I could go back . . . maybe there would be a way to fix things. But there's not. I know that. You do, too. Killing me isn't going to bring your family back."

"It will stop anyone else from dying," Hector said in a low voice. "It will stop anyone else from having to bury bodies marked by a pale handprint."

Beru closed her eyes. So many times, she'd pictured what must have happened that day after she and Ephyra fled. Hector returning to find his father's cold body. She felt sick every time she thought of it.

"I never wanted any of them to get hurt," she said quietly. "Your mother and father. Marinos."

Hector's shoulders tensed. "Don't say his name."

Hector's brother had been seventeen when he died. He'd been patient and affectionately teasing to his kid brother, riling him up with a few choice words and placating him just as easily. At the tender age of eleven, Beru had been hopelessly in love with both of them.

She could still remember how she and Hector used to beg Marinos to climb the rocky sea cliffs near their home or sneak into the vineyards of Sal Triste to taste the sweet grapes. On the few occasions Marinos had relented to their mischief, they were triumphant, invincible. Marinos had been Hector's hero.

Until Beru and Ephyra had taken him away.

"You don't have the right to speak about him," Hector said.

"I see his face every time I shut my eyes," Beru replied. "Do you still remember it? His smile was ever so slightly crooked—the left side of his mouth pulled up more than the right. He had that little scar just above his right eyebrow. I never found out how he got that."

"*Don't.*" Hector was shaking.

"I can't imagine," she said, her voice low, "what it must be like for you. To see me like this, alive and well, when your family—"

His fist slammed onto the table, cutting her off and startling the few people around them. Hector kept his eyes lowered until the other passengers lost interest and went back to their tea and chitchat.

"You think I want your *pity?*"

Beru flinched at the cutting disdain in his voice. "It's not about pity, Hector. I loved your family."

"*Stop* it," he said. "Just stop—Stop pretending that you're not—"

"Not what?" Beru demanded, the long fuse of her temper now alight. "A monster?"

Hector gripped the edge of the table hard enough to crack it. "You rose from the dead. Ever since then, you and your sister have been traveling down a path that leads to darkness. You'll pull the whole world into it with you."

"What are you talking about?"

Hector's words filled her with dread. She couldn't make sense of them, but they felt true in a way she couldn't explain. As though she'd dreamed them once, and now was remembering.

"It's time for this to end," Hector said. In his coal-dark eyes, Beru saw the pain and grief that stoked the flames of his fury. "I am the only person who knows what you are. That means I'm the only person who can stop you. No one else will suffer because of you. I want you to see the cost of every breath you've taken on this earth."

"I don't need you for that," Beru said. "Every night, I see them. The faces of everyone who's ever died so I could live."

"Then why?" he asked, desperation breaking his voice. "Why do you let her do it?"

Beru made herself meet his gaze. He wanted the revenant, he

wanted the specter of his grief. But the only thing she could offer Hector was the truth. "I wanted to live."

Hector looked as lost as she felt. "And now?"

An hour ago, she would have given the same answer. But the moment she'd seen Hector standing in the crypt, something had changed. As if the truth of what she and Ephyra had done had grown heavier. No longer something she could carry.

She had come to Pallas Athos to find Eleazar's Chalice, so she could finally be free of the curse of her second life. But now, sitting across from Hector Navarro as the train snaked its way along an endless coast, Beru knew that she would never be free.

"Now," she said, "I want to go home."

32

JUDE

SOMEONE WAS SHAKING JUDE. AND SAYING THINGS. JUDE DID NOT KNOW WHAT things they were saying, but they seemed to be saying them at him.

Groaning, he opened his eyes. Bright white stars danced in front of his vision before slowly resolving into the features of a face.

"Oh, good. You're not dead."

Warm peat-dark eyes blinked down at him from beneath unkempt sand-colored hair. Faint freckles dotted a narrow nose and pale cheeks. Jude wondered if he should count them. But before he could embark on this task, a jolt of panic shot through him as he remembered just how he had ended up lying here in a dark, dank sanctum.

He lurched forward, pushing himself upright. Pain screamed through his left arm. "Hector, he—Where did he—?"

"He's gone," the stranger said flatly.

"Gone? But—" Jude looked back at the stranger. Only he wasn't quite a stranger, he realized as they locked eyes. Like a faint imprint, he could see those eyes staring up at him, wide with fear, from the floor of the crumbling mausoleum. They had held on Jude then, lingering in a way that had prickled at his skin.

"You're the other prisoner," Jude said. "You—This is—"

"Anton," the boy supplied.

Jude's mind, fuzzy with pain and disorientation, stuttered to a halt. "What?"

"My name," the boy said, leaning toward him, "is Anton."

"Anton," Jude echoed, and then sucked in a breath. He was worse off than he thought. Sitting up took most of his energy. Clasping a hand over his bleeding shoulder, he said, "This is your fault."

"*My* fault?" Anton sounded like he might laugh, though Jude couldn't imagine a less appropriate response.

"You told Hector where to find the Pale Hand's sister." Jude sucked in another labored breath. "You led him to her."

"He was going to kill me."

Jude didn't believe that. "He wouldn't have hurt you."

Anton gaped. "Did he tell you that before or after he threw you off a roof?"

"I fell," Jude corrected stiffly, but even he knew it was a poor defense. Anton was right. He didn't want to think about what he'd seen in Hector today. How could the person who had leapt from waterfalls with him, who'd snuck wine from the Order's storerooms and broken curfews to talk and laugh with him until dawn, be the same person who had cursed his friendship and left him to bleed on the floor of a crumbling mausoleum?

"Fine," Jude said at last. "I'm not blaming you for your cowardice—"

"Well, that's awfully generous—"

"But now Hector and the girl are *gone*."

"That," said Anton, "is not actually my problem."

"Then why are you here?"

Anton's jaw clenched, and when he spoke again, his amusement was gone. "Look. Whether you think your friend was really going to kill me or not, you did save my life. I'm just doing my part to make sure you don't die. If you don't want my help, fine. We can part ways here."

Jude said nothing.

Anton sighed. "Let me at least take you to a healer. There's a row of tavernas near the marina. We can start there."

"I don't need—" Jude began, but a tremendous wave of dizziness overtook him and he had to close his eyes.

When they opened again, Anton was staring at him. "Can you even stand?"

"I'm fine."

"You fell off a roof," Anton said again. "You're not fine. I'm surprised you're even in the vicinity of fine. You should probably be dead."

"I have the Grace of Heart."

"I noticed," Anton answered blandly, sweeping his eyes over Jude in a way that made his skin prickle again. "Doesn't make you invincible. Someone needs to look at that shoulder."

"It'll heal. I need to find Hector. I need to—"

"He's long gone by now, and aside from that, you'll be no help to him in your current state." He huffed, clearly annoyed. "Let me just help you."

Jude closed his eyes and breathed in deeply, summoning the strength to move through a koah. He fanned out his hands and began to lean into his back foot, but another wave of dizziness hit him and he wavered. When he opened his eyes again, Anton was right beside him.

"Jude. It's Jude, right?" Anton asked, blinking down at him.

Jude grunted in agreement.

"All right then, Jude. Stop being an idiot and let me help you."

Jude let out a breath. He was not in the practice of accepting help from . . . whatever this boy was, but he didn't have many other options. Tucking himself under Jude's injured arm, Anton helped him stand. They hobbled out of the sanctum and onto the scorched steps of the mausoleum. Exhaustion hit Jude like a train as soon as the hot morning sun touched him. His knees buckled.

"Whoa!" Anton cried, struggling to keep his own balance as Jude started to fall. Carefully, he leaned down so Jude could sit on the steps. "Wait here."

Jude lolled his head back against the broken pillar behind him. He wasn't sure how much time passed, but when he opened his eyes again, Anton had returned with a package wrapped in crinkly white paper. The scent of sugar and nuts hit him as Anton unwrapped it.

Jude stared down at the triangle of golden-brown dough, sprinkled with sesame seeds and crushed pistachios. "Did you—Is that *dessert?*"

"They're selling them up the road, near the city gates. Here." He shook the pastry in front of Jude's face. "You need to eat to recover your strength. Unless you're too busy bleeding on everything."

"I'm not bleeding anymore," Jude said, although he didn't actually know if that was true. His entire side throbbed, every breath harder than the last. He did not have the stamina to both argue with Anton and stay conscious. He ate the pastry. Rich syrup oozed over his tongue, just this side of too sweet. But the flaky texture as he bit through the layers was nothing short of delightful.

"Good, right?"

Jude licked a bit of pistachio off his thumb. "I've never eaten street dessert before." He'd never eaten street anything before. Pallas Athos was the first city he'd ever been to.

Anton beamed.

"All right," he said when Jude was done. "Let's try this again."

To Jude's surprise, the sugar helped. Aided by Anton, he was able to stand up and hobble down the stairs. He stopped at the bottom to catch his breath. The pain in his side had dulled to an ache. He wiped the sweat from his brow and then looked up.

The white tiers of the High City rose up before him like a great monument of marble and limestone. Crowning the top was the Temple of Pallas. The home of the Order of the Last Light. It felt a world away.

"It's this way," Anton said, tugging Jude toward a narrow road that led away from the High City and down toward the docks.

Jude gazed over his shoulder at the temple. He thought about how he'd felt, only two days ago, making that long journey up the Sacred Road to the Temple of Pallas. Leading the Order of the Last Light back to the City of Faith. Finding the Last Prophet. He was finally walking the path he'd been meant for his entire life.

The path was never supposed to take him here. He didn't know how he could have gotten so off track. He knew he had to go back. He just didn't know how he could do it without Hector.

So he allowed Anton to lead him down the street, the low sun at their backs. He focused on the steady beat of his own heart, the gentle pressure of breath in his lungs. And tried to think of nothing at all.

33

ANTON

THE LATE AFTERNOON CROWD AT THE HIDDEN SPRING WAS ALREADY PLENTY drunk when Anton and Jude arrived. The swordsman's strength had deteriorated considerably, and by the time they stepped through the colonnaded entrance, he was leaning heavily against Anton. He had lost a lot of blood. Anton knew that, because much of it had soaked through Anton's tunic.

"Just a bit farther, I promise," Anton muttered.

The taverna was laid out like a horseshoe around a large central courtyard, with zigzagging stairs and walled walkways that led to rooms stacked in tiers, mimicking the city itself. A crumbling fountain dribbled water into a murky pool in the center of the courtyard, where sailors, dockworkers, and Sentry cadets gathered on stone benches around card tables.

The Hidden Spring was one of many tavernas that lined the docks of Pallas Athos, in an area particularly popular with passing sailors looking for cheap food, copious amounts of wine, a semisoft bed and someone to keep that bed warm. Anton preferred the tavernas closer to the marina square, but it seemed wise to avoid his usual haunts.

The scent of roasting meats and burning valerian wafted over Anton and Jude as they stumbled through the crowd, avoiding serving girls carrying trays of watered-down wine and muddy ale. Anton's gaze inevitably found an open sack of coins sitting on a card table, surrounded by what looked like a contentious game of canbarra.

One of the players was bearded, bald-headed, and so tall that even sitting he nearly matched the height of the serving boy at his elbow. Dark, swirling tattoos climbed up from his wrists to his shoulders, bare to the sun. A healer.

Anton shoved Jude down onto the edge of the crumbling fountain. "Wait here."

Jude nodded, listing to the side.

Anton caught him and put one of Jude's hands on the edge of the fountain. "Hold on to this."

He turned away, craning his neck over the crowd to find the card-playing healer again.

A thump and a sudden splash sounded behind him. Anton whirled. One of Jude's legs was flopped over the edge of the fountain. The rest of him was in the water.

"There's a swordsman in the fountain," someone called with mild concern.

Two large sailors were already heaving Jude out of the water as Anton dashed over.

"This yours?" one asked. Before Anton could answer, they shoved the sopping swordsman at him.

Anton stumbled as Jude slung his arms around his neck, blinking up at him. His eyes were grassy green in the light of the courtyard.

"The water," he informed Anton gravely, "is not for bathing."

"Oh no?" Anton asked, biting back a laugh. "Easy now. Let's sit down."

Jude didn't seem to realize his arms were still around Anton, and as he collapsed to the ground, he dragged Anton with him.

"I've had some time to reflect," Jude said, slumping back against the fountain, "and I think I may need a healer."

"Yeah," Anton said, disentangling himself. "Working on it."

He heaved himself to his feet. The healer was dead ahead. Anton marched over, squeezing between two stout sailors who goaded the card players on. With as much bravado as he could manage, he demanded, "How much is the pot?"

"It's too late to get dealt in. You'll have to wait for the next hand," the healer said, waving him off.

Anton lifted the sack of coins from the table.

"Hey," exclaimed the healer's opponent, a scrawny, rough-looking fellow. "What in the Wanderer's name do you think you're—?"

"Forty virtues?" Anton asked, tossing the sack back down. "I'll give you fifty-five if you put your cards down right now and come upstairs with me."

The sailor behind Anton choked out a laugh.

The healer leaned back in his chair, raising one thick eyebrow. "Well. That *is* an interesting proposition. But I'm not sure my husband would approve." He inclined his head at the scrawny man across from him, who gave Anton a smile that managed to be both pleasant and threatening.

"What? No. I'm not asking you to *come up to my room*," Anton stuttered. "I mean. I *am* asking you to come up to my room. But not like—"

"Is that blood?" The healer's husband pointed.

Anton looked down at himself.

"It's blood," the healer confirmed.

"So," Anton said. "Are you going to help us out, or what?"

"Us?"

Anton glanced back at Jude, who was still slumped by the fountain.

"Behezda's mercy," the healer muttered. "Is that who I think it is?"

"Oh no," the scrawny man said. "I know that look. You're not getting us mixed up in whatever this mess is, Yael."

The healer dropped one large hand onto his husband's shoulder and leaned in, kissing him briefly on the cheek. "Relax, dear," he said. "There'll be plenty of time for you to cheat me out of whatever money I earn after I'm done earning it."

"Oh, all right," his husband replied waspishly. "I was getting bored of beating you, anyway."

The healer rolled his eyes as he swept toward the fountain, Anton at his heels. Together, they lifted Jude awkwardly from the ground. The crowd parted easily for Yael, who was so tall he had to stoop to wrap his arm around Jude's waist as they maneuvered up the zigzagging stairs.

Once Jude was safely curled up on the bed of one of the taverna's open rooms, Yael turned back to Anton.

"I'll do it for eighty virtues," he said.

That was nearly all the money Anton had left. Enough for a train ticket and a good meal.

Or enough to pay a cranky healer of questionable moral rectitude.

"I said fifty," Anton pointed out.

"You said fifty-five, and if you wanted charity, you should have taken him to the Temple of Keric."

A temple would have been too conspicuous. By now, Illya had surely found out that Anton had escaped the citadel, and he'd be scouring the city for signs of him. This required discretion. And discretion always had a price.

"Sixty," Anton countered.

"Seventy-five."

Gritting his teeth, Anton dug out his coin purse.

Yael smiled as Anton plopped the purse in his large palm. "Your friend thanks you for your generosity, I'm sure."

He knelt beside Jude's pallet and laid out the necessary accoutrements of his trade—cuttings from the blood garden, which would provide the *esha* to heal Jude, and oils to draw the patterns of binding.

Anton's eyes traced the intricate lines of ink that ran along Yael's long arms in fractal spirals. All healers tattooed the patterns of binding onto their skin to keep their powers focused.

Yael painted out those same patterns on Jude's pallid skin. Placing his broad hands on Jude's arm, he closed his eyes. Anton watched, transfixed, as the bloodied flesh began to knit itself back together. When he looked back at Yael, he found the healer looking down at Jude with a thoughtful expression.

"You know," he said conversationally, "there's a rumor going around that the silver-sailed ship sitting in the Pallas Athos harbor belongs to none other than the Order of the Last Light. Your friend here know anything about that?"

He sounded merely curious, but Anton couldn't help being wary.

"He's not really my friend," he said.

"You sure? You went through a lot of trouble to get him a healer."

Anton looked down at his bloody tunic. The trouble he'd gone through for Jude had nothing to do with friendship. He barely knew Jude. But something had rooted him to the ground when Jude had arrived at the mausoleum. As he fought with Hector on the roof.

It was the way Anton's Grace reacted to Jude's *esha*. It scared him, especially now that he knew just who that stormlike *esha* belonged to. But there was another feeling, beyond fear. That unconscious pull that wove its way around Anton and made it impossible to turn away.

Whatever it was, he didn't like it. Yael was right—Anton had gone through a lot of trouble to help Jude. But now that he had, he didn't need to stick around. He didn't need to succumb to that pull.

"Looks like my work here's done," Yael said, unfolding his long limbs and standing to his full height in the middle of the room.

"Wait," Anton said, struck with an idea. "The sailors you're with. Did they just cast anchor, or will they be blowing out soon?"

"Tomorrow evening," Yael said. "Remzi likes to keep a tight schedule."

"Remzi?"

"My husband," Yael replied. "Skinny fellow you almost started a fight with?"

"Oh, the canbarra player."

Yael's eyes crinkled. "You play?"

Anton smirked.

Yael laughed. "That good, eh? I'd say you should come down and join us for a hand, but you've nothing to stake, do you?"

He laughed again, tossing and catching Anton's coin purse in one palm as he ducked out of the room.

Anton was left with a newly healed, unconscious swordsman and the edged, flighty panic that said it was time to get out of this city. For more than one reason.

He turned back toward the door and stopped. There, lying against the wall, was Jude's sword. He vaguely remembered that it had fallen from Jude's belt, and Anton had tossed it into the room before laying Jude down on the cot. It gleamed at him now, weighty, elegant. A testament to fine craftsmanship. Anton stared at it a moment longer and realized that Yael was wrong. He did have something to stake. Something expensive, rare, and, best of all, would cost Anton absolutely nothing.

Anton had done bad things before—ruthless things, selfish things—and while guilt always followed, it was never enough to stop him from doing such things again. He'd been repentant the first time he'd stolen, from an innocent family who'd been kind enough to take him in. He'd told himself he had no other choice when he held a knife to the throat of a man who had once protected him on the canals of Valletta. But none of these things, nor the thousand other tiny wrongs that made up his life, had been enough to make him turn back.

He wouldn't turn back now, either. He would leave this city behind, get as far away as he could, until Pallas Athos was just a bad memory he could let fade. He would go somewhere with no Pale Hand, no monstrous brothers, and no swordsmen named Jude. He could let go of them all, like stones sinking to the bottom of the sea. Still there, but no more significant than the thousands of others that lay unturned below dark water.

He picked up the sword.

34

HASSAN

"WE DON'T HAVE MUCH TIME."

Khepri's voice was brisk and urgent as she looked around the table at Penrose, Osei, and Hassan. For hours the four of them had been here in the villa's library, maps and books and papers spread out across the table. Petrossian, Yarik, and Annuka had gone up to the agora to meet with the refugee army.

Over the course of the afternoon, Khepri had given Hassan a run-down of the army, and indeed their numbers were small. Three hundred men and women had pledged themselves, although according to Khepri, more and more had been coming as the rumors that the prince was in Pallas Athos reached the camps in other cities.

Even with the addition of the four hundred Paladin from the Order of the Last Light, they were still far outnumbered by the Witnesses. Khepri and the other refugees had estimated that the Hierophant had several thousand soldiers in Nazirah—his own die-hard followers and Herati citizens who had turned traitor.

But the refugee army and the Paladin had Grace and the element of surprise on their side.

The problem they faced now was time.

"When Reza was held captive by the Witnesses with Godfire, he said he heard them talk about something called the Day of Reckoning," Khepri said. "There are other refugees who say they'd heard them talk about this, too. That's what they call the day they're planning to unleash their Godfire on the Graced."

"And you know when it is?" Penrose asked.

"We think the Hierophant is planning it for the Festival of the Flame," Khepri said.

"Fitting," Petrossian said grimly.

"It's a day of celebration in Herat," Khepri explained. "The festival that commemorates the founding of Nazirah, and the first time the lighthouse was lit."

"That's ten days from now," Hassan said. If he were back in Nazirah, if the Hierophant had never seized it, he would be helping his mother and father prepare—decorating the palace with lily and pearl, inviting dancers and poets, sampling the menus for the citywide feast that would last for three days.

But there would be no dancers this year. No poetry. No feast.

"Ten days," Penrose said. "It's three days sailing to Nazirah, if the good weather holds. We'd need to leave in less than a week."

"Will it be enough time for the Order to get here?"

"We'll need a few days to provision that many ships. Even with Grace-woven sails, it will be almost five days to sail here," Penrose replied. "And that's before they go on to Nazirah."

Hassan worried the edge of his lip. If Khepri was right about the Festival of the Flame, they couldn't afford to wait for the Order. If they set sail too late, they'd arrive in a city of ashes.

As Penrose and Khepri continued discussing the tight timeline, Hassan's gaze drifted to the wall, where a marble relief stretched from floor to ceiling, depicting the famous Reconquest of Pallas Athos from over a century ago. It was one of Hassan's favorite stories. Desperate to win her city-state back from King Vasili and his invading Novogardian army, the priestess Kyria had snuck into the city with a small band of loyal soldiers dressed in plainclothes and successfully retook the stronghold of the citadel. When the Novogardian troops figured out what was going on, their forces poured into the High City, leaving the harbor defenseless. That was when Kyria's ally and lover, the Princess of Charis, arrived with a fleet of ships to capture the harbor. In the marble depiction, the priestess and her princess stood together on the steps of the Temple of Pallas wearing crowns of laurel set with gold leaf, looking down at a sea of lapis.

A seed of a plan rooted in Hassan's mind. He turned to Penrose. "Tell the Order not to come to Pallas Athos. Tell them to sail straight for Nazirah."

"Straight for Nazirah?" Penrose asked. "Prince Hassan, we only have one ship here in Pallas Athos. It's not enough to carry the Herati army. We still need more ships."

"I believe I can be of some help."

Hassan whirled toward the entrance of the library to find Lethia standing there. "Aunt Lethia." He pushed himself from the table and strode toward her at once. "I thought you wanted no part of this."

Lethia had never been a humble woman by any stretch, but in this moment, she looked humbled. "I took some time to think everything over and . . . I owe you an apology. All of you." She turned to the Guard. "Earlier, when I questioned your motives, it was only because I feared for what all of this means for Hassan. He only barely made it out of Nazirah. My brother and his wife were not so lucky. I worry about them every day, and I suppose, rather selfishly, I didn't want to have to worry about Hassan, too. I apologize for how I reacted."

Penrose bowed her head. "Thank you."

Hassan swallowed and turned to his aunt. "I owe you an apology, too. I spoke harshly, and I should have realized how difficult the past few weeks have been for you. Herat is your country, too."

"You're right," she said. "Herat is my homeland. That's why I am going to do everything I can to help you return. Luckily, I know exactly how."

"What are you talking about?" Khepri asked, moving toward them.

"I'm talking about a small fleet of ships with top-of-the-line defenses," Lethia replied. "And a loyal merchant who will dedicate them and their crews to saving Herat."

Hassan blinked at her in surprise. "Aunt Lethia—are you sure?"

"Of course," she replied, striding toward the map table and drumming her fingers between the port of Pallas Athos and the harbor of Nazirah. "Cirion is my son. Even if he was raised here in Pallas Athos, Herat is his country, too."

"No," Hassan said. "I mean, are you sure you want to help us?"

Lethia's hand paused on the map. "Hassan," she said, more seriously. "If this is what you've decided you need to do, then I stand alongside you."

He knew she meant the words. Lethia could seem flippant and insincere at times, but she was never one to go back on her word. Whatever had changed Lethia's mind, Hassan trusted that she would get him back to Nazirah, no matter what it took.

"When can you speak to your son?" Khepri asked.

"They're returning from a voyage tomorrow. I'll send word now," Lethia replied, rising to leave. "I know he'll help."

"There's one more thing," Hassan said as Lethia turned to go. "I know there are other refugees who fled Herat. Most of them went to Charis. Someone should go to them, make sure they're safe."

"And ask them to join us," Khepri added. "They won't get there in time to take part in the initial assault, but once we've secured the city, they can return to help us rebuild."

On the other side of the room, Lethia paused. "Send me."

All four of them turned to the door.

"You?" Osei asked.

"Why not?" she replied, turning toward them. "I have contacts in Charis. I can make arrangements to go there and tell the other refugees what you're doing."

Gratitude washed over Hassan. "There is no one I trust more than you to do this. Thank you."

He didn't just mean for this task. He couldn't put into words how much her support meant to him—even after her own doubt and apprehension about the prophecy and his role in it, she had still risen to the occasion to help him in every way she could. From the look she gave him, he saw that she understood. With a brief nod, she left the room.

As afternoon stretched into early evening, Hassan retreated to his dressing room to ready himself to go to the agora, where the rest of the Guard were waiting. Together, they would stand on the steps of the Temple of Pallas and reveal the secret of the Prophets' unfinished last prophecy, and tell the refugees how Hassan, at last, had completed it.

Lethia's servants adorned him in brocade silks of wheat gold and river green, and anointed him with sandalwood and myrrh oil. Atop his brown curls, they set a woven crown of real laurel leaves. It wasn't the gold and emerald of the Crown of Herat. Not yet. But that crown would be his again soon enough. He had seen it.

When the servants finished dressing him, Hassan dismissed them and walked out to stand alone on the balcony overlooking the peristyle garden. A lone figure stood among the flowers, enclosed by a white marble colonnade. It was Khepri, surrounded by young saplings, with figs and olives swelling sleek and dark on their branches.

Before he could reconsider, Hassan descended the staircase, strode across the tiled walkway lined with white and purple hyacinths, and drew up beside Khepri at the edge of the reflecting pool. A thin fan of water flowed down to the delicate silver water organ, its tune lilting gently over them.

He followed Khepri's gaze to where it rested on the pale blue blossoms that drifted lazily on the water's surface, perfuming the air with their sweetly musky fragrance. The blue lily of Herat. Some of the blooms had begun to close, furling their petals tight to sink below the surface of the water, where they would wait, hidden, to resurface in the light of morning.

"They're beautiful, aren't they?" Hassan said. "When my father was courting my mother, he sent three barges of these blossoms up the Herat River to her door. He told her that when they married, he would put fresh blue lilies in every room of the palace."

Khepri closed her eyes, breathing in deeply. "They smell like home."

"Al-Khansa, right?" he asked. Al-Khansa was smaller than Herat's capital, a vibrant town to the south of Nazirah on the bank of the Herat River. It was always the last stop on the royal family's tour down the river at the beginning of the flood season.

Khepri nodded. "Every year during the Festival of the Flood, the whole city is perfumed with the scent of blue lilies. Vendors sell them by the side of the road for people to send into the river with their votives. They say the flowers promise a fruitful year."

Hassan plucked a blossom off its lily pad gently. He remembered the last time he'd been alone with Khepri like this—overlooking the camps and the children playing. How she'd touched his hand and leaned into him like a date palm bowing to a desert wind. He had drawn back, afraid of letting anything happen when his lie about who he truly was still stood between them. But she knew now. He had nothing to hide from her. He reached to tuck the lily into her hair.

Khepri flinched back, and the flower fell to the ground between them.

"I—Your Grace—" she stammered.

Those words—*Your Grace*—instantly diffused the warmth and familiarity between them. There was nothing of the easy laughter, the instinctual intimacy they'd had in the Herati camps that first night in the agora.

Hassan was reminded that he hadn't been the only one hiding something that night.

His hand was still hovering by Khepri's cheek. He let it drop to his side. "What did you mean yesterday, when you said that it was selfish not to tell me about the Godfire when we first met?"

"We should go," Khepri said, ducking her head. "The others are waiting."

"Khepri."

She sucked in a breath, shaking herself slightly. Her amber eyes, always disarming to Hassan, held something in them he hadn't seen there before. Something like regret. Guilt.

"The days after I arrived in Pallas Athos were some the worst of my life," she said. "If I wasn't worrying about the other refugees, I was terrified about what was happening back in Nazirah. I fixated on all the awful stories I heard about the Hierophant and what he and his Witnesses were doing. It was all I thought about."

It was what those first weeks had been like for him, too.

"But when you showed up in the agora, it felt like, for a few short hours, despite all of that anger and worry, I could breathe again."

Hassan stared, stunned to hear her voice the thoughts that had run through his own mind, as though she had reached inside him and grasped them at their roots.

"I didn't tell you about Godfire or what the Witnesses were planning because I wanted to keep that feeling," she said. "I didn't want to ruin it with all that pain and horror. It was selfish. *I* was selfish, for wanting that when my friends—my *brothers*, are—" She choked on the next word.

"I get it," Hassan said softly. "In a way, it's the same reason I didn't tell you who I was. Because all of the responsibility and the weight of who I am would have drowned out everything else. That was selfish, too."

"I hated myself. For thinking about something that wasn't saving my brothers." She swallowed, her eyes searching his. "For wanting something else."

It was too much. He couldn't let her leave it at that. Catching her hand in his, he said, "I wanted it, too."

She bowed her head toward his, but didn't speak.

"Now," Hassan said, eagerness creeping into his voice. "Now you know who I really am."

"You're right." Her eyes met his. "Now I know who you really are. You're the key to saving Nazirah." She pulled her hand away slowly. "You are the prince. The Prophet. And I am your soldier."

As her fingers trailed from his, Hassan understood. He bowed his head, feeling foolish.

From the moment he'd met Khepri, Hassan had felt the many ways in which they were the same. Both driven from the home that they loved. Both seeking a way to return to it. He'd thought the only thing standing between them was the lie he'd told her about who he was. But now he saw how the truth stood between them even more powerfully. Even a prince in exile had power over a soldier, and the more he tried to pretend that wasn't true, the less he could be what she really needed him to be. What they all needed him to be.

"Prince Hassan."

He and Khepri both turned toward the edge of the garden, where Penrose and Osei stood, their midnight blue cloaks swept over their shoulders.

"It's time," Penrose said. "The army and the refugees are all waiting for you."

Hassan glanced back at Khepri, but she was already leaving the garden, her back to him. He took a breath and followed.

There was no going back after tonight. Plans had been made, ships were on their way, and a century-old prophecy would soon be fulfilled. It still felt strange to even think it. That he would return to his country not just a prince, but a Prophet. That the vision he'd seen in his dream would soon be real.

He pushed aside all thoughts of Khepri and blue lilies as he reached the edge of the garden where the others waited.

"I'm ready."

35

EPHYRA

"WAKE UP."

Ephyra blinked slowly in the dim light. She tasted salt. Her face felt scrubbed raw, her eyes dried out and stinging. Had she been crying? She wasn't sure. She wasn't sure of anything—not how long she'd been in the cell. Not how much time had passed since the swordsman had left her here.

Not whether her sister's life was now in the hands of a man who wanted Ephyra dead.

Polished black boots clicked against the cut stone of the cell. Ephyra sat up. In the doorway stood a man dressed in a fine charcoal coat. A man she was supposed to have killed.

"Nice place," Illya Aliyev commented, his gold eyes sweeping over the bare cell before coming to rest on Ephyra. She was chilled by the coldness of his smile. "I suppose they save the best cells for the most notorious murderers. Like you—the Pale Hand."

Ephyra froze. Had Hector done it, then? Had he proven to the Sentry what they both knew she was?

But Illya waved his hands. "Just a rumor, of course. But the guards certainly believe it. They warned me at least three times not to come in here."

"Maybe they're right," Ephyra replied, her voice hoarse from disuse. Or perhaps from crying. "You sure you want to be in here with me?"

"I'll risk it."

"What in the Wanderer's name do you want?"

"Now, there's no reason to be rude."

She glared. "That was me being polite. In case you forgot, you are the reason I'm in here."

"Is that so?" he asked, drawing farther into the cell. "I seem to remember it was my brother who took you to that temple."

Ephyra leaned back against the wall and pushed herself to her feet. "And was it your brother who tipped the Sentry off about alleged thieves? I'm not stupid. I know you set us up."

"I had nothing to do with that," Illya said. "You just got unlucky."

Ephyra snorted, turning away. "You don't know the half of it."

He leaned an arm on the wall, blocking her. "Then how do you feel about changing your luck?"

She eyed him. "What does that mean?"

"It looks like one of the Paladin broke my brother out of here. I don't know the details. But I think you do."

Panic rose in Ephyra's throat. He was talking about Hector.

"Ah," Illya said. Her alarm must have been plain on her face. "I'm right."

If Anton had convinced Hector to let him out of his cell, it could only mean he'd led him to Beru. And if Hector figured out what role Beru had played in his family's deaths, he would kill her. Ephyra knew it. She still remembered how Hector's father had turned on them, his grief transformed into murderous rage.

Illya's gold eyes were pinned on her. "You know where they went, don't you?"

"If I did, I wouldn't tell you."

He raised his eyebrows. "That's too bad, because I think we could help each other."

"How is that? You don't have anything I want."

He cocked his head in a way that made him look eerily like his brother. "You're stuck in this cell. I could change that."

Ephyra let out a laugh. "The Sentry isn't going to just let a suspected murderer go free."

"Then it's a good thing I know for a *fact* you couldn't have committed those murders," he replied breezily.

"What are you talking about?"

"The night the Pale Hand killed the priest Armando Curio, you were with me," he said. His expression changed, and suddenly he was cloyingly sweet. "Weren't you, darling? I think I'd know if my wife was a murderer."

"Your wife?" she choked out.

He shrugged. "My intended, if you prefer."

She wanted to tell him she'd prefer he never speak to her again, but he was offering her an alibi and freedom, and that was hard to pass up. If it wasn't a bluff.

"Why would the Sentry of Pallas Athos believe the word of some foreigner?"

"My word is very good here in Pallas Athos," he said with a guileless smile. "I have a few friends in high places. High enough that I can get a prisoner released on my word."

She didn't doubt that this was true. It explained how he'd managed to gain access to her cell.

"I'll be happy to tell the Sentry all of this," he went on. "If you help me find my brother."

"Why do you need to find him so badly?"

There was a pause, and when he spoke again, his tone was different. Quieter. "You don't have a lot in this life you care about, do you?"

Ephyra looked away. She supposed it was obvious how little regard she had for the rest of the world. Beru had always been enough.

"It's the same for me," Illya said. "Sure, I can dress up and play the rich foreigner. I can enjoy a well-made meal, a well-played tune, a well-built woman." His gaze swept over Ephyra. "But those things . . . none of them matter. Not truly. There are precious few things that do. You know that, don't you? I suppose it took me a long time to learn. Too long, perhaps."

Ephyra watched his face soften until he looked just like the young man he was. Until she could almost believe that his words were as earnest as they sounded.

"But now . . ." Illya let out a breath. "I see it. My brother is one of those rare things that truly matters. I will give anything to find him. To earn his forgiveness."

With the silent grace she'd learned as the Pale Hand, Ephyra drew closer until she was a breath away. "Oh, Illya," she said softly. "I must look like the easiest mark in the Six Cities if you think I'm going to buy that horseshit."

Illya flinched. "I'm not lying."

She remembered he'd said the same thing to Anton. "What do you really want with him?"

"I want to protect him."

"From *what?*" Ephyra asked. "I'm not going to pretend I know him that well, but I know what fear looks like, and the only thing that kid's truly afraid of is you."

"Why else would I spend *years* trying to find him? Why would I spend half a fortune hiring scryers to track him down? Why would I race from city to city with nothing more than a *whisper* that he might be there?"

Ephyra held her tongue. She did not want to have anything in common with the manipulator who stood in front of her, but she couldn't help but compare his story to her own. She had traveled what felt like the world over to find a cure for her sister. Illya had done the same to find his brother.

But just because they seemed the same didn't mean they were.

"Fine," Illya said, stepping back. "You still think I'm lying. I'll find him again on my own."

He turned toward the door and the corridor beyond, boots clicking sharply against the stone floor.

Ephyra cursed. She needed to find Anton just as much as Illya did. If anyone knew what had happened to Beru, whether Hector had found her, it was Anton.

"Wait," she called. Illya turned with a polite smile that barely hid the smugness underneath. "I wasn't lying when I said I don't know where they went. But I can take you to where we were staying in the city. Maybe he'll still be there. Maybe he won't."

"That's not promising."

"It's better than nothing, and you know it," Ephyra shot back. "Look, I don't know what your game is, and I certainly don't trust you, but I need to get out of here. Do we have a deal, or not?"

Illya waved a hand. "Trust me, don't trust me. It doesn't matter. I need you, and you clearly need me, which makes us natural allies."

She snorted. "Natural allies? I tried to kill you."

"But you didn't."

"Still might."

He smiled again, his expression half-wolf, half-pup. "I'm willing to take that chance if you are." He held out his hand. "Allies?"

She took it, swallowing as she looked into his honey-gold eyes. She'd spent most of her life bargaining with dark forces. It had never felt like this.

"Allies."

36

JUDE

JUDE WOKE SLOWLY, HIS AWARENESS EBBING AND FLOWING LIKE THE WASH OF a tide. He was inexplicably damp, and the back of his mouth tasted sharply bitter. A dull ache pulsed through his shoulder as he tried to roll over, as if someone had tried to wrench his arm from his body. In a terrible flash, he recalled his sudden, violent fall from the mausoleum roof, and the broken stone that had cut through his shoulder. But when he pressed his fingers there, he found that the flesh had knitted back together, as though the wound had never been.

He stared up at a low, sloping ceiling of cracked white plaster. A square of night sky peeked through the window beside him. The memory of the past day coalesced in his mind as he sat up on the narrow cot, burying his face in his hands.

He was a fool, a fool, a fool. And Hector was gone.

Jude would return to the villa. Tonight. The Guard and the Prophet would know now what had been so clear to him. He wasn't worthy to be Keeper. He would beg the forgiveness of the Prophet, kneel at his feet, lay the Pinnacle Blade on the ground—

The Pinnacle Blade.

He shot to his feet, stomach plummeting when he didn't see the sword beside him. He tried to think. He'd had it after falling from the roof, hadn't he? And when they'd reached the Hidden Spring, Jude shaking with exhaustion, held upright by that boy—Anton—he'd had it then, too.

He had already lost Hector. He could not lose the Pinnacle Blade, too.

Panic pumped through his veins as he dashed out the door and down the stairs. Raucous laughter, overlapping voices, and clinking glasses filtered from the courtyard. Jude paused, considering. The thought of stepping foot out there filled him with unease. Cities and crowds were challenging enough for him, after spending his first nineteen years in the company of the same few hundred people in their remote fort in the mountains. But this went above even braving the crowds in the marina and in the streets. This was the type of place home to criminals and castoffs, ruffians and scoundrels. He could barely believe such a place existed in the City of Faith, and yet here he was. Just one more thing that had turned out nothing like he'd imagined.

But if he was searching for a sword thief, he knew he'd do well to start here. Bracing himself against the damp smell of sweat, smoke, and spit, Jude stepped through the arched entrance. Strings of incandescents drenched the courtyard in a tawny haze. Between stone benches and laurel bushes, clusters of drunken sailors and Sentry cadets sloshed sweet wine and ale onto one another. Around them, coquettish women giggled and young men preened, their draped tunics all but baring their chests to the warm evening air.

"Careful there." A slender young man in a short tunic pushed past Jude with a wink, two pints of muddy-brown ale sloshing in his hands. Jude's gaze followed him to the fountain in the middle of the courtyard, and then, as if drawn there, landed on a familiar figure a few tables away. Anton.

He hadn't left after all.

He was gulping down a pint of ale with no small amount of enthusiasm, face flushing as one of the onlookers goaded him on. When the pint was empty, Anton raised it triumphantly. His eyes held briefly on Jude's and a small smile flickered across his face.

Not a smile. A *smirk*. The kind worn by someone who was used to stares that lingered.

He seemed to be engaged in some sort of card game that had gathered quite a bit of attention from the surrounding drinkers. His gaze dropped from Jude's as his cohort thumped him hard on the shoulder. He ducked down to face his opponent.

And then Jude saw it. The familiar curve of the sheath, the gleam of the inlaid star at the perfectly balanced hilt. The Pinnacle Blade, sitting on a table strewn with cards, coins, and empty glasses.

Jude's vision went white. Anger pulsed like a hot fist in his chest as he charged across the courtyard. The rowdy patrons seemed to press in from all sides—stumbling, jostling, shoving—until at last Jude had threaded through the crowd to the card game.

"You sure you want to risk it?" the man sitting across from Anton said, over the din of drunken chatter.

Anton laughed. "I'll take my chances."

"I wouldn't," Jude said darkly.

Anton flinched but didn't turn to face him.

"Well, now," Anton's opponent said, leaning his chin on his hand as he raked his eyes over Jude like a cat with a pretty bird in its clutches. "Who is this?"

Jude wasn't about to be intimidated by a taverna ruffian. "Jude Weatherbourne. And that is my sword."

The man raised his eyebrows. "Well, that's interesting," he said, "because your young friend here just staked it on a hand of cards."

"He—*what?*"

Anton turned around slowly, his face a mask of innocence, which did not, for one second, fool Jude. "Shouldn't you be upstairs, sleeping off your mortal wounds?"

"Shouldn't *you* be sitting in a cell?" Jude shot back. "Clearly, that's where you belong."

Anton grimaced, dragging a hand through his already disheveled hair. "Could you possibly say that louder, just in case any of the off-duty Sentry here didn't hear you?"

"You're a thief."

"I don't know what you're talking about," Anton replied primly.

"You stole the Pinnacle Blade!"

"What—your sword? I was going to return it."

"You wagered it!" Jude retorted, voice high with disbelief. "How are you planning on returning it if you lose?"

"Oh, Jude," Anton said with a laugh. "I don't *lose.*"

"That sword has been passed down in my family since the dawn of the Prophets. It has one purpose, and one purpose alone. And it is *not* to be wagered in a drunken game of cards!"

"Well, if the sword is so important to you, maybe you shouldn't leave it lying around where anyone could take it."

In that moment, faced with the smirk on Anton's lips and the faint freckles that dotted the bridge of his nose, Jude felt he had never despised a single person more in his entire life.

"You have no idea," he said, his voice trembling with the strain of keeping it even, "*no idea* what you've done. Do you care for no one but yourself?"

Anton's jaw went tight, and Jude saw quite plainly that this accusation had wounded him. "If it weren't for me," Anton said tersely, "you'd still be bleeding out in that mausoleum."

Beside his opponent, a bearded man who wore the marks of a healer spoke up. "I helped, too."

Jude glanced from the healer back to Anton, remembering the look of determination that had crossed his face when Jude had questioned his motives back in the mausoleum. The missing Pinnacle Blade had driven everything else from his thoughts, but now he was forced to consider the fact that this loathsome, selfish thief who sat before him may very well have saved his life.

"If you're quite done," Anton went on coolly, "I have a game to win."

"No, I'm not done," Jude sputtered. "*You* are done. I'm taking my sword."

"Now, boys." Anton's opponent leaned over the table. "I'm afraid the wager's already been set."

Jude narrowed his eyes. "And what exactly has my sword been wagered for?"

"A ticket out of Pallas Athos," Anton replied steadily. "Remzi here is captain of a ship."

"The *Black Cormorant*," the captain said cheerfully. "She's like a Vallettan shop girl. Not much of a looker, but she sure gets around."

Jude flushed at the comparison, but embarrassment only kindled his anger. "You would allow someone like this on your ship? A proven thief? A boy who, until this morning, was a prisoner in the citadel of Pallas Athos?"

The captain blinked at Anton in surprise and then turned to Jude and shrugged. "A bet is a bet. The sword against free passage to Tel Amot."

The sailor sitting beside Anton leaned toward him eagerly, cheeks flushed pink with alcohol. "What were you imprisoned for?"

"Wrongfully imprisoned," Anton corrected loftily. "It was a misunder—"

"Wait," Jude said suddenly, his thoughts catching up with what the captain had just said. "Did you say Tel Amot?"

I will follow the revenant all the way to Tel Amot if I must. That was what Hector had said inside the mausoleum.

Once the possibility of it bloomed in Jude's mind, he found he could not leave it be. He knew, *he knew*, that was where Hector was going. The next words were out of his mouth before he could stop them. "You'll take me aboard, too."

He could feel Anton's eyes on him, but Jude kept his gaze fixed on the captain.

"The initial wager was for a single spot aboard the ship," the captain said, spreading his fingers apart. "I like to think I'm a lenient man, but you can't simply change the terms in the middle of the game."

"It's my blade, so it's my passage you'll be providing."

"Sure," the captain replied lazily. "If you'd like to play for it."

"Play cards?" Jude had never gambled before in his life. He eyed the complicated layout of cards and drinks lined up like battlements. This did not seem like the time or place to start.

"Or perhaps you'll convince your friend to play for your passage instead of his own. He does seem like a good-hearted fellow."

Jude almost never swore, but he felt like doing so now. He wanted to invoke the crudest, most uncouth string of adjectives he could think of. Even if Anton had helped him before, he'd done so only grudgingly, and Jude doubted his capacity for more acts of selflessness.

But that didn't mean that Jude couldn't make a wager of his own. He swallowed the anger building in his throat and brought his hand to his neck, running his fingers along the ribboned gold ring of his torc.

He couldn't be considering this. He wasn't considering it.

Yet, deep in his gut, he knew the decision had already been made. It had been made standing in Hector's empty quarters that morning in the villa. Revenge had been more important to Hector than his duty was.

And Hector was more important to Jude.

He had done everything his father and the Order had ever asked of him, and still, after all of it, he had fallen short. He would fail. He had already failed. He'd abandoned the Prophet. Not for the threat of the Pale Hand and the third harbinger. He'd done it for Hector, and he hadn't hesitated. Lacking in discipline, wavering in his devotion, full of doubt and uncertainty and dreadful longing—Jude was not fit to bear the title of Keeper of the Word. Just as he could hear truth in the hearts of others, he knew that this was the truth of his own.

His fingers found the fastener of the torc at his throat and twisted it open.

"This is pure gold, forged by the Smith King himself," he said, holding it out for not only the captain but also the rest of the gathered sailors to see. "It will more than pay for passage aboard your ship."

Leaning over a white-faced Anton, Jude placed the torc in the center of the card table.

"If you win the wager, the sword and the torc are yours," he said. He focused on keeping his voice even. Authoritative. "If you lose, you will provide passage and board for myself and your opponent. Are these terms acceptable?"

The captain smiled, slow and satisfied. "Well, I do believe this game just got interesting."

37

ANTON

ANTON LEANED OVER THE TABLE THAT SEPARATED HIM AND CAPTAIN BEDRICH Remzi of the *Black Cormorant*, studying the cards between them.

Trove and River had been a favorite card game among sailors, watchmen, and ruffians trying to stave off boredom since the dawn of time. In every city he'd ever been to, the rough element (and Anton counted himself among them) always knew Trove and River. Each hand began with both players drawing six cards, then keeping three in their hand (their trove), and playing one to each of the three communal piles in the center (the river). Players built hands of five using the three cards in the river and two of their trove cards. The best Trove and River players were adaptable, able to change strategies on the fly. It wasn't as elegant as canbarra, Anton's preferred game, but he took what he could get. And what he could get was usually every last one of his opponent's coins.

"I hold," Captain Remzi said, placing down his trove cards.

Around them, some two dozen sailors, already drunk or approaching it, let out jeers and low whistles. Jude stood apart from them, his silent glower louder than any of the sailor's hollers. Anton was all too aware of the swordsman, his *esha* swirling like a thundercloud, tugging at his attention.

He gritted his teeth and played his ace on top of a higher-value poet card. Now was not the time to lose focus.

"Oh, no, you don't want to do *that*." Captain Remzi leaned back in his chair, his eyelids at half-mast in an expression of languid confidence.

He had every reason to be confident. After two contentious rounds, Remzi firmly had the upper hand. Though they wouldn't reveal their cards until the end, Anton had a good idea what cards Remzi had in his trove, based on the ones he'd already played. They would be hard to beat.

"Anton." Jude's voice was stiff and nervous behind him.

Anton didn't even glance at him. If Jude didn't like the way he played, then maybe he shouldn't have bet on him. Anton still didn't understand why he'd done it. One moment, Jude had been yelling at him for borrowing the sword, and the next, he was stripping the golden torc from his throat and demanding passage aboard Remzi's ship. In one instant, he'd tied their fates together—at least until the game ended.

Anton had just wanted to win and sail far away from Pallas Athos and everything in it, including Jude. And yet here Jude was, hovering in thunderous silence over Anton's shoulder. It was unnerving. *Jude* was unnerving.

And he was making Anton lose.

"What's wrong?" Remzi drawled as he played a ten on top of the ace. "Make a mistake?"

Anton knew Remzi could tell he was rattled, though the captain no doubt assumed *he* was the cause.

Anton hated that his discomfort was so obvious. He was usually much better at hiding it. And if Remzi could tell he was unsettled, then Jude must see it, too. That bothered Anton even more than the thought of losing.

He plucked a card from the deck. A herald. The highest card in the game. A good, safe play would be to hold on to this card and keep it in his trove.

"Hurry up," Remzi said, "before your swordsman decides to reconsider betting on you."

Anton felt Jude's intense gaze prickling at the back of his neck. He wasn't about to let a surly swordsman fluster him. And he wasn't about to let a wine-soaked sea captain beat him. If he couldn't regain his composure, he would just have to bait Remzi into losing his, too.

Relaxing his shoulders, Anton peered up from his cards. "Does it trouble you?"

"Does what trouble me?" Remzi replied, looking for all the world like he'd never had a trouble in his life.

"That you have the better hand," Anton said, "and yet you're still going to lose."

"You can bluff as much as you like," Remzi said with an easy smile.

"Who's bluffing?" Anton played the herald.

It was a bold, risky move, but Anton saw immediately that it had worked, knocking Remzi off kilter just enough to let something slip. A mere flicker in his expression, one that anyone else might have missed. But Anton knew how to read the slightest shifts in mood, to predict how someone would react to every tiny disruption. These were things he'd learned long before he'd proved himself at the canbarra table. It was how he'd survived his brother's wrath all those years.

And those same instincts told him that Remzi had just given the game away.

Remzi recovered quickly, playing his next card, a seven of swords.

The herald remained faceup between them. "You and I both know, in the end we all have to play the cards we're dealt."

"Captain," Anton said, playing his next card, "if you really believe that, then I've already won."

A smirk crossed Remzi's face as his eyes scanned the cards left in the center of the table. "A herald and two sevens. I hold."

Anton could take another turn, or hold as well, ending the game. He knew Remzi expected him to take another turn, buying more time to get back on even footing.

Anton smiled. "I hold."

Remzi covered his surprise better this time, his eyes flitting to the cards in front of him. "All right then. Reveal." He turned over his first card. Another herald, which Anton had expected.

Behind him, Jude let out a huff of agitation. "Are you sure you know what you're doing?"

"Hardly ever," Anton said. He couldn't resist tossing a wink over his shoulder as he reached for the cards. He flipped over his first card. A seven of cups.

Remzi turned over the final card to complete his hand—a scribe. The second-highest card in the deck. He picked up his glass of ale, toasting Anton with a smirk. "Better luck next time, kid."

A hand on Anton's shoulder wrenched him abruptly back. Jude loomed over him, his expression stormy. "I can't believe you—"

Anton plucked Jude's hand from his shoulder and flipped over his final card. The fourth herald.

A hushed silence fell over the onlookers.

"Two heralds, three sevens," Yael said. "To Remzi's three heralds, high scribe."

Remzi choked on his ale. "You," he gasped, coughing. "How did you—?"

"Just lucky, I guess," Anton said with a shrug, and then turned to find Yael's beaming face in front of his own.

"I guess you *are* that good," he said. "Well done. Not many can beat the captain at this. I thought he really had you there."

Remzi coughed harder. "Yael, stop flirting with the boy and get me some water!"

"Wait, so," Jude started, his hand still clamped around Anton's shoulder. "You won?"

Anton met his gaze smugly. "Of course. I told you I would."

Jude's expression wavered between annoyed and impressed. Anton leapt to his feet, seizing the sword from the center of the table and holding it up like a victory laurel. Jude's expression landed firmly on annoyed as he snatched it back, his other hand closing around the torc.

"Here you are," Remzi said to Anton, setting down a sloshing glass filled with wine, which, in the tawny light of the courtyard, looked almost gold. "And one for your swordsman."

"Oh no. I don't—"

But Remzi ignored Jude, setting down a second glass full to the brim.

"Drink up," Yael advised from his other side. "The only way to survive a journey on a rat-infested pile of driftwood crewed by the world's strongest-bladdered sailors is to drink more than they do."

"I prefer my faculties unimpaired," Jude replied.

"He always this much fun?" Remzi asked, arching an eyebrow at Anton.

Anton smirked. "I'll let you know when I find out."

Remzi guffawed. Jude was less amused, his lips pursing into a frown and his thick eyebrows drawing together.

Anton let his gaze linger on the swordsman, almost challenging. He knew exactly what he was doing. It was the same thing he'd just done to

Remzi at the card table—provoking a reaction to hide his own unease. Because the thought of being stuck aboard a ship with Jude for six days, in close quarters with that overpowering *esha*, felt like a threat. And not the kind Anton could sweet-talk or run from.

Remzi squinted at Jude. "You know, I swore for a second you were one of those swordsmen. The Paladin. Rumor says, they returned to Pallas Athos."

Jude's frown deepened.

Anton's mind whirred, trying to produce a plausible lie. "He's—"

"Then I thought to myself, 'Remzi, you idiot! A swordsman from the Order of the Last Light slumming it in a dump like this?'" Remzi thumped Jude hard on the back, managing to spill about a third of his wine in the process. "Could you imagine?"

He laughed uproariously, and Anton laughed along with him, relieved.

Jude looked like he might be ill as he stepped out of Remzi's reach and ducked back through the crowd.

"Ah, well," Remzi said, tossing back the rest of Jude's wine and throwing an arm around Anton. "Now, you—you may have beaten me at Trove and River, but let's see how you hold up in a good old-fashioned drinking contest."

38

HASSAN

HASSAN'S STOMACH TWISTED IN ANTICIPATION AS HE SNAKED UP THE ROAD TO the agora. In a few short minutes, he would stand on the steps of the Temple of Pallas as the Guard proclaimed him the Last Prophet. There would be no turning back after that.

Hassan didn't want to turn back. He was certain of their plan, certain of the people he'd chosen to trust. He glanced at Khepri, several paces ahead of him, deep in conversation with Osei about the finer details of the plan to return to Nazirah.

Part of Hassan wondered if Khepri, after her not-quite rejection in the garden, was looking for an excuse not to talk to him. Though it hurt, he was determined to give her space and adhere to the boundary she'd drawn. Besides, he had other matters to worry about.

He turned to Penrose, who strode beside him. "There's something I wanted to discuss with you," he said. "Captain Weatherbourne. He still hasn't returned."

The way Penrose stiffened was slight but unmistakable. Hassan was sure his hunch was correct. Penrose was hiding something about her captain's absence.

"Is he coming back?" he asked. "The truth."

Penrose closed her eyes. "The truth is, I don't know."

"What aren't you telling me?"

"It's nothing about the prophecy," she said. "Nothing about the Witnesses. What I said before is true. It's nothing you need to worry about."

He could see the conflict playing across her face. "You feel loyalty toward him. Not because he is your captain, but because you care for him. I can understand that."

"You are the Prophet. My loyalty to you comes before anything else. Always."

"I know." If he demanded to know why Captain Weatherbourne had left, Penrose would tell him. "That's why . . . I want to name you captain of my Guard."

Penrose hesitated. "Jude is still captain," she said haltingly. "The Prophecy names him Keeper of the Word. That isn't me."

"I know what the prophecy says. But now that I know what we must do to stop the Age of Darkness, I need someone to command the Paladin in Nazirah and coordinate with the Order. If Captain Weatherbourne doesn't return—"

"I understand," Penrose said. "I wish I didn't have to, but I accept."

Hassan saw what it had cost her to say yes. But the words did come, unflinchingly, and he knew it was the right decision.

"Thank you," he said. "There's one other thing. I wanted to ask you about the ship you brought to Pallas Athos."

"What about it?"

"I don't want it to sail to Nazirah with us," Hassan said. "I want to send it back to Kerameikos Fort with the rest of the refugees from Herat—the ones who can't fight. The Order will pledge to protect them while our forces fight to take Nazirah back."

He'd thought long about what might happen to vulnerable refugees like Azizi and his mother if they were left behind in Pallas Athos. Would the Witnesses attack the refugees in retribution? Would the people of Pallas Athos grow tired of their presence and convince the priests to expel them?

Penrose stared at Hassan for a long moment, her expression inscrutable.

"What is it?" he asked.

She shook her head. "Your Grace. It's just that—I've spent my whole life thinking about the Prophet, and how he would stop the Age of Darkness. I always knew the Prophet would be a savior, a bringer of light, but—"

"But?"

"You are those things," she said. "But you're something else, too. A good man."

Hassan didn't quite know what to say. Penrose didn't seem like someone who showed her emotions easily. But he could see the pride and gratitude in her eyes.

"I'm just trying to do what's right," he said.

They were only about a quarter mile from the agora when Khepri and Osei came to an abrupt stop in the middle of the road. Penrose halted, too.

Hassan followed Penrose's gaze. In the distance, two people barreled toward them. "Is that Yarik and Annuka?"

They were calling out as they ran, but still too far away for Hassan to make out their words.

"What are they saying?"

He glanced at Penrose, but it was Osei who replied in a heavy tone. "They're saying, turn back."

Hassan's stomach dropped. He could hear them now, their shouts growing louder in the street. "What's going on?"

"Nothing good," Khepri said darkly. Her hand went to the hilt of the curved blade at her belt. Hassan saw that Osei and Penrose had their hands on their swords, too.

Annuka and Yarik slowed their pace as they approached.

"The Witnesses," Annuka said, out of breath. "They're at the temple."

Khepri cursed. "I knew they'd be back. How many this time?"

Yarik shook his head. "More than we even thought there were in this city. Two, three hundred, maybe."

Hassan went cold, his eyes flickering to the outline of the Temple of Pallas in the distance.

"They came with torches," Annuka added. "They say they're going to burn down the temple. There are people trapped inside."

Rage built in Hassan's throat.

"All right," Khepri said briskly. "Penrose, take the prince back to the villa. The four of us will continue on to the agora."

"No," Hassan said at once. "I'm not going back."

Penrose stepped toward him. "She's right."

A curl of smoke spiraled into the twilit sky, sending a jolt of panic through Hassan. "I'm not going to hide from them. I'm not going to leave while the rest of you—"

"We don't have time to argue," Khepri cut in. "Don't let him out of your sight. Osei, let's go."

They took off running.

"*Khepri!*" Hassan lunged after them, but Penrose seized him by the arm before he could get far.

He tried to wrench himself from her grip, but he was no match for her Graced strength. "I have to do *something*!"

"What you'll do is stay safe," she replied. "Trust in the people you've chosen to fight for you."

Hassan understood the wisdom of her words, but his heart railed against them. The memory of the coup bubbled to the surface of his thoughts like flame-blistered skin. After everything, he was as helpless now as he'd been then. Twice, the Witnesses had come for his people, and twice, he had hidden, useless, as others fought for their lives.

He pulled harder against Penrose's grip.

"Your Grace!" she exclaimed as he twisted away from her furiously.

"Let me go! I am not going to stay here while the others risk their lives."

"You putting yourself in danger is the last thing any of us need!" Penrose replied. She was beginning to sound winded.

Hassan stopped pulling and then slammed into her sideways as hard as he could. She caught him with a grunt.

"I'm not going to give up," he warned her. "And you're going to have to hurt me if you want to stop me."

He could feel her hesitation.

"Penrose," he said. "Please."

"Behezda's mercy," she muttered. "All right. But you don't leave my side, understand?"

"I won't," he promised.

"And if I say run, you *run*. No second-guessing."

Hassan nodded.

"Then let's go," Penrose said.

They took off, Penrose keeping pace with him along the curve of the street, through the Sacred Gate.

Ahead, Hassan could hear angry, fearful voices crying out, indistinguishable from one another.

When they reached the edge of the agora, he came to a sudden stop. A sea of black and gold robed figures stood on the temple steps. Smoke poured from their torches, obscuring the crowd around them.

The scene looked almost like the one in Hassan's vision. Except they were in Pallas Athos, not Nazirah, and their torches did not burn with the pale flame of Godfire, but blazed bright orange against the night sky.

Between the crowd and the Witnesses, three dozen Herati soldiers stood with their curved blades held at the ready. At the front was their leader, her energy poised and palpable even from a distance. Khepri.

Before Penrose could stop him, Hassan began pushing his way through the crowd.

"Prince Hassan!"

He ignored her. One of the Witnesses was shouting at the others on the steps. As he shoved through the crowd, Hassan began to make out his words.

"Do not let them make you afraid!" the Witness cried. "They are the ones who should fear us! We will make them tremble! The Immaculate One will know of our courage here today, and he will reward us in the Reckoning to come."

Hassan stepped into the space between them and the soldiers. "Leave this temple in peace," he called out.

Khepri turned toward the sound of his voice. "Prince Hassan, *no!*"

He strode up the temple steps.

"Your Grace!" Penrose emerged behind him. "Get back!"

The other members of the Paladin Guard advanced as well. Hassan kept his eyes on the Witnesses.

"Lay down your weapons and leave this temple in peace."

The Witnesses' leader had his attention focused on Hassan now. "We will not be commanded by an abomination!"

The other Witnesses shouted their agreement.

Hassan did not slow. "I am the Last Prophet," he called out, mounting the steps. "I have seen what lies ahead on the path you walk. I have seen the flames of your Reckoning go out. Lay down your weapons."

The shouts of the Witnesses and the crowd behind him drowned out his voice, but the words spilled forth anyway. As if by the very force of them he could drive the Witnesses back. As if the fact of his identity was enough to bring them to heel. This was what he had come to the temple to say, and he said it now in front of the very people who sought to stop him.

A crash shattered through the air. One of the Witnesses had knocked over the marble font of consecrating oil at the temple threshold. The oil spilled out onto the portico.

"*No!*" Hassan lunged, realizing what was about to happen.

Three Witnesses lowered their torches to the spilled oil.

Someone seized Hassan's arm, throwing him back. The Guard and Khepri launched themselves at the Witnesses, the fragile standoff now shattered.

Hassan landed hard on the temple steps. A frantic melee raged above him. The Guard was a whirl of silver and blue, fending off the Witnesses. The temple threshold rippled into flame.

Hassan staggered to his feet and turned. "Get back!" he hollered at the crowd below. "Stay back!"

Someone collided with him. He caught himself against a stone pillar and turned to his attacker. It was one of the Witnesses, his robes smeared with blood and soot. Hassan realized he'd seen his face before. This was the same pale, round-faced youth whom he'd confronted on the steps of the temple when Hassan had first arrived in Pallas Athos.

"You," the Witness rasped, bracing himself against the side of the archway. Blood dripped from a fresh wound in his side. His eyes were wide and wild as his lips moved rapidly in some incoherent catechism.

Silver flashed toward Hassan. He threw his arm over his face. The Witness's knife ripped through his palm.

Pain tore through Hassan's hand. His legs buckled beneath him. Catching himself in a half crouch, he looked up, ready for the next blow.

"Prince Hassan!"

He turned toward the sound of Khepri's voice. Before he could so much as blink, she brought her blade down on the wounded Witness.

The temple, the crowd, and the flames swirled and dipped around him. Hassan closed his eyes to steady himself, but the image of the Witness, blood trickling from the corner of his mouth, remained like a stain. The world spun again, white and green and blood red.

Then nothing but black.

39

EPHYRA

"THEY'RE NOT HERE," ILLYA SAID.

Ephyra glared. Did Illya think she didn't have eyes?

She ignored him, shouldering her way into the alcove. Dread twisted her stomach at the sight of the buckled-in table in the center of the room.

"I'm guessing that's new," Illya said. "Whose handiwork do you think this is?"

Ephyra shook her head. "I don't know." But she had a prickling suspicion.

Maybe Beru had left before Hector had gotten here. Or maybe the broken table was evidence of something more sinister.

"No blood," Illya mused, pacing a half circle around the room. "That's probably good."

It wasn't good. None of this was good. Beru was gone, and Ephyra had no idea where she was. No idea where Hector was. No idea what Hector would do to her if he found out what she really was.

She closed her eyes and sank down against the stone wall with a heavy sigh. She heard Illya move toward her.

"We'll find them," he said, his voice strangely sincere.

Ephyra opened one eye. Illya was leaning against the wall next to her, slouched there in a way that reminded her of Anton in this very alcove that first night. Concern pinched his features, drawing his brows together over bright gold eyes.

"He wanted me to kill you," Ephyra said. Illya's expression didn't change. "Doesn't that bother you?"

Illya blew out a breath. "I wasn't a very good brother to him. When we were growing up . . . there's a lot I wish I'd done differently."

She watched him carefully. He was difficult to read—even more so than Anton. Was this true remorse? Or was it, like Anton believed, all a show?

"You say you want to protect him now, but why didn't you then?" she asked.

"Because I didn't realize he needed protecting," he answered. He shook his head, looking almost irritated—although with Ephyra or with himself she couldn't tell. "He was the chosen son. He was Graced. I wasn't. My grandmother and my father never let us forget it. It was all they cared about."

"But why?" Ephyra asked. "I mean, I know that Anton's Grace is powerful, and he told us that things are different in the north than they are here, but—"

"What else did he tell you?"

Ephyra tried to recall. "That you and your father and your grandmother were all Graceless," she said slowly. "That they thought he was special because of his Grace, and you resented it."

"They thought he was more than just special," Illya said. "Do you know anything about the prophecy of Vasili the Raving?"

Ephyra peered up at him. She was hardly an expert in Novogardian history, but everyone knew the story of the Raving King. "I know it's the last prophecy the Prophets made before they disappeared, about some asshole king losing his mind."

"Yes," Illya said. "The Prophets predicted three things about Vasili: that he would be the last emperor of the Novogardian Empire, that he would go mad, and that there would never be a Graced heir to his line."

"And that has something to do with you?"

He gave her a meaningful look.

After a moment, she realized. "Are you saying that you and Anton are the descendants of the Raving King? That the prophecy was wrong?"

"My grandmother certainly believed it," Illya replied. "The people in the north aren't like the ones in the Six Cities. They never worshipped the Prophets. When they disappeared, my grandmother's family thought it meant it was finally time for their line to rise again. To undo the prophecy of the Raving King and restore the Novogardian Empire to its former glory."

"And she thought that . . . that *Anton* was going to be the one to restore your family to power?" Ephyra asked. "Anton? The kid who gets beat up over cards and can't scry without nearly drowning?"

"She was convinced of it," Illya replied. "She'd waited her whole life for a Graced child. And finally, she got one. The day we discovered Anton's Grace was the worst day of my life."

"Did he hurt you somehow?" It wasn't uncommon for children just beginning to control their Graces to cause accidents. Ephyra had always suspected it was one of her parents' biggest fears, and the reason they tried to hide her Grace and begged her not to use it. In hindsight, maybe they'd been right to be so scared.

"No," Illya replied. "He saved my life. Used his Grace to lead our grandmother to me after I'd gotten lost in a storm. And the moment she saw me there, shivering and terrified, she turned her back and threw her arms around Anton, weeping because she knew he was the Graced heir she'd been waiting for. It was like I didn't exist."

"So Grandma didn't love you, and you took it out on him," Ephyra said drily. But her chest clenched—she couldn't help but see how something like that could mess a kid up. If it was even true.

"Yes," Illya replied. "She and my father gave him all their attention, remembering me only when they needed something to scream at. So when their backs were turned, I would hurt Anton. He was the special one, and yet that was one power I could wield. He didn't deserve it, but back then I couldn't see that."

"And now?"

He rubbed a hand over his face. "He's been alone this whole time, and it's because of me. Everything he's gone through—I should have been there alongside him. I'll never have that back."

She *wanted* to believe him, she realized. It would make her feel better if she could tell herself that helping Illya wasn't betraying Anton.

"What changed?" she asked.

"I found . . . purpose," Illya replied. "Somewhere to direct all the pain of that neglect. Somewhere I could feel useful, for once."

The words struck a strange chord with Ephyra. She, too, had found purpose. Keeping Beru alive. It hadn't mattered what she'd had to do in pursuit of that purpose. It still didn't. In the cell, she'd told herself she wasn't like Illya. Calculating. Cold. Ruthless. But whether Illya's remorse was real or not, whether he truly wanted to protect Anton or do something much more sinister, Ephyra knew she would have made the same choice to help him.

She could only fool herself for so long. Maybe it was time she recognized the person she'd become.

She looked back to the remains of the broken table. Beneath a splintered leg, something glinted. She leaned over, reaching for it. It was a bracelet—Beru must have finished it after their argument. A string of colored pottery shards surrounded one tiny glass bead. It was the bottle stopper Ephyra had brought Beru the night she'd killed the priest.

She slipped the bracelet onto her wrist and stood up. "Come on. If Beru and Anton were here, they must have left through the sanctum. There could be more clues up there. Something we missed."

"The sanctum is all rubble and ashes," Illya replied. "How exactly are we going to find clues in there?"

"I don't know, but I'm not giving up," she said. "If you really want to make up for what you did in the past, you won't, either."

She held her hand out like he'd done inside the cell. He took it, long fingers clasping her palm.

She hadn't really allowed herself to look before, but now that they were standing close in the dimly lit alcove, Ephyra could admit that Illya's face was rather striking. He and Anton shared similar features, but where they were boyish and pretty on Anton, on Illya they were regal, elegant. It wasn't difficult at all to believe he was descended from a line of northern emperors.

"It's this way," she said after a moment, realizing she'd been staring too long.

She led Illya up the stairs slowly and emerged into the dark shrine. She didn't know exactly what she expected to find there. *Something.* Some sign that Beru had gotten away, that she was all right. But just like Illya had said, all they found was ash and rubble. A once-holy place now given to decay, like the city itself.

She stood in the center of the shrine, in front of the scrying pool and beneath the hole in the roof. Behind her, she could hear Illya shifting loose rubble, picking around the shrine. The sound of his footsteps moved farther away, toward the gaping threshold.

"I found something!" he called.

Ephyra whirled around, scrambling over the piles of rubble to the main steps, where Illya stood, frowning down at something between his hands.

He glanced at Ephyra as she drew up beside him. "Never mind," he said apologetically. "I thought it was a note, but it's just trash."

In his hands was a sheet of crinkled white parchment paper. He started to ball it back up, but Ephyra quickly snatched it out of his hands.

"Wait," she said. "Trash isn't just trash."

As the Pale Hand, Ephyra had often found creative ways of tracking her victims. The kills had to be meticulously planned, which meant taking whatever was at her disposal to learn more about her targets and using it to her advantage. Over the years, she'd discovered that one of the best ways to learn about someone was to look at what they threw away.

She brought the crinkled paper to her face and sniffed it. Sugar and nuts. When she lowered it, Illya was looking at her like she had done something truly objectionable. Ignoring him, she flipped the paper over, scanning for the ink stamp she was almost certain she would find.

In the bottom corner of the paper, she could make out a light green stamp in the shape of an olive.

She looked up at Illya, who was still staring at her askance. "This is from the bakery up the road," she told him. It was a favorite of Beru's, though Ephyra had warned her against going there too frequently, lest the baker begin to recognize her.

His expression didn't change, and Ephyra tucked the paper away impatiently. "The baker might have seen something that could point us in the right direction."

Illya waved his hand toward the empty street. "It's the middle of the night. I'm pretty sure anyone who *might* have seen anything is asleep."

"So we wake them up," Ephyra said, starting down the steps and pulling him after her.

The baker was not particularly happy about being woken up at half past midnight, but being the Pale Hand had taught Ephyra that there were certain advantages to appearing as harmless and innocent as a normal eighteen-year-old girl. Once she had finished spinning her sob story about her missing sister (leaving out a few key details) and Illya had smoothed things over with an artfully creased brow and a perfectly placed catch in his words, the baker had softened like a fig on the vine.

He studied the parchment wrapper. "I'm sorry," he said. "This is mine. But I didn't see your sister."

Ephyra's heart dropped. This had been a long shot, she knew, but it was *all she had*. She was so tired of running into dead ends. First, with the search for Eleazar's Chalice, and now, trying to find Beru. She was tired of constantly being one step behind.

"We're sorry to have bothered you so late," Illya said gently, drawing Ephyra away, his hand at the small of her back. "Thank you for your time."

He started to lead her back down the hall.

"I didn't see your sister," the baker called after them. "But I did see a northerner like you." Ephyra and Illya stopped. The baker was looking at Illya.

"You did?" Ephyra asked.

"Yeah," the baker said. "I remember him because he was covered in dirt or soot or something. He passed by again with another fellow practically falling asleep on him."

Ephyra whirled back on the baker. "Another fellow? What did he look like?"

The baker shrugged. "Didn't see him too close. He was wearing dark blue, maybe?"

Dark blue, like the cloak of the Paladin.

"Did you see where they went?"

"Sure," the baker replied. "Down the road, probably headed to the tavernas by the docks. I remember I was worried whether they were gonna make it. The fellow in blue wasn't looking too great."

Ephyra hurriedly thanked the baker again and bid him a good night. When she turned back around, Illya was still standing where she'd left him, a few steps down the hall.

"Come on, what are you waiting for?" she asked, whirling past him. "There can't be that many tavernas down there. We can find the right one."

He didn't move. "I think . . . maybe you should go without me."

"What? But we found Anton! Why would you—?"

"I can't stop thinking about what he said the last time I saw him." He ran a hand through his hair. "I don't want this to go the same way. Maybe if you talk to him first, tell him what I told you . . ."

She was used to his effortlessly composed demeanor, and this sudden uncertainty threw her. Could Illya's remorse be real after all?

He lowered his gaze. "I don't want him to be scared."

Ephyra watched his expression for a moment, the fatigue and concern etched into his forehead. She had been so quick to believe the worst of him—but perhaps that was just one more way that being the Pale Hand had warped her. Seeking out monsters had chipped away at her ability to see the good in people. That was always something Beru had been better at. She knew what her sister would do if she were here.

"All right," she said at last. "If that's what you want. I'll go in first and talk to him. Find out what happened to Beru. Then maybe he'll agree to talk to you again."

Illya nodded. "Thank you."

Seized by a sudden impulse, Ephyra reached out and touched his shoulder. "He's all right. At least you know that."

His eyes fell to her hand, his face half illuminated by a slant of moonlight coming in through the window. He looked lost.

Ephyra pulled her hand away and turned, hurrying down the stairs and back into the night.

40

JUDE

THE FESTIVITIES IN THE COURTYARD LASTED LONG PAST MIDNIGHT, THOUGH Jude left the sailors to their own devices after the third rendition of "The Wanderer and the Lovesick Mariner." He'd lost track of Anton at some point in the midst of the revelry and retreated to the tiny room up the stairs where he'd woken only hours before with a healed arm and a missing sword.

He held the Pinnacle Blade in his lap, polishing the hilt. His thoughts pitched and rocked like a ship on the waves, but the weight of the sword grounded him.

Anton was nowhere to be found, which probably meant he'd passed out downstairs. Unbidden, Jude's mind called up the image of the flushed-faced sailor boy cheering Anton on at the card table. Maybe Anton had simply found another bed to spend the night in.

Footsteps sounded from outside the room. Jude's fingers curled instinctively around the Pinnacle Blade.

The door creaked open, flooding the room with moonlight and the faint fragrance of sweet oil. Anton shuffled inside, wearing linen trousers and a half-laced undershirt, scratching lightly at his ribs. The shirt rode up, exposing a bare strip of skin beneath his navel.

"Oh," Anton said, spotting Jude. He lowered his hand, and Jude watched the pale crease of his hip bone disappear beneath the soft fabric.

"You're awake," Jude said stupidly.

"So are you," Anton returned, suppressing a tiny yawn. "Couldn't sleep?"

Jude gave a hesitant nod. "I . . . It happens, sometimes."

Anton rubbed a hand over his dust-colored hair, making it stand up in spiky tufts. It was damp, Jude realized.

"You were at the baths?" he guessed.

"Had to wash off all that prison muck. It was that or the fountain in the courtyard, but you already tested that out."

"What?"

Anton smiled, a private smile like there was some joke Jude wasn't privy to. "Never mind."

"I didn't think you'd be using the room," Jude blurted as Anton busied himself with lighting a paraffin lamp. "I *was* going to try and sleep here, but . . ." He trailed off awkwardly. His instinct, always, was to be polite, but none of his interactions with Anton had included courtesies. Beginning them now felt like playacting.

"I don't mind," Anton said, the lamp flame flickering to life beneath his hands. "If you want to share my bed, though, that'll cost."

Heat flooded Jude's face, and he was distinctly glad for the dimness of the flame so that Anton could not see. "I—That isn't—I wouldn't—"

"That was a joke," Anton said, setting the paraffin lamp on the small table between their two cots. "You know, people tell them to make each other laugh?"

"I know what a joke is." Jude's voice was too sharp in the soft light of the room.

Anton shrugged one slim shoulder. "Seemed like maybe you weren't familiar with the concept."

"Meaning what?"

"Well, you know, just that you're very—" Anton affected an exaggerated scowl, straightening his back and squaring his shoulders.

Jude frowned.

"Yes, like that," Anton agreed. He flopped down on the cot across from Jude in a languid half sprawl.

Jude took in Anton's relaxed pose, the practiced ease with which he carried himself—so at odds with the boy who'd cowered in fear before Hector.

"I've given it more thought," Jude said after a moment.

"Oh?" Anton replied, raising an eyebrow.

Candlelight leapt across his face, illuminating the faint freckles sprinkled along his nose and cheeks. There was a certain kind of intimacy to candlelight that was lost with artificed incandescent light, Jude thought.

"I believe that you meant to return my sword to me," he decided. "If you'd meant to steal it outright, you wouldn't have wagered it in the very same taverna where I was sleeping."

"No," Anton said. "I guess not."

"And," Jude went on, "you did see me back here safely and find a healer for my shoulder. I ought to thank you."

"Saying you ought to thank someone isn't the same as a thank-you," Anton pointed out wryly.

"You did still try to wager my sword."

A half smile crinkled the edge of Anton's mouth as he pushed himself up on one elbow. "I suppose I ought to apologize."

"Saying you ought to apologize isn't the same as an apology."

Anton's smile widened, crooked and disarming.

Jude felt his own mouth tug up in response. He quickly looked away, out the window at the ink-black sky. "I've been wanting to know—what were you doing with the Pale Hand?"

The smile dropped from Anton's face. "She was . . . she was trying to help me."

"Help you?"

"It doesn't matter anymore."

"She's a murderer," Jude said. "That doesn't scare you?"

Anton didn't say anything for a long moment, scratching at a splintered piece of wood on the table. Finally, he said, "Do you know what it's like to feel fear, Jude? I mean, real fear."

Jude didn't answer. He knew fear, of course. He had felt it in his lungs when he faced Hector on top of the roof. He had felt it before that, too—like the flutter of a sparrow's wings in his chest the moment he had laid eyes upon the Prophet.

"It feels like drowning," Anton went on, looking down at where he'd gouged a small wound in the wood. "It feels just like drowning, and you can either let yourself sink or you can fight and claw your way to the surface. The thing is, I'm not really sure there's a difference, in the end."

Jude's pulse leapt, and he thought again of how Anton had looked, cowering in the dark shrine with Hector standing over him. He remembered how Anton's gaze had landed on Jude, how he hadn't looked away. Something in the boy's eyes had unsettled him.

He realized now what it was. At the mercy of Hector's anger, Anton hadn't seemed frightened. Fear had appeared on his face only when he'd looked at Jude.

"So, no," Anton said. "The Pale Hand doesn't scare me. That's not what I'm afraid of."

"But something does," Jude said carefully. "And that . . . fear . . . is that why you're so eager to get out of Pallas Athos?"

Anton lifted one shoulder. "Sure, I guess." His eyes flickered back to Jude. "What about you? You were this close to maiming me for wagering your sword, but when Remzi said where they're sailing next, you suddenly threw in your own bet."

"That city . . . Tel Amot." Jude paused. "That's where Hector said he was going."

"He almost killed you," Anton said. "If I were you, I'd be trying to get as far away from him as possible."

"Well, I'm not like you," Jude snapped, growing irritated. "I have a responsibility to him. I am his leader. I chose him, and if he dishonors himself, he dishonors me."

There was a pause, and then Anton leveled his gaze at him. "That," he said, "sounds like horseshit."

Jude's hand clenched around the Pinnacle Blade. He was not certain of much anymore, but he was certain he no longer wanted to talk about Hector, and he particularly did not want to talk about him with this peat-eyed boy.

"What would you know about it?" Jude said acidly. "You've more interest in gambling than in honor."

Anton arched an eyebrow, amused. "You could learn a thing or two from the card table. A good player knows when to cut his losses and walk away."

Jude met his challenging gaze. "I will not give up on him."

Anton cocked his head to the side. "Oh." The weight of that one syllable settled over Jude, and he felt how Remzi must have felt facing off against Anton, waiting for him to turn over the last card between them. "So. It's like that."

Jude opened his mouth to respond and then sealed it shut again.

"You're in love with him, aren't you?"

It was the question Jude had never allowed himself to ask. It was the question he'd heard in his father's voice when he'd warned him not to choose Hector for the Guard. The one that had been reflected in Penrose's eyes when she begged him not to go after him. The one that had hung between him and Hector on the roof of the mausoleum before Jude's fall.

The Paladin didn't fall in love. The oath was clear—duty to the Prophets before their countries, their livelihoods, their hearts. They never took lovers, and the sole exception to their sacred vow of chastity was the Ritual of Sacred Union, performed to produce an heir to the Weatherbourne line. Anything outside of that was a desecration of their vows, the same as if they'd abandoned their duty altogether.

"I'm not." Jude's throat was suddenly dry. "I'm—He's—"

"Maybe you *are* better off keeping away from the card table," Anton said. "You're a shit bluffer."

"It's not like that," Jude said swiftly. "I wouldn't expect you to understand. It's—I have a duty. A purpose."

A duty he'd abandoned. A purpose he'd failed. The words hung in the air, taunting him. Every accusation he'd leveled at Hector— that he'd let himself be distracted by emotion, that he lacked true devotion to the Prophet—was true of Jude, too. The Keeper of the Word didn't fall in love, and the Keeper of the Word didn't succumb to doubt.

But Jude had done both.

"Well, you're right," Anton said. "I don't know anything about that. I don't know about duty and purpose. But I know what people want. You may think you're different, that you live by some special code that sets you apart, but everyone wants something, Jude. Even you."

Anger flashed through Jude like a hot oil flame. Who was this boy, who presumed to know the truths of Jude's heart better than his Guard, better than his father, better than Jude himself?

"All I want," he said, his voice shaking with the effort of keeping it calm, "is to find Hector. To bring him back here, where he belongs."

Anton did not blink or look away. He stared back at Jude, and it was almost like those dark eyes could see beneath his skin, beneath his flesh, beneath the bones of his ribs, to the lie that beat inside his chest.

The sound of footsteps striding down the hall stole Jude's attention. He was relieved for the distraction, for the excuse to tear his eyes away from Anton.

But his relief tightened into fear. Jude counted five sets of footsteps, and they were quicker and more purposeful than the gait of drunken sailors stumbling to their beds.

"What is it?" Anton asked.

"Footsteps. Someone's coming."

Anton's eyes darted to the door, and then he went still. A small tremor went through him, as though he'd just recalled a bad memory.

"Why do you look like you know who it is?"

Anton's eyes were wide and terrified. "They're here for me."

"The Sentry?"

Anton shook his head, fear flickering across his face.

The footsteps drew nearer. Jude stood and crossed the room in three easy steps, his hand on the hilt of the Pinnacle Blade.

"Go out the window," he told Anton. "I'll hold them here and find you after."

He wasn't sure who the men outside the door were or what they wanted with Anton, but he didn't question the instinct that told him to protect the boy. Anton had talked about real fear, and Jude could see that fear plainly in his eyes now.

Anton froze with one leg slung over the edge of the open window.

"Whatever happens," Jude said, "I'll protect you."

Anton met Jude's eyes across the candlelit room, staring at him like he could not quite comprehend the words.

The door burst open. Jude had never drawn the Pinnacle Blade before, but now he didn't hesitate. It scraped free of its sheath with a surge of power that gusted through the room like a sudden windstorm. The five men standing in the doorway were blown back by its force.

For a moment, Jude stood still, stunned by the sword's sheer power. He'd heard the tales of the Pinnacle Blade's strength before, but he'd never *felt* it. The sword felt almost alive in his hands, thrumming through his Grace, strengthening and focusing it like a koah.

The men staggered back to their feet, charging into the room. With the Pinnacle Blade in his hands, Jude leapt forward to meet them.

41

ANTON

THE DROP FROM THE WINDOW WAS FARTHER THAN ANTON HAD ANTICIPATED IN the dark. As his feet hit the rough limestone roof, his knees buckled.

Jude's *esha* thundered through the air, flattening Anton. It surged over him, stronger than he had ever felt it. He lay there, disoriented, awash in the storm.

Run, his mind screamed at him, and he lurched to his feet, racing across the roof. His brother was here, somewhere. If not with the men that just burst into the room, then lurking somewhere outside. Beneath the tempest of Jude's *esha* he could feel his brother's, dissonant and jarring, like the sound of glass shattering. Unmistakable.

And he'd brought his hired swords, the same ones that had shown up at Anton's flat. But Anton didn't think his brother would have accounted for Jude. A few sell-swords were no match for a Grace as powerful as his.

Then again, this was Illya. Anton had learned early on not to underestimate his brother. Somehow, Anton always wound up at his mercy.

Anton dropped down to the next level of terraced rooftops, keeping to the shadows as he tried to think of a plan. If he left the Hidden Spring, he'd miss his best shot at getting out of Pallas Athos. He could circle back in the morning to meet up with Remzi and his crew—but who was to say that Illya wouldn't be waiting with even more mercenaries?

He edged to the other side of the roof and then dropped down onto the walkway below. The marina, then. That was the only option. He had to make it there and hide out until the *Black Cormorant* set sail.

"Anton." The hissed whisper stopped him in his tracks. He turned to find Ephyra standing at the top of a stairway. Surprise and relief flooded him.

"Ephyra?" he said. "You—How did you find me? How did you get out of the citadel?"

Her eyes flashed fiercely in the moonlight. "How did *you?*"

Guilt churned in his gut.

"I know Hector Navarro broke you out," Ephyra said. "And I know he went after Beru. Tell me where they are."

"I tried to help her," Anton said. "I *swear*. I—I managed to distract Navarro to give Beru time to get away. She did—she went to the train station, to go to Tel Amot. But there was a fight. Navarro got away. After that, I don't know."

He expected her anger, her panic, her disgust. What he got was none of these things. It was her face crumpling, her eyes flickering away from his. Then she nodded, firm.

"He's going to find her, isn't he?"

"I don't know," Anton said. "It doesn't matter. Ephyra, we have to get out of here. My brother—he's here. He found me somehow. He . . ." He stared at Ephyra, at the tight set of her jaw and the way she did not quite meet his gaze.

He realized she had never answered his question.

"How *did* you get out of the citadel, Ephyra?"

To her credit, she didn't look away. "It was the only way," she said. "The only way to save Beru."

Of course. Of course Ephyra was the one who'd brought Illya here. Panic twisted his stomach as his brother's rattling *esha* drew closer.

"I know this isn't what you wanted." There was more emotion in Ephyra's voice than Anton had ever heard. "But I think you're wrong about him. I don't think he's what you think he is."

"He's exactly what I think he is. And you just—you—"

His throat closed as another figure emerged at the top of the stairwell.

Illya.

Ice shot down Anton's spine at the sight of his brother's face—the pale skin stretched tight, dark shadows under his golden eyes. He looked back at Ephyra, still not certain, unwilling to be certain, that she had betrayed him.

"You never bid me farewell, Anton," Illya said, sorrow permeating his voice as he descended toward him.

Ephyra glanced between them uncertainly. "I thought you were going to wait for me to talk to him."

"I changed my mind," Illya said dismissively. He turned those gold eyes back on Anton. "You didn't bid me farewell the first time you left, either. When you stole away in the middle of the night. Grandmother and Father blamed me, you know. Gave me the worst beating of my life."

"Well, they had it right. I was running away from you."

"No, you weren't," Illya said softly. "Perhaps that's what you needed to tell yourself back then. Perhaps it was easier that way, to think that all your fears could be traced to your cruel, jealous brother. But that's not the truth, and deep down, you know that."

Illya's words froze him. He wanted so badly to run and not look back. But he couldn't will himself to move.

He sucked in a shaking breath. "I ran away because you were going to kill me."

"You mean the lake?" Illya asked. "No, Anton. I didn't try to kill you, but something did happen that day. Something that scared you more than I ever could. Something that, even now, you can't face."

"I know what happened."

"Do you?"

"I—" Anton shut his eyes. He was in the lake again, his muscles frozen rigid. Hands pulling him down. "I'm—"

You still don't know what you're running from, do you?

He couldn't let the water in, no matter how much his lungs burned for release. He couldn't give in. Couldn't let himself sink. Couldn't face what waited for him at the bottom of the lake.

"I don't—"

Stop!

STOP!

"Anton!"

His eyes flew open to find Jude's face just in front of him. Anton wasn't sure where he'd come from.

"Are you all right?" Jude asked.

The storm of Jude's *esha* rang out around them as Anton stared at the slight gap between Jude's front teeth, the thick lines of his brows drawn together, the green eyes bright with earnest concern. He didn't know how to answer.

Jude's gaze flickered past Anton to Ephyra. "You," he said in surprise. "I don't understand. Anton said you were trying to *help* him."

"It's simple," Anton said. "She decided to betray me instead."

"Could you be any more dramatic?" Ephyra said. "I didn't *betray* you. I came to find Beru."

"And led *him* here in the process," Anton said. "Along with his mercenaries."

"Mercenaries?" Ephyra said. "What mercenaries?"

"Oh," Illya said mildly. "After we parted ways, I may have invited a few friends to join us."

Five men rounded the corner. They were dressed in uniforms almost like the Sentry, but gray and red instead of blue. Two of them wielded huge crossbows with brass gears and heavy silver chains wound around them. The rest held swords. Anton couldn't sense Grace in any of them. These were average, run-of-the-mill fighters. Their brute force would have been more than enough to overpower him alone.

But for the first time, Anton wasn't alone.

Jude stepped forward to fill the space between Anton and the approaching mercenaries, gripping the hilt of his sword tight even as confusion clouded his features.

"What?" Ephyra said, glancing between them and Illya. "But you— you said—"

"He lied to you, Ephyra," Anton said. "All he does is lie."

"I do a little more than just that," Illya said. With a flick of his hand, the mercenaries descended.

Jude was a blur. One second, he was at Anton's side, and the next, he was a flurry of motion—a swirl of blue cloak, the flash of moonlight on a silver blade.

Jude met the first mercenary, sending him stumbling back. He spun, fending off another. The next few seconds were a furious clash of blades as Jude drove back the mercenaries' attacks, keeping himself, always, between them and Anton.

Anton met Ephyra's gaze across the chaos of the fight as he pressed himself back against the wall. There was no regret or guilt in her eyes. Just ruthless determination. She started to turn away, toward the low wall that led out into the courtyard.

"Get her, too," Illya growled. "All three of them."

Two of the mercenaries lunged at Ephyra. One grabbed hold of her arm, dragging her away from the wall.

She struggled against the mercenary, arms pinned at her sides. "Let *go!*"

Anton watched her eyes find Illya again, cold fury in them.

"What happened to *allies?*" she spat.

His brother smiled—a smile that chilled Anton to the bone. "You made a good ally. But you'll make an even better prisoner."

Ephyra's face twisted. "I should have killed you when I had the chance." She stomped down on her captor's foot. He let out a howl of pain, and a moment later, she was slipping free of his hold and launching herself toward Illya. In a flash, she knocked him to the ground, pinning his chest with her knee, her palm pressed to his throat like the edge of a knife.

"Call them off," she cried. "I can stop your heart before you take your next breath, and I don't need a weapon to do it. Call. Them. Off."

Anton heard a low cranking noise, and in the time it took him to realize what was happening, one of the crossbow-wielding mercenaries fired.

Ephyra threw herself to the side, rolling off Illya. The bolt and chain flew past her, over the low terrace wall.

Ephyra stared at it, wide-eyed, and then took off at a run, vaulting over the wall and onto the next roof.

"Go after her!" Illya cried, and then turned his attention back to Anton.

Jude was now the only person standing between the brothers. But before either of them could make a move, the two mercenaries flanking Illya hefted their crossbows and fired.

Anton flinched. Jude's sword whirled in front of him, blocking one of the bolts. He dodged past the other, his blade cutting through the air toward Illya.

The second bolt struck the wall beside Anton, embedding itself into the stone. The attached chain whipped after it and then released, wrapping around Jude's wrist, pulling taut and stopping his blade inches from Illya's throat.

The mercenary yanked on the chain, wrenching Jude's arm back with a sick pop. Jude staggered, crying out. He looked up, his green eyes burning fiercely as he sat back on his heels to move through a koah.

"I don't think you want to be doing that," Illya warned.

Jude cried out and stumbled again, collapsing to his knees. Anton felt Jude's *esha* shudder. He wanted to go to his side, but his instincts screamed at him to stay put.

Illya stepped up to Jude's crumpled form. Jude let out a low groan.

"What did you do to him?" Anton demanded.

"Nothing permanent," Illya assured him. "These chains were forged in Godfire. They won't burn out your Grace like the flames themselves, but they will make it unimaginably painful to use it."

Jude jerked his head up. "Godfire? That's impossible. You're . . ." He let out another hiss of pain. "The Witnesses sent you?"

Anton whipped back toward his brother. All along, he'd thought Illya was here to bring vengeance on him, but—this? Illya, one of the Witnesses?

He'd been so stupid. Illya had never cared about their family's supposed bloodline. He'd always resented Anton for his Grace. It made sense, then, that he'd turned to the people who validated that. Who had taught him that the very thing he hated—Anton's power—was the thing that condemned him.

"You catch on quick," Illya said. "I'm almost impressed."

Jude groaned again. "What do you want with Anton?"

"I thought that would be obvious," Illya replied mildly. "After all, it's the same thing *you* want with him."

Jude looked back at Anton, his expression clouded with agony. "What is he talking about?"

"Oh," Illya said, amusement lightening his tone. "Interesting."

"Let him go," Anton said, turning back to his brother. "He's not who you want."

"Oh, but he is," Illya replied. "You both are."

He knelt down to Jude, tugging the brooch from his cloak. The dark blue fabric pooled around Jude's form.

"Keeper of the Word," Illya said, looking down at the brooch. "I've a feeling the Hierophant will be plenty pleased with me when I deliver the leader of the Order of the Last Light to him."

They were cornered. There was no bargain, no wager Anton could offer. No trick he could pull. No choice he could make. The fear that had pushed him from city to city, that had sharpened his mind and hastened his step for years suddenly dissolved. In its wake was defeat.

Perhaps he had known all along that Illya would one day win. Anton had managed to put it off for years, but he had ended up here after all—with nowhere left to run and no way to stop himself from sinking.

42

EPHYRA

THE MERCENARIES WERE EASY TO KILL. EPHYRA HAD ENDED SO MANY LIVES, she barely even registered the moment when the *esha* left them, when they crossed that narrow pathway between life and death.

She didn't know anything about these men who'd been hired to capture her or what choices had led them to this moment on the roof of the taverna. She didn't care. With her hand on his throat, she looked down at the mercenary's glazed eyes and bloodless face and pictured Illya Aliyev instead.

The anger she felt at being tricked was as sharp and bitter as blood. Illya had made a fool of her, gaining her trust, with downcast eyes and a few soft words. Of course he didn't want to *protect* Anton—Anton had told her as much, and she'd dismissed him. Because despite everything she'd done, she still had a stupid tender heart that didn't let her believe there was someone who would turn on their own brother. He'd played her.

She was the Pale Hand. She didn't *get* played.

But Illya was the least of her concerns. When the second mercenary dropped to the ground, Ephyra redirected her anger where it belonged—on Hector Navarro. She had to get to Beru. That was the only thing that mattered.

Footsteps echoed up from the walkway below. There were at least two sets, plodding and uneven.

"Sweet Endarra, how are you still so terrible at holding your liquor?" a gruff voice grumbled.

Ephyra dropped to her belly as two figures turned the corner below. One of them was taller than any man she had ever seen before, and he seemed to be supporting half the weight of his smaller companion. Ducking her head, she prayed they wouldn't look up.

"I'm perfectly fine, *darling*."

"You say that now, but I'm the one who's going to have to tend to you tomorrow when you're sick and in a hateful mood. You know, it's really not becoming for a sea captain to begin each voyage throwing up over the side of his own ship."

"What did I do to deserve a husband capable of such cruelty?"

The tall man's laughter boomed out from below as they passed directly beneath Ephyra and the dead mercenaries. In the soft moonlight, she could make out dark markings on the taller man's skin. A healer.

"I'll make it up to you when we get to Tel Amot," the healer said slyly. As he leaned down to whisper something in his companion's ear, Ephyra's heart thudded hard.

Tel Amot.

Before she'd thought it through, she crawled away from the edge of the roof and dropped down to a shadowed alcove between the stairs and the wall. The laughter and teasing of the two men drew closer.

When they were nearly on top of her, Ephyra stepped out from the shadows, nearly bowling them over.

"I'm so sorry!" she cried as they stumbled back.

"Quite all right," the tall healer said. "Remzi here can hardly walk straight, anyway."

The shorter man pouted. "That's just hurtful."

"I was just coming down the stairs," she said, gesturing, "and I overheard you say you have a ship headed to Tel Amot?"

The two men exchanged a glance that Ephyra couldn't quite parse.

"We are *not* taking any more charity cases aboard," the tall one said. "Or wagers. Definitely no wagers."

"Excuse me?"

"What Yael means to say is that we can't help you get to Tel Amot," Remzi said. "Sorry."

They maneuvered around her to continue down the walkway.

"I would pay, of course," she called after them.

They stopped. The smaller man turned around, brightening.

Ephyra held out a coin purse. "Will this cover it?"

She'd stolen it off the two mercenaries. They had no need for it anymore.

Ephyra let the purse fall from her hand, and Remzi reached forward to catch it. His eyes grew wide as he peered inside.

"That's nearly two hundred virtues," she said. "And if that's not enough, I'll work for it, too. Whatever you need done."

Remzi closed the purse and handed it to Yael over his shoulder. "I think this should cover it. Yael?"

Yael balanced the purse on one broad hand. "Should do it."

"Happy to have you aboard," Remzi said, beaming as Yael tucked the purse away. "We leave at first light."

"You won't even be sober yet at first light," the tall healer said, ushering him away. Over his shoulder, he said, "We leave at midday."

Ephyra would have preferred dawn, but she'd take what she could get. Soon, she would be on her way to Tel Amot. And from there, back to the place she never thought she'd return.

Ephyra was going home.

43

HASSAN

HASSAN WOKE TO THE WOODY SCENT OF BURNING INCENSE FILLING HIS LUNGS. Warmth enveloped him as he slowly opened his eyes. Slivers of sunlight penetrated through the layered palm fronds above him.

"Glad to see you're awake."

A cool hand pressed against his forehead. He turned his head and saw Lethia, her eyes creased with weary concern. "Easy now. You're all right."

He sat up woozily, taking in his surroundings. He was in the healer's tent in the agora.

Penrose rose from a cushion at the foot of his pallet. "Prince Hassan."

Hassan wrenched the thin blanket off and simultaneously tried to get up. The blanket tangled, and he furiously tried to kick it away.

"What happened?" he asked. "Was anyone else hurt?"

"What were you thinking, charging at the Witnesses like that?" Lethia said. "You were nearly killed!"

"I told you to stay put," Penrose admonished.

"I see you two have decided to get along," Hassan muttered. "What happened to the temple?"

The image of flames billowing from its doors blazed in his mind.

"They put out the fire," Penrose replied. "The Sentry showed up, and the rest of the Witnesses fled. Several were killed, including the one who hurt you."

"Was anyone else hurt?" Hassan asked again.

Penrose didn't answer. Lethia was silent, too.

Hassan's heart lurched. He couldn't stand not knowing a second longer. The image of Khepri's face as she'd raced away from him hung in his mind. She had to be all right. She had to be.

He strode past the two of them, pushing his way through the curtains that separated his sickbed from the rest of the tent.

And ran straight into Khepri.

"Prince Hassan!" she cried in surprise, but did not pull away. He took in her face, the dirt and grime and horror of the fight still fresh.

Before he knew what he was doing, his hands wrapped around her shoulders, drawing her close, pressing his face into the crease between her shoulder and neck.

"Hassan," she said, her voice coming out softer, shakier, more unsure than he'd ever heard it before.

"You're safe," he murmured into her throat. The sight of her charging into the agora had made his gut clench and his pulse thunder in his ears. He couldn't stand the thought of her leaping into battle and not coming out of it alive.

He stepped back, hands trailing up her shoulders to cup the sides of her face. Her eyes closed at his touch. Dried blood caked over a scrape on her forehead, dirt streaked her cheeks, and Hassan was certain that she was the most beautiful thing he'd ever seen.

"Khepri," he breathed, drawing toward her, powerless against her pull. Her eyes fluttered open, and he saw that they were red. Tear tracks streaked through the dirt on her face. "What happened?"

"It's Emir. The acolyte. There—The fire." She let out a shaking breath. "Emir was in the temple, defending the other acolytes, trying to get them out safely."

He knew what she was going to say before she said it.

"He didn't make it out."

Hearing the words aloud was like a blow to the chest. Emir, the old acolyte he'd defended from the Witnesses. Who'd discovered who Hassan truly was. Who'd brought the Order here.

Emir, whom Hassan had seen in his vision, standing at his side on the lighthouse of Nazirah.

It couldn't be. Hassan had *seen him*.

"Are you sure?" The question scraped out of his throat.

She nodded, eyes as hollow as Hassan felt. "I just found out. I came to tell you."

It was impossible. Emir had been in Hassan's vision. He was supposed to be with them when they retook Nazirah. He couldn't be dead.

The sound of raised voices from outside the tent broke the ensuing silence. It sounded like a crowd had gathered. Hassan glanced at Penrose.

"What's going on?" he asked her.

"Go on," Penrose said gently. "They're waiting for you."

Hassan glanced back at Khepri, stomach twisting with trepidation. There were still tear tracks on her cheeks. He didn't move.

"Go," Khepri said, releasing him.

Numb, he stepped outside, where the rest of the army and the refugees were gathering. One voice rose above the rest, and Hassan's gaze fell to Osei, who stood facing the others. The rest of the Guard stood behind him.

"One month ago, the Witnesses took the city of Nazirah under the command of a man who calls himself the Hierophant," Osei said. "He believes that the Graced are a plague, one that he has promised to end. He has filled his followers' ears with evil lies, lies that continue to spread throughout the land of Herat and beyond. Lies that have separated families and sown fear into the hearts of many. Lies that have exposed the Hierophant for what he truly is."

Hassan looked around. The refugees and soldiers were transfixed, captivated by Osei. Slowly, with dawning horror, Hassan realized what the swordsman was doing.

"But the Prophets foresaw the Hierophant's rise to power," Osei said. "They saw the darkness he would bring. For the good of mankind, we kept it a secret until now, but it is real. A prophecy that foresaw the Hierophant's rise and the Age of Darkness that will follow."

Whispers of shock and fear rippled through the crowd. Hassan just stood there, his own thoughts whirling madly. He had to stop Osei. He had to keep him from saying what was about to come next.

But his legs were lead. His mouth, empty of words. He could only stand there and listen.

"But the Seven Prophets' last prophecy spoke of more than just darkness. They also saw light. A new Prophet, born almost a century after the Seven disappeared. A Prophet who can see into the future and stop the Witnesses. A Prophet who lives among us." Osei held out his hand, his eyes boring into Hassan. "He is here. Prince Hassan Seif, the heir to the throne of Herat, is the Last Prophet."

The crowd turned from Osei to face Hassan. There was awe in their faces. Some even had tears in their eyes.

Hassan could barely breathe.

"Our Prophet has seen into our future and glimpsed our destiny to stop the Hierophant and the Age of Darkness. This is a fight for the future of a kingdom. Stand with the Prophet, and help us free the people of Nazirah and protect the Graced. Stand with the Prophet, and all of us—the people of Herat, of Pallas Athos, of the other Six Cities and beyond—can step out of the darkness and into the light."

"The Witnesses won't get the best of us!" someone cried from within the crowd. "We'll defeat them. I stand with the Prophet!"

As one, the crowd cried, "I stand with the Prophet!"

The call reverberated through the crowd. The Guard and the soldiers and refugees alike. Everyone who believed in Hassan.

"I stand with the Prophet!"

Their gazes crashed over Hassan like waves, so powerful that he had to look away. Their voices faded to a low drone in his head as something whispered out from the darkest part of his mind.

You are not the Prophet.

If Emir standing beside him in the vision was false, what about the rest of it? What had Hassan really seen—a vision or a dream?

You are not the Prophet.

It couldn't be a lie. He had *seen it.* It had felt real. It had felt *true.*

Or had he only convinced himself it was? Emir was dead. The vision couldn't be true. So what did that make Hassan? If he wasn't the Last Prophet, what was he?

A prince without a kingdom. A boy without Grace.

A liar.

III

THE TOWER

44

BERU

MEDEA WAS NO LONGER A VILLAGE—IT WAS A GRAVE.

The bodies of the villagers lay exactly as they had fallen when they died, but by now they'd all decayed to bones and dust. None of them had been disturbed; not even the jackals and the wildcats came to this place anymore. The trees were silent from the call of songbirds. The ants and cicadas had fled.

Beru had come a very long way to reach the place where she had begun.

Hector had honored her request to return to the village. It was Beru who had hesitated, Beru who had dawdled after their train pulled into Tel Amot Station. Not because she feared what lay ahead, but because she couldn't face what she'd left behind. Now, in this place, her past and her future converged—two ends of a single thread, an impossible beginning and an inevitable end.

The crunch of hard-packed dirt beneath their feet was the only sound as they made their way to the empty square. This was where the villagers used to set up market stalls to sell their goods and wares to caravans passing through. Beru could still remember the smell of roasting meat and fried dough, could almost hear the laughter of children and the mingling voices of neighbors gossiping and traders bargaining.

Now, it was silent. Sandstone archways flanked each edge of the square. Flat-roofed shops, their draped awnings stripped away, stood empty.

Hector stopped at Beru's side.

"There's no one here," Hector said, dark eyes sweeping the square. Past the Temple of Behezda and the old clock tower that was forever frozen at twelve o'clock, a twisted sycamore burst from the cracked earth.

Five skeletons lay half buried in the dirt around it. One was small—the child it had belonged to would have been no older than eight.

"They're all dead," Hector said.

Beru wasn't ready to see the look on his face. She could barely comprehend the scene around her, and she'd known exactly what awaited them in this village. She had *chosen* to come here, to come home, even knowing what was left of it.

"Your parents and your brother weren't the first innocent people to die because of me," she said.

Hector inhaled sharply.

"This is what it took to bring me back." Only now did she meet his gaze.

"How did it happen?" Hector asked, his voice rough.

It took all of Beru's dwindling strength to think back on that awful day. "She didn't mean to kill them," she whispered. "When she saw me lying dead, she grabbed my arm and—"

"No," Hector said. "Not that. How did you die?"

The question surprised her. What possible difference could it make to him? Maybe it was just the last piece in a puzzle Hector had spent the past five years putting together. What one tragedy could he trace the death of his family back to? What one choice had toppled into the next, and the next, and the next, that had led them here?

"I got sick," Beru replied. "Our parents, too. And many of the other villagers. There was a famine that year, and the lack of food made us all more vulnerable."

"That's not it, is it?"

She looked away. There was more, but she had never spoken it aloud. It wasn't anything she knew to be certain, only a lingering question she'd never been brave enough to ask. Her illness had not come over her quickly. It had been slow, gradual, just like all the times of fading that had come after it.

"Ephyra tried to heal me," Beru said. "She had done it before, for others. Our parents had forbidden her from using her Grace—they tried to keep it a secret from the other villagers—but sometimes we'd hear about sick kids and . . . she'd help them. But for some reason, this time, it didn't stick. I'd get better for a few days at a time, but then suddenly, I'd be sick again. Worse than I was before. It kept taking more and more to heal me. Ephyra has always blamed herself for failing to heal me before I died."

She looked out into the empty square. It was only here, in this place that held her past and her future, that she could face this last unanswered question. "But I think maybe it was me all along. Maybe there was always something wrong with me, something Ephyra couldn't fix. Something no one can fix. Maybe it wasn't being brought back to life that made me what I am. Maybe I was always meant for death."

In Hector's eyes, she saw not horror or confusion, but resolve. He looked down at the sword in his hand. Whatever answers he had been searching for, he had them now. And Beru, even in her fear and guilt, felt relief.

"I'll give you a proper funeral," he said. "Like I gave to my family."

Beru nodded, no longer trusting herself to speak. *I want to go home,* she had told Hector on the train from Pallas Athos. Now she was here. And she was scared. She didn't want to die. But neither could she bear the burden of what her life cost any longer.

Beru stood with her back to the sycamore and faced the end of her life. She didn't look away as Hector's sword scraped free of its sheath. Only as he raised his sword did she close her eyes.

She held her breath as the blade sang toward her.

45

JUDE

THE FIRST THING JUDE FELT BESIDES PAIN WAS THE SUDDEN COLD RUSH OF water splashing over him.

He shot to his feet. The whole world lurched, sending him stumbling back against a wall. His head swam. The floor rocked beneath him. He must have passed out at some point. The last thing he remembered was cold metal against his skin, a burning pain—

"At last, he wakes!"

Jude struggled to right himself, leaning against the wall. Heavy metal cuffs circled his wrists. Two men, both fair-skinned and taller than he, stood in a rectangle of light. He recognized them from the Hidden Spring. Mercenaries.

Fear spiked in his blood, and on instinct he shifted forward to move through a koah. But the cuffs seared against his wrists, and a flare of pain ripped through him. He slumped back again, gasping. He turned to the side to retch. His insides felt like they'd been turned to ash. His skin burned with the same white-hot pain that he'd felt from the mercenary's chain. These metal cuffs must have been forged in Godfire.

Jude was cut off from his Grace.

"Look at him," one of the mercenaries said, tilting his head to the side. A long scar ran down from beneath his eye to his jaw. "They're really quite pathetic when you take away their Grace. He can barely stand."

The other mercenary smirked and walked over to Jude. Something at his waist caught Jude's eye. The damascened hilt of a sword, etched with a familiar pattern.

"Oh, you like my sword, do you?" the mercenary asked, laying a hand on the hilt. "I think it rather suits me."

The Pinnacle Blade. Without thinking, Jude lunged toward the mercenary. His chains strained, yanking him to the floor.

The mercenary tutted, reaching down to grab him roughly by the hair. He dragged him up, jerking his head back and baring his throat.

"Maybe I'll sell it, though," he mused, his breath hot against Jude's cheek. "I bet it would fetch a fine price. Almost as fine a price as you."

Jude shuddered as he met the mercenary's cruel gray eyes.

"'Ey!" the scarred mercenary shouted. "We're not supposed to hurt him."

"Aww, not even a little?" He turned Jude's head one way and then the other.

"Illya said not to cause more damage," the scarred mercenary said. "I don't want to give that snake any reason not to pay up, do you?"

The gray-eyed mercenary's face twisted with displeasure. "What do you think the Hierophant will do with him?"

Jude choked in a breath as the mercenary's grip tightened. He had never been as helpless as he was now.

"Whatever it is, I hope I'll get to watch," the gray-eyed mercenary said, lowering his voice as if he meant the words for Jude.

"Let's just give him his food and get out of here," the scarred mercenary said.

The gray-eyed mercenary threw Jude to the ground.

"Eat up," he said with a nasty smile as the other mercenary dropped a bowl to the floor. An unappealing brown liquid sloshed out. Sniggering, the two mercenaries left.

The door clanked shut again, and a breath burst from Jude's chest like a punch. He sucked in another as he curled himself inward, pressing a fist to his teeth, willing himself to stay calm. He was falling apart, his seams ripped out, leaving him empty and ragged.

He took a shaking breath, and then another, and tried to focus on his surroundings. He was in a damp, dark enclosure—a cell? The wood of the wall pressed into his spine. It wasn't just his bleary head—the floor really was rocking.

He was aboard a ship.

"So you're awake."

A voice croaked through the fragile silence. Jude turned toward the side wall of his cell, which was less of a wall and more like a row of simple wooden slats nailed together. Through the finger-sized gaps between the slats, he could make out another figure. Anton.

He hadn't even known there was someone else here with him. If he'd been able to use his Grace, he would have heard Anton's heartbeat, his breath. Jude felt blind.

"How long was I—have we—?"

There was the sound of shifting on the other side of the wall. "You were out for . . . a while. I didn't know what they'd done to you back at the Hidden Spring. Those chains . . ."

"Godfire," Jude said. "That man said they were forged in Godfire. It's the Witnesses' weapon. It burns the Grace out of you."

He tried to keep his tone flat, but pain lingered in his voice. He remembered the rumors he'd heard about the Hierophant, even before coming to Pallas Athos. That somehow, he could block people from using their Grace. At least now, Jude knew how that rumor had started.

It was a moment before Anton replied. "It's not . . . Is it permanent?"

"I don't know." Jude closed his eyes. He didn't want to think about that. The possibility that this pain, this *emptiness*, would persist even after the chains were taken off.

"But it hurts you, doesn't it?" Anton's voice was timid now. "I could see, back at the Hidden Spring. And now, you sound . . ."

Jude knew how he sounded. Defeated. He was. He was completely at the mercy of these men. If they wanted, they could keep him subdued and in pain for the rest of his life.

Though that might not be much longer anyway.

"What about you?" he asked after a moment, turning his head back toward the wall between them. "Did they hurt you?"

"No," Anton replied. "They didn't hurt me."

The slight pause between his words settled uncomfortably in the stale air. The image of Anton's fearful face back at the taverna flashed through Jude's mind.

"You knew they were coming for you," Jude said. "Back at the Hidden Spring, you didn't even question it. What do the Witnesses want with you?"

"I don't know," Anton said.

It had to be a lie. Jude knew it, even without his Grace to help him hear the hitch of Anton's breath, the acceleration of his heartbeat.

"Tell me the truth, Anton," he said. "You were found with the Pale Hand. You're being hunted by someone connected to the Witnesses. Why?"

"I don't *know*."

"You're lying," Jude said, growing angry. "That man, Illya—"

"Don't." Anton's voice trembled. "Don't say his name."

Jude's anger wilted. "You know him, though." He thought again of Anton's face when Jude had leapt between him and Illya. It was terror—terror that had cut through Jude's own confusion as clean as a blade.

"He's my brother," Anton answered after a long moment. "But I didn't know he was connected with the Witnesses. I swear."

Jude pressed his head against his knees.

"I'm sorry," Anton said, his voice quiet against the background of Jude's harsh breath.

"Don't," Jude bit out. A fragile silence strained between them.

He wished he could blame Anton, but this wasn't his fault. Any of it. Jude was the one who'd recklessly thrown his lot in with him at the Hidden Spring. What had he been thinking, chasing Hector halfway across an ocean? Chasing a man who'd abandoned him, broken his oath, turned his back on Jude like he meant nothing to him?

He should never have left the Prophet's side.

No—he should never have come to Pallas Athos at all. He should never have accepted the title of Keeper, when he knew he would only disgrace himself, the Order, his father. Every doubt in his heart had been right. He'd abandoned the Prophet. He'd lost the Pinnacle Blade. He had carried one hundred years of legacy and hope on his back, and he had let it all come crashing down.

"I failed him," he said quietly, the realization settling over him.

"Navarro made his own choices," Anton replied. "It wasn't your job to stop him, no matter what you think."

"Not Hector." Relief washed over Jude in speaking the words, as though now, finally, he was unburdened of the lie he'd told himself for so long. The lie that said he was equal to the duty he'd been raised to carry out, that said he would one day be able to set aside every doubt and misstep, and devote himself to the one thing—the only thing—that should have mattered. For nineteen years, he'd carried around that lie, and now he let it slip away. "The Prophet."

A hitch of breath was Anton's only reply. The silence deepened between them.

And then: "Jude . . ."

A tension that sounded almost like pain wracked Anton's voice. A staccato breath punctured the air. Then silence again.

Jude turned away from the wall separating them. There was nothing Anton could say that would change the truth. Jude had failed. It didn't matter what happened to him now.

46

HASSAN

HASSAN LED THE PROCESSION FROM THE STEPS OF THE TEMPLE OF PALLAS TO the site below the agora where they'd dug the grave. The refugees and other acolytes kissed their palms and held them out as they passed along the weaving path.

Earlier, Hassan had stood in the temple as they washed Emir's body in the scrying pool. Just as every squalling baby was washed in the temple scrying pool, so was every still and silent corpse. The First and Last Waters.

When the washing was done, an acolyte with the Grace of Blood drew the patterns of unbinding on Emir's body with sweet-smelling chrism oil. The others dressed him in the traditional lilac robes of the acolytes, and tied the sash into a special knot that symbolized the flow of *esha* from the body back into the world. They cut a lock from his gray hair and sealed it in a bottle of chrism oil.

"He would have wanted you to have it," the acolyte said as he pressed the blue jeweled bottle into Hassan's hand.

Hassan didn't deserve this reliquary, the last token of Emir's life.

He took it nonetheless, slipping it into his breast pocket, beside his father's compass and his heart.

The sun was high and hot above as they reached the grave and laid Emir inside. Seven torches were lit and planted in the ground beside it.

Hassan wiped the sweat trickling from his brow as one of the other acolytes faced the mourners and began to speak.

"We bless this *esha*, the sacred energy that was Emir, and pray for its release and safe return into the earth. May it be guided by the Grace of the Prophet without a name, who wandered the Earth, the protector of all the forgotten, the nameless, the lost."

The blessing had been spoken in some form at funerary rites all over the world for centuries, but today Hassan felt like it was meant for him, too. What was he, besides lost? He thought he'd been following a path, one laid out for him by the Prophets a century ago, only to find he'd been led astray.

He thought he'd seen his destiny before him, clear and vivid, but it had dissolved like smoke. Emir was supposed to stand beside Hassan when they took back Nazirah from the Witnesses. Instead, he was in a grave. He'd been wrong about Hassan. And it had cost him his life.

Afternoon deepened into twilight as they filled Emir's grave with earth. Those who'd followed the procession to the gravesite slowly departed back to the agora. Hassan remained. The Guard kept their distance, perhaps in deference to Hassan's grief. But it was guilt, not grief, that kept him beside the grave. Guilt and shame.

The scent of earth and citrus perfumed the air as someone drew up beside him. Khepri. They stood for a moment in silence, faces to the disappearing sun.

"I know it's hard," Khepri began haltingly. "I cared for him, too. But Prince Hassan, please—now is not the time to lose sight of what we're doing."

Hassan didn't look at her. He knew what was coming. He'd avoided her and everyone else as much as he could over the past few days. He didn't know what to say to any of them. How to unravel the things he'd set in motion with his hope and hubris and *lies*.

"You've missed strategy meetings," Khepri said. "You've barely spoken to the soldiers, even though now is when they need to hear from you most. The Order has already set sail, and your aunt's ships are ready. As awful and as cruel as it is, we don't have time for you to grieve, Hassan."

"I know." His voice came out hoarse, unfeeling.

"Emir believed in you and in our cause. He wanted us to fight. He would still want that now, when we're so close to the future that you saw. You can't—"

"He was there," Hassan said. "In my vision. Emir was there. Beside me, on the lighthouse. He was *there*."

Shock and disbelief flickered in her eyes.

"I saw him there, with me, watching our forces take on the Witnesses," he went on. "But now he is *gone*. How can the vision be true if I saw myself standing beside a man whose body we just buried?"

"That—that doesn't mean anything. It doesn't mean that *none of it*—"

"*It does!*" Hassan roared. Everything he'd been hiding since the Witnesses' attack came bubbling to the surface. Every thought that had chased through his mind. Every doubt he hadn't allowed himself to have before. They poured out of him, soaked in days of guilt and shame and rage. "I believed that what I saw was the future, my destiny, a way to stop the Age of Darkness. But it was a ridiculous, naive dream. Lethia was right. I wanted so badly to believe that dream, but I can't any longer." He closed his eyes. He knew what he had to do, but it meant giving up everything.

"What are you saying?" Khepri asked, her voice trembling in desperation.

"I am not the Last Prophet, Khepri," Hassan said. "I don't have any answers—not for you, not for the Guard, and not for the people who stand behind me. If I were the Prophet, I would know it. If I had a Grace, I would feel it. But I don't. There's nothing powerful in me. It's time I stop pretending there is."

"You want to give up on fighting the Witnesses?" Betrayal cracked through her words. "Hassan, you *can't*. The Order is the key to winning Nazirah back. If you tell them this, it's all over. They won't fight for us, not if they don't believe it will fulfill their prophecy."

"I know. I know what I am giving up." Without the Guard behind him, without Khepri at his side, without their army standing before him, he had nothing. "But I can't lie to them and send them into battle in the same breath."

"You don't *know* it's a lie! Just because part of your vision was false doesn't mean you're not—"

"I know enough," Hassan said. "Enough to doubt. Enough that I know I should tell them, rather than let more people lose their lives for the sake of a lie."

Emir, who had given his life for a lie, who had believed in him, had told him he fit all the signs of the prophecy. Now when Hassan thought back on that conversation, he wanted to laugh. The lights in the sky. The prophecy of Nazirah. Had he really been so convinced by a handful of coincidences? Had he been so eager to believe it?

People believed what they wanted to believe. When it seemed like the Last Prophet had come at last, the Order of the Last Light had not questioned it. They had wanted him to be the Prophet, to believe their savior had come. Hassan had wanted it, too. And it had been so easy to convince himself it was true.

"Even if you aren't the Prophet, you are still the Prince of Herat," Khepri said fiercely. "We don't need a vision of the future to tell us it's our destiny to stand against the Witnesses. It is already our destiny. It was written when they took Nazirah. When they used their Godfire to torture our people. When they attacked us here. As long as the Witnesses have the Godfire flame, and the Hierophant walks the Earth, all the Graced are in danger. Think of your family, Hassan. Your parents. If you do this . . . the lives of every person with Grace living in Herat will be forfeited."

"Do you think I haven't considered that?" Anger burst in his chest. Anger was so much easier, so much simpler, than the grief that threatened to rend his heart in two.

But Khepri lifted her chin, refusing to be cowed. "I think you are still afraid. Whether that vision was true or false, I bound my fate to yours when I came here to Pallas Athos." She reached out and cupped his face between her hands, the same way he had done to her after the Witnesses' attack. "You may not be the chosen Prophet, but you are still the one *I* chose. So tell me—was that a mistake, too? Did I choose the wrong man?"

I don't know, he thought helplessly, swallowing hard. With careful, measured motions, he raised his hands to hers and pulled them away from him.

"I don't know why you chose me," he said. "I don't know why you would choose me, even now." He pressed her hands back against her chest and released her. "But the others deserve to have the same choice."

Hurt and betrayal clouded her face.

"I want you to gather the army and the Guard outside the temple tonight," Hassan said. "I will speak with them. We will see what they decide."

He started to walk away from her, past the ancient stone markers that lined the graveyard. Ahead, a bright torchlight wobbled, picking its way through the gravesite toward him.

"I thought I would find you here." It was Lethia. The light cast shadows on her long face.

"Is everything all right?" he asked.

"Yes," Lethia replied. "I came to tell you the ships are ready to set sail for Nazirah tomorrow morning. I'll depart for Charis then, too, as planned."

Tomorrow morning. There was no time. No time to think this through, any of it.

"Khepri, go gather the others." He didn't look at her as he spoke. "The army and the Guard. I need to speak with my aunt."

Khepri didn't move. "Hassan, think about what you're doing, *please*—"

"Khepri."

She stiffened at his brusque tone. "Yes, Your Grace."

The honorific twisted in his gut, but Hassan didn't let it show as Khepri stalked off into the night.

He turned to Lethia once they were alone. "There's something else, isn't there?"

"There's been word from Nazirah," Lethia said hesitantly. "A source inside the city."

The words jolted through Hassan like lightning.

"And?"

Lethia's expression was grave. "The Hierophant ordered the execution of the king. The sentence was carried out two days ago."

Hassan's heart stuttered. That couldn't be right. His father was waiting for him, waiting for Hassan to free him from the Witnesses. Together, they would take their country back.

"Your father is dead, Hassan," Lethia said softly. "I'm so sorry."

The words echoed hollowly around him, drowning out every other sound. He thought of the Hierophant, of the Godfire burns on Reza's body, of the flames licking at the Temple of Pallas. The image of Emir's face swam before him—pale and still in death. The image morphed, and it was not Emir's face that he saw, but Hassan's father's. The laughter and wonder in his eyes when he'd watched Hassan and his mother spar in the palace training yard. The crease of his brow as he'd shaped gears and wire and glass together in the palace workshop. The small, private smile that told Hassan he'd done something to please him. A smile Hassan would never see again.

Each memory made his blood burn hotter.

"Hassan?"

He looked up at his aunt, the stern set of her features made soft by wide, concerned eyes. Eyes the same color as her brother's. As Hassan gazed into them, he saw his father looking back.

He touched a shaking hand to the compass in his breast pocket.

He knew exactly what he would do.

"I swear," he said, "I will do everything in my power to make the Hierophant pay for this. We sail for Nazirah tomorrow. And he better be ready for us."

47

BERU

THE CRACK OF STEEL STRIKING WOOD SPLIT THE AIR.

Beru's eyes flew open. Inches from her head, Hector's sword hung, half buried in the trunk of the sycamore.

She was unharmed. Shock and relief overwhelmed her, buckling her knees. She slid to the ground, shaking. Her eyes found Hector standing beside the tree, face turned away, body held in tension, breath coming in ragged bursts.

"I can't," he said, his voice wracked with pain. He, too, was shaking. "I can't."

Tears bit at the corners of her eyes. She could not speak.

Hector slowly raised his dark eyes to hers. "I can't kill you. Why can't I kill you?"

She shook her head. Hector pulled his sword free from the tree trunk.

"I have to do this," he said, his voice quavering. "If I do . . . I can stop it."

Stop what? Beru wanted to ask, but nothing came out of her mouth.

His eyes met hers again. "What was it you said? That killing you won't bring my family back? I know that. You think I came after you for revenge. That's what Jude thought, too. But you're both wrong. The death of my family is what brought me to you, but they're not why you have to die."

"Then why?" she asked at last. She needed to know. Not why she had to die, but why she was alive. Somehow, she knew the answer was the same.

Hector took a shaking breath. "I was brought to the Order of the Last Light after my family died. They raised me, trained me, and when the time came, I took an oath and joined their ranks. I learned the secret they've been keeping for a century. A prophecy."

A chill shivered through her, as though the heat of the evening sun had momentarily evaporated.

"There's another prophecy?" The idea was too huge to wrap her mind around.

"The prophecy predicts an end to the Graced and the destruction of the world as we know it," Hector said. "An Age of Darkness, brought by three harbingers. A deceiver. The pale hand of death."

A gasp rose in her throat.

"And the last harbinger of the Age of Darkness," Hector said slowly. "'That which sleeps in the dust shall rise.'"

It was her. The moment the words left his lips, she *knew*. The truth of what she was obliterated all other thought.

She was a creature of darkness.

"I should do it." Hector gripped his sword tighter. "I should end your life. Kill you to stop the Age of Darkness from coming."

He moved suddenly toward her. Beru flinched instinctively. But when she looked back, it was his hand, and not the sword, he held out to her.

She took it, hesitant, and let him pull her to her feet.

He sheathed his sword. "But I can't. I can't end a life, even one that shouldn't be here."

Beru stood facing him, her hand hooked around her wrist, covering the dark handprint by habit. It was a moment before she found her voice. "I'm going to die soon anyway. It doesn't matter if it's you or . . ." She shook her head. "Ephyra was the thing keeping me alive. Without her, I'm going to die."

His dark eyes were locked on hers, and Beru could still see pain and grief there. And something else.

"Then I'll stay with you," he said. "Until the end."

Beru closed her eyes. She thought about the silent village around them. About the bodies marked with the pale handprint. About Ephyra—her loud bark of a laugh and the way they'd traded barbs and shared gripes, carving out a life together in the rotten, forgotten corners of cities.

She thought about her sister's blood-soaked hands, her own bone-tired weariness, and the slow whittling down of their hope.

"Until the end," she echoed.

In the village of the dead, they waited.

48

HASSAN

HASSAN TRACED HIS FINGER OVER THE MAP TO THE IMAGE OF THE LIGHTHOUSE. "This is where we drop anchor."

The others—Petrossian, Osei, Penrose, Khepri, and Lethia's son Cirion, looked at him with various expressions of exhaustion. They'd been at this for hours now, and hours the day before, hashing and rehashing the plan. By now, they'd all grown tired of the cramped, seasick navigation room of the *Cressida*. More than that, they'd grown tired of the endless discussion. They'd gone over every detail of their attack a dozen times.

"The *Artemisia* will dock before sunrise. Yarik, Annuka, and Faran will wait for the Order's ships to arrive, then lead the assault on the harbor," Hassan said, pointing. "Meanwhile, we'll be behind the lighthouse, so we won't be visible from the palace. Khepri and I will go up into the lighthouse to scout the palace and the harbor. We'll signal you to disembark and make your way to the palace."

"The Witnesses are either keeping the Godfire flame in the High

Temple or somewhere in the palace, I'd bet," Khepri added. "We can start there."

Penrose nodded. "The Order's ships will arrive at dawn. They'll wipe out the Witnesses' forces on shore and take the harbor while we search for the Godfire flame."

"There's no margin for error," Petrossian said.

"We all came here for the same reason," Cirion said. "Myself and my crew included. By this time tomorrow, Nazirah's rightful ruler will reign."

Hassan glanced at his elder cousin, whom he remembered from his visits to the Palace of Herat, when Hassan was very young. Yet Cirion—now Captain Siskos—had answered Hassan's call for aid without hesitation and at great personal risk. He may have been only half-Herati, but he was as loyal as any countryman.

"We'll be in sight of land soon," Cirion went on. "We should all try and get some rest in the next few hours."

Every muscle in Hassan's back stiffened in protest when he straightened up from hunching over the map. He nodded farewell to the others as they shuffled out of the navigation room. Hassan stayed. Tomorrow, he would see his city again for the first time in over a month.

Departing Pallas Athos had been bittersweet. Many of the soldiers had bid farewell to their families, who had boarded the Order's ship to sail for the Gallian Mountains and seek protection at Kerameikos Fort. It was difficult but necessary to part with them. If Hassan failed—and only he and Khepri knew how possible failure was—then it would be more important than ever for his people to have somewhere safe to go.

Azizi, his mother, and his baby sister were among the refugees who'd departed for Kerameikos.

"I want to go home, too," Azizi had said to Hassan as they waited on the docks to board the ship. "Why can't we come with you?"

The words had twisted in Hassan's gut. "You will. I promise. You will. That's why I'm going—to make Nazirah safe for you to return to."

"But I'm not scared," Azizi protested. "I want to help."

Hassan had crouched down to Azizi's level, putting a hand on the boy's bony shoulder. "You *are* helping. This—getting on this ship with your mother and sister to sail to an unfamiliar land—it's just as important as what I'm doing. Just as brave. To keep our home inside your heart, right beside your hope, even when you're far away—it's one of the bravest things there is. I'm going to make Herat safe for you, Azizi."

He hoped.

Then it had come time for Hassan to say his farewells to Lethia. Part of him wished she were coming with him instead of boarding a ship headed to Charis, bringing word to the Herati refugees there.

There were not enough words, he thought, in all the languages of the world to thank her. Not just for the ships, but for everything she had done and everything she'd been to him since the coup. Even when she'd kept him from the agora, even when she'd questioned the Order, she had never doubted *him*.

"Lethia—"

She had cut him off with a look. "Be safe, and I will see you soon, my prince."

She'd kissed his cheek and nodded at Cirion to take him aboard the *Cressida*.

Now, in the ship's navigation room, Hassan traced the distance from Pallas Athos to Nazirah. It was hardly any distance at all, yet it had taken everything he had to cross it.

"You should get some rest, Hassan."

Khepri. Some small part of him had hoped she would stay behind after the strategy meeting, too. In the days leading up to their departure,

Hassan had noticed how often he'd sought her out, even in the midst of their planning and strategy with the rest of the army and the Guard. He'd caught himself staring at her, hoping she'd look back. Every time she did, he was hit with an unexpected lightness in his chest, a deep pull in his belly. Herat and Nazirah were what Hassan thought of the moment he awoke each day, but Khepri was what he saw when he closed his eyes at night.

She leaned her hip against the table beside him.

He shook his head, spreading his hands over the map. "There's so much that could still go wrong. Our ship could be spotted from shore. There could be a blockade we don't know about, or the Order's ships might be delayed—"

"Stop," Khepri said, stilling his hands with her own. "We've gone over the contingencies a thousand times. There's nothing left to do except trust in yourself, and in us." She put her palm against his cheek, tilting his face to her. "But that's not really what you're worried about, is it?"

He let himself look at her, unable to hide the desperation on his face. "Tell me I'm doing the right thing," he said, helplessness clawing at his throat. "Tell me this is what I must do. That I have no other choice than the path in front of us."

Her gaze was steady as she moved toward him, into him, cupping his face in her hands. "We always have choices, Hassan."

And then she pressed her lips to his. Hassan barely had time to react before she was drawing away, her brows creased in concern. Her hand pressed down on the curve between his neck and shoulder like an anchor.

"I'm sorry," she said, with a shake of her head. "That was—"

He did not wait to hear the rest of it. He surged toward her, one hand in her hair and the other enclosing her against the table as his mouth found hers. They'd almost been here twice before. Once, he had drawn away. The second time, it had been she who'd shied from this.

But now, they came together. Now, he kissed her like it was the only thing in the world he was meant for. Like prophecy and bloodshed and battle did not matter. Just this—lips against lips, his pulse beating against her thumb, her hair like silk through his fingers.

Khepri broke the kiss with a soft gasp, and then swept her hand across the table behind her, scattering maps and papers and plans. She pushed herself up onto it and drew Hassan toward her, kissing him again, frantic and hungry and hopeful.

Heat surged through Hassan, and he thought incongruously of their sparring match in the agora, of how luminous Khepri had looked while yelling at him in the villa courtyard, of her fierce and unbreakable spirit in the face of the Witnesses' attack.

Did I choose the wrong man? she had asked him beside Emir's grave.

No, he thought desperately now, clutching her closer, consumed by his need for this, for her. He wanted all that fire and grit and steel directed at him, and him alone. He wanted to know every part of her. And he wanted her to know every part of him, because no one else could. He'd lied to her about who he was the first time he'd met her. But here in the ship's belly, on the eve of battle, she was the only person in the world who knew the truth of who he was. He wanted her to know the truth of this, too—how she made him feel, how her touch and her gaze and her words took him apart. How they pulled him back into something whole and new and *more.*

Her fingers curled around the back of his neck, tugging slightly at the short hairs there until he lifted his lips from her pulse point and pressed his nose against her cheek.

"I can hear your heart beat," she whispered against his ear.

Hassan trailed his thumbs down her sides, reveling in how she shivered against him.

"It's very fast." He could hear the smile in her voice.

He let out a helpless laugh.

"It's all right," Khepri said. She reached for his hand and pressed it to her heart. He felt it beat against his palm. "So's mine."

"I thought," Hassan gasped, pressing his forehead against hers. "I thought you didn't want this. I thought—"

She cut him off with a kiss, her hands leaving trails of warmth down the planes of his chest. When she pulled back, her eyes were damp. "I tried not to. But I don't care if it's selfish anymore—I want this. I want you."

His lips found her pulse, the line of her jaw, the hollow of her throat, eliciting sweet sighs and the sound of his name, like a breath. "*Hassan.*"

And then her body went rigid against his. "What was that? Did you hear that?"

It took Hassan a second to pull away. Khepri's eyes were wide and alert. He hadn't heard anything, but he stepped back nonetheless, allowing her to slide from the table back onto her feet.

"Something's wrong," Khepri said, grabbing her sword from where it leaned against the wall.

The door burst open.

"Prince Hassan!" It was the ship's first mate, out of breath and frantic. Two other crew members stood behind him in the shadowed corridor. "Come quickly."

Hassan straightened, desperately hoping he didn't look like he'd been doing what he'd just been doing. "What is it?"

"Something's been sighted in the harbor," the first mate said, leading them out into the corridor and toward the stairs.

"Ships?" Hassan asked, hastening to keep up.

The first mate shook his head. "I'm not sure. The captain just asked us to come fetch you immediately."

It was then that Hassan realized Khepri was no longer keeping pace behind them. She'd stopped in the middle of the corridor, illuminated by the incandescent light spilling out of the room they'd just left, the two other crew members at her back.

"Khepri?"

"You're lying," she said suddenly to the first mate. "I—Your heart rate just sped up. You *do* know what's going on."

"Come, they're waiting above decks," the first mate replied briskly.

Khepri shook her head. "You're *lying*."

She reached for her sword, but not quickly enough. Before Hassan could comprehend what was happening, the two crew members behind Khepri leapt forward, wrapping a chain around her, pinning her arms to her sides.

"Khepri!" Hassan did not think. He lunged, slamming one of the crew members sideways into the wall. The other grabbed Hassan, dragging him back down the corridor.

With that moment of reprieve, Khepri threw the chain off. It dangled free from a metal cuff that had been locked around her wrist. Khepri slid into a strong lunge, her arms bent at the elbows in front of her. Hassan recognized the stance as the starting position of the koah for strength. A desperate cry escaped her lips as she began to move, and she fell back into the wall.

Rage poured into Hassan's lungs as he surged against the crew members who held him. In his anger, he was blind to anything but the sight of Khepri's face, warped in pain.

"What's happening?" Hassan demanded, his voice a hoarse shout. "What have you done to her?"

Khepri tried another koah, and again cried out. Two more crew members pinned her against the wall, binding her arms behind her back.

"Don't touch her!" Hassan roared, ripping himself free from his captors. "Get off—"

Someone slammed into him from behind, pinning him face forward against the wall beside Khepri. He could hear the sounds of her struggle, and the choked-off whimper she let out.

As they bound his hands, Hassan struggled to make sense of what was happening. Anger clouded his mind. Was this a misunderstanding? Mutiny?

But as the first mate marched them down the corridor and up through the hatch to the deck, the truth became clear.

In the bruised violet-blue light of the dawning morning, Hassan's soldiers were lined up along the side of the ship, hands bound with chains and mouths gagged with cloth. A dozen crew members stood in front of them, crossbows trained.

They had been betrayed.

The click of boots sounded behind him, and then a firm hand clamped down on his shoulder.

"Well, Hassan," Cirion said. "I have to admit, you had a pretty fine plan laid out."

Wordless with rage, Hassan turned to face his eldest cousin. His eyes were exactly the same shade as Lethia's.

"It just so happens that ours was better."

49

ANTON

THE PALACE SERVANT'S ROOM THEY KEPT ANTON IN WAS ACTUALLY VERY NICE. Nicer than his tiny room in Pallas Athos, and certainly nicer than the cramped, rotting cell in the hull of the ship where he'd spent the last few days.

Pale sandstone walls and iron scaffolding stretched up to a sloped ceiling. A lofted bed was tucked beneath one narrow window, where he could stare out at that white strip between sea and sky. Every so often, he would catch a glimpse of sails on the horizon and imagine it was a ship that was coming to save him.

It never was.

Twice a day, a guard dressed in green and gold brought him plates of crumbly white cheese sprinkled over olives and sun-risen bread and a cup of lukewarm tea.

"Wait," Anton said one night as the guard began to shuffle out.

The guard stopped, uneasy.

Anton leaned forward, trying to strike the right balance of eagerness and boredom. "Do you have any cards?"

Halfway through their sixth game of canbarra, the door swung open again and in strode Illya.

The guard jumped to his feet from where he'd been sitting on the floor with Anton, sending the cards in his hand flying. Illya nodded almost imperceptibly to the door, and the guard hastily retreated.

Only after he was gone did Illya look at Anton. "I think you'll agree these accommodations exceed the ones in Pallas Athos."

Anton hadn't seen his brother since the fight at the Hidden Spring, but he'd known this moment was coming. Illya always made Anton feel powerless, but now he truly was. With everything else stripped away, with no hope of escape, there was only one way left for Anton to stand up to him. He could deny Illya that which he wanted the most—Anton's fear. He'd spent most of their childhood learning how to extract it, but here, with Anton completely at his mercy, he wouldn't get the satisfaction of seeing just how deep that fear ran.

Anton shuffled the deck idly in his hands. "I guess in Herat they like to comfort their lambs before they slaughter them."

"A lamb?" Illya said, mirth in his golden eyes. "Is that what you think you are?"

He circled his brother and sat down in the place the guard had just vacated. Tossing one of the olive pits they'd been using as counters into the air, he asked, "Canbarra?"

Sitting this close, Illya looked startlingly young. A memory came to Anton, of the two of them on the thick wool rug beside the hearth in their grandmother's home, heads bent together as they peered down at a fanned-out deck of cards and a pile of dried white beans.

Anton blinked the memory away. There were so few peaceful memories of his brother that he was surprised he'd held on to any of them at all. The terror hadn't been constant, which made it all the more insidious. He had never been able to tell when he would be faced with an older brother teaching him how to play cards and throw snowballs, and when he would be faced with a creature of rage and wrath.

Illya shuffled the cards and then dealt them, four cards each and one faceup in the middle. He picked up the olive pit and shuffled it between his hands before holding both fists out to Anton.

"Choose."

Warily, Anton pointed at the left hand. Illya opened it. Empty.

"So tell me, Anton," Illya said, drawing a card from the deck. "How are you finding Nazirah?"

Anton's voice was measured as he took his own turn. "Well, I'm being held prisoner by the person I despise more than anyone in the world, so I can't say it's recommended itself to me."

Illya sighed wearily. "I suppose it was too much to hope that you might have learned some manners since we were children."

"Oh, I did. I just must've missed the lesson where they teach you to be polite to murderous older brothers."

"Murderous?" Illya flipped an ace of cups over. "I'm not sure that's fair. I know what you think happened that day on the lake, but I'm afraid your mind has played tricks on you."

"I know what I remember." It wasn't the first time that Illya had tried to convince Anton his own perception was false, or that the pain he'd inflicted on him was somehow Anton's fault. *You shouldn't have made me angry, you shouldn't have been in my way, you shouldn't have looked at me like that.* "You hid it so well from Grandmother and from Father, but we both know what you were really like. What you did."

"I don't deny that I hurt you when we were young," Illya said, placing a counter on a pair of sixes. "I'm sorry for that. I was stupid back then. Jealous, inconsolable."

"Psychotic," Anton offered, placing his card.

"That's all in the past."

Anton looked up. "Then let me go." He hated to plead, but there was nothing else he could do. "Let me go, and just stay away from me."

Illya looked down at his cards, taking his time in drawing and discarding. "I can't do that," he said at last. "Not now that I finally see what Father and Grandmother tried so hard to teach me. What they told me, over and over until I could barely stand it anymore."

His eyes flashed, and his words tightened to a growl. It was the first hint of the Illya Anton knew, not the one he'd tried to be in Pallas Athos, so sorrowful and filled with regret. Not the one who moved through the world with riches and finery. Not even the one who lied and manipulated with cold, effortless efficiency. Those were not the truth of Illya. This was. This snarling, howling creature who tore and bit, and wanted, above all, to *destroy*. This was what Illya had worked so hard to conceal, even when they were young. He couldn't afford to let anyone see what he truly was—a monster who wore the face of a man.

"They were right," Illya said, his calm facade sliding back into place. "You are special, Anton. They didn't even realize how much. They thought you were the chosen heir of a dead, raving king, but you're more than that."

Nausea rose in Anton's throat. Illya's words pulled at him the same way the memory of the lake did. He refused to let them pull him under.

"Well, dear brother, it looks like that's the game," Illya said pleasantly, tossing down his cards faceup.

Anton looked at them. Illya had won. He had not, he realized, expected any other outcome.

Illya rose. "Time to go."

He swept over to the door, nodding to the guards who stood by.

They seized hold of Anton. He didn't bother to struggle as they led him after Illya, up the winding stairs and down a long hallway lit by flickering torchlight. Mosaics stretched down the walls, depicting scenes of tall-stalked wheat, a flowing river, and exotic wildlife—crocodiles and herons, and an elephant with tusks of inlaid pearl.

The sitting room that Illya led him to was decorated to much simpler taste. A few plush seats in dark violet and dusk rose surrounded a glass and silver filigree table. As they entered, Illya nodded to a man that stood beside an open door that led out onto a balcony.

A woman's voice floated in with the sea breeze. "Leave us."

The man at the door bowed his head and exited. Behind him, the door clicked shut.

The woman stepped in from the balcony. She wore a patterned black kaftan, belted with a gold sash inlaid with rubies and other bright gems. They caught the light of the flickering flames that lit the corners of the room. She held herself like royalty—back straight, chin up, floating across the floor toward them. Her thin, stern face was punctuated by a black mole just above her upper lip. In one hand, a lit cigarillo trailed a thin stream of smoke.

"Lady Lethia," Illya said, sweeping into a tidy bow. "I trust your journey from Pallas Athos was tolerable."

She inclined her head, turning her piercing gaze to Anton. "Is this him?"

Illya nodded, stepping back to present him. "It is."

Lady Lethia prowled a circle around Anton, a lioness closing in on her prey. "The Hierophant may believe your word, but my own confidence in you is waning," she said to Illya. "Last we spoke, you said you would deliver the Pale Hand along with this boy. Yet you let her slip through your hands. Thanks to your carelessness, I'll have to expend more valuable resources finding her again."

Anton turned sharply to look at his brother. In the chaos of the fight at the Hidden Spring, he hadn't paused to think about why, exactly, Illya had tried to capture Ephyra, too. Now, though, he wondered. What could the Witnesses want with the Pale Hand?

"There was a complication," Illya replied, his gaze dropping to the ground. "She killed two of my mercenaries."

"*Your* mercenaries? Whose money was it that paid for them?"

Anton recognized the mild smile that graced Illya's lips. It was the same smile he used to wear as their grandmother berated him, sometimes for hours on end. To Anton, that smile had been a warning that his own torment would come next.

"Yours, of course, Lady Lethia," Illya replied lightly. "And need I remind you what that generosity got you?"

Lethia's gaze returned to Anton. "You'd better be sure about him. You can't afford another mistake."

"Don't worry," Illya replied, haughtiness creeping into his voice. "I'm sure."

"I suppose we'll find out soon enough. You did well in delivering the Keeper, at least."

Jude. Anton's heart lurched. It had been three days since they'd been taken off the ship and separated. Anton had tried not to think about the swordsman, though his mind had stubbornly returned to him time and again. Guilt clawed at his chest. He didn't even know if Jude was still alive.

"It was mere luck they were together," Illya said.

Lady Lethia smiled. "The Prophets would have called it fate."

"Then fate is on our side."

"Of that, we can be sure," Lady Lethia replied. "But your job isn't over yet. Find the answers we seek. If the Hierophant is satisfied, then we all get what we want. I will have Nazirah, the Hierophant will have his Reckoning, and you will have your place at his side secured."

Illya bared his teeth in a smile. "It will be done."

Anton shivered. Illya meant to do what their grandmother had tried to do—use Anton's power, a power he had never wanted, in order to gain his own.

"Now, if you'd be so kind, I have other business to attend to," Lady Lethia said, turning back toward the window that faced the sea. "My nephew will be arriving in Nazirah soon, and I must prepare his warm welcome."

50

EPHYRA

THE NIGHT MARKET OF TEL AMOT WAS EXACTLY AS EPHYRA REMEMBERED IT.
Violet-hued lights and sweet-smelling smoke cast a soft haziness over
the square where the artisans and craftsmen of the city set up their
shops to catch the incoming sailors and tradesmen from across the
Pelagos. It sat at the junction of four roads that led out of the city to
the surrounding villages. Tel Amot was the channel that funneled the
Six Prophetic Cities to the Seti desert and the Inshuu steppe, and the
night market was the gate between these worlds.

It had been over five years since Ephyra had set foot on this
stretch of coast. She remembered their last day here, she and Beru
huddled on the docks with the other orphans, waiting to board a ship
that would take them all to Charis, the City of Charity. Beru had been
quiet, but Ephyra had filled the silence for both of them, telling her
sister all the wonderful things that waited for them in Charis. There
would be ocean everywhere, all around them. More trees than they'd
ever seen in their lives. And best of all, a family that would take them
in. A new start.

The crease of Beru's mouth had made it clear that none of Ephyra's pretty words had convinced her for a single moment. But she'd let her sister keep talking anyway, seeming to understand that Ephyra needed to convince herself.

"You got somewhere to stay tonight?"

Ephyra shook off thoughts of the past as she turned to face the healer from the ship. She had kept her distance from him during the journey. She'd never spent much time around anyone else with the Grace of Blood. It put her on edge, as if somehow he could tell what she was. As if one small slip was all it would take, and then she would be faced with his horror and disgust at how she'd twisted the Grace of Blood into something terrible.

"I'm not staying here," Ephyra replied, shouldering her bag and turning away from the market. "I have somewhere I need to be."

Too much time had passed already. It had been more than six days since she had last seen Beru. Over two weeks since she'd killed the priest inside his extravagant room at Thalassa and used his *esha* to heal Beru. She would be growing weak. She'd need to be healed again. Ephyra didn't know exactly how long she had, but if she didn't reach Beru in time—

No. She would not think of it. She would find Beru. She would heal her, as she always did.

And then what? a treacherous part of Ephyra's mind asked.

"You're not planning on traveling outside the city tonight, are you? Marauders roam the roads at night. You don't want to be caught traveling alone."

Ephyra glanced back, realizing with irritation that the healer was still keeping pace with her up the dirt path that led out of town. "It's funny, I don't actually remember asking your opinion."

He barked out a laugh. "That's true—you didn't. But you paid for passage on our ship, so now you get my opinion free of charge. Where are you in such a hurry to get to, anyway?"

"None of your business," Ephyra replied. She took a right to head down a well-remembered road, quickening her pace. It was dark, unlit except by the moon above.

"Hang on, now," the healer protested. His height made it easy for him to match her speed, but Ephyra sped up anyway, hoping he'd get bored and give up. "Hey, stop!"

Her foot caught on a hole in the cracked road, and she went flying to the ground. Her knees crashed against the dirt, and she let out a gasp of pain.

"I told you to stop," the healer admonished, crouching beside her.

"I can't," Ephyra said from the ground, her voice coming out broken. If she stopped, even for a moment, then she'd have to think about where she was going. She would have to think about what was waiting for her there. And she would have to think about the fact that Beru was the one who had brought her back to it.

Hector wasn't the one who'd bought those train tickets. Beru had, after telling Ephyra she wanted to give up. Coming back here, to the place where this nightmare had started, was her way of trying to convince Ephyra. Because for five years, Ephyra had warped herself into something cold and lethal, brushing aside her guilt and burying her remorse. It had been the only way to keep going, to keep being the Pale Hand, to keep Beru alive.

But now she stood on the road that led back to the very worst of her sins. To return meant unearthing all of her guilt. It meant seeing the truth of what she was. It was the cruelest thing Beru could do to her.

Maybe Ephyra deserved it. Maybe this was the punishment for all the terrible things she had done. If it was, she would bear it. She would face whatever horrors waited in Medea. For Beru.

The healer let out a heavy sigh and settled down on the ground beside her. "Look. Wherever it is you're going—"

"Medea," Ephyra said. She shifted so she, too, was sitting, side by side with the healer. "I'm going to Medea."

In the moonlight, his face flashed with recognition. "Medea? But that's . . ." He let out a sigh, pressing one broad palm against his face. "I'm sorry to be the one to tell you this. That village is gone. Everyone in it is dead."

Ephyra turned away. She knew this, yet his words still hollowed her.

"No one knows for sure what happened," he went on softly. "Some say a plague."

It wasn't a plague. It was me, Ephyra wanted to say. *I am the one who killed them.* A sharp sob clawed at her throat. She swallowed it down.

"If that's where you're trying to go, then I don't think anything's waiting for you there," the healer said. "I'm sorry."

Ephyra got to her feet. Maybe the healer was right. Beru had made her choice. She had fled back here, to the one place Ephyra could no longer ignore what she was and the things she had done. She had returned to the beginning, because she wanted an end.

"Thank you," she said to the healer. "But I still need to go."

She turned toward the road. Toward Beru. If this was truly the end, they would face it together.

51

HASSAN

WHEN HASSAN HAD PICTURED HIS FIRST STEPS ONTO NAZIRAH'S SHORES AFTER two months, he hadn't imagined himself blindfolded and bound.

Though he could not see, he knew every step of the journey from the harbor to the Palace of Herat. The spiced sweetness of blue water lilies hit him as the Witnesses led him through the palace gates, the familiar tune of the water organ in the central courtyard lilting around them. They passed beneath the shadow of the gaping arches that rose over the main steps of the palace and mounted the stairs.

The climb was the longest Hassan had ever endured. Each step felt like a lifetime. Is this what his father had felt like, only days ago, making his way to his own execution? He couldn't bear to think of it. He focused on his feet, on the repetitive motion of each step that brought him closer to whatever fate awaited.

At the top of the stairs, on the grand portico that led into the throne room itself, one of his captors ripped the blindfold from his face. In the flickering torchlight, Hassan could make out the Witnesses' close-shaved heads and white robes. And on the backs of their hands, the symbol of a black eye with the pupil a sun.

The Witnesses.

"You've been summoned by the queen," one of them said.

For a blind, wild moment, Hassan thought they meant his mother. But the smug, almost excited look on the Witness's face told him otherwise. Which meant the Hierophant had not been alone in deposing Herat's royal family. Someone else had played a part. Someone who now called herself queen.

The massive doors of the throne room eased slowly open. Hassan turned to take one last glance at Nazirah, spread out before him from the harbor to the distant bank of the Herat River, some twenty miles west. Couched in the river's embrace, the sandstone and tile of Nazirah's homes, shops, market squares, and stadiums were laid out in a dizzying crosswork cleaved by the broad paved Ozmandith Road.

This was the city he loved. This was the city he had failed.

A low crunch signaled that the great doors were open. Hassan's captors shoved him forward, and then he faced the gaping threshold to the throne room.

It looked exactly as it had in his dream. The gilded columns leading to the golden pyramid. The animal-shaped spigots, spewing water out from the pyramid to the moat below. The painted falcon spanning across the back wall. But instead of returning in triumph to claim his throne, Hassan was here as a prisoner.

The Witnesses led him to the edge of the moat that surrounded the throne. Clear water rippled over the iridescent black and green mosaic scarab at the bottom of the pool. Hassan slowly raised his eyes from this familiar creature to the one sitting on his father's throne.

"Prince Hassan," Lethia said warmly. "Welcome home."

She looked the same as she had the day Hassan had left Pallas Athos. When she'd kissed his cheek and told him she would see him soon. A promise she hadn't broken.

"Aunt Lethia." Anger and disbelief ribboned through each syllable. It was like the world had tipped on its side, and no matter which way Hassan shifted, it would not right itself.

He'd known what it had meant when Cirion and his crew betrayed them on the *Cressida*, but he hadn't been able to accept it. Even now, face-to-face with his aunt perched on his father's throne like she belonged there, he felt there must be some mistake, some cruel joke had been played, some secret which, once revealed, would make all of this make sense.

"Aunt Lethia?" she echoed with a thin smile. "Come now, Hassan. You know how to address your new queen."

"My mother is the queen," he hissed. "Whatever you've done with her, you are still nothing but a jealous usurper."

She pressed two long fingers to her temple, massaging it like he'd given her a headache. "I told you, Hassan, that anger does not serve you."

"What have you done with the rest of my soldiers?"

"You mean the rest of your scraped-together band of misfits?" Lethia asked. "Don't worry. They're all alive. Imprisoned, but alive. You'll be seeing them shortly."

They were prisoners now. Because of him. "I put my trust in you," he growled. "I put all their lives in your hands. And you—you betrayed all of us."

"No," Lethia replied. "*You* did. By leading them here, telling them that you were the Prophet they'd been waiting for. When we both know that couldn't be further from the truth."

Hassan's mouth went dry, his anger momentarily replaced with cold dread. He hadn't told Lethia what he'd discovered after the Witnesses' attack in the agora. He hadn't told anyone, save for Khepri.

Lethia let out a laugh—it was the same sound he had heard on numerous occasions, but it was laced now with cruelty. "If there is one thing that has surprised me, Hassan, it's that you carried on the farce for so long. You certainly played your part well. You were exactly what they wanted you to be. A leader. Smart, charismatic. Yet, when they find out what you truly are, do you think any of that will matter?"

"How—how did you—?"

Lethia clucked her tongue, pity in her eyes as she sat back on the throne. "I was more surprised than anyone when you had your dream that night. For a moment, I almost believed it. That you were the long-awaited Prophet, come at last."

"That's why you didn't want me to come back here," Hassan said, his heart sinking. "You never wanted to protect me. You were just afraid that if I proclaimed myself the Prophet, true or false, I would come to Nazirah with an army, reclaim the throne, and undo everything you and the Witnesses had done." Everything suddenly felt so clear. "You . . . you'd been buying time for *weeks*. Refusing to tell me what was happening here. Hiding me away from anyone who might be able to help me." He stopped suddenly, a new and terrible thought dawning. "No one else even knew I was in Pallas Athos. Why didn't you just kill me? It would have been simpler."

She gave him a withering look. "No matter what you might think of me, I'm not a monster, Hassan. You are still my blood."

"So was my father," he bit out.

"And I didn't want him to die, either. He forced my hand, when he would not abdicate the throne."

Fury rendered Hassan speechless. His heart lurched at the thought of his father, steady to his last, refusing to bow to his treacherous sister even when it cost him his life. Hassan could not waver, either.

"To be honest, I didn't expect it from him," Lethia went on. "I'd always thought of my brother as weak-willed in the face of conflict. But at the end of his life, he proved me wrong."

Hassan swallowed his anger. "So you murdered my father but kept me alive because you knew you could make me useless. Cut off from the world. But then the Guard arrived and ruined everything."

"It was a slight hiccup, I'll confess," Lethia said. "I never intended you to return to Nazirah. In fact, I would have let you remain safe in Pallas Athos after I finally took Nazirah for myself. But you insisted on getting in my way. So I came up with a new plan."

"That's why you offered Cirion's ships," Hassan said. "When you realized I was going to come back here no matter what you said, you made sure I would return as a prisoner."

She smiled. "You are the brilliant little strategist, aren't you? I saw how I could use your supposed prophecy to my advantage, and so I did. You made it too easy, Hassan. By then, I knew your dream was just that. A dream. Even before you knew it."

"How?" he asked.

"Someone came to me, telling me they knew where to find the true Prophet. I only needed to provide a ship and a few favors."

"You're lying."

Lethia laughed. "That's rich, coming from you."

"No one came to you," Hassan said. "They couldn't have. Only the Order of the Last Light knows about the prophecy."

Lethia's lips stretched into a thin smile. "They *think* they're the only ones who know of the prophecy. Arrogant, as always. But we have the true Prophet here in Nazirah. That was the Hierophant's price. He promised me Nazirah, and in return I helped deliver the Prophet to him. Now that he has him, Nazirah is mine."

Hassan took a step back. He could see so clearly every step that Lethia had taken to counter him and the Order. But he still couldn't fathom it. "How could you do it? How could you sell our country to the Hierophant?"

"You of all people should understand," Lethia said. "It's the same reason you believed you were the Prophet. I was tired of being told I had to please people like my parents—like my inferior brother, my useless husband, and those selfish priests in Pallas Athos. Tired of knowing I would always fall short, because of a chance of birth." She fixed her green eyes on him. "Just as *you* will, Hassan. You will never be enough, and you know that."

"You're wrong." He met her gaze with defiance.

"Whether or not you agree with the Witnesses, you cannot deny that you have been held back by the rules set down by the Prophets centuries ago. That the Graced will rule, and the rest of us will merely be footnotes in their stories."

Hassan didn't say anything. There was a seed of truth in her words, and as much as he wanted to bury it, he knew it would only fester there, waiting to grow in the deep dark of his mind.

"I've always known I would make a better ruler of Herat than my brother," Lethia said. "He was more interested in tinkering with toys than ruling a kingdom. But despite our ages, despite my skill at strategy, at politics, at everything that makes one fit to rule, no one ever considered that I would be the better choice. Because there wasn't ever going to be a choice. Not when my brother had Grace and I did not."

"So you gave up our country to a sadistic zealot?" Hassan demanded, fury raising his voice to a shout.

"You may call him a zealot, but the Hierophant is much more than that," Lethia said. "One of his many gifts is that he sees things as they should be. He saw that in a just world, I would be Queen of Herat. And he made it so. He understands that the rules of our world are not immutable, and he dares to change them."

"He will destroy this city," Hassan hissed. "And you will watch it happen."

"He will *change* this city," Lethia replied. "We will create a new age for a broken world. Finally, people like us will be able to wield our own power. And don't worry—you'll have a role to play, too."

Before Hassan could reply, the massive doors of the throne room let out a tremendous groan as they were pushed open again. Two women dressed in the uniform of the palace watch entered. If they were surprised to see Hassan there, they didn't show it.

"Queen Lethia," said the first, an older woman, sweeping down to one knee.

The other followed suit.

"Rise," Lethia commanded. "What is it?"

Hassan watched Lethia carefully but could not read the expression on her face.

"You told us to alert you if any ships were spotted from shore."

Ships? Hope bloomed in his chest.

Lethia's expression hadn't changed. "How many?"

"At last count, six frigates and three smaller vessels coming from the northwest," the watchwoman replied. "All of them have silver sails."

The Order of the Last Light was here. There was still hope. There was still a chance.

But when Hassan looked back at Lethia, hope faded. Her expression was far from grim. She looked nearly smug.

"It looks as though your friends have arrived," she said to him. "Right on schedule."

"They'll destroy you," Hassan said between clenched teeth. "And the Witnesses. The Order will take this city back from their clutches, just like we planned."

"Oh, I don't think they will," Lethia said lightly, dismissing the watchwomen with a wave. "After all, they would never risk launching an attack when it would endanger the thing they care about the most."

"What are you talking about?"

"What do you think?" Lethia asked. "You."

"But I'm—" Hassan swallowed the thought. *Not the Prophet*, he was about to say. Of course, he knew that, and Lethia knew that.

But the Order of the Last Light did not.

"I couldn't stop you or the Guard from sending word to the rest of the Order," Lethia said. "But once again, I knew how to turn it to my advantage. As I said, you have a role to play, too. Just not the one you thought."

It was a setup. He'd been used as bait to draw the Order of the Last Light away from their fortress in the mountains and into the Witnesses' clutches.

He'd thought he was Nazirah's salvation. Instead, he was its ruin.

"Come now," Lethia said, rising from the throne and descending the stairs. "It's time you met the man who started all this. The Day of Reckoning is here, and the Hierophant is waiting."

52

ANTON

DARKNESS MADE THE TOWERS OF THE ROYAL PALACE LOOK LIKE THE SHADOWS of gods. The smell of earth and a hint of the sea beyond surrounded them as Illya led Anton into the lush outer courtyard. Anton's heart beat in time with the steady susurration of waves washing in and out.

"Nazirah is really quite an impressive city," Illya said as they trekked along the edge of the outer wall of the palace grounds, guards at their backs. "The very first rulers had the Grace of Mind, and they used their abilities to build their capital city into a technological marvel. It was the first city to apply artificery to infrastructure, and, of course, the construction of the lighthouse itself was one of the most impressive feats of its day."

Anton stared at his brother. "I thought you were supposed to hate the Graced."

Illya laughed. "Should I discount the ingenuity of my enemies simply because I seek to best them?"

At Anton's answering silence, Illya took up his original topic with gusto. "But the most impressive thing about Nazirah is not its light-house, its roads, or even the Great Library. It's something no one even sees. Beneath our very feet, under the streets and houses, lies a complex of ancient wells and cisterns, almost a city unto itself. During the annual floods, water flows from the Herat River through a series of underground canals and into these wells and cisterns. This is how the city keeps its supply of fresh water during the dry months."

"Doesn't sound that impressive," Anton muttered. He couldn't stand Illya's cheerful chattering, playing tour guide in the city where he'd brought Anton as his captive.

"No? Well, perhaps when you see it for yourself you'll change your mind."

They had stopped in front of the entrance to a watchtower, one of several they'd passed along the walls of the palace. A torchlight burned at its entrance, which struck Anton as strange until he realized that the Witnesses wouldn't use incandescent lights. They wouldn't use anything that had been made by the Graced.

The guards lit their own torches and led the way inside the tower. Shadows flickered against cut stone walls as they passed a set of stairs that led up to the watchtower itself, and entered another chamber. The low ceiling sloped toward another set of stairs that led down into darkness.

Anton's dread turned cold as they began their descent, footsteps echoing against stone. The air grew damp and chilly, smelling of mildew and wet earth.

Once, when they were children, Illya had locked Anton inside a wooden chest. He'd refused to let him out even when Anton sobbed and begged, pounding his tiny fists against the lid over and over and over.

He felt now like Illya was leading him into a tomb, and once Anton was inside, he would seal it off, brick by brick by brick, until no one could hear him beg.

But when they reached the bottom of the stairs, Anton saw that it wasn't a tomb. They were let out into an enormous chamber, with a high, vaulted ceiling, reinforced by thin arches like the ribs of some ancient subterranean creature. Columns rose from the depths of mirror-dark water. Marble walkways lined with torches crisscrossed their way between them, some raised high on arches and some hovering just above the water like ice floes.

The sound of trickling water echoed through the chamber as Illya led Anton down crumbling marble stairs to a walkway and then brought them to a halt.

"What am I doing here, Illya?" he asked.

Illya turned back to him. "In Pallas Athos, you said that I once tried to drown you in the frozen lake where we grew up."

Anton rasped out breath. The lake wasn't a far-off memory. It was here, beneath the dark water of the cistern.

"Do you want to know the truth about that day?" Illya said.

Anton knew the truth. But there was something in his brother's voice, something beyond cruelty and malice, that prickled at Anton's skin like the chill of ice.

Illya drew his brows together. "I never tried to drown you." He looked nothing like the cruel, smirking beast of Anton's nightmares. Nothing like the creature who'd held him, thrashing, beneath the water. "I found you outside during the last snow of the season."

Anton closed his eyes, as though blocking out the light would some-how mute the sound of Illya's lies, but his brother's voice washed over him in the dark. The cistern faded away and he was back in the snow, by the lake. But it was not the dream-dark chaos of his nightmares.

This was a memory, rendered to him now as though he were watching from afar.

The sky hung heavy and gray above, early morning flurries falling lightly, ice crystals catching in Anton's fine fair hair. He was a figure in monochrome—dark eyes, pale hair, pale skin. The frozen-over lake was an unmarred oval of white, the trees beyond it just dark shapes in the distance. Only the tracks of his bare feet broke the surface of the new snow.

A voice called to him, hesitant. *Anton?*

He stepped out onto the lake. The thin ice creaked beneath his weight. He kept going.

Footsteps behind him.

Stop! Anton!

Arms around him, dragging him back as he kicked and clawed. Snow bit his skin as he fell forward.

He crawled to his feet, away from his brother, farther onto the lake, and ran. Wind stung his face, his limbs aflame with some sickness that carried him on and on, until he was in the center of the lake, ice splintering beneath his feet.

He plunged into icy darkness. All became silent and still and frozen.

"I *saved* you from the lake."

His brother's face above him, fearful, crying, reaching down to grab at him before he slipped away. Anton thrashed against his hold, but Illya's grip was fierce and he did not let go. He hauled him up and onto the melting ice.

"You grabbed my arm and you looked at me."

Anton opened his eyes and stared at his brother's face now, and in the flamelight of the cavern it looked like it was flickering, features shifting until Anton felt like he was looking at his own reflection.

"You begged me to let you drown."

Anton's voice was barely a croak. "You're lying."

But now that the floodgates of memory had been forced open, Anton knew that he wasn't.

This was the truth. Something more sinister than his brother had brought him to the middle of the lake that day. Had pushed him beneath the ice and held him under. Had made him run away from home, never to return. Had kept him running ever since.

Something that, even now, he could not bear to face.

"You saw something that day, Anton."

The water lapped up at him. He gasped, choking, an icy cold gripping his lungs.

"It was only later that I realized what it meant," Illya went on. "That you're not just the Graced son of a cursed line."

Anton closed his eyes, heart thumping.

"You saw something no one has seen in a hundred years," Illya said. "You saw the future."

Illya's words echoed through him, reverberating like the thrum of his Grace.

As impossible as they were, Illya's words were the truth. Anton knew it, in some deep, hidden part of himself. A part of his mind he had tried to wall away so he wouldn't have to face it. So he could pretend that he was just what he appeared to be—some boy on the street, a wayward son with loose morals and a quick tongue.

But now the truth rang out, deafening, cracking through the fragile walls that he'd built. He had seen something that day. Something impossible.

"That's what really happened that day," Illya said. The guards advanced around them. "What you were too afraid to admit to yourself. Now I want to know something. I want to know what you saw."

Anton shook and shook and shook until he felt as though he might crack in two.

"Illya, please, *please* don't do this," he begged as the guards dragged him to the edge of the water and forced him to his knees. "Please don't do this to me."

"I wish I didn't have to. You've been through enough, haven't you?"

Liar. Anton didn't believe his contrition for a moment. But as he watched Illya's gaze soften, he wondered for the first time if *Illya* believed it. If, like Anton, he had managed to hide what he was so well he'd even deceived himself.

"Illya," he said, and he hated the way his voice sounded—high, panicked, desperate. A lamb pleading for a wolf to take pity.

"You *can't* tell me, can you?"

Anton had buried the memory of the vision so thoroughly it was no longer somewhere he could access by will. Even now, faced with torture and maybe worse, he did not know if he wanted to. In the pit of his gut, he knew that the vision, whatever it was, would be worse than anything Illya could do to him.

"The memory of the lake is the gateway," Illya went on. "I figured it out when I saw you in Pallas Athos. The way you reacted when you spoke of it. You went back there. I saw it in your eyes. You were there, drowning—"

"Stop."

"—drowning like you did five years ago, trying to escape what you saw in your vision—"

"I said *stop*."

"I remember what you were like that day." Illya's voice went distant and soft. "You were in a trance. I couldn't reach you, no matter how hard I tried. The vision had a hold on you, and I couldn't break you out of it."

The guard pushed his head down so his face hovered just above the surface of the water. Anton sucked in breath on a whimper. He was so close to that memory now. A thin sheet of ice was all that separated his past from the future. The black depths of the water gaped up at him, ready to consume him.

"What did you see, Anton?" Illya's voice was a whisper in his ear, so close that he couldn't be sure it was truly his brother's voice at all. "What did you see that made you want to die rather than live with it in your head?"

53

JUDE

THE CHAINS AROUND JUDE'S WRISTS AND THROAT BURNED AS TWO WITNESSES led him up a twisting stair of dark rock. The cell he had occupied since arriving in Nazirah was a narrow, windowless vault in the base of the city's lighthouse. They'd fed him chunks of stale flatbread and a few mouthfuls of water, and fitted him with new chains forged in Godfire that bound him, wrists to ankles to neck.

Before that, it had been three grueling days of sea travel, trapped in a cold, dark space that offered little room for movement. At least on the ship, he'd had the solace of another voice to drown out the one inside his head. The one that wouldn't stop counting all the ways in which he'd failed.

But Jude didn't know what had become of Anton after they'd left the ship. Maybe he was in another cold, damp cell. Or maybe Anton was already dead.

Jude swallowed down the guilt that followed that thought. Failing to protect Anton was just one more broken promise.

"Hurry up, swordsman," one of the Witnesses sneered.

A sharp tug at his chains sent him stumbling up the next step. Jude could barely see his feet, so dark was the stairwell. He still had not gotten used to what darkness felt like without his Grace—the koah to sharpen vision was among the first he'd ever learned. The sensation of blindness was overwhelming. The weakening of his other senses only made him feel more blind. He could smell only the pervasive salt and brine, could hear nothing past the crash of waves against a rocky shore.

At last they reached a landing. The massive sandstone walls of the lighthouse's main atrium towered above them. Sweeping golden staircases and metalwork spiraled up in curved patterns. At the apex of the tower, like a distant star, the torch emitted a cold white light.

Jude's stomach dropped as he realized what burned at the top.

Godfire.

The pale flame drew shadows as immense as the monoliths of the Circle of Stones in Kerameikos. The silhouette of a towering, shrouded figure, its head crowned with thin spires, flickered on the walls. For a moment, Jude thought he was seeing some kind of apparition, a ghostly creature of shadow.

But when he blinked, he saw the source of the shadows was a man. Unlike the other Witnesses, this man's robes were pure white. On his face was a mask of dark gold, glimmering in the flamelight. A ring of black powder surrounded him. Around it, dozens of figures dressed in white robes patterned with black and gold stood stock-still, their eyes fixed on their master.

The two Witnesses led Jude forward, through the ring of black powder, and shoved him to his knees. They knelt beside him, foreheads to the ground.

"Immaculate One," the one on Jude's right said. "We have brought you the Keeper of the Word."

Jude raised his eyes to the man who stood before him. The Hierophant's mask curved sharply over the sides of his face, tapering into jagged points at his chin. A flaming black sun was carved into the forehead, its wheeling arms stretching up above the mask like a crown. The only part of the Hierophant's face that Jude could see clearly were his eyes—a bright, almost unnatural blue.

"You have done well, my dear disciples," he said, his voice melodious. He placed a hand on each of the Witnesses' heads, the touch almost reverent. The Witnesses closed their eyes. "Do not think your service has gone unnoticed."

"T-Thank you, Immaculate One," the first Witness stuttered. They rose together and retreated back.

Then the Hierophant's pale blue eyes fell on Jude, and all the breath went out of Jude's chest. A wave of fear rolled through him. Whatever hid behind that mask was something dark and twisted. The first harbinger of the Age of Darkness.

"Jude Weatherbourne," the Hierophant mused. "I've been looking forward to this meeting for a long time."

It did not seem impossible, somehow, that this man would know his name. But it was the way he said it—*Jude Weatherbourne*—that made him feel like the Hierophant had cracked open the vault of Jude's self.

"Each of us has a part to play in the Reckoning. Even you, Jude Weatherbourne," he said. "It is a gift to know one's purpose. That's one thing the Prophets were right about."

"I know what my purpose is," Jude said. He'd always known, even when he'd abandoned it.

"No, you don't," the Hierophant said gently. "What you think you know is a lie. You see, I was once like you. I served the legacy of the Prophets, keeping their wisdom alive. But I had questions. Questions that led to doubts. We all have doubts from time to time, don't we? Even the Keeper of the Word must."

The Hierophant's tone was soft, but the words hit Jude like a blow. As if the Hierophant had plunged his hand into Jude's chest and torn it asunder, exposing all his fears and desires to the harsh and unforgiving light. As if he knew that Jude's doubts were the very reason he'd ended up here, a prisoner.

"My doubts led me to answers I never could have imagined," the Hierophant went on. "You would never let the names of your Prophets pass your lips again if you knew the secrets I have learned about them. Once I opened my eyes to the truth, I saw how Grace had corrupted this world. And I saw that my purpose was to purify it."

As Jude watched the flickering Godfire cast jagged shadows over the Hierophant's mask, a deep hatred swelled like a storm inside him. This man believed he knew better than the Prophets, that he had a right to determine the fates of others. He may have convinced his followers he was a simple man speaking simple truth, but Jude saw his arrogance lurking beneath.

"Today, at last, that purification can begin." The Hierophant closed his eyes and breathed in, as if the thought brought him deep peace. In the same measured tone, he commanded, "Bring forth the others."

The doors of the lighthouse opened again. Robed Witnesses dragged forth five familiar figures bound in a single line by Godfire chains. A fresh wave of guilt wracked Jude as Penrose, Petrossian, Osei, Annuka, and Yarik stumbled forward.

His eyes sought Penrose's. Betrayal flashed across her face, then grief. She turned away.

Jude had failed them. He had failed them all.

The Hierophant spoke again, "The Order of the Last Light. Servants of the Prophets. Keepers of the final prophecy."

Horror thundered through Jude. *The final prophecy.* He *knew.* How could that be? The Order had kept the prophecy a secret for a century. No one else was supposed to know the prophecy even existed.

But the Hierophant had known about the Age of Darkness all along. Had known about the harbingers.

And he knew about the Last Prophet.

"You thought you were meant to protect the Last Prophet." His cold blue gaze settled on Jude as another figure advanced from the edge of the atrium. "But instead, you've delivered him right into our hands."

54

HASSAN

THE ATRIUM WAS DARK AND FULL OF FLICKERING SHADOWS AS LETHIA LED Hassan inside the lighthouse. He looked up and saw with sinking dread that the bright torch at the top had been replaced with pale Godfire flame.

This was the flame they would use to eradicate the Graced. They'd put it here, at the top of the lighthouse that symbolized Nazirah's legacy and the wisdom of the Prophets.

In the center of the atrium, five members of the Paladin Guard stood chained before the tall, pale figure of the Hierophant. There was another prisoner beside them, bound with chains from neck to ankles. It took Hassan a moment to recognize that it was Jude Weatherbourne. The Keeper of the Word. Hassan had not seen him since the night he'd had the dream.

Above, more prisoners were lined up on the tiered balconies. His army. He scanned the rows, searching for one soldier in particular. But it was too dim to make out anyone's face.

At last he let his gaze fall on the man illuminated in the center of the room. The mask on his face glinted in the light of the Godfire, and Hassan felt a wave of fury roll through him. This man, standing placidly in the center of a ring of chained prisoners, was the cause of every fear and horror Hassan had endured in the last four weeks. This man caused pain and fomented violence everywhere he went, and dared to call it salvation. Hassan's fury lashed like a creature inside him, longing to be set free.

"It's time now you knew the truth," the Hierophant said, looking out at all the prisoners.

"The truth?" Penrose cried out. "You hide your face behind a mask and then presume to speak of truth? We know what you really are. You are the Deceiver."

The Hierophant turned to her slowly. She flinched but didn't look away. Hassan felt a surge of pride in her as she stared down the Hierophant.

"Ah, yes, the Deceiver. The first harbinger of our new age, according to the prophecy. You believe it is I?" the Hierophant asked mockingly. "What falsehood have I spoken?"

"You've told your followers lies about the Graced, convincing them to hate us," Penrose spat. "You claim you were once an acolyte, but there's no trace of you at any of the temples. You have slandered the names of the Prophets and led these people all astray."

"My followers are not the ones who have been led astray," the Hierophant said calmly. "And I have preached no lies. But there is someone here who has. Someone whose deception led you all here."

Hassan's whole body went tense. The Hierophant's eyes were on him now.

"Tell them, Prince Hassan."

Hassan's mouth was bone-dry. He didn't think he could draw breath, let alone speak.

"Or perhaps . . . you cannot admit it, even now. Perhaps you'd rather these people face the Reckoning without knowing the true reason they are here."

A breath punched out of Hassan. "No. I'll tell them."

All eyes in the tower were on him now. He knew what he needed to do. It was what he should have done days ago, when they were back in Pallas Athos, standing before Emir's grave. What he'd intended to do, before fury and grief had changed his mind.

He took a breath and turned toward the six members of the Guard, the people who'd fought for him and believed in him. He faced them and did not look away.

"The truth," he said, "is that I am not the Prophet."

Penrose looked stricken, her mouth a half-moon of surprise. "I—You're lying."

"I thought that I was the Prophet," Hassan went on slowly. "I believed it—for much longer than I should have. But my vision was nothing more than a dream. And even when I realized the truth, I let the lie continue. For that, I—I have no excuse."

Osei moved toward him, straining at his chains. "The day you were born, the sky lit up—"

"A coincidence," Hassan said firmly.

"But the prophecy of Nazirah," Petrossian said. "It was undone when the Witnesses took the city."

"Wrong," Lethia said from beside Hassan. "The lighthouse stands, and the Seif line still rules this kingdom. *I* am the heir of my mother. I am the Queen of Herat."

Penrose looked at Hassan, her eyes pleading. "But—the vision. The vision that showed us how to stop the Age of Darkness."

"It was a dream," he said as steadily as he could manage. "Nothing more."

Disbelief faded from Penrose's face as she took in the truth. Accepted it. Beside her, Jude Weatherbourne's expression was inscrutable, his eyes wide but focused, his mouth set in a tight line.

"You're not the Last Prophet," he said slowly, as though turning the thought carefully over in his mind. "It was never you."

"He is but a false Prophet," the Hierophant said. "A Deceiver."

All the breath left Hassan's chest. The words of the prophecy echoed in the back of his head. *The deceiver ensnares the world with lies.*

"Prince Hassan is the first harbinger of the Age of Darkness."

55

ANTON

ILLYA WAS CAREFUL. HE LET THE GUARDS PUSH ANTON'S HEAD BELOW THE
water to drown and drown and drown, but just before Anton felt his
lungs would burst, they pulled him back and let him cough and choke
and gasp for breath.

And then they began again. On and on it went. Drowning. Gasping.
Retching. Crying.

Anton didn't even try to stop the tears now. Sobbing and gasping
and gagging all seemed to bleed together, all obstacles to the only thing in
the world that mattered.

Breath.

The guards wrenched his head back yet again, and Anton collapsed
onto the marble platform. He could barely hold himself up on shaking
hands and knees as he emptied his stomach of bile and tried to gasp in
a tiny sip of air.

"Please." His voice was wrecked. "Please, no more."

He didn't know how long he sat there, head bowed, counting every
breath a victory.

A shadow fell over him.

"You want this to stop?" Illya said.

Anton closed his eyes, shaking. *Stop me, Anton,* Illya's voice taunted in his head. *If you're so powerful, then you can stop me.*

"Tell me what you saw."

"You're going to kill me," Anton croaked. He did not want to die. Oh, he did not want to die. But he could not keep drowning. "I always knew you would."

"Tell me what you saw, and this will all be over."

A low whimper escaped Anton's throat. "I *can't.* I don't know what I saw, why I tried to—" He couldn't say it, even now. "Why are you doing this?" he whispered, his voice so low he was sure only Illya could hear him. "Why do you need to know what I saw?"

Illya knelt, his face grim in the low shadows of the chamber as he placed his hand on his brother's shoulder, as if comforting him. "Before you begged me to let you drown, you said something else. You said, 'It's coming. The darkness.'"

Anton shivered. His brother's words gripped him like cadaverous hands pulling him below the surface of the lake.

"I didn't know what it meant, then," Illya said. "But after I joined the Witnesses, the Hierophant shared with me his most closely kept secret. A secret that few others know. But he trusted *me* with it."

Illya's voice dripped with pride. For once, Illya had been deemed special. For once, *he* had been chosen. Anton knew there was nothing Illya could have wanted more.

"Before the Prophets disappeared, they made a final prophecy," Illya told him. "A prophecy that predicted the end to those who stand against the natural order of the world. A Reckoning that would restore the world to the way it was before the Prophets. They called it the Age of Darkness. The Prophets didn't know how this new age would come about. But you do. You saw what they could not. You saw the Reckoning, Anton. You saw it all."

Anton's lungs flooded with ice.

"No." Gasping in a burning breath, he choked, "I don't—I don't know about a reckoning. I don't know anything—"

An image flashed through his mind, like lightning silhouetted against dark clouds.

"No!"

His voice reverberated through the cavern. This is what he'd tried to protect himself from. This was the vision his mind had drowned beneath the nightmare of the frozen lake.

He looked up at his brother and saw a small, satisfied smile on his face.

"We're getting closer," he said. He seemed to be speaking not to Anton, but to the guards behind him. "Keep going."

Anton struggled against the guards' hold, thrashing. The vision hovered at the edges of his consciousness, and if he didn't keep his mind here, in the dark, cavernous chamber with his sadistic brother and his loyal mercenaries, he would be lost to it.

His struggle was futile. The guards' grip on him barely buckled as they forced Anton to the edge of the platform. With one hand gripping him by the hair, another locked around his neck, the guard plunged him below the water again.

Anton had spent so much of his life building up walls between himself and his Grace. It was the only way he knew to stave off the darkness that waited for him in his dreams.

As he breached the surface of the water, the walls crumbled.

The thrum of his Grace, that pulse that swelled like a tide within him, the one he had pushed back again and again, burst through him like a torrent.

Now, in the dark underbelly of the cistern, Anton let go. He sank into the fold of his Sight, into the shivering fabric of the world. His Grace unfurled within him, spooling out in all directions like ripples from a cast stone.

Scrying was seeking, using one's Grace to find the *esha* that vibrated at a particular frequency.

This was not scrying. Anton's Grace reverberated through the currents of *esha*, disrupting their patterns with an echo of itself.

He wasn't seeking. He was calling out.

Help, he cried into the black, shivering world. *Help me.*

56

JUDE

WHITE LIGHT FLARED AT THE TOP OF THE TOWER. JUDE RAISED HIS EYES TO SEE lines of Witnesses marching down the curved staircases, torches alight with Godfire.

"Retribution is here," the Hierophant said, his voice echoing against the tower walls. "Our Godfire will end the corruption of the Graced and cleanse the world of the Prophets' sins. Once you have been purged of the powers that corrupt you, you will begin to see the truth, too. Some of you will not be able to face it. That is the price of the Reckoning."

The Hierophant's tone was somber, as if he truly grieved the thought.

"But the rest of you will be remade as part of a new and pure world," he went on. "A world much like the one that existed long ago, before the Prophets warped it. The sacred *esha* of the world will flow in harmony once more, without the Graced to manipulate it for their own selfish ends. And we will witness a true and lasting peace."

The torches floated ghostlike along the spiral stairs, until they reached the atrium, forming a ring around the Paladin Guard in the center.

The Hierophant spread his arms, raising his voice. "Let the Reckoning begin."

Shadows flickered at the edge of Jude's vision. He willed himself not to tremble, not to show the slightest indication of his fear, as the Hierophant stepped toward him.

"Jude Weatherbourne. Keeper of the Word. Most loyal of the Prophets' followers."

Guilt sank through Jude. The Hierophant's words taunted him. He was not the most loyal of the Prophets' followers. He had failed them, and never had that been clearer than in this moment.

He stiffened as the Hierophant took his chin between two cold, delicate fingers. The touch was gentle, but it crackled against Jude's skin. The sharp scent of anise and ash surrounded him.

The Hierophant waved a hand, and one of the Witnesses brought him a torch burning with Godfire.

"You will be the first to face the Reckoning."

Jude couldn't take his eyes off the pale flame as it drew closer. The light swallowed his gaze.

Pain tore through him, sudden and fierce. He doubled over, his vision fading out, a shout of agony bursting unbidden from his chest. It felt exactly the same as when he'd tried to use his Grace while wearing the Godfire chains.

For a moment, he thought the fire had burned him. But when his vision cleared, he saw that the Hierophant had drawn the torch back.

The pain lessened but lingered. Jude focused on the Hierophant's face in front of his, illuminated by the Godfire torch. He was frozen, his blue eyes wide behind the mask.

Another burst of fiery pain wracked through Jude. It radiated out from his chest and against his skin, like he was burning from the inside out. It faded again, faster this time, and in its stead, he felt a slow and gentle pulse, expanding and contracting like a blinking star.

It surged through him like his Grace, but it was not. It was something else, something that thrummed inside his chest, as sure as his own heart, growing from a gentle tug into an undeniable pull, the way a koah pulled *esha* through him, the way the pole of the Earth pulled the needle of a compass north.

He closed his eyes, and as another warm pulse rippled over him, he realized what it was. The echo of another Grace that was not his own. He had felt this before, though he had been too young to know what it was. In the shadow of a monolith, beneath a radiant sky, Jude had felt a thrum tremble through the earth. A cry ringing through him, calling out to its keeper.

Now, sixteen years later, the Last Prophet's Grace called out again.

57

JUDE

THE HIEROPHANT WAVED THE TORCH, THE FLAME BLAZING TOWARD JUDE. ON instinct, Jude leapt back, forgetting that his wrists and ankles were still bound.

The chains jerked, and he fell to his knees. He closed his eyes and let out a breath. He could still recall the intensity of the pain he'd felt from the Godfire chains, a deep burning that pitted his bones.

But that was before everything had narrowed to a single purpose. Pain seemed like such an irrelevant thing now. The Grace of the Last Prophet—the *true* Last Prophet, not the Prince of Herat—had called to him. Nothing would stop him from answering it.

Jude breathed in and focused on the call of the Prophet. His Grace surged within him, and with it, the heat of the Godfire chains. He leaned into the pain, into its scorching heat. It lapped at him like a tide, but it didn't swallow him. He could withstand it.

He performed a koah for strength, letting the fire of pain fuel him, drawing his *esha* more powerfully through him. With a burst of strength, he snapped the chains at his wrists, ankles, and throat. The

Hierophant stood with the torch held in front of him, his mouth round with disbelief.

"Get him!" he barked to the Witnesses. Two of them closed in on Jude, their torches held aloft.

But Jude was unshackled now, and he was ready for them. With Graced speed, he ducked beneath the flame and caught the Godfire torch in both hands. Shoving hard, he shook off the Witness who wielded it and then spun. If Jude closed his eyes and ignored the heat of the flame, he could pretend the torch was just like the bowstaves the Paladin used to train at Kerameikos Fort.

He expected to find the other torch-bearing Witness behind him, but was surprised to find instead that the Prince of Herat had leapt onto that Witness, arms locked around his neck.

"The Guard!" the prince cried.

Jude understood at once. Pivoting, he swung the torch. Another Witness scrambled out of its path. But Jude hadn't been aiming at him—instead, the flame found its target on the chains that bound the five members of the Paladin Guard together. He met Penrose's wide-eyed gaze for a moment, and then both of them focused on the point where metal met flame. She gave a slight nod.

"Stop them!" the Hierophant cried.

Movement flurried around them. Without looking, Jude could tell that the guards that had entered the lighthouse with the prince and Lady Lethia had charged into the fray.

Jude tossed the torch into his left hand and, without missing a beat, reached behind himself to grab the hilt of a charging guard's sword and draw it from its sheath. Penrose raised her arms, pulling the Paladin Guards' chains taut, and Jude brought the blade down on the weakened metal.

The chains snapped and fell away. Yarik, Annuka, Petrossian, and

Osei drew themselves into protective positions, fending off the advancing guards and Witnesses. Jude darted through the fray to Penrose's side.

"Penrose," he said breathlessly. There was so much he had to say to her. But right now, only one thing mattered. "The Prophet. The Prophet is here."

Penrose shook her head slowly. "We were wrong, Jude. The prince isn't—"

"No," Jude said, stilling her with a hand on her shoulder. "Not the prince. The true Prophet. I—I felt his Grace. I can still feel it."

Penrose's eyes widened.

"They have him," Jude said. "Somewhere near."

"You're sure?"

"More sure than I've been of anything in my life."

Her gaze hardened. "Then find him. Whatever it takes. That is our duty, and all of us would gladly give our lives to see it done. The Order's fleet is in the harbor. Get him aboard one of our ships."

Jude hesitated. He didn't want to abandon the Guard again. But the Prophet's Grace was an undeniable force inside him, echoing Penrose's words. *Find him. Whatever it takes.*

He turned away from her, catching sight of the Hierophant lowering his torch to the ground. Jude did not think; he only reacted, flipping backward onto his feet. Before his eyes, a blazing white ring of fire rippled to life around the other members of the Order. A wall of Godfire separated them from Jude.

With one last glance at Penrose's bright, determined face, he turned and locked eyes with the Hierophant.

He was utterly unprotected, the Witnesses around him distracted by the unexpected melee. The Hierophant's eyes held on Jude, as if he knew exactly what thoughts were running through his mind. How easy it would be to push the Hierophant into the flames and turn his own weapon against him.

But the Prophet's call thrummed through Jude louder than ever, demanding an answer. Jude turned away from the Hierophant and fled, battling his way through more Witnesses and guards until he was bursting out of the lighthouse doors.

Echoing shouts and footsteps pursued him as he emerged into the night. Clenching his jaw against the burning ache in his legs, he flew over the viaduct that connected the lighthouse to the mainland. The stars stretched over him. The call of the Prophet's Grace strengthened to a steady pulse. It grew with each stride, pulling him like a lodestone.

His whole life, Jude had let his faith guide him. His faith in the Prophet, in the Order, had been unshakable. His faith in himself, less so. He'd spent so much time struggling to put his doubts to rest, to hide his fear.

But he saw now that they were a part of him as true as his Grace. He would never be rid of them. But he would fulfill his duty anyway. Even if he wasn't worthy of it. Even if his devotion wavered.

The Prophet's Grace was calling out to him, and Jude would answer.

It grew even stronger as he skirted the cliffs below the Palace of Herat, his feet swift and sure even on the slippery rock.

Tucked into the side of the dark rock face, he saw the black mouth of a cave. As he approached, the Prophet's Grace amplified even more, like a warm hand beckoning. He followed on pure instinct and the blind faith that this strange pull would lead him where he needed to go.

Moonlight spilled over the stone walls as he entered the cave. Inside was dark, but Jude's Grace allowed him to see that beneath a stone overhang, a set of stairs led down into gaping blackness. The pulse of the Prophet's Grace pounded in his ears, but it was now joined by another pulse, beating in exact synchrony. At first, Jude thought that somehow it was echoing on the cavernous passage, but slowly he realized the truth.

He could hear the Prophet's heart beating. The Prophet was down there.

He still had the sword he'd taken off the guard. Its curved shape and peculiar balance were unfamiliar to Jude, but he no longer had the Pinnacle Blade, and this was better than being unarmed. He gripped the hilt tighter as he began his descent. The stairway was cold and damp, but his Grace was warm within him.

He reached the bottom of the stairs quickly and found himself in a damp, narrow tunnel that took him farther underground. He did not want to think about why the Prophet might be so far down here, so he focused on the sound of his own breath and the Prophet's real, thumping heartbeat, as he descended deeper.

They were joined by more sounds—the echoing splash of water, followed by a voice, terse and impatient.

"Keep going until I say stop."

It was Illya Aliyev's voice. Jude quickened his pace around the curve of the tunnel and then stopped. The tunnel ended abruptly, opening out to a cavernous chamber with a high, vaulted ceiling. About twenty feet below was a floor of smooth black glass, like a night sky devoid of stars.

No, not glass, he realized. Water. An underground lake. Marble platforms stretched out over the surface of the water, some raised on arches, some crumbling and eroded.

And on one of these platforms, Jude saw eight guards standing around a figure lying on its side.

The Prophet. His Grace rose to a crescendo. Jude let its power take him through a familiar sequence of koahs, for speed, strength, and balance.

He leapt off the edge of the tunnel and onto the platform below. The guards turned at the sound of his landing.

"There's someone here!"

"Get rid of him," Illya's cold voice rang out.

Jude vaulted over three guards rushing to meet him, landing behind their backs.

"What? Where'd he—?" One guard lurched around, his sword slicing toward Jude's chest. Jude danced back. The guard thrust again, and Jude met the guard's blade with his own. The sound of clashing steel echoed off marble and water.

A second guard lunged at Jude from the other side. With a flick of his wrist, Jude withdrew his sword, sending the first guard toppling off the high platform, and spun to meet the second, striking her in the arm. She stumbled back with a gasp, and Jude dropped to a crouch, sweeping her legs from beneath her. She collapsed into the water with a splash.

The third guard reeled back as the remaining five caught up to them. "He's too fast!"

The others held back, swords drawn, trepidation in their eyes. "You're the swordsman," one of them said. "The one we caught in Pallas Athos."

"I am Jude Weatherbourne of Kerameikos, captain of the Paladin Guard, Keeper of the Word," he said. "And you are in my way."

With a sword in his hand, *esha* flowing through his body, and the drum of the Prophet's pulse, close and rabbit-fast, Jude was without equal in this fight. He dispatched the guards readily. His way cleared, he raced along the torch-lined walkway, boots sliding over the slick marble stones. His vision narrowed to a single point—the small figure lying crumpled on the edge of the platform, whose pulse pounded in Jude's ears.

The Prophet.

Jude reached his side and knelt. Turning him over gently, he pressed his palm against the side of the Prophet's face.

His breath caught. He knew that face.

Once, across a dim, smoke-filled courtyard, he'd seen those lips twist into a teasing smile. Once, in a crumbling shrine, he had woken to see that forehead like a pale moon above him.

The Prophet was Anton.

Anton was the Prophet.

The certainty of it struck him like the edge of a blade. Then the boy who was both Anton and the Prophet sighed out a breath and opened his eyes.

Once, as the rest of Jude's world had crashed down around him, his gaze had been drawn to the warm, dark eyes of a strange boy hunched over the side of a scrying pool.

Now, their eyes met again.

And Jude's true north was found.

58

HASSAN

THE LIGHTHOUSE FLASHED WITH WHITE FLAME AS A RING OF GODFIRE BLAZED to life. The brief melee in the center of the atrium had ended with Hassan and the Paladin Guard trapped inside the circle of Godfire, their hopes of escape dashed.

A sudden, violent cough wracked Hassan's lungs as foul-smelling black smoke spilled from the flames. Hassan threw his sleeve over his nose. He watched his aunt, outside of the circle of flames, secure a scarf over her nose and mouth.

"Your Keeper has fled," the Hierophant said. "He has shown himself to be a coward, rejecting the truth that I have offered him. But he will not escape the Reckoning—none of you will. Today, you will face your destinies."

The flames glinted on the jagged curves of his mask as he turned to the Witnesses. "Light the rest."

Hassan watched in horror as two Witnesses strode across the atrium to the foot of the balcony that wound up the sides of the tower. They lowered their torches to the ground, where the same black powder was spread in a line along the balcony. The powder caught flame, igniting all the way up. Cries and gasps echoed as the flames spiraled around the Herati soldiers, trapping them against the edge of the balcony.

"The smoke you're breathing right now contains the noxious fumes of black rock," the Hierophant said. "Slowly, these fumes will fill the lighthouse. One by one, each of you will fall to the poison."

Hassan pressed his nose harder into his sleeve, lungs seizing.

"But you don't have to die here," the Hierophant said. "There is another choice. To be free, you need only walk through the Godfire flames. Purge yourselves of the sins of the Prophets, and you will be welcomed into our new city, transformed. Live, and let your bodies be purified of the corruption of Grace. Those are your choices—salvation or death."

The Hierophant glanced at the Witnesses as he made his way to the staircase. That was all the direction they needed. Torches aglow, they followed him out of the lighthouse.

Hassan's eyes fell on his aunt, who stood watching the flames.

"Lethia," Hassan said, unable to hide the fear and desperation in his voice. "Lethia, please. Don't do this."

Over the silk of her scarf, her eyes met his. There could be no question of her conviction. He watched the shadows flicker across her face as he realized she was going to let everyone in the lighthouse either burn or die.

Slowly, she turned away, following the Witnesses out. A moment later, the tower resounded with the sound of the doors closing.

They were trapped inside.

The smoke thickened. Hassan and the Guard stood in a tightly packed circle, their backs to one another and their eyes on the ring of Godfire that surrounded them.

Hassan couldn't stop coughing, his lungs working to expel the foul-smelling smoke.

"Cover your nose and mouth," Penrose said, voice muffled by her cloak.

Hassan shrugged out of his thick brocade overshirt and tore off a strip of his soft cotton undershirt with his teeth. He tied the fabric around his face. It wouldn't make much of a difference when the smoke filled the whole tower, but for now it provided some relief.

"Prince Hassan," Penrose said from his left. "You can cross the Godfire flame. You can save yourself."

She was right, of course. He could cross the flames and suffer only a few minor burns. He could get out of the lighthouse before the smoke killed him. But he would be the only one.

"I'm not going to leave you," Hassan said. "I . . . I'm the reason you're all here. I *lied* to you. If it weren't for me—"

"It is your fault," Penrose said harshly. "If you want to sacrifice your life out of guilt, then so be it. But you and I both know that is the coward's way out. And despite everything you've done, I don't believe you are a coward. If you truly feel remorse for your lies, you will find a way to atone."

She was right. If Hassan perished in the lighthouse, there would be no one left to stop the Witnesses from burning the rest of Nazirah. But the thought of leaving everyone inside, to choose death or worse, made him feel sick. He looked up through the thickening smoke at the rows of Herati soldiers trapped on the balconies.

It was only because he was Graceless that Hassan could save himself. The others were trapped here by the power he had always wanted. The power he'd always thought he needed in order to lead his people.

But maybe he'd never needed it. Maybe whether he had Grace or not had nothing to do with who he was or what kind of leader he could be. Maybe all that mattered were the choices he made.

Salvation or death. Those were the choices the Hierophant had left them with. Burn out their Graces or die.

But those weren't the only choices Hassan had.

He closed his eyes and summoned his courage. Then he took a step back. And another, until he was at the edge of the flames.

Only he could do this. Only he could cross the Godfire.

He opened his eyes, ran across the ring, and leapt. His skin seared. Tucking his legs beneath him, he hit the ground at a roll, and kept rolling to smother the flames.

He got to his feet, whirling back around to face the Guard through the Godfire, singed but alive.

"I'm not leaving you," he said again. "I'm going to get you out of here. All of you."

He didn't have a plan. He had, at most, a glimmer of one. But it would have to be enough. He looked down and spotted a coil of chains—the Godfire chains that had been discarded after Captain Weatherbourne had cut the Guard free. Hassan gathered the chains, looping them over his neck before racing up the stairs. When he judged that he was high enough, he threaded one chain through the stair railing. There was no way to fasten it, so he'd anchor it himself.

"Penrose!" he called down to her. He raised the rest of the chain up in one hand. She seemed to understand quickly. With a nod, she turned to Osei beside her, and after a short conference, they got in position—Penrose at the far edge of the circle, her back to the flames, and Osei kneeling in the center with his hands cupped.

"Ready?" Hassan called down.

"Ready."

He tossed the other end of the chain toward her. Penrose took a running leap. The chain swung down. Penrose launched up from Osei's hands. She caught the end of the chain just as it started to rebound, arcing back toward Hassan.

He braced against the added weight. For a few precarious seconds, Penrose swung wildly on the suspended chain. Then it steadied, and Penrose let go on the backswing, sailing over the flickering fire below and flipping to catch herself on the railing of the stairs beneath him.

"You all right?" he called down to her.

"Keep going!"

Hassan refocused himself, gathering up the chain again and preparing to toss one end of it down to the next member of the Guard. With the same dexterous poise as Penrose, Petrossian made it to safety.

But the fumes of the smoke were beginning to affect Hassan. He fell into a coughing fit that left him light-headed and dizzy. He was running out of time.

When he'd recovered, Penrose was standing beside him. "If we can get everyone out of the lighthouse, there might be a way to get to the Order's ships. But we need to move quickly."

Hassan craned his head to look at the upper levels of the tower. The smoke was rising rapidly—down here, he and Penrose could breathe all right, but he could see that already on the topmost levels, there were people who'd collapsed to the ground.

"Get the rest of the Guard," he said, shoving the chains into Penrose's hands. She flinched at the contact with it.

"What are you going to do?"

"I'm going to get them out."

When he'd let a false vision of victory guide him, he'd led everyone to this terrible fate. He hadn't been good at being a Prophet, but he was good at this—making things up as he went.

And one way or another, he was going to get everyone out.

59

ANTON

ANTON WASN'T DROWNING.

He woke gasping, water choking his lungs, his stomach heaving to expel everything inside of it. He wasn't drowning, but he still felt like he was about to die.

His retching subsided, and slowly he became aware of warmth, of the gentle press of hands against his side. For a moment, he was utterly paralyzed, awash in the sensation of his pulse pounding through every inch of his body, like a gong that had been struck clear and true. He blinked away water to find a pair of wide green eyes staring back at him. Jude.

His *esha* was undeniable, as it had been the first time Anton had felt it in the marina of Pallas Athos, and again in the mausoleum. Now, every particle of air in the cavern seemed charged with it, warm and thick like a thunderhead. Anton's own Grace tuned to it, the two ringing together in harmony, reverberating out from the place where Jude's hands lay.

"It's *you*," Jude said.

A shadow moved behind him, and Illya appeared. Something gleamed in his hand, a dangerous silver in the low torchlight.

Anton drew in a sharp breath.

Without turning, Jude caught Illya's wrist, seconds before the knife in his hand would have plunged through Jude's back. His grip tightened until Anton heard a low crack, and Illya let out a howl of pain. The knife clattered onto the marble.

Jude released Illya's wrist and stood to face him. "You are never going to hurt him again."

Anton pushed himself to his knees and clambered to his feet. Over Jude's shoulder, he could see Illya cradling his wrist. Gold eyes flickered to meet Anton's gaze.

Jude's stance shifted, as if trying to block Anton from view.

"I told you," Illya said. "You can't run from this anymore. You can't run from what's inside your own head."

Anton shivered. *What did you see?* His brother's voice hissed in his head. *What did you see that made you want to—*

He gasped in a breath.

"For five years, you've delayed this," Illya said. "But the truth cannot stay buried. If it's not me that unearths it, it will be them." He nodded at Jude. *Them* meant the Order, the Paladin Guard.

Illya was right. Following Jude was just another path to the same outcome. Jude could lead him out of here, but he couldn't help him escape from what truly haunted him.

Jude turned, meeting Anton's eyes. "Whatever happens," he said, "I'll protect you."

Jude had said those words before, as Illya's men had ambushed them in the Hidden Spring. Before Jude had even known what Anton was. The words had stunned him. They'd seemed impossible, for no one in his life had ever said them before. But then there was Jude, with his serious face and his intense green eyes and his *esha* swirling like a windstorm. And when he said those words, Anton believed them.

He took Jude's arm.

"You can't run from this, Anton." Illya's voice echoed as they turned away from him. "Not anymore."

Anton suppressed another shiver as Jude pulled him along the walkway toward the cavern's entrance. Suddenly, Jude drew up short, throwing his arm out to stop him in his tracks. More guards, these ones wielding crossbows, were lined up above them, aiming their weapons down.

Ahead, at the top of the stairs, the bright flare of torches appeared. But the flames weren't like any Anton had seen before—they were pale like moonlight.

"What is that?" he asked as the men carrying the torches spilled out onto the marble platform.

"Godfire," Jude said grimly.

The flames were hypnotic, flickering like ghosts in the dark. Anton found himself unable to tear his gaze away. They were eyes, blazing like a sun, piercing him.

The guards above fired their crossbows. A dozen bolts sailed toward them. The Godfire flames flickered at his periphery as Anton dropped into a crouch, trying to make himself as small a target as possible. But Jude didn't cower.

He turned, his sword a glint of blurred silver. His Grace surged like a roll of thunder. The crossbow bolts fell from the air at once, as though they'd been met with a gale-force wind.

Jude sheathed the sword at his belt before wrapping a hand around Anton's wrist and hauling him to his feet. Together, they raced along the walkway, deeper into the cistern. Boots pounded against the marble as the guards followed.

"Jude?" Anton said uneasily. They were coming up quickly to a wall. "I don't think this is a way—"

"This way," Jude said, dragging Anton up a stairway cut into the rock. It ended abruptly on narrow platform. Three stone levers jutted out from the wall.

Faintly, Anton heard the sound of trickling water. He reached out and felt a thin stream of water flowing down the rock face.

"Stand back," Jude warned, wrapping his hands around one of the levers.

Anton barely had time to react before he heard a great crunch. About three feet above his head, a stone panel in the wall opened and a deluge burst out, rushing past him and down the stairs. The flood lasted only a few seconds, after which Anton found himself staring up at the black mouth of a tunnel.

"They're up there!" a guard shouted from below.

Jude laced his hands together in front of him. "Climb up." Over his shoulder, Anton saw the bright flicker of Godfire torches as the guards ascended the stairs. "I'll be right behind you."

With a nod, Anton put his hands on Jude's shoulders and stepped up. He grabbed onto the slick ledge of the tunnel. He could hear the guards drawing closer. Digging his fingers into the wet stone, Anton pushed off Jude's hands and hoisted himself into the tunnel.

He turned back. "Jude!"

The guards were nearly on top of him. Jude unsheathed his sword just in time to meet the blow of a guard's blade. He kicked the guard hard, and then turned to leap after Anton. But his foot slipped off the edge of the rock.

Anton dove forward, catching Jude under the arms. They stayed there for an unsteady moment, Anton trying desperately to hold Jude up without slipping on the wet stone.

A loud crunch sounded, and Anton caught sight of a guard with his hands wrapped around one of the levers on the platform. Squeezing his eyes closed, he sucked in a breath and pulled, dragging Jude into the tunnel just as the stone panel crashed shut, sealing them within.

Anton fell back, Jude's solid weight falling beside him. It was pitch-dark, which made everything feel less real—like he was floating, like at any moment the world could slip out from beneath him.

The brush of Jude's arm against his brought him back. "Where are we?" he asked.

"Underground canal," Jude answered. "The water comes in from the aqueducts, and I guess they either divert it into the cisterns or let it flow through this tunnel. I imagine during the flood season this would be completely submerged."

Anton recalled Illya's lecture on Nazirah's waterways and decided he'd heard enough about it for the rest of his life. "Then let's be thankful it's not the flood season," he said. "How do we get out?"

Jude helped him to his feet. "We start walking."

Anton could see absolutely nothing in the darkness, but he trusted that Jude could. "So was this your plan?" The sound of his own voice in his ears kept him grounded. "Wander around in the dark until we find a way out? I've heard worse, I guess."

"I didn't really have one," Jude admitted. "All I know is that I—I heard you, and I knew I had to find you."

"You heard me?"

"Your Grace. Like it was calling out to me."

It had worked. The reverse scrying, or whatever it was that Anton had done, sending an echo of his Grace out as a call for help.

A call that Jude had answered.

"I can't explain it exactly," Jude went on haltingly. "But it led me to you."

Though Anton couldn't see Jude's face, he felt his gaze on him, and he felt his own pulse tapping against Jude's palm. It felt like they were standing at a precipice, the split second before leaping. But Anton wasn't ready to face whatever lay below. Not yet.

"Anton—"

"Please just—Please, let's just get out of here."

Jude didn't press. Anton kept his attention on his pulse, the rhythm of his feet against the wet stone, and the pressure of Jude's fingers locked around his wrist, leading him through the dark.

60

HASSAN

HEART POUNDING IN HIS HEAD, HASSAN RACED UP THE STAIRS TOWARD THE trapped Herati soldiers. There were almost fifty still up on the balcony. A few had made it over the railing, but they were trapped there, hanging off the side, unable to jump to safety. One of them, he realized with a start, was Khepri.

"Hassan!" she cried in surprise when he appeared at the stairwell across from her.

He looked down at the chain in his arms, "Use this," he called to her. "But be careful. It's a Godfire chain."

"Throw it to me," Khepri replied.

Hassan tossed one end to her. She caught it, letting out an audible hiss of pain when the chain touched her hand. Her grip on the balcony slipped.

"Khepri!" he cried, instinctively moving toward her.

She caught herself just in time. "I'm all right," she said shakily. She threaded the Godfire chain through the railing, letting one end dangle so it formed a kind of pulley. Then she glanced back up at the other soldiers and waved them down.

"Come on." One by one, they used the pulley chain to lower themselves over the flames, their teeth gritted and their eyes watering with pain by the time they reached Hassan.

When the last one was down from the balcony, he beckoned to Khepri. "Your turn."

She grabbed the end of the chain, swinging herself from the rail with considerable force. She let go midswing, sailing across the divide between the balcony and stairs to land squarely on top of Hassan.

His arms went around her automatically, and he braced himself to bear her weight.

Khepri looked down at him, her knees squeezing his sides. "Nice catch. You can let go now."

Swallowing, Hassan unwound his arms from her waist.

"We have to get everyone down to the atrium," he said.

"Not all of them can make it that far. The smoke—it's so much thicker up here."

"We're not going to leave anyone behind," Hassan said. "Do you think they can make it up just two flights?"

"Up?"

He nodded and pointed two floors above, at a set of doors that opened to the platform that circled the outside of the tower. "The observation deck. There's a set of stairs that leads down from the deck to the ground."

"They'll make it," Khepri said, like she could will it true just by saying it. She directed the limping, stumbling soldiers toward the stairs. She and Hassan brought up the rear of the group, dodging through falling debris and coughing up the smoke that grew thicker the higher they climbed.

A cry came down from the first of their group who'd reached their destination. "The doors are locked!"

Heart sinking, Hassan shouldered through the crowd, Khepri at his back. The soldiers had cleared a space in front of the door, and two of them were trying to break it down through sheer strength.

The black smoke curled around them, thickening the air with its poison. Violent rattling coughs echoed through the tower. One soldier's legs gave out, and he collapsed to his knees. Some soldiers were carrying those too weak to stand. Others crawled forward on shaking hands.

Time was running short. If they didn't get outside quickly, they would all succumb to the smoke.

He had led them all up here, thinking this would be the way to get out. But he may have just doomed them all over again.

The two soldiers rammed against the door with their shoulders again. It didn't budge. With a determined look on her face, Khepri stepped right up to Hassan, chest to chest, her eyes locked on his. For a wild moment, he thought she was about to kiss him. Instead, he felt her hands at his waist, unknotting the sash threaded through the top of his pants.

Logically, he understood that this was a dire situation that they might not make it out of. But at the same time, he couldn't help the way his body reacted to a beautiful woman suddenly undressing him.

"What are you—?" He choked on the rest of the question as she stepped away, the sash in hand. He stared mutely as Khepri ripped it in half with her teeth. She handed one half to him.

"Do you still have the reliquary?"

"What?"

"Emir's reliquary," Khepri said. "They gave it to you after the funeral, didn't they?"

He blinked and touched the bottle that hung tied from a loop in his pants. It held the chrism oil that had been used to anoint Emir in death.

Blue jewels and glass glinted in his palm as Hassan handed the bottle to Khepri. She flipped open the latch and stuffed the cloth inside, leaving a few inches to spill out the top.

"Light that with Godfire," Khepri said to him, nodding at the other half of his sash, which was still in his hands.

Bewildered, he took the cloth and climbed down the stairs until he was close enough to the flames. The fire was uncomfortably hot on his skin, but Hassan withstood it until the end of the sash was lit.

He ran back to Khepri.

"Clear the way!" Khepri called, motioning to the soldiers standing in front of the door. They hastily stepped aside.

Khepri held the bottle beneath the burning sash that dangled from Hassan's hands. She kept it there long enough for the cloth inside the chrism oil to catch fire, and then threw the entire thing—oil, cloth, and flame—against the doors before dropping to a crouch and pulling Hassan down.

An earth-shattering *boom* shook the tower.

Hassan looked up in time to see a small white inferno expand and then quickly dissipate, leaving a charred black opening in its wake.

A cheer went up, and Khepri looked over at him, grinning. They got to their feet and ran from the debris and smoke, into the open air. The rest of the prisoners were already through to the deck by the time they emerged.

"We made it." There was a giddiness in Khepri's voice.

Hassan looked over at her, breathing in deeply. Each lungful of fresh air was sweeter than the one before. As relief washed over him, he tugged her into his arms. Khepri's arms looped easily around his neck, and he leaned in. When Khepri had kissed him on the *Cressida*, it had been desperate and full of the fear and guilt that had plagued them both. But here, now, with the night stars spread above them, Hassan kissed her, full of promise and hope.

They broke apart, and Hassan tried to memorize her face as it was in this moment—lips slightly parted, a flush suffusing her bronze skin, eyelashes fanning delicately out from those captivating amber eyes. It was strange that any part of Khepri—bold, brave Khepri with sunlight in her eyes and steel in her spine—could be delicate. But there were parts of her he had not yet come to know, and he could only hope that he would have time to learn them.

She smiled at him and then leaned back in to steal a tiny kiss that took Hassan by surprise and made him answer with a grin that he knew must look ridiculous.

"Come on," she murmured.

Hassan folded her hand in his own. They followed the rest of the soldiers down the stone stairwell that wrapped around the outside of the lighthouse.

"How did you know that would happen?" he asked as they descended. "The chrism oil, I mean. You knew it would react with the Godfire."

Khepri's face hardened. "I saw it happen before, remember? When we tried to put out the source of the flame in the High Temple. The temple exploded when the Godfire touched the chrism oil."

Hassan had forgotten that detail, so preoccupied with the other horrors he had seen and heard about that day. But Khepri had lost three comrades that night. Those memories, he knew, were burned into her mind.

"Well," he murmured, "your quick thinking saved us."

They reached the bottom of the stairs to find three familiar figures racing toward them.

"Penrose!" Hassan cried.

She, Petrossian, and Osei halted before Hassan's group. They were sooty and damp from sea spray, but otherwise looked unharmed.

"You made it out," Penrose said in relief. "Thank the Prophets. We were about to go back in to find you."

"We got out through the observation deck," Hassan explained. "Did everyone else make it out?"

Penrose nodded. "After you went up into the tower, we helped the others escape through the atrium. The Hierophant left some guards outside the lighthouse, but we took care of them. Annuka and Yarik are signaling the Order's ships at the seawall to let them know to dock there. The harbor is too dangerous and overrun with Witnesses. But we have to go now if we're going to meet them before the Witnesses figure out what they're doing."

Hassan nodded. He turned to the rest of the soldiers. "Everyone, go with Penrose. She will take you to the Order's ships. You'll be safe with them."

Khepri stepped up to him. "Why does it sound like you aren't going?"

He looked past her toward the lighthouse. "The Godfire flame is still burning up there. As long as that's true, Nazirah is in danger. I won't leave my kingdom again. Herat doesn't need a conqueror, and it doesn't need a Prophet. It needs someone who will fight for it no matter what." He thought of his father, who had faced execution rather than give in to the Witnesses. "Even die for it if necessary."

Herat still needed its prince. Hassan had never needed Grace or a prophecy to save his kingdom. He'd only needed the belief that he could, and all the rage and hope that had brought him here.

"You're serious," Penrose said, a pang of disbelief in her voice. "You're going to stay here? With the Witnesses? Your aunt?"

"They're going to burn the city, Penrose. Unless someone stops them."

"But how?"

"I have a plan." He looked up at the lighthouse. The symbol of Nazirah's past. The tower that was his kingdom's heart. The light that had guided him home. "You told us in Pallas Athos that there's only one source of Godfire," he said to Khepri. "If that's it up there, then there's only one way to put it out. We have to destroy the lighthouse."

This was a conclusion Hassan had reached hours ago, when he'd first seen the pale flame burning at its top.

"It's the only way," he said.

"But Hassan—" Khepri began.

He silenced her with a look. "You told me on the *Cressida* that we always have choices. This is what I choose, Khepri. I'm going to stop the Witnesses."

This would be his salvation.

Khepri held his gaze. "Then I'll help you."

"I can't ask you to—"

"Of course I'm helping you," she said. "You know that. My brothers are still here in Nazirah. If there's hope we can save them, I'll do whatever it takes."

He peered into her eyes, his heart at war with itself. He wouldn't be able to bear her getting hurt. But neither could he let her go.

"I bound my fate to yours, remember?" She squeezed his hand. "I already made my choice, Hassan. I choose you."

"We do, too."

Hassan looked up and saw Khepri's lieutenant, Faran, standing in front of him. "We're not leaving, either, Prince Hassan."

The soldiers gathered behind him nodded in agreement.

"No," Hassan said. "You should get to safety, to give our people a chance outside of this kingdom."

Faran shook his head. "What is a people without their homeland? We came here to fight at your side, Prince Hassan, to stand up to the Witnesses. To reclaim our kingdom. So that's what we'll do."

"You heard what the Hierophant said about me," Hassan said. "What I am. I deceived all of you. All of this, it's my fault. What I've done . . . it's beyond forgiveness."

"It's the Hierophant's fault," Faran said fiercely. "And the fault of everyone who followed him. It doesn't matter what they say you are, Prince Hassan. *We* know who you are. We want to fight beside you. For Nazirah."

"For Nazirah," the others murmured.

Hassan couldn't quite believe it—despite everything, despite what he'd done, his people still trusted him. Still *believed* in him.

He turned to Penrose. "I guess this is it, then."

She stepped toward him, grasping his forearm. Surprised, he wrapped his hand around hers.

"May Nazirah's light guide you, Your Grace," Penrose said, her tone fierce.

He bowed his head. "You, too."

With a final nod, the remaining members of the Guard retreated, until they were three smudges against the dark sky.

Hassan turned toward the soldiers who stood ready to take his orders. "At dawn, the lighthouse falls."

61

EPHYRA

EPHYRA WAS THIRTEEN YEARS OLD WHEN SHE BROUGHT HER SISTER BACK from the dead.

It was a terrible, hungry year of drought and famine. The usual scatterings of caravans that passed through their town on the trading route from Tel Amot to Behezda had dried up like rain from the cracked earth.

Sickness began to spread. Ephyra and Beru's parents succumbed to it quickly.

But when Beru had taken ill, Ephyra no longer cared about her parents' warning about using her Grace. They were gone, and she wasn't going to lose Beru, too. So she had healed her.

But Beru took ill again. And again. And again.

And then came the morning when Ephyra had gone to her sister's room and found her lying cold on the bed. Ephyra had never known a more powerful grief than the one that overtook her that morning. It burst forth from her lungs and her throat, and shook her very bones.

Her cries drew her neighbors, who came and discovered Beru's body. Ephyra knew they would burn it, just like the others. She kicked and fought as they dragged her away. The moment she couldn't feel her sister's cold fingers in her own, Ephyra blacked out.

She would never know what had happened in the time she was unconscious. Perhaps for the best. When she came to, she was lying beside her sister's body. No—beside her sister. Because Beru was breathing again. Short, shallow gasps, her eyes twitching under her lids. And when Beru opened her eyes, Ephyra realized everything around them had gone quiet. The only sound was the breath on her sister's lips.

And then, the first words of her second life: "What did you do?"

They never spoke about that day again. They never spoke of the slow walk from their home through the silent town square, the bodies of their friends and neighbors lying like broken dolls around them. They never spoke of the empty eyes and the suffocating silence.

It was the last time Ephyra had set foot in this village. Now she had returned, hoping to save her sister again.

Only she feared she was too late.

She stood at the base of the clock tower at the center of town, shielding her eyes against the rising sun. A thick cloth covered the bottom half of her face, to protect it from the dust storms.

Someone had been here. The evidence was in the loosened dirt above the market's hard pack, in the freshly gouged wound in the trunk of the sycamore that stood at the edge of the village's main square.

Yes, someone had been here. Ephyra touched the rough bark of the sycamore. There was no blood, nothing to suggest that there had been violence. She refused to consider the possibility. Instead, she moved past the tree, following the path away from the square, down the windy dirt road she knew well. The road that led home.

The house was exactly as she remembered it, down to the crack that ran from the top of the window up to the flat roof. She could almost believe that if she walked up the cobbled walkway and through the arched doorway, she would find her father sketching in the sitting room amid his stacks of journals. That if she walked into the kitchen, she would find her mother chiding Beru for her bruises and dirty fingernails.

But when Ephyra stepped through the threshold, the memory flickered and vanished like a ghost.

"Beru?" she called into the dark, dusty house. "Beru, are you in here?"

The crunch of footsteps broke the silence. Ephyra shot through the main sitting room and into the kitchen. The door that led to the yard swung open.

"Beru!"

But the person standing on the other side of the door wasn't her sister. It was Hector Navarro.

He stared at her, frozen.

"What have you done to my sister?"

Hector stiffened, anger flashing across his face. "I've done nothing to her."

"Where is she?"

"She's where she belongs. Where you should have left her, all those years ago. Before you—"

Ephyra couldn't listen anymore. She shoved past him, streaking out into the yard, her heart a frightened animal in her chest. "Beru!"

Beru lay beneath the acacia tree, her limbs folded beneath her like a straw grass weave.

Ephyra choked on her next breath, a raw, wounded sound bursting from her throat as she stood in the yard, her body frozen. She had crossed the sea to come back to her sister's side, but she could not make herself cross this last distance.

"I didn't do this." Hector's voice scraped through the air behind her. "You never should have brought her back. You never should have tangled the lines of life and death. You delayed this moment for over five years. You took countless lives. Now it will finally be set right."

The words broke over her like waves, but Ephyra could barely hear them over the pounding in her head.

Beru couldn't be dead. Not before Ephyra could get to her.

Her legs carried her across the yard to Beru's side. She slid to her knees, taking her sister's limp hand and pressing it to her cheek. Silent, aching sobs shook her.

Beru's fingers twitched, curling around Ephyra's thumb.

Ephyra sucked in a desperate breath, pressing her thumb to Beru's wrist, above the black handprint. Beru's pulse fluttered faintly.

She was alive. There was still time.

"I'm here," Ephyra said desperately, combing a curl from Beru's peaceful face. "I'm here, Beru. I'm here."

"You should say your goodbyes. It's over now."

Ephyra startled at the sound of Hector's voice, quiet and close behind her.

Why was I spared? Hector had asked her in the cell in Pallas Athos. Ephyra had taken his whole family but left him alive.

And now Beru needed another life.

Ephyra's fingers tightened around her sister's wrist. Hector was not like the people she'd killed as the Pale Hand. His death would not be an accident. And there would be no going back from it.

But without Beru, there was no way forward.

She shook herself and got to her feet, facing Hector. "It's not over. This is not how it ends."

Everything in their lives had led to this moment.

"It's you or her. I choose her."

Panic flashed in Hector's eyes as she leapt toward him. He grabbed at the hilt of his sword, unsheathing it quicker than Ephyra could react. It sliced past her, and she stumbled back, her hand flying to where the blade had nicked her cheek. Warm blood gushed between her fingers.

Hector looked from her to the blade, his expression stunned. "I—"

Ephyra charged again, but Hector was ready for her. With Graced speed and strength, he pinned her to the ground, his sword at her throat.

"It's over," he said again.

She gasped out a ragged breath.

He lowered the sword. "Give up."

For a moment, the world was still as they stared at each other. Two people who had lost everything. Neither of them able to let go.

With every bit of strength she had, Ephyra surged up at him, reaching wildly to clasp her palm around his arm. His eyes were locked on hers as she took a breath and focused on drawing the *esha* from his body.

His grip on her began to slacken. At first, it seemed he didn't understand what was happening. But as he looked from her face to the hand around his arm, his eyes widened in panic. Her other hand shot up, her thumb finding the hollow of his throat. He gasped, his lungs heaving out desperate breaths, each shorter and shallower than the last. His pulse pounded wildly and then began to slow. The light drained from his eyes as he choked and went silent. Beneath her palm, his pulse stopped.

He slumped over, his weight pressing down on her. With a great cry of effort, Ephyra pushed him onto the dirt. She lay beside him for a moment, sucking in breath after breath. Hot tears stung her face. She was shaking.

She scraped herself off the ground and forced herself to look down at Hector's body beside her, and the pale white handprint marring his skin.

Grief and guilt clawed at her throat, but she swallowed them down. Beru needed her.

The rest of the job went quickly. Ephyra had done this so many times it was like her body knew what to do without her direction. The blade, the blood, her hand.

And her sister, dying beneath the acacia.

Ephyra knelt at Beru's side, brushing the curls from her forehead with her clean hand. She wrapped the other, dripping with fresh blood, around Beru's wrist, over the dark handprint. She closed her eyes and focused on sending Hector's *esha* into Beru. Filling her back up with life.

Please . . . please. It can't be too late. Please.

A soft gasp of breath broke the silence. Ephyra opened her eyes and met Beru's gaze.

"Ephyra?" she mumbled. "Ephyra, you're hurt."

She brushed her fingers against the blood that dripped from Ephyra's cheek.

"I'm fine." Ephyra couldn't help the smile that spread across her face—one of relief and exhaustion. "I'm fine, Beru. And so are you."

Beru looked up at her, brows bunched together in confusion.

"I'm . . ." Her eyes fell to Ephyra's bloody hand, still locked around Beru's wrist. In a flurry of movement, Beru pushed herself up. Ephyra saw the moment Beru's gaze caught on the corpse that lay in the yard. Her expression rippled with confusion and anger.

"Ephyra," Beru said, her voice full of dread. "What did you do?"

62

JUDE

JUDE HEARD THE WAY OUT BEFORE HE SAW IT. THE HIGH, FLUTING SOUND OF wind through a tunnel whistled through the damp air.

He turned to Anton. "Do you hear that?"

They'd been journeying through the underground waterways for what felt like hours. Anton had kept close to his side. Jude wasn't sure if that was because he was frightened or simply because he couldn't see in the dark.

Anton tensed beside him, slowing. But Jude tugged him forward, quickening his steps.

"I think it's an exit." He took off, dragging Anton behind him.

Ahead, wan light marked the mouth of the tunnel. Dawn had broken while they were underground. The scent of salt and sea gusted in with the strengthening wind.

They reached the end and stopped short. The tunnel let out beneath a viaduct that jutted from the cliff, supported by cut-stone arches. Nothing but a sharp drop separated them and the waves of white and dark gray that crashed against the rocks below.

"This must be where the water drains to the sea," Jude said, raising his voice over the sound of the wind and the ocean. He scanned the viaduct above them. He could easily climb up, but it would be more difficult with Anton.

And then Jude realized that Anton was no longer right beside him. He'd stepped up to the edge of the tunnel, his eyes locked on the churning water below. He started to lean forward, slowly, like someone was tugging him down.

"Anton!" Jude scrambled to his side, locking an arm around his chest to drag him back. Anton's dark eyes looked dazed, disoriented.

He blinked, his vision focusing slowly.

Jude's breath came in short bursts, panic still suffusing his body.

"Sorry," Anton said quietly. Jude felt his chest rise and fall, and then Anton's warm breath against his cheek. "I didn't think . . ."

But he didn't finish the thought. There was a part of him, Jude realized, that was still inside the cistern. He didn't know exactly what had transpired there, but from the state Anton was in now, he had enough guesses to fuel a thousand nightmares.

The sooner Jude could get him out of here and safely aboard the Order's ship, the better.

"You can let go," Anton said. "I'm all right."

Jude withdrew his arm warily and turned his attention back to the viaduct. There was a narrow ledge of rock protruding from the cliff face, and supports on either side of the viaduct that one could reasonably climb onto from there.

"I'll go first," he said. "You follow behind. Don't look down."

Anton looked up from the water. He nodded.

"I won't let you fall," Jude said.

He picked carefully over the rough, slippery rocks, pausing here and there to help Anton across a particularly tricky stretch. He didn't breathe until they reached the viaduct supports, which were full of ledges and handholds that made it much easier to climb than the wet rock face. He reached the edge of the parapet first and pulled Anton up after him. With his face against the wind, Jude looked out across the span of the viaduct to the sea.

Silver sails on the gray horizon. Relief coursed through him. "The Order of the Last Light. Just like Penrose promised."

He turned back to Anton and saw that his eyes had gone distant and dazed again, trained on the lighthouse tower that stood at the end of the viaduct.

Jude followed his gaze, and all of his relief fled. Smoke poured from the top of the tower. The Godfire torch burned brightly against the bleak sky.

The Guard. The other prisoners. They might still be in there.

Wind buffeted him as he stood there, torn once again between what he knew his duty to be and what his heart would break to lose. He had to get Anton—the Prophet—to safety. He knew that. But he couldn't leave the others to die.

He turned to tell Anton to stay put, to run for the beach if he saw anyone coming. But once again, he realized Anton was no longer there.

A sharp spike of panic went through him, one that did not subside when he spotted Anton's fair hair against the dark gray sky, racing toward the burning lighthouse. A stone staircase spiraled down the side. Jude watched as Anton began to climb. Toward the Grace-destroying flames of Godfire.

Heart in his throat, Jude raced after him.

63

HASSAN

THE PLAN WAS VERY SIMPLE.

Under the cover of darkness, they had split into groups of six and hit every temple that stood along Ozmandith Way, collecting chrism oil and all the cloth and drapery they could find.

The streets of Nazirah were ominously empty. Most of the Witnesses, it seemed, were concentrated around the harbor, anticipating the Order's ships, but small groups of two or three walked the streets of the city. One of these patrols had spotted Hassan and Khepri's group leaving their third temple. Hassan had waited, heart pounding in his ears, while Khepri went after the Witnesses. They would lose every advantage they had if Lethia and the Hierophant discovered they'd escaped the lighthouse.

Khepri had returned unharmed, with one of the patrolling Witnesses in tow.

"What happened to the other one?" Hassan had asked.

"He won't get very far on a broken leg," she'd said.

"There's no telling who else might have been spotted," Hassan had said. "We should hurry."

When they returned to the lighthouse, the others had already started soaking the cloth in chrism oil and packing it into wooden crates.

"Do you think it will be enough?" Hassan asked Khepri.

They were crouched down along the seawall that ran perpendicular to the lighthouse peninsula.

"It'll have to be," Khepri said, watching the other soldiers stack the crates against the sea-facing side of the lighthouse. With enough force against it, they hoped they would be able to destabilize the tower and send it crashing down into the waves.

"It's time," Hassan said when the soldiers had finished stacking and began to retreat across the peninsula. He stood, slinging a long coil of rope over his shoulder.

The most dangerous task fell to him. He was the only one who could safely get near enough to the Godfire flame without risking anything more than flesh. He would be the one to set the fuse and light it.

"Wait," Khepri said, rising with him. For a moment, Hassan was afraid she was going to demand to go with him, though they both knew that was too dangerous.

But instead, Khepri simply slipped her arm around him and leaned in with a brief but fierce kiss that left him reeling.

"I believe in you," she told him. She placed a glass bottle into his hand and, with a gentle shove, sent him away from the seawall.

He hitched the rope higher on his shoulder as he made his way toward the lighthouse. Several of the Herati soldiers passed him, going in the opposite direction. They stopped upon seeing him and turned in a single, coordinated motion, touching their fists to the center of their chests in the royal salute of the Herati Legionnaires. Prophet or not, Deceiver or not, Hassan was still their prince.

He nodded to them in acknowledgment, and they went on their way toward the seawall, where Khepri waited.

Hassan continued to the lighthouse alone. When he reached the stacks of crates full of chrism oil, he unwound the rope and ran it between them. Then he unscrewed the top of the glass bottle Khepri had given him and poured its contents over the rope and crates.

He picked up the free end of the rope and let it spool out as he walked along the side of the lighthouse toward its entrance. He could already smell the acrid smoke within. Tightening his grip on the rope, he slipped his makeshift mask back over his nose and mouth.

He opened the doors, and smoke bellowed out. Hassan stumbled back, his eyes watering. The smoke was so thick he couldn't even see the pale light of the Godfire flames within. Sucking in a great breath of air, he shut his eyes and charged inside. Heat and smoke assaulted him, pressing against him like a solid weight. He fought through the dark clouds, head growing thick with the fumes.

Trusting that he was headed toward the flames, he pushed forward blindly. The rope unwound as he ventured farther inside. A deep, hot ache wrenched at his chest.

At last he saw a white tongue of flames against the smoke. His eyes stung, and his stomach heaved as he dragged himself toward it. With as much strength as he could muster, he took the last of the rope gathered in his arms and threw it into the flames.

The fire flickered, and Hassan fell to his knees, violent coughs wracking his body. Shutting his eyes against the burn of the smoke, he crawled away, following the rope to find the exit.

The heat grew more intense. The rope had caught fire, burning quicker than he could crawl.

He rolled to the side to avoid being scorched and tried to follow the line of white fire. But the smoke was pressing in on him. He could no longer see. He could no longer breathe. The smoke was in his lungs, in his mouth, in his eyes, filling up his head. His chest felt like it would burst open.

Soon the fire would reach the chrism oil and set the whole tower alight. Hassan had done what he needed to do. He had no more strength.

Just like his father, he would die protecting his people.

He closed his eyes, and the smoke enveloped him.

64

ANTON

ANTON CLIMBED.

It was like he was in a trance, following the dizzying stairs that wound farther and farther up the lighthouse. The crashing of waves against rock grew fainter as he climbed higher.

The Godfire at the top had been just a far-off light when he'd begun, but now he could see its pale flames and the whirring glass panes that protected it from the wind. His legs burned in protest as he passed the observation deck. The stairs narrowed. The flame grew nearer, its light consuming his gaze.

Flames licked out against the gray sky as he careened onto the stone platform surrounding the torch. Heat scorched his back as he edged along the parapet.

A tumult of dark green and gray waves raged below. Hands shaking, Anton raised himself onto the slick surface of the stone, climbing slowly, carefully, up from the platform onto the parapet. He wavered there for a moment, the wind buffeting him. Then, slowly, he reached toward the flame.

"What are you doing?"

A voice. Its sharp edge pierced through Anton's daze. A torrent of *esha* crashed over him like a breaking storm. He turned.

Jude stood at the top of the stairs, aglow in the light of the pale flame. His face was its own storm, his eyes the same perilous green as the tempest sea.

"Don't come any closer." The wind swallowed Anton's plea.

Jude strode toward him. "Come down."

Anton looked back at the Godfire flame. He shook his head. "I have to do this." The flame was hot on his skin, but inside, he was as cold as the day he'd plunged beneath the ice. He had to get rid of it, the thing that had haunted him since that day. "This is the only way."

He had to burn out his Grace.

"Either come down here," Jude said, voice rising over the wind, "or I'm coming up there."

Anton didn't move. A moment later, he felt Jude's warmth beside him on the parapet. Wind cut across Anton's cheeks, blowing wet strands of hair into his eyes.

"Look at me," Jude said.

Anton shook his head, focusing on the bright flame. He just had to touch the flame, and then, he knew, all of this would end. The nightmares. The memory. This was the only way he would find salvation. The only way to be free. "You shouldn't have followed me."

"Anton," Jude said, trying again. "The reason I found you in that cistern. The reason the Witnesses wanted you. It's because—"

"I'm a Prophet," Anton said, meeting Jude's eyes at last.

A Prophet. It was impossible. It was the truth.

"Yes," Jude said steadily. "Your birth was foretold. Before they disappeared, the Seven Prophets knew that you would arrive. They told us the signs. 'Born beneath a light-streaked sky. An heir with the blessed Sight. A promise of the past undone.'"

"'The shadowed future made bright,'" Anton said, the words coming to him unbidden, like something he'd heard in a story once. But he hadn't.

Jude's bright eyes widened in surprise. "Yes. You are the Last Prophet, Anton. It is my duty to protect you. I won't let anyone hurt you. Not Illya. Not the Witnesses. No one."

Anton looked at the dark line of Jude's brow and then down at his hand, where it was clenched, white-knuckled, at his side. "They're not the ones I'm afraid of."

Jude faltered. When he spoke again, his voice was barely audible above the howl of the wind. "Then what?"

Anton shook his head. "I—I saw something. A long time ago. But I—"

"What? What did you see?"

"A vision," Anton said at last. "I was so young, but even then, I—I knew, somehow, that what I saw was something that hadn't come to pass. But that it would. And that when it did . . . no one could stop it. Least of all me."

Something dark was coming for this world, and Anton had seen its shadow.

"A vision?" Jude repeated. "You mean you—you saw it? The end of the prophecy? The future that the Seven couldn't see?"

Was that what it was? A vision that the Seven Prophets themselves hadn't been able to see?

He shook his head. "I don't know. I can barely remember it. It put me in some kind of trance, I think, and I went out onto the lake. I remember falling through the ice. Then—just flashes. Darkness. When my brother pulled me out of the water, I ran. I couldn't face it, whatever it was." He still couldn't. He looked away from Jude, casting his gaze toward the horizon. "Feels like I've been running away from this thing my whole life." Running from something in his own head. Running from something he would never escape.

"Then maybe it's time to stop." Jude's voice was quiet and earnest, and so close beside him.

Anton heard it over the wind, over the crash of waves against the barren rock. He would, he thought unsteadily, be able to hear that voice over anything.

He turned. Jude's eyes were bright and dangerous.

A crack split the air, louder and nearer than thunder. The lighthouse lurched beneath them. Anton wavered at the edge of the parapet.

"Jude!"

The sky, the wind, and the sea held their breath for a silent moment. Then a flash of light burst from below and lit the world to white flame.

The lighthouse swayed. Flames licked through the air. Anton stumbled back. Jude leapt forward.

Together, they fell.

65

JUDE

JUDE'S BLOOD SEARED AS HE LEAPT THROUGH THE GODFIRE.

He ignored the pain, ignored the fire that raged in his veins and the wind that whipped at his face as he threw his arms around Anton, shielding him from the flames. His Grace surged as he held the Prophet tight and pushed off from the edge of the lighthouse parapet, arcing their fall toward the sea.

The water rushed up to meet them. Bright light filled his vision. Godfire ignited his Grace, setting his body ablaze with pain. The scorching white heat consumed him until he could hold on no longer.

He could feel nothing, see nothing, but he could still hear the soft sound of Anton's breath rising over the howling, pitiless wind.

They splashed down into the water, and everything was silent.

66

ANTON

THE SEA FOLDED ANTON INTO ITS EMBRACE.

Fire burned behind his eyelids. Darkness reached up, closing around him. It had chased him since the day on the frozen lake.

He'd done everything he could to protect himself from it, but the vision had always been there, waiting. In the water, in the darkness, he couldn't run anymore. He couldn't fight. He let it in.

And sank.

He was in a city of ruins. Ash and dust choked a red sky. A shadow eclipsed the light of the sun.

A curl of black smoke beckoned Anton along an eroded path, past crumbling pillars and collapsed arches.

Anton . . . Anton . . . Prophet . . .

The smoke led him to the heart of the ruined city. To the broken tower—rubble, a skeletal frame, and one standing wall rising up like a great monolith.

Four black twists of smoke spiraled up from each crumbled wall, joining in the center like the points of a compass.

A low hum permeated the air, growing louder until it resolved into a voice, crackling like flames.

The final piece of our prophecy revealed.

In the ruin of the tower lay a body, twisted unnaturally among the crumbling stones. The smoke wound around it. The figure began to crack, like a stone statue broken. White light poured out from the fissures.

In vision of Grace and fire.

The smoke rippled and curled together into a single form, rising up from the figure, blocking out the bleeding sky.

Anton looked up.

Two bright eyes, searing with light. Eyelids of rippling black smoke.

To bring the age of dark to yield.

They saw him. Saw inside him. He could not *move*, could not *think*, could not see anything but those eyes. Eyes of cold flame and light.

Or break the world entire.

He stood at a precipice, overlooking a city he'd never seen before, a city of lush green palms and cerulean water tucked in the embrace of rolling dunes. An immense gate carved of red rock towered over the edge of the city. A crack split the air, and suddenly the gate collapsed. The entire city began to waver, as the shifting sand beneath swallowed it.

Another city rose in its place. This one he knew by the two great statues that flanked its harbor. Tarsepolis. Light and fire rained down from the sky, igniting the city in a blazing inferno.

From the ashes, Pallas Athos rose. Anton stood at the highest tier, on the steps of the Temple of Pallas, watching as a wave of blood flooded in, turning the once-white streets and buildings red.

One by one, the Six Prophetic Cities fell.

He returned to the broken tower where he'd started. Only now, he was standing within the ruin, beneath the blood-red sky. Smoke twisted around him.

He looked down. The body lay there, face twisted up toward him.

Her eyes opened, and Beru let out a shattering scream. The vision dissipated in a blast of bright light.

Anton woke.

67

BERU

BERU STOOD BESIDE HER SISTER IN THE RUIN OF THEIR HOME, STARING AT THE
body of the boy who'd brought her there.

Hector lay spread out in the dirt, his eyes gazing blankly up at a
cloudless sky. Beru knew the last thing those eyes had seen was Ephyra's
face.

"What did you do?" she said. Warm blood trickled down her wrist.
She tore her eyes from Hector's still body to watch the drops of blood
splash down into the dust at her feet.

What have we done?

"Beru." Ephyra's voice was wracked with pain. "I had to. I *had* to. He
brought you here to die. I couldn't let that happen."

"He was innocent," Beru said, her voice hollow. "He was innocent,
and you killed him. You *murdered* him, Ephyra."

"To save *you*."

Dirt, blood, and tears stained Ephyra's cheeks. Beru stared at her
sister, feeling like she was seeing her as she truly was for the first time.

"I would rather die than be the reason you become a monster."

Beru's voice caught on the edge of those words. She felt a wave of nausea and the pressure of tears behind her eyes. "But I think it's too late."

"Beru—"

"I told you, Ephyra, I can't do this anymore."

"We can still find the Chalice," Ephyra said, reaching for her. "Just because Anton couldn't help us doesn't mean—"

Beru pulled away. "No more. No more searching. No more Pale Hand. No more people dead because of what I am. It's over."

"It's not over," Ephyra said fiercely. "You're still breathing. Beru. Please—"

"Hector told me there's a prophecy," Beru said haltingly. "A prophecy that says that an Age of Darkness is coming, and . . . we're the ones who will cause it. The pale hand of death. And one who rises from the dust."

Ephyra let out a humorless laugh. "Are you serious? A prophecy? There are no more prophecies. The Prophets are *gone*, and they aren't coming back. You don't really—"

"That's what he told me. And I believe him. I do. Because he's right, Ephyra. Look at what you've done. This place . . . our home . . . we *destroyed* it. If we're capable of this, I don't need a prophecy to tell me that we're capable of much worse."

"Is this what you really think?" Ephyra stepped toward her. "That we have some sort of destiny to cause *evil?*"

Beru swallowed. "All I know is that there's something dark inside of us. I can't ignore it anymore."

"What are you saying?" Ephyra asked desperately. "What are you going to do?"

Beru raised her chin and looked past her sister, across the yard and toward the distant sun. "I'm saying that I'm leaving. And this time, you aren't going to follow me."

Ephyra stepped toward her. "Beru."

"I'm saying goodbye."

"No," Ephyra said. "No, you don't get to—"

"I don't get to?" Beru echoed. "I didn't get a choice in dying. I didn't get a choice in being brought back. But I get a choice now. I'm not going to let us become monsters. I choose to leave."

"Beru, you can't do this." Ephyra's voice cracked. "*Please.*"

Beru curled her hands around her sister's arms. "You're my sister, and no matter what you've done I'll always love you." She stepped back, releasing Ephyra. "But this is the last time you'll ever see me."

Beru watched as her sister's heart broke. She could see it in the way her face crumpled, in the way her body shook. She made herself watch until she couldn't anymore, and then she turned away.

She needed to do this. Hector had known that, and now she did, too. This was about more than his death. More than the lives the Pale Hand had taken. More than the village Beru's resurrection had destroyed.

Ephyra loved Beru enough to tear the world apart to save her. And Beru loved Ephyra enough not to let her.

So she turned, and she walked from the shade of the acacia and into the light.

68

HASSAN

THE FIRST THING HASSAN BECAME AWARE OF WASN'T A SENSATION, BUT THE lack of one—pain. His eyes no longer stung. His chest no longer felt like it was about to collapse. Air moved through his lungs with ease—in and out, in and out.

Somehow, he was alive.

The next thing he felt were cool hands against his cheek. The scent of citrus and earth tickled his nose beneath the stench of smoke. He wanted to fall into it. Lips brushed his forehead, and he moved, catching the kisser with one hand and pressing his lips to hers.

Khepri let out a small noise of surprise, and then a sigh as they separated. Hassan blinked his eyes open and sat up. Khepri was kneeling beside him, her face sooty but wide open with relief. The other soldiers stood around them.

"What happened?" he rasped out. His throat, he realized, was still sore from the smoke.

Khepri hesitated before answering. "When you didn't come out of the lighthouse, I went in after you."

"Khepri," he said, meaning it to be a reproach.

But she didn't look the least bit sorry. "You were just inside the door. You'd almost made it out before you collapsed."

"She carried you on her back."

Hassan looked up and saw Faran standing over both of them, arms crossed over his chest.

"You two barely made it clear of the explosion."

Hassan sat up. "The lighthouse?"

"It's gone," Khepri said gently.

"I want to see."

Khepri pressed her lips together but dutifully stood and helped pull Hassan to his feet. He was still a little weak, but after a moment of swaying, he was able to stand and look beyond the seawall to the ruins of the lighthouse.

The legacy of his family. The pride of his kingdom. It was gone now, and no matter what happened next, no matter if they succeeded in driving out the Witnesses and deposing Lethia, this piece of his people's history would never be the same. The lighthouse that had stood for over a thousand years now lay beneath the sea. And Hassan would be remembered as the prince who had brought it down.

It was difficult to find triumph in that.

"Prince Hassan."

He turned. Behind him stood the Herati soldiers, their faces tired and streaked with soot, some of them wounded. Dozens fewer than the full force that had come to Nazirah.

"Prince Hassan, what do we do now?"

There was no telling what would happen to them here. They would be hunted. They could be executed.

But they had stopped the Witnesses together. They had kept the city from being burned to ash. The lighthouse of Nazirah was no longer standing, but these people were. And so was he.

"We find shelter," Hassan said. "We regroup. And soon, we strike."

He wasn't on anyone's path anymore—not his father's, not the Order's, not Lethia's. Nothing was promised, except the girl beside him and the people who believed in them both. The Kingdom of Herat was more than a lighthouse. More than a prophecy. Now that Hassan was back on its shores, he would do whatever it took to keep it safe.

In the distance, the Order's silver-sailed ships turned, gliding away into the sea.

Hassan lifted his face to the sky. There, in the east, the sun broke over the horizon.

69

EPHYRA

A BREEZE STIRRED THE ACACIA LEAVES OVER EPHYRA'S HEAD. THE SUN HAD SET on the village of the dead.

Beru was gone. Ephyra was alone, after everything she'd done to prevent it.

"Hello, Ephyra."

Ephyra whipped toward the sound of her name. Not so alone. Not yet.

She didn't recognize the woman who stood at the edge of the yard, but something told her she should.

She wore brown trousers and a simple shift of sky blue, the same type of clothing the people in Medea would have worn. A pale orange scarf, the color of the blushing sunrise, covered her dark curls. She was beautiful, Ephyra could see that—deep-brown skin a shade or two lighter than her own, eyes the color of dark liquor.

"Who are you?" Ephyra asked as another breeze rustled past them.

The woman stepped into the yard, making her way toward her with fluid grace. "Well, I never did tell you my real name."

"Mrs. Tappan?"

That's not her real name, you know. That's what Anton had said, that night that felt like an eon ago, standing in his flat in the City of Faith. Now that Ephyra was finally face-to-face with her, she knew Anton had been right. Whoever this woman was, she wasn't just a bounty hunter. And now she'd tracked down the village of the dead, where Ephyra had begun.

Ephyra clenched her fist. "What are you doing here?"

"I came to help you," the woman replied.

"*Help* me?" Ephyra said. "You've done nothing but ruin my life. You are the one who sent us to Pallas Athos. You are the reason Hector found us there. All of this is your fault!"

The woman watched her impassively. "I may have put you in Hector Navarro's path, but it is your actions, and your sister's, that brought you here. Those who cannot own their choices will always be mastered by fate."

"Is this just some sick game to you?" Ephyra choked out. "Sending us on a wild chase to find some legendary Chalice? It doesn't even really exist, does it?"

"Oh, the Chalice does indeed exist. And it can help you save your sister. Is that still what you want?"'

Ephyra dragged in a harsh breath. Saving Beru had been the one constant in her life for so long. There was never *room* for anything else. There was only the next city, the next kill, the next line of ink on Beru's skin.

She didn't know a life without it. She didn't know *how* to want anything else.

"Come with me," the woman said, tilting her head toward the house. The house where both of Ephyra's parents had perished. The house where Beru had taken the first breaths of her second life.

Ephyra followed.

The woman glided through the draped doorway and into the small sitting room, with its low table surrounded by worn cushions and the tall bookshelves that lined the walls. Ephyra couldn't help reaching out to trip her fingers over the spines of the books, the way she used to when she was young. Nostalgia hit her like a sudden ray of sun, for a moment blasting through her grief. She felt just like a little girl again.

The woman turned to one of the bookshelves and pulled something out. Ephyra recognized it instantly. It was one of her father's sketchbooks. He used to take it with him on long caravan journeys, capturing within its pages the faces of the people he'd met and the sights he'd seen. She remembered many evenings, tucked warm against her father's side, exclaiming, *What's that!* each time her father turned a page to reveal a herd of camels or a strange artefact he'd encountered from another merchant caravan.

The woman opened the sketchbook and began paging through it. Ephyra bit back a cry of protest. Her father's sketches felt like something private. Sacred.

The woman stopped on a sketch of Beru. In the picture, she looked about ten or eleven, a gangly sprite of a kid. Her arms were stretched above her head, diving to catch a falling kite. Ephyra remembered that day. The village kite festival. Beru had caught more kites than any other kid. She'd been so proud. It was only a few weeks before Beru had gotten sick.

Tucked between that page and the next was a piece of loose parchment, folded into quarters. The woman held it out to her.

With shaking hands, Ephyra unfolded it. It was another drawing, but not of a person.

It was a cup. She brushed her fingers over the fine detailed pencil strokes depicting a cup of elaborate silver filigree, studded with tiny jewels. It looked like it belonged on the table of an ancient king of Behezda.

Not a *cup*. A chalice.

She slowly raised her eyes from the chalice to the woman's face. "Is this—?"

"Look at the other side," the woman said.

There, Ephyra found a map of the Seti desert, stretching from the eastern Pelagos coast to Behezda, and from the northern Inshuu steppe all the way to the South Sea. Tiny ink *x*'s marked off dozens of desert villages, some she'd never even heard of.

Clipped to the bottom corner of the map was a scrap of parchment with words written in an unfamiliar hand.

Aran, it read. Her father's name. *I'm afraid we can't help you with this one. If the Chalice exists, you don't want to go looking for it. The only thing you'll find is a quick death.*

Ephyra read the words three times over, as if they might change. Long before she even knew it existed, her father had been searching for Eleazar's Chalice. All those times he'd left with a caravan to trade in the desert, was this really what he'd been doing? Her heart thudded in her throat.

"What is this?" she croaked. "Why was my father looking for Eleazar's Chalice?"

The woman didn't answer.

Ephyra lunged forward, smacking her father's sketchbook out of the woman's hands.

"Answer me!" she cried. "If my father was looking for Eleazar's Chalice, it had something to do with me, didn't it? Why I'm . . . why my Grace is like this."

The woman tilted her head. "Like what?"

"Powerful," Ephyra said. The word felt strange on her tongue. She didn't think of herself as powerful, but the proof was here, in this village, and burned into the skin of every person she'd ever killed.

Had her father known, somehow, what Ephyra was capable of? Did he believe the Chalice would help her control her Grace?

The woman swept her gaze over the room. "You and your sister did not start this. The Pale Hand and the one who rises. But you will be the ones to finish it."

Ephyra flinched. Beru's words about the last prophecy came back to her. *An Age of Darkness is coming. And we're the ones who will cause it.*

"All I wanted was to save my sister," Ephyra said, her voice breaking. "None of this was supposed to happen."

"But it did," the woman replied. "And now, knowing that, knowing what it costs, do you still want to save her?"

Ephyra closed her eyes. "Yes."

"Then you'll have to finish what your father started," the woman said. "Make your choice."

Ephyra looked at the map in her hands. If she could find the Chalice, she could save Beru once and for all.

And she might doom the world in the process.

As she met the woman's unwavering gaze, Ephyra made her choice.

70

ANTON

ANTON HADN'T DROWNED.

His head throbbed. The world rocked and swayed. He needed to throw up, but he couldn't seem to figure out which way was up. He wrenched his eyes open. Bright light drilled into him.

In a flash, it all came back—the cistern, the lighthouse, his brother, *Jude*—and he sat back, panting.

"Let's try and take it easy for now, all right?"

A hand pressed flat against his chest. He felt the hum of *esha* suffusing the room, pleasant and brassy. Calm. Focused. Powerful.

Anton stared blearily up at the woman. She was pale and muscular, tawny freckles dotting her face and what he could see of her neck and arms. Her copper curls were gathered into a thick braid, hiding part of a silver twist of metal around her neck. Her dark blue eyes seemed to warm when they met his. But there was an edge of unease beneath them.

Anton's stomach heaved, and he flopped to his side, emptying its contents onto the wooden floor.

The woman didn't even blink.

"Water," he rasped when he was done.

There was a bowl sitting beside the cot. The woman carefully held it to his lips, tipping his chin back to help him drink. The touch was unexpectedly tender. Reverent, almost.

Anton shuddered and lay back against the pillows, closing his eyes. Groaning, he threw his arms over his face, trying to block any light.

"Do you know where you are?" the woman asked. "Can you tell me your name?"

"Anton," he mumbled underneath his arms. "We're on a ship."

"That's right," she said gently. "My name is Penrose. I know you must be very confused right now, but I can promise that you're safe here. Very safe."

"Where is Jude?" The last thing he remembered was falling, Jude's arms around him, shielding him from the Godfire, the two of them splashing down into the sea, and then—

Penrose's lips pressed into a thin line, and her face, already pale, went white. Anton's stomach swooped low, and he leaned over, certain he was going to be sick again.

At last, Penrose answered, "He's on the ship."

A breath rushed out of him, choking in its relief.

But Penrose wasn't finished. "I saw you both fall from the light-house. I saw you go into the sea. We dove in after you—Annuka and I—and pulled you out as quickly as we could. Jude wasn't breathing when you came out. The healers are doing everything they can."

Anton's head thumped with a rush of hot blood, and he felt dizzy all over again.

"Anton." Penrose's voice was still soft, but there was new urgency beneath it. "What were you and Jude doing on top of the lighthouse?"

Anton didn't say anything for a long moment. Then, when he

sensed Penrose was growing restless with his silence, he said, "You're one of them, aren't you? The Order of the Last Light?"

She nodded.

He drew in a shaking breath. There was no point anymore, hiding from this, running from it. He'd proved that on top of the lighthouse. And it had nearly gotten him killed.

It had nearly gotten Jude killed.

"I want to see him," he said abruptly.

Penrose hesitated.

"Please. Take me to him, and I'll tell you whatever you want."

It took three tries for Anton to make it out of his cabin. Penrose was patient, supporting most of his weight as he stumbled to the door and down the narrow, creaking hallway. They paused every few hundred steps so he could lean against the bulkheads and stop his head from spinning.

When they finally reached the sick bay, there were four more people in the hallway, two dark-skinned men, and a fair-skinned woman and man who looked so similar they had to be siblings. They all wore the same dark blue cloak and silver torc as Penrose.

"Is that—?" the fair-skinned man began, staring openly at Anton.

Penrose cut him off with a meaningful look. "He wants to see Jude."

The hatch eased open, and the pale light of the sick bay spilled into the hall. Anton swallowed, hesitant now that he was standing so close to where Jude lay broken and helpless.

He pushed the door open and entered. A row of cots lined the room, half of them curtained off. Wan light suffused the room. Penrose led him to one of the curtains and swept it back.

Jude was small and pallid against the gray sheets of his cot. His arm was wrapped in bandages, and pale scars crept up the side of his throat like the cracks in shattered glass.

All because of Anton. Because he'd been a coward, running to the top of the lighthouse because he hadn't been able to face what he was. What he had seen.

He was going to be sick again. He ran from the room, pushing past the hatch and the people in the passageway. He made it all the way to the main deck before his stomach heaved. He emptied it over the side of the ship.

When he was done, he laid his head against his arms, slumping over the gunwale. The inside of his mouth was hot and astringently bitter. A hand fell tentatively against his shoulder and he felt Penrose's brassy *esha* again.

"The Godfire," Anton said hollowly. "At the top of the lighthouse. Jude leapt through it to get to me." He could still remember the heat, the serpentine twist of flames that cracked like a whip through the air between them.

"When you hit the water, the flames were put out," Penrose said haltingly. "The burns are minor. There's a chance—" She stopped, emotion swallowing her next word. "There's a chance the water doused him before the Godfire could burn out his Grace. We won't know until he wakes up. We just have to wait."

Wait to see if Jude's body could withstand what Anton had done to it.

"Jude was still using his Grace as you fell," Penrose said. "He used it to leap away from the falling lighthouse and swim away from the undertow."

Anton looked up, not sure what she was getting at. She was looking at him carefully.

"It must have taken a lot of will," Penrose went on, "for him to use his Grace with that much pain. I've touched chains forged in Godfire, and that alone was almost more pain than I could bear. I can't imagine what it would feel like to try to use my Grace with the flames themselves scorching me. Whatever he was fighting for . . . it must have been very important."

Anton raised his head, meeting her gaze and the unspoken question in it.

"I'm a Prophet." He'd said the words to Jude at the lighthouse. They didn't sound any less strange now. "The Prophet, I suppose."

Penrose held herself very still. "It's true, then."

"You knew?"

"You're the right age," Penrose said quietly. "And when I saw Jude—" Her voice caught.

Anton waited.

"Jude abandoned the Order in Pallas Athos. He turned his back on his duty and betrayed his vows. For a Paladin, to betray your vows is to forfeit your life."

"Oh."

Anton thought of the Hidden Spring, and the grim set of Jude's mouth when he'd set down the golden torc and declared he, too, would come aboard the *Black Cormorant* and sail to Tel Amot. He thought of the sound of Jude's voice—broken, defeated—aboard the ship Illya had held them captive on, saying that he'd failed.

Shame flooded his chest. Jude had risked his life, in more ways than one, to keep Anton safe. He thought he had failed, that he'd betrayed everything he believed in. He'd told Anton as much, in the hold of the ship on the way to Nazirah. But it wasn't Jude who'd failed to live up to his destiny. It was Anton. By trying so hard, for so long, to escape it, he had nearly doomed the both of them.

"When I saw Jude in the lighthouse he said he knew you were in Nazirah," Penrose said. "He said he could feel your Grace. Can you tell me what happened?"

Anton took a shuddering breath. He was suddenly so very tired. But he thought of Jude, lying half-dead in the sick bay, and he knew that this—the secrets he'd kept his whole life, the vision his mind had tried to erase—were what had put him there.

So he started to speak. The more he talked, the more he wanted to keep going—to get it all out, dig it up from the deep, dark place inside him.

At some point, the chill of the night air grew too cold, and he and Penrose retreated to the cramped space of his cabin.

"When we were down in the cistern, my brother told me that the Prophets made a final prophecy before they disappeared." He could still see Illya's face in front of his, gold eyes gleaming in the dark. "That's why they wanted me, I think. Somehow, I'm part of it all. The Witnesses— the Hierophant, I guess—wanted to get inside my head, to know what I saw all those years ago."

Penrose drew in a sharp breath. "What did you see?" she asked, her voice barely a whisper but taut with urgency. "Anton, did you see how to stop the Age of Darkness?"

The words tugged at him like a memory. "Stop *what?*"

"The prophecy," Penrose said in a rush. "The Last Prophet is meant to complete it. *You* are meant to complete it. To see how to stop the Age of Darkness."

Anton shook his head, his heart plummeting like a stone to the bottom of a dark sea. "I saw something. The Age of Darkness. I saw it unfold. But not . . ."

Penrose's fist tightened in her lap. "Tell me what you saw."

He closed his eyes. The shadow over the sun. The broken tower. The dark smoke. And those bright eyes, pinning him in place, ripping him open. The ruins of the Six Prophetic Cities. The vision surged behind his eyes—he could see it, could *smell* the smoke and the blood-red sky.

He could see Beru's face, her eyes the same bright white as the Godfire flames.

"Ruin," Anton said at last. "I saw the whole world in ruin."

Anton haunted the ship like a living ghost as they sailed across the Pelagos Sea. A sickness had settled heavy in his stomach, a sickness that no amount of sailor's wine seemed to be able to cure.

The Order members stared when they encountered him in the narrow corridors, and whispered among themselves when they saw him on the mess deck. They spoke in hushed tones of the boy who'd climbed to the top of the lighthouse to spread his light. The boy who was their savior. Their Prophet.

He didn't return to see Jude in the sick bay after that first night, even when days passed and Jude still didn't wake. Anton took to staying in his room, sleeping during the day when the light was brightest. Penrose would wake him for supper, bringing flatbread and dried figs to his cabin. He ventured out only in the middle of the night, when he was sure that only a bare-bones crew would be awake.

The Guard did not raise any protests, though Anton could tell they weren't pleased whenever he slipped out in the middle of the night. Nevertheless, one of them was always waiting outside his door, ready to trail after him like an imposing shadow.

Tonight, Penrose was on watch, standing in silence behind him as he bent over the rail, leaning into the wind as the ship raced into the night's black embrace.

"Penrose."

Anton stilled. Eight days had passed since he'd last heard that voice.

"Should you be up here?" Penrose asked. "You're barely on your feet."

Anton turned. Jude stood a few paces away, dressed in a simple linen tunic and pants. The moon washed him in pale light.

"I'm all right," he said to Penrose. "Why don't you get some rest? I can watch over him for the rest of the night."

A tense silence fell between them. But then she nodded. Anton watched her retreat, only looking back to Jude once she'd disappeared down into the ship's cabin.

"You're awake," Anton said stupidly.

"So are you," Jude returned, limping toward him.

Penrose hadn't said anything about Jude waking up. None of them had. But then, Anton hadn't asked. Seeing Jude like that—pale, small, helpless—had brought out that sick feeling in his gut.

Guilt.

He felt it again, now, as his eyes trailed over the sickly tinge of Jude's face, the faint purple beneath his eyes, the shattered-glass scars that crept up his throat.

He met Jude's gaze again, and Jude's eyes softened as he answered the unasked question. "I'm fine." The ghost of a smile quirked his lips when he added, "Well, somewhere in the vicinity of fine."

He was lying. Anton had been attuned to Jude's *esha* since before he'd met him. He'd felt it like a storm gathering in his bones. He felt it just as acutely now, but it was weak, like a trembling breeze. Broken.

The Godfire had damaged Jude's Grace, that was almost certain. But to what extent, Anton didn't know. And he couldn't bring himself to ask.

Jude stepped toward him. "What about you? Are you—?"

"Going to throw myself off the side of the ship?"

Jude's face went stony.

Anton turned back to the water, and the darkness beyond. "I survived this long. I guess I'll just—keep doing that."

Jude drew up beside him as Anton scratched at the wooden gunwale in front of him.

"I don't know what to say to you anymore." There were many things Anton wanted to say. Things he probably should say. "You saved my life. I called for your help, and you heard me. You came. And on the lighthouse—"

"It wasn't a choice," Jude replied. "You are the Prophet. It is my duty to protect you, at any cost."

It was the same thing he had said to Anton on top of the lighthouse, right before proving the truth of those words.

"I know." Anton didn't know how to complete the thought. It was more than anyone had given him before. It was too much, or maybe not enough. He shook his head and looked out toward the water, uneasy beneath Jude's gaze. "Penrose told me about the last prophecy. About the Age of Darkness. You all believed that when I completed the prophecy, we would know how to stop it."

"Anton—"

"I saw it, Jude," Anton said, fighting to steady his voice. "I saw the breaking of the world. That's what my vision was. The Reckoning that the Witnesses want, the Age of Darkness the Prophets saw—it's coming. But I have no idea how to stop it."

Beside him, Jude drew in a breath. Anton felt a gentle pressure over his hand where it rested on the gunwale. The touch was light, but as sure as a promise.

Whatever happens, I'll protect you.

Someday, maybe, Jude would have to break that promise. Someday, Anton would have to face something no one could protect him from.

But for now ... Anton looked down, curling his thumb gently around Jude's fingers. For now, there was this. The press of a hand on his, the comfort of another heartbeat close enough to hear.

They stayed like that, side by side against the wind, as the ship sailed on into the dark.

ACKNOWLEDGMENTS

The journey of getting a book from brain to shelf is a long and arduous one, but I am fortunate enough to have had some truly incredible people help me along the way.

To my agents, Hillary Jacobson and Alexandra Machinist: If this book was a Disney princess, you two would be its badass fairy godmothers. Thank you for seeing its potential and mine, and for putting in the work to get us there. You plucked me out of obscurity and made my dreams come true. And thank you to the rest of the team at ICM and Curtis Brown, with special thanks to Tamara Kawar, Ruth Landry, and Roxane Edouard. I appreciate everything you do!

Thank you to Brian Geffen, my brilliant editor—your thoughtfulness, enthusiasm, and unwavering support have truly humbled me. I never thought I'd be lucky enough to work with someone who gets this book as completely as you do. To Jean Feiwel, Christian Trimmer, Rachel Murray, Rich Deas, Mallory Grigg, Elizabeth Johnson, Starr Baer: thank you for all your hard work, and for giving this book such a wonderful home. And a huge thank-you to the incredible publicity and marketing team at MCPG: Molly Ellis, Brittany Pearlman, Ashley Woodfolk, Johanna Kirby, Allegra Green, Melissa Croce, Mariel Dawson, Julia Gardiner. Jim Tierney, thank you for lending your talent to this incredible cover!

To the writer cult: Janella Angeles (my publishing twin!), Madeline Colis, Erin Bay, Christine Lynn Herman, Amanda Foody, Kat Cho,

Amanda Haas, Mara Fitzgerald, Ashley Burdin, thank you all for your friendship, feedback, and vats of wine. Axie Oh, Ella Dyson, Alexis Castellanos, Claribel Ortega, Tara Sim, Melody Simpson—thank you for endless salt, cute pet pictures, and heart-trash. I could not imagine navigating this publishing thing without all of you, and I am so grateful I don't have to. Akshaya Raman, thank you for being the best revision trenches/book event/writing date buddy, and for that one Skype call that actually helped. And Meg RK, you brilliant star, this book owes so much to your patience, your humor, and your insights. When I'm on the floor doubting every word, you always know how to pick me up.

Traci Chee, Swati Teerdhala, Hannah Reynolds, Chelsea Beam, and Julie Dao, your advice and friendship mean the world to me. The KELT girls, Lucy Schwartz and Teagan Miller, I will never forget your encouragement when this book was just a few dozen terrible pages. Melina Charis, thank you for sticking around for the last decade (and for the use of your last name!). Scott Hovdey, forever movie date and fabulous friend—thank you for believing in me every step of the way.

To my family: Mom and Dad, thank you for parenting me by basically sticking me in the backyard and letting me run free. Those backyard days shaped my imagination and forged me into a writer. Sean, thank you for letting me read your D&D books, even if you never let me play. David, my brother, you are in my heart always. To Julia Pool, for making sure I savor every moment. To Riley O'Neill, for celebratory cocktails and book club chats. Kristin Cerda, thank you for SSWS, camping in the redwoods, and endless discussions about language, meaning, and sometimes cults. I would not be the woman I am today if it weren't for you. To Mary Shelley's sassy teenage spirit!

Erica, you're my dearest sister and the other half of my brain. If there's anyone in the world who has put more into this book than I have, it's you. You have seen this thing through the earliest days of brainstorming to the very last commas. When I'm lost in a sea of plot twists and magic system conundrums, you are the compass that guides me back to the story. This book is for you—and so are all the next ones. Now go finish yours!

Finally, my deepest thanks to every reader, every blogger, every librarian, every bookseller who has picked up this book. I am honored to share it with you.

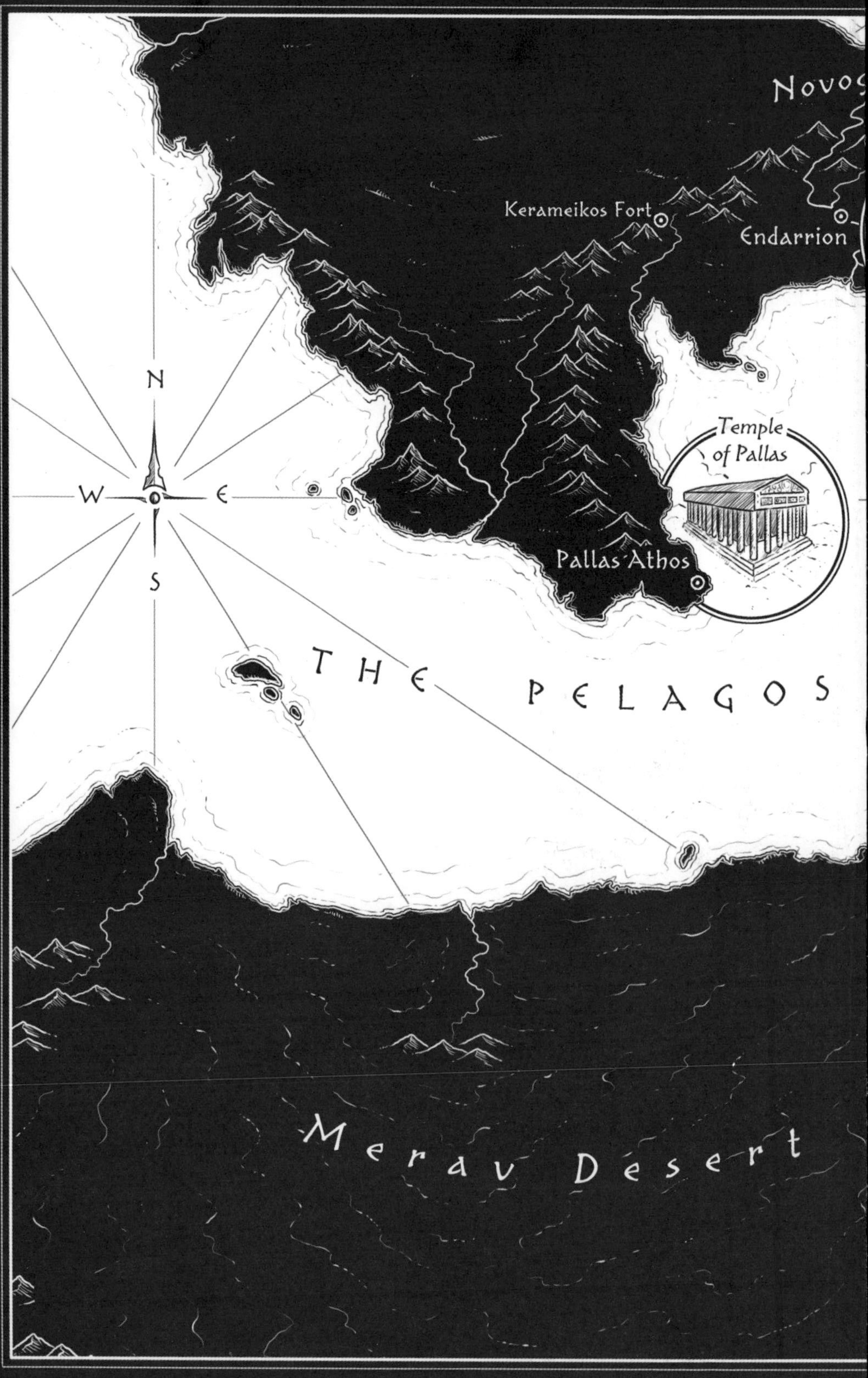
Novos
Kerameikos Fort
Endarrion
N
W
E
S
Temple of Pallas
Pallas Athos
THE PELAGOS
Merav Desert